THE DIAMOND AS BIG AS THE RITZ

and other stories

◆

F. Scott Fitzgerald

Introduction and Notes by
STUART HUTCHINSON
University of Kent

WORDSWORTH CLASSICS

2

Readers who are interested in other titles from
Wordsworth Editions are invited to visit our website at
www.wordsworth-editions.com

For our latest list and a full mail-order service contact
Bibliophile Books, 5 Thomas Road, London E14 7BN
Tel: +44 0207 515 9222 Fax: +44 0207 538 4115
e-mail: orders@bibliophilebooks.com

This edition published 1994 by Wordsworth Editions Limited
8B East Street, Ware, Hertfordshire SG12 9HJ
Introduction and Notes added in 2006

ISBN 1 85326 212 9

Typeset by Antony Gray
Printed in Great Britain by Clays Ltd, St Ives plc

CONTENTS

GENERAL INTRODUCTION

Wordsworth Classics are inexpensive editions designed to appeal to the general reader and students. We commissioned teachers and specialists to write wide ranging, jargon-free introductions and to provide notes that would assist the understanding of our readers rather than interpret the stories for them. In the same spirit, because the pleasures of reading are inseparable from the surprises, secrets and revelations that all narratives contain, we strongly advise you to enjoy this book before turning to the Introduction.

General Adviser
KEITH CARABINE
Rutherford College
University of Kent at Canterbury

INTRODUCTION

The stories of Francis Scott Key Fitzgerald (1896–1940) represented in this volume offer abbreviated treatments of his recurrent themes, namely men's and women's problematical relationships with one another; whether the possession of great wealth increases human happiness, there being in Fitzgerald's view no viable alternative even to the Darwinian ruthlessness of capitalism; and the significance of the artist when his productions too (it is always a man) become as complicit in the market as Fitzgerald's stories were themselves. The main period depicted begins with the liberating years after World War 1, the so-called 'Jazz Age' of the 1920s, and ends with the post-1929 Wall Street crash, leading to the Depression of the 1930s, a decade 'some people would consider themselves lucky to've missed'

(p. 213). Significantly, this quotation from 'The Lost Decade' (*Esquire*, December 1939) is from a sketch about *not* engaging with the 1930s. It confirms that as far as the public world is concerned Fitzgerald's essential material during his short life was the 1920s and their immediate after-effects. As for short stories themselves, he apparently held them in low esteem, declaring in 1926, when he must have thought *The Great Gatsby* (1925) had confirmed his career as a great novelist: 'I hate writing short stories . . . and only do my six a year to have the leisure to write my novels' *(Letters*, p. 206). None the less, they 'sustained Fitzgerald financially' (Kuehl, p. 4), and he was eventually to write a hundred and seventy-eight. As I hope to show, some of them enhance a literary form that has been major in American literature since Poe.

II

'Evylyn. I'm going to give you a present that's as hard as you are and as beautiful and as empty and as easy to see through' (p. 2). So Evylyn Piper, the central character of 'The Cut-Glass Bowl' (*Scribner's Magazine*, May 1920), recollects the words of a suitor as he presented her with the bowl shortly before her marriage to another man. The story has begun seven years into this marriage to Harold Piper, with Evylyn about to bring one more affair to an end. Interrupted by Harold, she conceals the man, but he unintentionally betrays his presence by striking his arm against the fateful bowl. Thereafter the Pipers' marriage is dead, even though Evylyn discovers, at the very moment of her husband's humiliation, 'how much she loved [him]' and 'how indelibly she had hurt him' (p. 28). These deeper feelings are rebuffed by Harold and survive only in Evylyn's love for her son, who at the end of the story will be killed in World War 1, the formal letter from the War Department being temporarily placed in the cut-glass bowl by a servant.

'You see, I am fate,' the bowl supposedly declares to Evylyn at the end, 'and stronger than your puny plans; and I am how-things-turn-out and I am different from your little dreams, and I am the flight of time and the end of beauty and unfulfilled desire' (p. 40). Given this moral, which the story grimly enforces by also getting the bowl to cause a disfigurement to the Pipers' daughter, how responsible can Evylyn be for 'how-things-turn-out'? The man who gave her the bowl believed it symbolised her essential vanity, but in its small way the story presents Evylyn as being as trapped as Edith Wharton's Lily Bart in *The House of Mirth*. The social world of 'The Cut-Glass Bowl', together with Fitzgerald's omniscient authorial manner, is indeed very much a development of Wharton's. It is still a hierarchical America where it is difficult to get good servants, and in which recent immigrants to America ('these Swedes' [p. 29]) will feature only as servants. It also is a Darwinian world, where established families like the Pipers are being challenged by new business energies embodied in the admirably adaptable Ahearns and, even more distastefully from the Pipers' point of view, in a Jewish rival Fitzgerald teasingly chooses to call Marx. A central dinner scene reveals Harold incapable of rising to the new competition, so what can Evylyn, tied to such a husband, do? 'Nothing' is the story's implicit answer, though this verdict is compromised by Fitzgerald himself being committed to understanding Evylyn only in terms of the evanescence of her beauty, as when he curtly informs us: 'If Evylyn's beauty had hesitated in her early thirties it came to an abrupt decision just afterward and completely left her' (p. 37). Having romanticised a woman's beauty, Fitzgerald insistently records its loss, thereby victimising Evylyn for the primary quality he has given her. Wharton's precedent with Lily Bart notwithstanding, this procedure might be seen as conventional male misogyny, especially when the woman is addressed as 'Evie' (p. 26) and is a beguiler of men.

Contrivance shows in 'The Cut-Glass Bowl', but two months later Fitzgerald's technique and social realism expanded into the multi-focused 'May Day' (*The Smart Set*, July 1920) which, along with 'Babylon Revisited', remains the best of his short stories. Like the earlier piece, it also intimates a Darwinian world immediately evident in the two returning soldiers, Carrol Key and Gus Rose: 'tossed as driftwood from their births, they would be tossed as driftwood to their deaths'. The blood of the former has been 'thinly diluted by generations of degeneration' while the latter, presumably of Jewish descent, is 'swart and bandy-legged, with rat-eyes and a much broken hooked nose' (p. 53). Contrastingly, we have the rich Philip Dean: 'Everything about him radiated fitness and bodily comfort. He smiled frequently, showing large and prominent teeth' (p. 44). Like Tom Buchanan in *The Great Gatsby*, Philip seems destined to get, predatorily, whatever he wants from the world, but his difference from Carrol's and Gus's 'driftwood' is as much the predictable result of nourishing food and an unstressful life as it is the deserving survival of the fittest. He is presumably one of those 'that had the money to buy himself out of the war' (p. 55) from which Gordon Sterrett, his fellow student at Yale, has also just returned. Gordon will eventually shoot himself, but no more than Carrol's is his early death the entirely deserved fate of the weak. Significantly, Fitzgerald himself has a latent self-identification with both men, giving Carrol one of his own names ('Key'), and representing Gordon as an aspiring artist. Whatever their deserts, their expectations have been gratuitously blighted by the war.

A similar complication is evident in the presentation of Edith Bradin and Jewel Hudson, the rich woman and the poor woman in Gordon's life. Edith convinces herself she is 'falling in love with her recollection of Gordon' (p. 60), but when she actually meets him she cannot bear his alcoholic, wasted reality. Used to men 'in various stages of intoxication, from uncles all the way down to chauffeurs . . . here for the first time she was seized with a new feeling – an unutterable horror'. Accusingly she says to Gordon, 'you look like the devil' (p. 65), thus aligning herself with Philip's metaphysical and moral reach when he too found in Gordon 'a sort of evil' (p. 48). Jewel by contrast, kissing Gordon 'with soft, pulpy lips' (p. 74), might be seen as a girl from the lower social depths, entrapping him in entirely basic instinct. Yet it seems true that she is indifferent to Gordon's not having the money she had demanded, and that she is ready to take care of him. As befits her name, and even if she regards Gordon as a 'catch', her value is a humanity all the more to be prized in a world of false glitter. Whereas Philip hoped he could brush Gordon off with some money, she will give him the best of her love.

Not that 'May Day' is sentimental. Gordon kills himself because he knows the promise of his life is finished, whatever Jewel's comforts. Allied to its social range, the story is remarkable for an authorial objectivity which is neither detached from, nor indifferent to, its subjects. Fitzgerald himself had participated in a 'Mr In and Mr Out' routine at a dance at Delmonico's (Kuehl, p. 40) and undoubtedly is as amused by these two characters as he expects us to be, even as he appreciates the irresponsibility of a rich drunken young man, who 'reached over to a plate on the table beside him and picking up a handful of hash tossed it into the air' (p. 83). May Day, like the Twelfth Night in Shakespeare's play, is a time for festivity, bacchanal, riot, and the rich have as much right as the poor to let go, even though riot can always be dangerous. A drunken rich boy wants to 'beat up this waiter' (p. 83), and a rampaging mob of soldiers results in the death of one of their own number. Would socialism or communism, which May Day also celebrates, eliminate these tensions? Edith's brother is promulgating a version of these ideologies in his newspaper, but the soldiers, understandably, do not want to hear they have been duped into fighting a war on behalf of capitalism, and consequently have no time for such a creed. Nor has Fitzgerald, who dismisses it as the pouring of 'the latest cures for incurable evils into the columns of a radical weekly newspaper' (p. 62).

Finally, the story's title also refers to the international rescue call, 'May Day', which derives from the French *'m'aidez'*, meaning 'help me'. Gordon is making this plea, but the story suggests Philip, narcissistically 'polishing his body' (p. 45), and everyone else should be making it too. What significant basis do their post-war lives have? Was it for this America that Columbus made his great voyage, the story implicitly asks, as it presents 'magical, breathless dawn, silhouetting the great statue of the immortal Christopher' (p. 84). It is a similar question to the one implied at the end of *Gatsby*, and it leads to similar irresolvability. This America after all offers the consumer goods which may bring so much happiness, and to which Fitzgerald is apparently as attracted as are his characters. Witness Gordon's examination of Philip's shirts, ties and socks in Chapter 1, and the working girls looking into shop windows in the first two paragraphs of Chapter 2, when Fitzgerald writes of 'the wealthy, happy sun' (p. 50), as if materialism were necessarily in harmony with nature. The Prologue to 'May Day' may indicate a Belshazzar's Feast (with 'The Diamond as Big as the Ritz' presenting the writing on the wall), but in his American way Fitzgerald is sure that consumerism's expression of the right to life, liberty and the pursuit of happiness is better than anything communism offers.

Meanwhile, in 'The Lees of Happiness' (*Chicago Sunday Tribune*, December 1920) he writes a story in which characters, in contrast to those in 'The Cut-Glass Bowl', encounter fates recognised to be undeserved. 'What had he and Roxanne done that life should deal these crashing blows to them?' (p. 204), Harry Cromwell wonders. His own marriage is a mess, while Roxanne's husband and his friend, the writer Jeffrey Curtain, lies barely alive as a result of a blood clot breaking in his brain. Immediately prior to his affliction Jeffrey may have manifested a latent antagonism to Roxanne. Watching him

play cards at a poker party, Roxanne 'quite innocently . . . reached out
her hand, intending to place it on Jeffrey's shoulder – as it touched
him he started of a sudden, gave a short grunt, and, sweeping back his
arm furiously, caught her a glancing blow on her elbow' (p. 199).
This reaction, however, may signal no more than a discountable hair-
line fissure in 'a marriage of love' (p. 194), or may even indicate the
looming physiological quake in Jeffrey's brain. Similarly, Harry's
slatternly wife may well be at least OK with her second husband, who
has the money to give her whatever she wants and needs, including
domestic help. Because 'The Lees of Happiness' presents characters
in the grip of developments (external or internal to the self) over
which they do not have control, it is not interested in culpability.
Rather, it is aware of general vulnerability and even futility. These
are exemplified in how a writer such as Jeffrey (or Fitzgerald himself)
might be cut down before ever achieving what might have been his
prime, and only leave 'passably amusing stories, a bit out of date now,
but doubtless the sort that would then have whiled away a dreary
half-hour in a dental office' (p. 193). They are exemplified too in the
knowledge that even had Roxanne achieved the kind of fame available
to her, it would have been mainly associated with triviality: 'Why did
her name not linger in popular songs and vaudeville jokes and cigar
bands, and the memory of that gay old uncle of yours . . . whither had
she gone? What dark trap-door had opened suddenly and swallowed
her up?' (p. 194).

What is it but good fortune that keeps such a trap-door from our
path? In Roxanne's case her life is swallowed up attending the barely
alive Jeffrey. Giving him this care, she experiences 'the lees of
happiness', and perhaps the recipient experiences it also. Certainly
Harry as witness does. Life turns out to be a grim business for the
three main characters, but, as when Jeffrey found a use for Roxanne's cookies, they try to make it better rather than worse. In this
effort Roxanne travels far from when she was a young 'butterfly of
butterflies' (p. 193).

In 'The Diamond as Big as the Ritz' (*The Smart Set*, June 1922)
Fitzgerald returns from personal to national themes. As a fable it
contrasts with the realism of 'May Day', while complementing the
earlier story's account of America. In it the significantly named
Washingtons own the colossal diamond signifying that material
wealth which the American New World, and especially its western
territory (Montana in this case), has always seemed to proffer

human imagination. Ominously, the most significant theme of the story is what must be done to protect this source of the American good life, itself epitomised in all its splendour and comfort by the allusion to 'the Ritz-Carlton hotel' (p. 95). In the story the diamond must be guarded by violence, murder, and the corruption of any discourse ('survey', 'maps', 'compasses' [p. 99]) making an approach to it. Other races (blacks in the story) must be enslaved to preserve it, and nature itself perverted. So the 'wealthy, happy sun' in 'May Day', becomes 'the Montana sunset [lying] between two mountains like a gigantic bruise from which dark arteries spread themselves over a poisoned sky' (p. 96). No one currently worried about the exploitation of the planet could write a better line.

Regrettably, the story is not entirely successful. It begins with the account of Hades, 'a small town on the Mississippi River' (p. 93), apparently created to let Fitzgerald, like Twain at his weakest, do easy jokes for their own sake. Soon we find ourselves in the Washingtons' domain, where the relationship between John Unger and Kismine is uninteresting even as a fable, and where the story requires 'Negroes' to be naturally gullible and foolish. So the Washingtons' slaves not only believe the South won the Civil War, they also 'passed a vote declaring it a good thing and held revival services immediately' (p. 105). In her preface to *Playing in the Dark: Whiteness and the Literary Imagination* (Harvard University Press Cambridge, Mass., 1992), Toni Morrison argues 'The readers of virtually all American fiction have been positioned as white', and in this story, and others in this selection referring to blacks (see p. 23, p. 173, p. 212), readers may well find evidence for her case. Disappointingly, 'The Diamond as Big as the Ritz' does not live up to its powerful suggestiveness about the absolute corrupting power of great wealth. Consequently, Braddock Washington's offer of 'a bribe to God' (p. 125), if only he can be left immune (what else have the very rich ever done to placate a divinity imagined in their own image?), becomes too big a moment for the accompanying triviality involving John and Kismine.

Referring to Fitzgerald as 'poor Julian', a Hemingway character in 'The Snows of Kilimanjaro' remembers

his romantic awe of [the rich] and how he had started a story once that began, 'The very rich are different from you and me.' And how someone had said to Julian, Yes, they have more money. But that was not humorous to Julian. He thought they were a special glamorous race and when he found they weren't it wrecked him just as much as any other things that wrecked him.

Whatever it was that wrecked Fitzgerald, none of the stories so far in this volume expresses an author romantically captivated, only to be disillusioned, by the very rich, and who indeed would want to spend much time with fiction having so simple a theme? Rather we have pervasively in Fitzgerald a theme more central to his age and our own. He shows how material wealth may be celebrated as the only measure of life we have left, even though it be accompanied by human, not to say spiritual, impoverishment. 'The Rich Boy' (*Redbook Magazine*, January and February 1926), to which Hemingway's story explicitly refers, is a case in point, offering as it does a mainly expository account of the rich boy's, Anson Hunter's, incapacity for love, *because* he is very rich. Though Anson is to conclude life 'has made a cynic of me' (p. 144), it is the narrator's point that to be very rich is inevitably to be 'cynical where we are trustful' (p. 131). He also mordantly observes: 'Anson accepted without reservation the world of high finance and high extravagance, of divorce and dissipation, of snobbery and privilege. Most of our lives end as compromise – it was as compromise that his life began' (p. 133). A strength of the story is its dramatic substantiation of these enactive comments. 'Ask me – oh, Anson, ask me!' (p. 142), Paula Legendre's heart cries out, as she longs for his proposal of marriage, but he won't/can't, because he has no fund of idealism to draw on. Why should he commit when he can always exploit? Matched to 'his strong, attractive presence, the paternal, understanding stature of his mind' is his 'other face . . . gross, humorous, reckless of everything but pleasure' (p. 139).

Not surprisingly his own explanation for his eventual 'growing loneliness' (p. 157) is misogynistic. With appalling insouciance he tells Paula, now happily married: 'I could settle down if women were different . . . If I didn't understand so much about them, if women didn't spoil you for other women, if they only had a little pride' (p. 163). Earlier, with equal self-ignorance, he has priggishly destroyed the love affair his aunt Edna was having and caused the death of her lover: 'Cary Sloane's body was found next morning on the lower shelf of a pillar of Queensboro Bridge. In the darkness and in his excitement he thought it was the flowing water beneath him, but in less than a second it made no possible difference – unless he had planned to think one last thought of Edna, and call out her name as he struggled feebly in the water' (p. 155). Though no one is perfect in this story, least of all the infatuated Cary Sloane, they are all able to risk more of themselves than Anson can. Better to be head-over-heels with consideration, as Paula's last husband is, than routinely to break others' lives as Anson does, leaving even a Dolly Karger 'lying awake and staring at the ceiling, never again [to believe] in anything at all' (p. 149).

'The Rich Boy' ends with Anson leaving for Europe, and Fitzgerald writing so evocatively of Anson's ship moving off 'into the wet space between the worlds, leaving his principality behind' (p. 164). Momentarily, the story has a metaphysical dimension, causing us to wonder what the meaning of anyone's life journey is, and whether worlds connected only by 'wet space' can be anything other than futile. Will Anson wreck the life of the new girl he now chats up on board? Whether he will or not, Fitzgerald throughout the story offers us the possibility of being as sympathetic to him as is the shadowy narrator. Why else is there a narrator, if not to offer an implicit double perspective also giving readers the opportunity *not* to identify with the point of view of this version of 'poor Julian', though it is a long way from Hemingway's? Arguably, unless the narrator has this function, he is unnecessary, and Fitzgerald might as well have delivered the story in his own authorial voice. Author needs narrator, however, because responding to the rich is never as straightforward as Hemingway's character believes. Even as we may wish we too were born with Anson's immense wealth, we see that his 'principality', where he has had the liberty to pursue whatever happiness he likes, has been his prison.

If Anson settles in Paris, he will have too much pedigree to live there as wildly as Charlie Wales has done. The central figure in 'Babylon Revisited' (*Saturday Evening Post*, February 1931), Charlie finds life is bleak after excesses in Paris sustained by the power of the mighty dollar during the stock market boom years of the 1920s. Returning to the city, he meets a head barman who remembers him:

'I heard that you lost a lot in the crash.'
'I did,' and he added grimly, 'but I lost everything I wanted in the boom.'
'Selling short.'

'Something like that.'

Again the memory of those days swept over him like a nightmare – the people they had met travelling; the people who couldn't add a row of figures or speak a coherent sentence. The little man Helen had consented to dance with at the ship's party, who had insulted her ten feet from the table; the women and girls carried screaming with drink or drugs out of public places –

– The men who locked their wives out in the snow, because the snow of twenty-nine wasn't real snow. If you didn't want it to be snow, you just paid some money.   [p. 235]

Paris is now nearly empty of Americans, because so many lost their money in the crash that eventually came in 1929. Having now recovered financially, Charlie is left with the ironic self-knowledge that he lost everything he valued (his wife and daughter) in the earlier boom. Separated from reality by his money, he locked his wife out in the snow, probably contributing to her early death, which then resulted in his daughter being taken from him into the custody of his wife's sister. What are we to think of those hedonistic pre-crash years in Paris, when the barman Charlie is talking to 'had come to work in his own custom-built car' (p. 217)? Their desperateness must have caused Charlie and Helen, his wife, 'to abuse each other's love, tear it into shreds' (p. 229), so is not Marion, Helen's sister, right to be entirely disapproving? Is not Charlie implicitly supporting her in his shocked remembrance of the kind of people he and Helen had mixed with? Even though it is presented from Charlie's point of view, the story is a triumph of objectivity, reminiscent on its smaller scale of James's presentation of the world of *The Ambassadors* through Strether's eyes, and sharing one of that novel's themes, namely pleasure in Paris versus someone's sense of responsibility. A sentimental Fitzgerald, intent on justifying Charlie as a version of himself, would have given us only the Marion Charlie wants to see. Fitzgerald, however, writes: 'She was a tall woman with worried eyes, who had once possessed a fresh American loveliness. Charlie had never been sensitive to it and was always surprised when people spoke of how pretty she had been. From the first there had been an instinctive antipathy between them' (pp. 219–20). The antipathy, therefore, ante-dates all experience, and is either cause or effect of Charlie's lack of sensitivity to Marion. She and her husband (first-named 'Lincoln'

by Fitzgerald to affirm positive American qualities) have never had
it as easy as Charlie in Paris, though it should also be said Marion
is unlikely ever to have anything easy, sitting, as she does, 'behind
the coffee service in a dignified black dinner dress that faintly
suggested mourning' (p. 225). Charlie concludes: 'She had built up
all her fear of life into one wall and faced it toward him' (p. 228).

He may well be right, though Marion has cause to fear him and be
protective of his daughter, given his part in Helen's life and death.
At the end of the story we cannot entirely concur in his being
'absolutely sure Helen wouldn't have wanted him to be so alone'
(p. 236), for this self-reassurance may be a lingering self-deception
Charlie cannot penetrate. Another example might be his
remembrance of his and Helen's earlier life in Paris: 'We were a sort
of royalty, almost infallible, with a sort of magic around us' (p. 220).
No more than most of us can Charlie consent to all the humiliations
his past might bring.

'Crazy Sunday' (*American Mercury*, October 1932) and 'An
Alcoholic Case' (*Esquire*, February 1937) belong to Fitzgerald's stories
of art and artists, and thus relate to the account of Gordon Sterrett in
'May Day' and Jeffrey Curtain in 'The Lees of Happiness'. The first is
set in Hollywood, that Mecca for a generation of writers, where
Sundays have become no more than crazy interludes to weekdays,
offering 'the clash and strain of many personalities fighting for their
lives' (p. 167). The story is associated with the point of view of Joel
Coles, a young continuity writer 'not yet broken by Hollywood' (p.
167) but, as the phrase indicates, inevitably destined to be so. The son
of an actress, he has always been required 'to separate the real from
the unreal' (p. 167), and is, therefore, an appropriately central figure
in a story exploring the traditional theme of the relationship between
life and art. Arguably, and as in *The Last Tycoon*, this theme becomes
all the more problematic with cinema's seeming facility in
representing actual life, and 'in a nation that for a decade had wanted
only to be entertained' (p. 170) in order to forget actual life. What,
anyway, is the relationship between artistic talent and a talent for
living? This age-old question is posed in the account of Miles Calman,
a director Joel admires for his independence and integrity. He 'was
the only director on the lot who did not work under a supervisor and
was responsible to the money men alone' (p. 167). His life is a mess,
however, unless he can direct it like a movie: 'Once he wanted a
man with a long beard to drink tea with him, and he sent down to

the casting agency for one, and drank tea with him all afternoon'
(pp. 178–9). To his wife, Stella, he has been a Pygmalion, making
'her a sort of masterpiece' (p. 183), and the consequence is a woman
without a real self, who can only play a part requiring Joel in turn to
play a part as her lover. Even when news comes that Miles has been
killed in a plane crash, Stella wants Joel to take her: ' . . . if he
betrayed Miles she would be keeping him alive – for if he were really
dead how could he be betrayed?' (p. 183). Seeing through it all, Joel
is none the less complicit in her games. With 'a certain bitterness',
he concedes to Stella in the story's last line, 'Oh, yes, I'll be back' (p.
183). He is being broken.

Life breaks all Fitzgerald's artist figures in the stories in this
volume, a recurrence suggesting the author might have a sentimental
inclination to believe the artist is necessarily a martyr and more
prone than anyone else to suffering. The self-pity which is likely to
accompany this inclination might account for the undeniable insub-
stantiality of 'Crazy Sunday'. Everything in it is too straight-
forwardly illustrative, because there is not enough flesh on the
protruding bones of the story's ideas. Not so with 'An Alcoholic
Case', however, even though it presents the last nihilistic days of
another stricken artist, who is cared for by a woman telling him,
'You're too good a man to do this to yourself' (p. 186), and
eventually staring 'at his handsome face, weak and defiant' (p. 192),
while knowing 'there were three medals from the war in his jewel
box' (p. 191). Remembering how Roxanne served Jeffrey Curtain, we
might object to this set-up were it the case in either story that the
woman's service to the man was mere subservience. In 'The Lees of
Happiness', however, it marks Roxanne's development from 'a
butterfly of butterflies' (p. 155) to someone who knows her love for
what Jeffrey 'once was' cannot be discarded like any shallower
feeling, and to someone who grows in love 'for life, for the people in
the world, from the tramp to whom she gave food she could ill
afford, to the butcher who sold her a cheap cut of steak across the
meaty board' (p. 209). Similarly, 'An Alcoholic Case' is also the
woman's story. Neither for her nor the artist drinking himself to
death have the enchanting promises of American life been fulfilled.
After the nurse has swept up the broken gin bottle, we read:

> The glass was all collected – as she got out a broom to make sure,
> she realised that the glass, in its fragments, was less than a window

through which they had seen each other for a moment. He did not know about her sister, and Bill Markoe whom she had almost married, and she did not know what had brought him to this pitch, when there was a picture on his bureau of his young wife and his two sons and him, all trim and handsome as he must have been five years ago. It was so utterly senseless – as she put a bandage on her finger where she had cut it while picking up the glass she made up her mind she would never take an alcoholic case again. [p. 187]

The artist's marriage has collapsed, while for the nurse marriage has never happened, and who knows the fate of her sister? In their isolation artist and nurse need each other. He needs a woman who will do what he asks because she is paid to. She needs men who in their sickness are more dependent than Bill Markoe presumably was. Despite making her mind up 'never [to] take an alcoholic case again', and despite Mrs Hixon's warning ('some alcoholics are pleasant and some of them are not, but all of them can be rotten' [p. 189]), she will return, if for no more than 'the lees of happiness'.

She wants also to cling to the idealism she associates with 'Pasteur and . . . Florence Nightingale' (p. 189): 'she was going to take care of him because nobody else would, and because the best people of her profession had been interested in taking care of the cases that nobody else wanted' (p. 190). The story is set, however, at the time of Halloween, an event that may be more ominous, more prone to the 'utterly senseless', than the May Day of the earlier story. Indeed what might death confirm but the senselessness of life? It is precisely such an intimation that incapacitates this young woman, reducing her to the care of dying men. She hopes for victory, but always knows 'that you can't really help them and it's so discouraging – it's all for nothing' (p. 192). As for the artist, he is an alcoholic case because he convinced himself of futility long ago. Minimally, he still exercises his gift and kindly draws a cartoon strip for the nurse. Like his bottle of gin, however, he is a broken 'Sir Galahad', and so, in his and his story's smaller way, akin to Eliot's 'broken Coriolanus' (*The Waste Land*, line 417).

STUART HUTCHINSON
School of English
University of Kent at Canterbury

BIBLIOGRAPHY

Works Cited

John Kuehl, *F. Scott Fitzgerald: A Study of the Short Fiction*, Twayne Publishers, Boston, 1991

Andrew Turnbull (ed.), *The Letters of Scott Fitzgerald*, Scribner's, New York, 1963; The Bodley Head, London, 1964

Further Reading

*Walter Allen, *The Short Story in English*, Oxford University Press, 1981, pp. 141–6

Marius Bewley, *The Eccentric Design: Form in the Classic American Novel*, Columbia University Press, New York, 1963, pp. 259–69

Matthew J. Brucoli, *Some Sort of Epic Grandeur: The Life of F. Scott Fitzgerald* (revised edition), Carroll & Graf, New York, 1991

Jackson R. Bryer (ed.), *The Short Stories of F. Scott Fitzgerald: New Approaches in Criticism*, University of Wisconsin Press, Madison, 1982, pp. 23–38

*Alan Casty, 'I and It in the Stories of F. Scott Fitzgerald', *Studies in Short Fiction*, 9, Winter 1972, pp. 47–58

*Seymour L. Gross, 'Fitzgerald's "Babylon Revisited" ', *College English*, 25, November 1963, pp. 128–35

Ernest Hemingway, A *Moveable Feast*, Scribner's, New York, 1964

Ernest Hemingway, *Selected Letters, 1917–61*, edited by Carlos Baker, Scribner's, New York, 1981

John A. Higgins, *F. Scott Fitzgerald: A Study of the Stories*, St John's University Press, New York, 1971

*Richard A. Koenigsberg, 'F. Scott Fitzgerald: Literature and the Work of Mourning', *American Imago*, 24, 1967, pp. 248–70

*Roy R. Male, ' "Babylon Revisited": A Story of Exile's Return', *Studies in Short Fiction*, 2, Spring 1965, pp. 270–7

*Anthony J. Mazzela, 'The Tension of Opposites in Fitzgerald's "May Day" ', *Studies in Short Fiction*, 14, Fall 1977, pp. 379–85

*Thomas F. Stayely, 'Time and Structure in Fitzgerald's "Babylon Revisited" ', *Modern Fiction Studies*, 10, Winter 1964, pp. 386–8

Brian Way, *F. Scott Fitzgerald and the Art of Social Fiction*, Arnold, London, 1980

Essays marked * are collected in Henry Claridge (ed.), *F. Scott Fitzgerald: Critical Assessments*, *3*, Helm Information, Robertsbridge, 1991

The Cut-Glass Bowl

CHAPTER I

THERE WAS a rough stone age and a smooth stone age and a bronze age, and many years afterward a cut-glass age. In the cut-glass age, when young ladies had persuaded young men with long, curly moustaches to marry them, they sat down several months afterward and wrote thank-you notes for all sorts of cut-glass presents – punch-bowls, finger-bowls, dinner-glasses, wine-glasses, ice-cream dishes, bonbon dishes, decanters, and cases – for, though cut glass was nothing new in the nineties, it was then especially busy reflecting the dazzling light of fashion from the Back Bay[1] to the fastnesses of the Middle West.

After the wedding the punch-bowls were arranged on the side-board with the big bowl in the centre; the glasses were set up in the china-closet; the candlesticks were put at both ends of things – and then the struggle for existence began. The bonbon dish lost its little handle and became a pin-tray upstairs; a promenading cat knocked the little bowl off the sideboard, and the hired girl chipped the middle-sized one with the sugar-dish; then the wine-glasses succumbed to leg fractures, and even the dinner-glasses disappeared one by one like the ten little niggers,[2] the last one ending up, scarred and maimed, as a toothbrush holder among other shabby genteels on the bathroom shelf. But by the time all this had happened the cut-glass age was over, anyway.

It was well past its first glory on the day the curious Mrs Roger Fairboalt came to see the beautiful Mrs Harold Piper.

'My *dear*,' said the curious Mrs Roger Fairboalt, 'I *love* your house. I think it's *quite* artistic.'

'I'm *so* glad,' said the beautiful Mrs Harold Piper, lights appearing in her young, dark eyes; 'and you *must* come often. I'm almost *always* alone in the afternoon.'

Mrs Fairboalt would have liked to remark that she didn't believe this at all and couldn't see how she'd be expected to – it was all over town that Mr Freddy Gedney had been dropping in on Mrs Piper five afternoons a week for the past six months. Mrs Fairboalt was at that ripe age where she distrusted all beautiful women –

'I love the dining-room *most*,' she said, 'all that *marvellous* china, and that huge cut-glass bowl.'

Mrs Piper laughed, so prettily that Mrs Fairboalt's lingering reservations about the Freddy Gedney story quite vanished.

'Oh, that big bowl!' Mrs Piper's mouth forming the words was a vivid rose petal. 'There's a story about that bowl – '

'Oh – '

'You remember young Carleton Canby? Well, he was very attentive at one time, and the night I told him I was going to marry Harold, seven years ago, in ninety-two, he drew himself way up and said: "Evylyn, I'm going to give a present that's as hard as you are and as beautiful and as empty and as easy to see through." He frightened me a little – his eyes were so black. I thought he was going to deed me a haunted house or something that would explode when you opened it. That bowl came, and of course it's beautiful. Its diameter or circumference or something is two and a half feet – or perhaps it's three and a half. Anyway, the sideboard is really too small for it; it sticks way out.'

'My *dear*, wasn't that *odd*! And he left town about then, didn't he?' Mrs Fairboalt was scribbling italicised notes on her memory – 'hard, beautiful, empty, and easy to see through'.

'Yes, he went West – or South – or somewhere,' answered Mrs Piper, radiating that divine vagueness that helps to lift beauty out of time.

Mrs Fairboalt drew on her gloves, approving the effect of largeness given by the open sweep from the spacious music-room through the library, disclosing a part of the dining-room beyond. It was really the nicest smaller house in town, and Mrs Piper had talked of moving to a larger one on Devereaux Avenue. Harold Piper must be *coining* money.

As she turned into the sidewalk under the gathering autumn dusk she assumed that disapproving, faintly unpleasant expression that almost all successful women of forty wear on the street.

If I were Harold Piper, she thought, I'd spend a *little* less time on business, and a *little* more time at home. Some *friend* should speak to him.

But if Mrs Fairboalt had considered it a successful afternoon she would have named it a triumph had she waited two minutes longer. For while she was still a black receding figure a hundred yards down the street, a very good-looking distraught young man turned up the walk to the Piper house. Mrs Piper answered the door-bell herself, and with a rather dismayed expression led him quickly into the library.

'I had to see you,' he began wildly; 'your note played the devil with me. Did Harold frighten you into this?'

She shook her head.

'I'm through, Fred,' she said slowly, and her lips had never looked to him so much like tearings from a rose. 'He came home last night sick with it. Jessie Piper's sense of duty was too much for her, so she went down to his office and told him. He was hurt and – oh! I can't help seeing it his way, Fred. He says we've been club gossip all summer and he didn't know it, and now he understands snatches of conversation he's caught and veiled hints people have dropped about me. He's mighty angry, Fred, and he loves me and I love him – rather.'

Gedney nodded slowly and half closed his eyes.

'Yes,' he said, 'yes, my trouble's like yours. I can see other people's points of view too plainly.' His grey eyes met her dark ones frankly. 'The blessed thing's over. My God, Evylyn, I've been sitting down at the office all day looking at the outside of your letter, and looking at it and looking at it – '

'You've got to go, Fred,' she said steadily, and the slight emphasis of hurry in her voice was a new thrust for him. 'I gave him my word of honour I wouldn't see you. I know just how far I can go with Harold, and being here with you this evening is one of the things I can't do.'

They were still standing, and as she spoke she made a little movement toward the door. Gedney looked at her miserably, trying, here at the end, to treasure up a last picture of her – and then suddenly both of them were stiffened into marble at the sound of steps on the walk outside. Instantly her arm reached out grasping the lapel of his coat – half urged, half swung him through the big door into the dark dining-room.

'I'll make him go upstairs,' she whispered close to his ear. 'Don't move till you hear him on the stairs. Then go out the front way.'

Then he was alone listening as she greeted her husband in the hall.

Harold Piper was thirty-six, nine years older than his wife. He was handsome – with marginal notes: these being eyes that were too close together, and a certain woodenness when his face was in repose. His attitude toward this Gedney matter was typical of all his attitudes. He had told Evylyn that he considered the subject closed and would never reproach her nor allude to it in any form; and he told himself that this was rather a big way of looking at it – that she was not a little impressed. Yet, like all men who are preoccupied with their own broadness, he was exceptionally narrow.

He greeted Evylyn with emphasised cordiality this evening.

'You'll have to hurry and dress, Harold,' she said eagerly. 'We're going to the Bronsons'.'

He nodded.

'It doesn't take me long to dress, dear,' and, his words trailing off, he walked on into the library. Evylyn's heart clattered loudly.

'Harold – ' she began, with a little catch in her voice, and followed him in. He was lighting a cigarette. 'You'll have to hurry, Harold,' she finished, standing in the doorway.

'Why?' he asked, a trifle impatiently. 'You're not dressed yourself yet, Evie.'

He stretched out in a Morris chair³ and unfolded a newspaper. With a sinking sensation Evylyn saw that this meant at least ten minutes – and Gedney was standing breathless in the next room. Supposing Harold decided that before he went upstairs he wanted a drink from the decanter on the sideboard. Then it occurred to her to forestall this contingency by bringing him the decanter and a glass. She dreaded calling his attention to the dining-room in any way, but she couldn't risk the other chance.

But at the same moment Harold rose and, throwing his paper down, came toward her.

'Evie, dear,' he said, bending and putting his arms about her, 'I hope you're not thinking about last night – ' She moved close to him, trembling. 'I know,' he continued, 'it was just an imprudent friendship on your part. We all make mistakes.'

Evylyn hardly heard him. She was wondering if by sheer clinging to him she could draw him out and up the stairs. She thought of playing sick, asking to be carried up – unfortunately, she knew he would lay her on the couch and bring her whiskey.

Suddenly her nervous tension moved up a last impossible notch.

She had heard a very faint but quite unmistakable creak from the floor of the dining-room. Fred was trying to get out the back way.

Then her heart took a flying leap as a hollow ringing note like a gong echoed and re-echoed through the house. Gedney's arm had struck the big cut-glass bowl.

'What's that!' cried Harold. 'Who's there?'

She clung to him but he broke away, and the room seemed to crash about her ears. She heard the pantry-door swing open, a scuffle, the rattle of a tin pan, and in wild despair she rushed into the kitchen and pulled up the gas. Her husband's arm slowly unwound from Gedney's neck, and he stood there very still, first in amazement, then with pain dawning in his face.

'My golly!' he said in bewilderment, and then repeated: 'My *golly*!'

He turned as if to jump again at Gedney, stopped, his muscles visibly relaxed, and he gave a bitter little laugh.

'You people – you people – ' Evylyn's arms were around him and her eyes were pleading with him frantically, but he pushed her away and sank dazed into a kitchen chair, his face like porcelain. 'You've been doing things to me, Evylyn. Why, you little devil! You little *devil*!'

She had never felt so sorry for him; she had never loved him so much.

'It wasn't her fault,' said Gedney rather humbly. 'I just came.' But Piper shook his head, and his expression when he stared up was as if some physical accident had jarred his mind into a temporary inability to function. His eyes, grown suddenly pitiful, struck a deep, unsounded chord in Evylyn – and simultaneously a furious anger surged in her. She felt her eyelids burning; she stamped her foot violently; her hands scurried nervously over the table as if searching for a weapon, and then she flung herself wildly at Gedney.

'Get out!' she screamed, dark eyes blazing, little fists beating helplessly on his outstretched arm. 'You did this! Get out of here – get out – get *out*! *Get out!*'

CONCERNING MRS HAROLD PIPER at thirty-five, opinion was divided – women said she was still handsome; men said she was pretty no longer. And this was probably because the qualities in her beauty that women had feared and men had followed had vanished. Her eyes were still as large and as dark and as sad, but the mystery had departed; their sadness was no longer eternal, only human, and she had developed a habit, when she was startled or annoyed, of twitching her brows together and blinking several times. Her mouth also had lost: the red had receded and the faint down-turning of its corners when she smiled, that had added to the sadness of the eyes and been vaguely mocking and beautiful, was quite gone. When she smiled now the corners of her lips turned up. Back in the days when she revelled in her own beauty Evylyn had enjoyed that smile of hers – she had accentuated it. When she stopped accentuating it, it faded out and the last of her mystery with it.

Evylyn had ceased accentuating her smile within a month after the Freddy Gedney affair. Externally things had gone on very much as they had before. But in those few minutes during which she had discovered how much she loved her husband, Evylyn had realised how indelibly she had hurt him. For a month she struggled against aching silences, wild reproaches, and accusations – she pled with him, made quiet, pitiful little love to him, and he laughed at her bitterly – and then she, too, slipped gradually into silence and a shadowy, impenetrable barrier dropped between them. The surge of love that had risen in her she lavished on Donald, her little boy, realising him almost wonderingly as a part of her life.

The next year a piling up of mutual interests and responsibilities and some stray flicker from the past brought husband and wife together again – but after a rather pathetic flood of passion Evylyn realised that her great opportunity was gone. There simply wasn't anything left. She might have been youth and love for both – but that time of silence had slowly dried up the springs of affection and her own desire to drink again of them was dead.

She began for the first time to seek women friends, to prefer books she had read before, to sew a little where she could watch her two children to whom she was devoted. She worried about little things – if she saw crumbs on the dinner-table her mind drifted off the conversation: she was receding gradually into middle age.

Her thirty-fifth birthday had been an exceptionally busy one, for they were entertaining on short notice that night, and as she stood in her bedroom window in the late afternoon she discovered that she was quite tired. Ten years before she would have lain down and slept, but now she had a feeling that things needed watching: maids were cleaning downstairs, bric-à-brac was all over the floor, and there were sure to be grocery-men that had to be talked to imperatively – and then there was a letter to write Donald, who was fourteen and in his first year away at school.

She had nearly decided to lie down, nevertheless, when she heard a sudden familiar signal from little Julie downstairs. She compressed her lips, her brows twitched together, and she blinked.

'Julie!' she called.

'Ah–h–h–ow!' prolonged Julie plaintively. Then the voice of Hilda, the second maid, floated up the stairs.

'She cut herself a little, Mis' Piper.'

Evylyn flew to her sewing-basket, rummaged until she found a torn handkerchief, and hurried downstairs. In a moment Julie was crying in her arms as she searched for the cut, faint, disparaging evidences of which appeared on Julie's dress!

'My *thu*–mb!' explained Julie. 'Oh–h–h–h, t'urts.'

'It was the bowl here, the he one,' said Hilda apologetically. 'It was waitin' on the floor while I polished the sideboard, and Julie come along an' went to foolin' with it. She yust scratch herself.'

Evylyn frowned heavily at Hilda, and twisting Julie decisively in her lap, began tearing strips off the handkerchief.

'Now – let's see it, dear.'

Julie held it up and Evylyn pounced.

'There!'

Julie surveyed her swatched thumb doubtfully. She crooked it; it waggled. A pleased, interested look appeared in her tear-stained face. She sniffled and waggled it again.

'You *precious*!' cried Evylyn and kissed her, but before she left the room she levelled another frown at Hilda. Careless! Servants all that way nowadays. If she could get a good Irishwoman – but you couldn't any more – and these Swedes –

At five o'clock Harold arrived and, coming up to her room, threatened in a suspiciously jovial tone to kiss her thirty-five times for her birthday. Evylyn resisted.

'You've been drinking,' she said shortly, and then added qualitatively, 'a little. You know I loathe the smell of it.'

'Evie,' he said, after a pause, seating himself in a chair by the window, 'I can tell you something now. I guess you've known things haven't been going quite right downtown.'

She was standing at the window combing her hair, but at these words she turned and looked at him.

'How do you mean? You've always said there was room for more than one wholesale hardware house in town.' Her voice expressed some alarm.

'There *was*,' said Harold significantly, 'but this Clarence Ahearn is a smart man.'

'I was surprised when you said he was coming to dinner.'

'Evie,' he went on, with another slap at his knee, 'after January first The Clarence Ahearn Company becomes The Ahearn, Piper Company – and Piper Brothers as a company ceases to exist.'

Evylyn was startled. The sound of his name in second place was somehow hostile to her; still he appeared jubilant.

'I don't understand, Harold.'

'Well, Evie, Ahearn had been fooling around with Marx. If those two had combined we'd have been the little fellow, struggling along, picking up smaller orders, hanging back on risks. It's a question of capital, Evie, and Ahearn and Marx would have had the business just like Ahearn and Piper is going to now.' He paused and coughed and a little cloud of whiskey floated up to her nostrils. 'Tell you the truth, Evie, I've suspected that Ahearn's wife had something to do with it. Ambitious little lady, I'm told. Guess she knew the Marxes couldn't help her much here.'

'Is she – common?' asked Evie.

'Never met her, I'm sure – but I don't doubt it. Clarence Ahearn's name's been up at the Country Club five months – no action taken.' He waved his hand disparagingly. 'Ahearn and I had lunch together today and just about clinched it, so I thought it'd be nice to have him and his wife up tonight – just have nine, mostly family. After all, it's a big thing for me, and of course we'll have to see something of them, Evie.'

'Yes,' said Evie thoughtfully, 'I suppose we will.'

Evylyn was not disturbed over the social end of it – but the idea of Piper Brothers becoming The Ahearn, Piper Company startled her. It seemed like going down in the world.

Half an hour later, as she began to dress for dinner, she heard his voice from downstairs.

'Oh, Evie, come down!'

She went out into the hall and called over the banister: 'What is it?'

'I want you to help me make some of that punch before dinner.'

Hurriedly rehooking her dress, she descended the stairs and found him grouping the essentials on the dining-room table. She went to the sideboard and, lifting one of the bowls, carried it over.

'Oh, no,' he protested, 'let's use the big one. There'll be Ahearn and his wife and you and I and Milton, that's five, and Tom and Jessie, that's seven, and your sister and Joe Ambler, that's nine. You don't know how quick that stuff goes when you make it.'

'We'll use this bowl,' she insisted. 'It'll hold plenty. You know how Tom is.'

Tom Lowrie, husband to Jessie, Harold's first cousin, was rather inclined to finish anything in a liquid way that he began.

Harold shook his head.

'Don't be foolish. That one holds only about three quarts and there's nine of us, and the servants'll want some – and it isn't very strong punch. It's so much more cheerful to have a lot, Evie; we don't have to drink all of it.'

'I say the small one.'

Again he shook his head obstinately.

'No; be reasonable.'

'I am reasonable,' she said shortly. 'I don't want any drunken men in the house.'

'Who said you did?'

'Then use the small bowl.'

'Now, Evie – '

He grasped the smaller bowl to lift it back. Instantly her hands were on it, holding it down. There was a momentary struggle, and then, with a little exasperated grunt, he raised his side, slipped it from her fingers, and carried it to the sideboard.

She looked at him and tried to make her expression contemptuous, but he only laughed. Acknowledging her defeat but disclaiming all future interest in the punch, she left the room.

CHAPTER 3

AT SEVEN-THIRTY, her cheeks glowing and her high-piled hair gleaming with a suspicion of brilliantine, Evylyn descended the stairs. Mrs Ahearn, a little woman concealing a slight nervousness under red hair and an extreme Empire gown,[4] greeted her volubly. Evylyn disliked her on the spot, but the husband she rather approved of. He had keen blue eyes and a natural gift of pleasing people that might have made him, socially, had he not so obviously committed the blunder of marrying too early in his career.

'I'm glad to know Piper's wife,' he said simply. 'It looks as though your husband and I are going to see a lot of each other in the future.'

She bowed, smiled graciously, and turned to greet the others: Milton Piper, Harold's quiet, unassertive younger brother; the two Lowries, Jessie and Tom; Irene, her own unmarried sister; and finally Joe Ambler, a confirmed bachelor and Irene's perennial beau.

Harold led the way into dinner.

'We're having a punch evening,' he announced jovially – Evylyn saw that he had already sampled his concoction – 'so there won't be any cocktails except the punch It's m' wife's greatest achievement, Mrs Ahearn; she'll give you the recipe if you want it; but owing to a slight' – he caught his wife's eye and paused – 'to a slight indisposition, I'm responsible for this batch. Here's how!'

All through dinner there was punch, and Evylyn, noticing that Ahearn and Milton Piper and all the women were shaking their heads negatively at the maid, knew she had been right about the bowl; it was still half full. She resolved to caution Harold directly afterward, but when the women left the table Mrs Ahearn cornered her, and she found herself talking cities and dressmakers with a polite show of interest.

'We've moved around a lot,' chatted Mrs Ahearn, her red hair nodding violently. 'Oh, yes, we've never stayed so long in a town before – but I do hope we're here for good. I like it here; don't you?'

'Well, you see, I've always lived here, so, naturally – '

'Oh, that's true,' said Mrs Ahearn and laughed. 'Clarence always used to tell me he had to have a wife he could come home to and say: "Well, we're going to Chicago tomorrow to live, so pack up." I got so I never expected to live anywhere.' She laughed her little laugh again; Evylyn suspected that it was her society laugh.

'Your husband is a very able man, I imagine.'

'Oh, yes,' Mrs Ahearn assured her eagerly. 'He's brainy, Clarence is. Ideas and enthusiasm, you know. Finds out what he wants and then goes and gets it.'

Evylyn nodded. She was wondering if the men were still drinking punch back in the dining-room. Mrs Ahearn's history kept unfolding jerkily, but Evylyn had ceased to listen. The first odour of massed cigars began to drift in. It wasn't really a large house, she reflected; on an evening like this the library sometimes grew blue with smoke, and next day one had to leave the windows open for hours to air the heavy staleness out of the curtains. Perhaps this partnership might . . . she began to speculate on a new house . . .

Mrs Ahearn's voice drifted in on her.

'I really would like the recipe if you have it written down somewhere – '

Then there was a sound of chairs in the dining-room and the men strolled in. Evylyn saw at once that her worst fears were realised. Harold's face was flushed and his words ran together at the ends of sentences, while Tom Lowrie lurched when he walked and narrowly missed Irene's lap when he tried to sink on to the couch beside her. He sat there blinking dazedly at the company. Evylyn found herself blinking back at him, but she saw no humour in it. Joe Ambler was smiling contentedly and purring on his cigar. Only Ahearn and Milton Piper seemed unaffected.

'It's a pretty fine town, Ahearn,' said Ambler, 'you'll find that.'

'I've found it so,' said Ahearn pleasantly.

'You find it more, Ahearn,' said Harold, nodding emphatically, ' 'f I've an'thin do 'th it.'

He soared into a eulogy of the city, and Evylyn wondered uncomfortably if it bored everyone as it bored her. Apparently not. They were all listening attentively. Evylyn broke in at the first gap.

'Where've you been living, Mr Ahearn?' she asked interestedly. Then she remembered that Mrs Ahearn had told her, but it didn't matter. Harold mustn't talk so much. He was such an *ass* when he'd been drinking. But he plopped directly back in.

'Tell you, Ahearn. Firs' you wanna get a house up here on the hill. Get Stearne house or Ridgeway house. Wanna have it so people say: "There's Ahearn house." Solid, you know, tha's effec' it gives.'

Evylyn flushed. This didn't sound right at all. Still Ahearn didn't seem to notice anything amiss, only nodded gravely.

'Have you been looking – ' But her words trailed off unheard as Harold's voice boomed on.

'Get house – tha's start. Then you get know people. Snobbish town first toward outsider, but not long – not after know you. People like you' – he indicated Ahearn and his wife with a sweeping gesture – 'all right. Cordial as an'thin' once get by first barrer – bar–barrer – ' He swallowed, and then said 'barrier', repeated it masterfully.

Evylyn looked appealingly at her brother-in-law, but before he could intercede a thick mumble had come crowding out of Tom Lowrie, hindered by the dead cigar which he gripped firmly with his teeth.

'Huma uma ho huma ahdy um – '

'What?' demanded Harold earnestly.

Resignedly and with difficulty Tom removed the cigar – that is, he removed part of it, and then blew the remainder with a *whut* sound across the room, where it landed liquidly and limply in Mrs Ahearn's lap.

'Beg pardon,' he mumbled, and rose with the vague intention of going after it. Milton's hand on his coat collapsed him in time, and Mrs Ahearn not ungracefully flounced the tobacco from her skirt to the floor, never once looking at it.

'I was sayin',' continued Tom thickly, ' 'fore 'at happened' – he waved his hand apologetically toward Mrs Ahearn – 'I was sayin' I heard all truth that Country Club matter.'

Milton leaned and whispered something to him.

'Lemme 'lone,' he said petulantly, 'know what I'm doin'. 'At's what they came for.'

Evylyn sat there in a panic, trying to make her mouth form words. She saw her sister's sardonic expression and Mrs Ahearn's face turning a vivid red. Ahearn was looking down at his watch-chain, fingering it.

'I heard who's been keepin' y' out, an' he's not a bit better'n you. I can fix whole damn thing up. Would've before, but I didn't know you. Harol' tol' me you felt bad about the thing – '

Milton Piper rose suddenly and awkwardly to his feet. In a second everyone was standing tensely and Milton was saying something very hurriedly about having to go early, and the Ahearns were listening

with eager intentness. Then Mrs Ahearn swallowed and turned with
a forced smile toward Jessie. Evylyn saw Tom lurch forward and put
his hand on Ahearn's shoulder – and suddenly she was listening to
a new, anxious voice at her elbow, and, turning, found Hilda, the
second maid.

'Please, Mis' Piper, I tank Yulie got her hand poisoned. It's all
swole up and her cheeks is hot and she's moanin' an' groanin' – '

'Julie is?' Evylyn asked sharply. The party suddenly receded.
She turned quickly, sought with her eyes for Mrs Ahearn, slipped
toward her.

'If you'll excuse me, Mrs – ' She had momentarily forgotten the
name, but she went right on: 'My little girl's been taken sick. I'll
be down when I can.' She turned and ran quickly up the stairs,
retaining a confused picture of rays of cigar smoke and a loud
discussion in the centre of the room that seemed to be developing
into an argument.

Switching on the light in the nursery, she found Julie tossing
feverishly and giving out odd little cries. She put her hand against
the cheeks. They were burning. With an exclamation she followed
the arm down under the cover until she found the hand. Hilda was
right. The whole thumb was swollen to the wrist and in the centre
was a little inflamed sore. Blood-poisoning! her mind cried in terror.
The bandage had come off the cut and she'd gotten something in it.
She'd cut it at three o'clock – it was now nearly eleven. Eight hours.
Blood-poisoning couldn't possibly develop so soon. She rushed to
the phone.

Dr Martin across the street was out. Dr Foulke, their family
physician, didn't answer. She racked her brains and in desperation
called her throat specialist, and bit her lip furiously while he looked
up the numbers of two physicians. During that interminable moment
she thought she heard loud voices downstairs – but she seemed to be
in another world now. After fifteen minutes she located a physician
who sounded angry and sulky at being called out of bed. She ran back
to the nursery and, looking at the hand, found it was somewhat more
swollen.

'Oh, God!' she cried, and kneeling beside the bed began
smoothing back Julie's hair over and over. With a vague idea of
getting some hot water, she rose and started toward the door, but
the lace of her dress caught in the bed-rail and she fell forward on
her hands and knees. She struggled up and jerked frantically at the

lace. The bed moved and Julie groaned. Then more quietly but with suddenly fumbling fingers she found the pleat in front, tore the whole pannier completely off, and rushed from the room.

Out in the hall she heard a single loud, insistent voice, but as she reached the head of the stairs it ceased and an outer door banged.

The music-room came into view. Only Harold and Milton were there, the former leaning against a chair, his face very pale, his collar open, and his mouth moving loosely.

'What's the matter?'

Milton looked at her anxiously.

'There was a little trouble – '

Then Harold saw her and, straightening up with an effort, began to speak.

' 'Sult m'own cousin m'own house. God damn common nouveau rish.⁵ 'Sult m'own cousin – '

'Tom had trouble with Ahearn and Harold interfered,' said Milton.

'My Lord, Milton,' cried Evylyn, 'couldn't you have done something?'

'I tried; I – '

'Julie's sick,' she interrupted; 'she's poisoned herself. Get him to bed if you can.'

Harold looked up.

'Julie sick?'

Paying no attention, Evylyn brushed by through the dining-room, catching sight, with a burst of horror, of the big punch-bowl still on the table, the liquid from melted ice in its bottom. She heard steps on the front stairs – it was Milton helping Harold up – and then a mumble: 'Why, Julie's a'righ'.'

'Don't let him go into the nursery!' she shouted.

The hours blurred into a nightmare. The doctor arrived just before midnight and within a half-hour had lanced the wound. He left at two after giving her the addresses of two nurses to call up and promising to return at half-past six. It was blood-poisoning.

At four, leaving Hilda by the bedside, she went to her room, and slipping with a shudder out of her evening dress, kicked it into a corner. She put on a house dress and returned to the nursery while Hilda went to make coffee.

Not until noon could she bring herself to look into Harold's room, but when she did it was to find him awake and staring very miserably at the ceiling. He turned bloodshot hollow eyes upon her.

For a minute she hated him, couldn't speak. A husky voice came from the bed.

'What time is it?'

'Noon.'

'I made a damn fool – '

'It doesn't matter,' she said sharply. 'Julie's got blood-poisoning. They may' – she choked over the words – 'they think she'll have to lose her hand.'

'What?'

'She cut herself on that – that bowl.'

'Last night?'

'Oh, what does it matter?' she cried. 'She's got blood-poisoning. Can't you hear?'

He looked at her bewildered – sat halfway up in bed.

'I'll get dressed,' he said.

Her anger subsided and a great wave of weariness and pity for him rolled over her. After all, it was his trouble, too.

'Yes,' she answered listlessly, 'I suppose you'd better.'

CHAPTER 4

IF EVYLYN'S BEAUTY had hesitated in her early thirties it came to an abrupt decision just afterward and completely left her. A tentative outlay of wrinkles on her face suddenly deepened and flesh collected rapidly on her legs and hips and arms. Her mannerism of drawing her brows together had become an expression – it was habitual when she was reading or speaking and even while she slept. She was forty-six.

As in most families whose fortunes have gone down rather than up, she and Harold had drifted into a colourless antagonism. In repose they looked at each other with the toleration they might have felt for broken old chairs; Evylyn worried a little when he was sick and did her best to be cheerful under the wearying depression of living with a disappointed man.

Family bridge was over for the evening and she sighed with relief. She had made more mistakes than usual this evening and she didn't care. Irene shouldn't have made that remark about the infantry being particularly dangerous. There had been no letter for three weeks now, and, while this was nothing out of the ordinary, it never failed to make her nervous; naturally she hadn't known how many clubs were out.

Harold had gone upstairs, so she stepped out on the porch for a breath of fresh air. There was a bright glamour of moonlight diffusing on the sidewalks and lawns, and with a little half-yawn, half-laugh, she remembered one long moonlight affair of her youth. It was astonishing to think that life had once been the sum of her current love-affairs. It was now the sum of her current problems.

There was the problem of Julie – Julie was thirteen, and lately she was growing more and more sensitive about her deformity and preferred to stay always in her room reading. A few years before she had been frightened at the idea of going to school, and Evylyn could not bring herself to send her, so she grew up in her mother's shadow, a pitiful little figure with the artificial hand that she made no attempt to use but kept forlornly in her pocket. Lately she had been taking lessons in using it because Evylyn had feared she would cease to lift the arm altogether, but after the lessons, unless she made a move with it in listless obedience to her mother, the little hand would creep back to the pocket of her dress. For a while her dresses were made without pockets, but Julie had moped around the house so miserably at a loss all one month that Evylyn weakened and never tried the experiment again.

The problem of Donald had been different from the start. She had attempted vainly to keep him near her as she had tried to teach Julie to lean less on her – lately the problem of Donald had been snatched out of her hands; his division had been abroad for three months.

She yawned again – life was a thing for youth. What a happy youth she must have had! She remembered her pony, Bijou, and the trip to Europe with her mother when she was eighteen –

'Very, very complicated,' she said aloud and severely to the moon, and, stepping inside, was about to close the door when she heard a noise in the library and started.

It was Martha, the middle-aged servant: they kept only one now.

'Why, Martha!' she said in surprise.

Martha turned quickly.

'Oh, I thought you was upstairs. I was jist – '

'Is anything the matter?'

Martha hesitated.

'No; I – ' She stood there fidgeting. 'It was a letter, Mrs Piper, that I put somewhere.'

'A letter? Your own letter?' asked Evylyn, switching on the light.

'No, it was to you. 'Twas this afternoon, Mrs Piper, in the last mail. The postman give it to me and then the back door-bell rang. I had it in my hand, so I must have stuck it somewhere. I thought I'd just slip in and find it.'

'What sort of a letter? From Mr Donald?'

'No, it was an advertisement, maybe, or a business letter. It was a long, narrow one, I remember.'

They began a search through the music-room, looking on trays and mantelpieces, and then through the library, feeling on the tops of rows of books. Martha paused in despair.

'I can't think where. I went straight to the kitchen. The dining-room, maybe.' She started hopefully for the dining-room, but turned suddenly at the sound of a gasp behind her. Evylyn had sat down heavily in a Morris chair, her brows drawn very close together, eyes blinking furiously.

'Are you sick?'

For a minute there was no answer. Evylyn sat there very still and Martha could see the very quick rise and fall of her bosom.

'Are you sick?' she repeated.

'No,' said Evylyn slowly, 'but I know where the letter is. Go 'way, Martha. I know.'

Wonderingly, Martha withdrew, and still Evylyn sat there, only the muscles around her eyes moving – contracting and relaxing and contracting again. She knew now where the letter was – she knew as well as if she had put it there herself. And she felt instinctively and unquestionably what the letter was. It was long and narrow like an advertisement, but up in the corner in large letters it said 'War Department' and, in smaller letters below, 'Official Business'. She knew it lay there in the big bowl with her name in ink on the outside and her soul's death within.

Rising uncertainly, she walked toward the dining-room, feeling her way along the bookcases and through the doorway. After a moment she found the light and switched it on.

There was the bowl, reflecting the electric light in crimson squares edged with black and yellow squares edged with blue, ponderous and glittering, grotesquely and triumphantly ominous. She took a step forward and paused again; another step and she would see over the top and into the inside – another step and she would see an edge of white – another step – her hands fell on the rough, cold surface –

In a moment she was tearing it open, fumbling with an obstinate fold, holding it before her while the typewritten page glared out and struck at her. Then it fluttered like a bird to the floor. The house that had seemed whirring, buzzing a moment since, was suddenly very quiet; a breath of air crept in through the open front door carrying the noise of a passing motor; she heard faint sounds from upstairs and then a grinding racket in the pipe behind the bookcases – her husband turning off a water-tap –

And in that instant it was as if this were not, after all, Donald's hour except in so far as he was a marker in the insidious contest that had gone on in sudden surges and long, listless interludes between Evylyn and this cold, malignant thing of beauty, a gift of enmity from a man whose face she had long since forgotten. With its massive, brooding passivity it lay there in the centre of her house as it had lain for years, throwing out the ice-like beams of a thousand eyes, perverse glitterings merging each into each, never ageing, never changing.

Evylyn sat down on the edge of the table and stared at it fascinated. It seemed to be smiling now, a very cruel smile, as if to say: 'You see, this time I didn't have to hurt you directly. I didn't bother. You know it was I who took your son away. You know how cold I am and how hard and how beautiful, because once you were just as cold and hard and beautiful.'

The bowl seemed suddenly to turn itself over and then to distend and swell until it became a great canopy that glittered and trembled over the room, over the house, and, as the walls melted slowly into mist, Evylyn saw that it was still moving out, out and far away from her, shutting off far horizons and suns and moons and stars except as inky blots seen faintly through it. And under it walked all the people, and the light that came through to them was refracted and twisted until shadow seemed light and light seemed shadow – until the whole panorama of the world became changed and distorted under the twinkling heaven of the bowl.

Then there came a far-away, booming voice like a low, clear bell. It came from the centre of the bowl and down the great sides to the ground and then bounced toward her eagerly.

'You see, I am fate,' it shouted, 'and stronger than your puny plans; and I am how-things-turn-out and I am different from your little dreams, and I am the flight of time and the end of beauty and unfulfilled desire; all the accidents and imperceptions and the little minutes that shape the crucial hours are mine. I am the exception that proves no rules, the limits of your control, the condiment in the dish of life.'

The booming sound stopped; the echoes rolled away over the wide land to the edge of the bowl that bounded the world and up the great sides and back to the centre where they hummed for a moment and died. Then the great walls began slowly to bear down upon her, growing smaller and smaller, coming closer and closer as if to crush her; and as she clinched her hands and waited for the swift bruise of the cold glass, the bowl gave a sudden wrench and turned over – and lay there on the sideboard, shining and inscrutable, reflecting in a hundred prisms myriad, many-coloured glints and gleams and crossings and interlacings of light.

The cold wind blew in again through the front door, and with a desperate, frantic energy Evylyn stretched both her arms around the bowl. She must be quick – she must be strong. She tightened her arms until they ached, tauted the thin strips of muscle under her soft flesh, and with a mighty effort raised it and held it. She felt the wind blow cold on her back where her dress had come apart from the strain of her effort, and as she felt it she turned toward it and staggered under the great weight out through the library and on toward the front door. She must be quick – she must be strong. The blood in her arms throbbed dully and her knees kept giving way under her, but the feel of the cool glass was good.

Out the front door she tottered and over to the stone steps, and there, summoning every fibre of her soul and body for a last effort, swung herself half around – for a second, as she tried to loose her hold, her numb fingers clung to the rough surface, and in that second she slipped and, losing balance, toppled forward with a despairing cry, her arms still around the bowl . . . down . . .

Over the way lights went on; far down the block the crash was heard, and pedestrians rushed up wonderingly; upstairs a tired man awoke from the edge of sleep and a little girl whimpered in a haunted doze. And all over the moonlit sidewalk around the still, black form, hundreds of prisms and cubes and splinters of glass reflected the light in little gleams of blue, and black edged with yellow, and yellow, and crimson edged with black.

May Day

THERE HAD BEEN a war fought and won and the great city of the conquering people was crossed with triumphal arches and vivid with thrown flowers of white, red, and rose. All through the long spring days the returning soldiers marched up the chief highway behind the strump of drums and the joyous, resonant wind of the brasses, while merchants and clerks left their bickerings and figurings and, crowding to the windows, turned their white-bunched faces gravely upon the passing battalions.

Never had there been such splendour in the great city, for the victorious war had brought plenty in its train, and the merchants had flocked thither from the South and West with their households to taste of all the luscious feasts and witness the lavish entertainments prepared – and to buy for their women furs against the next winter and bags of golden mesh and vari-coloured slippers of silk and silver and rose satin and cloth of gold.

So gaily and noisily were the peace and prosperity impending hymned by the scribes and poets of the conquering people that more and more spenders had gathered from the provinces to drink the wine of excitement, and faster and faster did the merchants dispose of their trinkets and slippers until they sent up a mighty cry for more trinkets and more slippers in order that they might give in barter what was demanded of them. Some even of them flung up their hands helplessly, shouting: 'Alas! I have no more slippers! and alas! I have no more trinkets! May heaven help me, for I know not what I shall do!'

But no one listened to their great outcry, for the throngs were far too busy – day by day, the foot-soldiers trod jauntily the highway and all exulted because the young men returning were pure and brave, sound of tooth and pink of cheek, and the young women of the land were virgins and comely both of face and of figure.

So during all this time there were many adventures that happened in the great city, and, of these, several – or perhaps one – are here set down.

CHAPTER I

AT NINE O'CLOCK on the morning of the first of May 1919, a young man spoke to the room clerk at the Biltmore Hotel, asking if Mr Philip Dean were registered there, and if so, could he be connected with Mr Dean's rooms. The enquirer was dressed in a well-cut shabby suit. He was small, slender, and darkly handsome; his eyes were framed above with unusually long eyelashes and below with the blue semicircle of ill health, this latter effect heightened by an unnatural glow which coloured his face like a low, incessant fever.

Mr Dean was staying there. The young man was directed to a telephone at the side.

After a second his connection was made; a sleepy voice hello'd from somewhere above.

'Mr Dean?' – this very eagerly – 'it's Gordon, Phil. It's Gordon Sterrett. I'm downstairs. I heard you were in New York and I had a hunch you'd be here.'

The sleepy voice became gradually enthusiastic. Well, how was Gordy, old boy! Well, he certainly was surprised and tickled! Would Gordy come right up, for Pete's sake!

A few minutes later Philip Dean, dressed in blue silk pyjamas, opened his door and the two young men greeted each other with a half-embarrassed exuberance. They were both about twenty-four. Yale graduates of the year before the war; but there the resemblance stopped abruptly. Dean was blond, ruddy, and rugged under his thin pyjamas. Everything about him radiated fitness and bodily comfort. He smiled frequently, showing large and prominent teeth.

'I was going to look you up,' he cried enthusiastically. 'I'm taking a couple of weeks off. If you'll sit down a sec I'll be right with you. Going to take a shower.'

As he vanished into the bathroom his visitor's dark eyes roved nervously around the room, resting for a moment on a great English travelling bag in the corner and on a family of thick silk shirts littered on the chairs amid impressive neckties and soft woollen socks.

Gordon rose, and picking up one of the shirts, gave it a minute examination. It was of very heavy silk, yellow with a pale blue stripe – and there were nearly a dozen of them. He stared involuntarily at his own shirt-cuffs – they were ragged and linty at the edges and soiled to a faint grey. Dropping the silk shirt, he held his coat-sleeves down and worked the frayed shirt-cuffs up till they were out of sight. Then he went to the mirror and looked at himself with listless, unhappy interest. His tie, of former glory, was faded and thumb-creased – it served no longer to hide the jagged buttonholes of his collar. He thought, quite without amusement, that only three years before he had received a scattering vote in the senior elections at college for being the best-dressed man in his class.

Dean emerged from the bathroom polishing his body.

'Saw an old friend of yours last night,' he remarked. 'Passed her in the lobby and couldn't think of her name to save my neck. That girl you brought up to New Haven senior year.'

Gordon started.

'Edith Bradin? That whom you mean?'

''At's the one. Damn good looking. She's still sort of a pretty doll – you know what I mean: as if if you touched her she'd smear.'

He surveyed his shining self complacently in the mirror, smiled faintly, exposing a section of teeth.

'She must be twenty-three anyway,' he continued.

'Twenty-two last month,' said Gordon absently.

'What? Oh, last month. Well, I imagine she's down for the Gamma Psi dance. Did you know we're having a Yale Gamma Psi dance tonight at Delmonico's?[6] You better come up, Gordy. Half of New Haven'll probably be there. I can get you an invitation.'

Draping himself reluctantly in fresh underwear, Dean lit a cigarette and sat down by the open window, inspecting his calves and knees under the morning sunshine which poured into the room.

'Sit down, Gordy,' he suggested, 'and tell me all about what you've been doing and what you're doing now and everything.'

Gordon collapsed unexpectedly upon the bed; lay there inert and spiritless. His mouth, which habitually dropped a little open when his face was in repose, became suddenly helpless and pathetic.

'What's the matter?' asked Dean quickly.

'Oh, God!'

'What's the matter?'

'Every God-damn thing in the world,' he said miserably. 'I've absolutely gone to pieces, Phil. I'm all in.'

'Huh?'

'I'm all in.' His voice was shaking.

Dean scrutinised him more closely with appraising blue eyes.

'You certainly look all shot.'

'I am. I've made a hell of mess of everything.' He paused. 'I'd better start at the beginning – or will it bore you?'

'Not at all; go on.' There was, however, a hesitant note in Dean's voice. This trip East had been planned for a holiday – to find Gordon Sterrett in trouble exasperated him a little.

'Go on,' he repeated, and then added half under his breath, 'Get it over with.'

'Well,' began Gordon unsteadily, 'I got back from France in February, went home to Harrisburg for a month, and then came down to New York to get a job – one with an export company. They fired me yesterday.'

'Fired you?'

'I'm coming to that, Phil. I want to tell you frankly. You're about the only man I can turn to in a matter like this. You won't mind if I just tell you frankly, will you, Phil?'

Dean stiffened a bit more. The pats he was bestowing on his knees grew perfunctory. He felt vaguely that he was being unfairly saddled with responsibility; he was not even sure he wanted to be told. Though never surprised at finding Gordon Sterrett in mild difficulty, there was something in this present misery that repelled him and hardened him, even though it excited his curiosity.

'Go on.'

'It's a girl.'

'Hm.' Dean resolved that nothing was going to spoil his trip. If Gordon was going to be depressing, then he'd have to see less of Gordon.

'Her name is Jewel Hudson,' went on the distressed voice from the bed. 'She used to be "pure", I guess, up to about a year ago. Lived here in New York – poor family. Her people are dead now and she lives with an old aunt. You see it was just about the time I met her that everybody began to come back from France in droves – and all I did was to welcome the newly arrived and go on parties with 'em. That's the way it started, Phil, just from being glad to see everybody and having them glad to see me.'

'You ought to've had more sense.'

'I know,' Gordon paused, and then continued listlessly. 'I'm on my own now, you know, and Phil, I can't stand being poor. Then came this darn girl. She sort of fell in love with me for a while and, though I never intended to get so involved, I'd always seem to run into her somewhere. You can imagine the sort of work I was doing for those exporting people – of course, I always intended to draw; do illustrating magazines; there's a pile of money in it.'

'Why didn't you? You've got to buckle down if you want to make good,' suggested Dean with cold formalism.

'I tried, a little, but my stuff's crude. I've got talent, Phil; I can draw – but I just don't know how. I ought to go to art school and I can't afford it. Well, things came to a crisis about a week ago. Just as I was down to about my last dollar this girl began bothering me. She wants some money; claims she can make trouble for me if she doesn't get it.'

'Can she?'

'I'm afraid she can. That's one reason I lost my job – she kept calling up the office all the time, and that was sort of the last straw down there. She's got a letter all written to send to my family. Oh, she's got me, all right. I've got to have some money for her.'

There was an awkward pause. Gordon lay very still, his hands clenched by his sides.

'I'm all in,' he continued, his voice trembling. 'I'm half crazy, Phil. If I hadn't known you were coming East, I think I'd have killed myself. I want you to lend me three hundred dollars.'

Dean's hands, which had been patting his bare ankles, were suddenly quiet – and the curious uncertainty playing between the two became taut and strained.

After a second Gordon continued: 'I've bled the family until I'm ashamed to ask for another nickel.'

Still Dean made no answer.

'Jewel says she's got to have two hundred dollars.'

'Tell her where she can go.'

'Yes, that sounds easy, but she's got a couple of drunken letters I wrote her. Unfortunately she's not at all the flabby sort of person you'd expect.'

Dean made an expression of distaste.

'I can't stand that sort of woman. You ought to have kept away.'

'I know,' admitted Gordon wearily.

'You've got to look at things as they are. If you haven't got money you've got to work and stay away from women.'

'That's easy for you to say,' began Gordon, his eyes narrowing. 'You've got all the money in the world.'

'I most certainly have not. My family keep darn close tabs on what I spend. Just because I have a little leeway I have to be extra careful not to abuse it.'

He raised the blind and let in a further flood of sunshine.

'I'm no prig, Lord knows,' he went on deliberately. 'I like pleasure – and I like a lot of it on a vacation like this – but you, you're in awful shape. I never heard you talk just this way before. You seem to be sort of bankrupt – morally as well as financially.'

'Don't they usually go together?'

Dean shook his head impatiently.

'There's a regular aura about you that I don't understand. It's a sort of evil.'

'It's an air of worry and poverty and sleepless nights,' said Gordon, rather defiantly.

'I don't know.'

'Oh, I admit I'm depressing. I depress myself. But, my God, Phil, a week's rest and a new suit and some ready money and I'd be like – like I was. Phil, I can draw like a streak, and you know it. But half the time I haven't had the money to buy decent drawing materials – and I can't draw when I'm tired and discouraged and all in. With a little ready money I can take a few weeks off and get started.'

'How do I know you wouldn't use it on some other woman?'

'Why rub it in?' said Gordon quietly.

'I'm not rubbing it in. I hate to see you this way.'

'Will you lend me the money, Phil?'

'I can't decide right off. That's a lot of money and it'll be darn inconvenient for me.'

'It'll be hell for me if you can't – I know I'm whining, and it's all my own fault but – that doesn't change it.'

'When could you pay it back?'

This was encouraging, Gordon considered. It was probably wisest to be frank.

'Of course, I could promise to send it back next month, but – I'd better say three months. Just as soon as I start to sell drawings.'

'How do I know you'll sell any drawings?'

A new hardness in Dean's voice sent a faint chill of doubt over Gordon. Was it possible that he wouldn't get the money?

'I supposed you had a little confidence in me.'

'I did have – but when I see you like this I begin to wonder.'

'Do you suppose if I wasn't at the end of my rope I'd come to you like this? Do you think I'm enjoying it?' He broke off and bit his lip, feeling that he had better subdue the rising anger in his voice. After all, he was the suppliant.

'You seem to manage it pretty easily,' said Dean angrily. 'You put me in the position where, if I don't lend it to you, I'm a sucker – oh, yes, you do. And let me tell you it's no easy thing for me to get hold of three hundred dollars. My income isn't so big but that a slice like that won't play the deuce with it.'

He left his chair and began to dress, choosing his clothes carefully. Gordon stretched out his arms and clenched the edges of the bed, fighting back a desire to cry out. His head was splitting and whirring, his mouth was dry and bitter and he could feel the fever in his blood resolving itself into innumerable regular counts like a slow dripping from a roof.

Dean tied his tie precisely, brushed his eyebrows, and removed a piece of tobacco from his teeth with solemnity. Next he filled his cigarette case, tossed the empty box thoughtfully into the waste basket, and settled the case in his vest pocket.

'Had breakfast?' he demanded.

'No; I don't eat it any more.'

'Well, we'll go out and have some. We'll decide about that money later. I'm sick of the subject. I came East to have a good time.

'Let's go over to the Yale Club,' he continued moodily, and then added with an implied reproof: 'You've given up your job. You've got nothing else to do.'

'I'd have a lot to do if I had a little money,' said Gordon pointedly.

'Oh, for heaven's sake drop the subject for a while! No point in glooming on my whole trip. Here, here's some money.'

He took a five-dollar bill from his wallet and tossed it over to Gordon, who folded it carefully and put it in his pocket. There was an added spot of colour in his cheeks, an added glow that was not fever. For an instant before they turned to go out their eyes met and in that instant each found something that made him lower his own glance quickly. For in that instant they quite suddenly and definitely hated each other.

FIFTH AVENUE and 44th Street swarmed with the noon crowd. The wealthy, happy sun glittered in transient gold through the thick windows of the smart shops, lighting upon mesh bags and purses and strings of pearls in grey velvet cases; upon gaudy feather fans of many colours; upon the laces and silks of expensive dresses; upon the bad paintings and the fine period furniture in the elaborate showrooms of interior decorators.

Working-girls, in pairs and groups and swarms, loitered by the windows, choosing their future boudoirs from some resplendent display which included even a man's silk pyjamas laid domestically across the bed. They stood in front of the jewellery stores and picked out their engagement rings, and their wedding rings and their platinum wrist-watches, and then drifted on to inspect the feather fans and opera cloaks; meanwhile digesting the sandwiches and sundaes they had eaten for lunch.

All through the crowd were men in uniform, sailors from the great fleet anchored in the Hudson, soldiers with divisional insignia from Massachusetts to California wanting fearfully to be noticed, and finding the great city thoroughly fed up with soldiers unless they were nicely massed into pretty formations and uncomfortable under the weight of a pack and rifle.

Through this medley Dean and Gordon wandered; the former interested, made alert by the display of humanity at its frothiest and gaudiest; the latter reminded of how often he had been one of the crowd, tired, casually fed, overworked, and dissipated. To Dean the struggle was significant, young, cheerful; to Gordon it was dismal, meaningless, endless.

In the Yale Club they met a group of their former classmates who greeted the visiting Dean vociferously. Sitting in a semicircle of lounges and great chairs, they had a highball all around.

Gordon found the conversation tiresome and interminable. They lunched together *en masse*, warmed with liquor as the afternoon began. They were all going to the Gamma Psi dance[7] that night – it promised to be the best party since the war.

'Edith Bradin's coming,' said someone to Gordon. 'Didn't she used to be an old flame of yours? Aren't you both from Harrisburg?'

'Yes.' He tried to change the subject. 'I see her brother occasionally. He's sort of a socialistic nut. Runs a paper or something here in New York.'

'Not like his gay[8] sister, eh?' continued his eager informant. 'Well, she's coming tonight with a junior named Peter Himmell.'

Gordon was to meet Jewel Hudson at eight o'clock – he had promised to have some money for her. Several times he glanced nervously at his wrist-watch. At four to his relief, Dean rose and announced that he was going over to Rivers Brothers to buy some collars and ties. But as they left the Club another of the party joined them, to Gordon's great dismay. Dean was in a jovial mood now, happy, expectant of the evening's party, faintly hilarious. Over in Rivers he chose a dozen neckties, selecting each one after long consultations with the other man. Did he think narrow ties were coming back? And wasn't it a shame that Rivers couldn't get any more Welsh Margotson collars? There never was a collar like the 'Covington'.

Gordon was in something of a panic. He wanted the money immediately. And he was now inspired also with a vague idea of attending the Gamma Psi dance. He wanted to see Edith – Edith whom he hadn't met since one romantic night at the Harrisburg Country Club just before he went to France. The affair had died, drowned in the turmoil of the war and quite forgotten in the arabesque of these three months, but a picture of her, poignant, debonair, immersed in her own inconsequential chatter, recurred to him unexpectedly and brought a hundred memories with it. It was Edith's face that he had cherished through college with a sort of detached yet affectionate admiration. He had loved to draw her – around his room had been a dozen sketches of her – playing golf, swimming – he could draw her pert, arresting profile with his eyes shut.

They left Rivers at five-thirty and paused for a moment on the sidewalk.

'Well,' said Dean genially, 'I'm all set now. Think I'll go back to the hotel and get a shave, haircut, and massage.'

'Good enough,' said the other man, 'I think I'll join you.'

Gordon wondered if he was to be beaten after all. With difficulty he restrained himself from turning to the man and snarling out, 'Go on away, damn you!' In despair he suspected that perhaps Dean had spoken to him, was keeping him along in order to avoid a dispute about the money.

They went into the Biltmore – a Biltmore alive with girls – mostly from the West and South, the stellar débutantes of many cities gathered for the dance of a famous fraternity of a famous university. But to Gordon they were faces in a dream. He gathered together his forces for a last appeal, was about to come out with he knew not what, when Dean suddenly excused himself to the other man and taking Gordon's arm led him aside.

'Gordy,' he said quickly, 'I've thought the whole thing over carefully and I've decided that I can't lend you that money. I'd like to oblige you, but I don't feel I ought to – it'd put a crimp in me for a month.'

Gordon, watching him dully, wondered why he had never before noticed how much those upper teeth projected.

' – I'm mighty sorry, Gordon,' continued Dean, 'but that's the way it is.'

He took out his wallet and deliberately counted out seventy-five dollars in bills.

'Here,' he said, holding them out, 'here's seventy-five; that makes eighty altogether. That's all the actual cash I have with me, besides what I'll actually spend on the trip.'

Gordon raised his clenched hand automatically, opened it as though it were a tongs he was holding, and clenched it again on the money.

'I'll see you at the dance,' continued Dean. 'I've got to get along to the barber shop.'

'So long,' said Gordon in a strained and husky voice.

'So long.'

Dean began to smile, but seemed to change his mind. He nodded briskly and disappeared.

But Gordon stood there, his handsome face awry with distress, the roll of bills clenched tightly in his hand. Then, blinded by sudden tears, he stumbled clumsily down the Biltmore steps.

CHAPTER 3

ABOUT NINE O'CLOCK of the same night two human beings came out of a cheap restaurant in Sixth Avenue. They were ugly, ill-nourished, devoid of all except the very lowest form of intelligence, and without even that animal exuberance that in itself brings colour into life; they were lately vermin-ridden, cold, and hungry in a dirty town of a strange land; they were poor, friendless; tossed as drift-wood from their births, they would be tossed as driftwood to their deaths. They were dressed in the uniform of the United States Army, and on the shoulder of each was the insignia of a drafted division from New Jersey, landed three days before.

The taller of the two was named Carrol Key, a name hinting that in his veins, however thinly diluted by generations of degeneration, ran blood of some potentiality. But one could stare endlessly at the long, chinless face, the dull, watery eyes, and high cheek-bones, without finding a suggestion of either ancestral worth or native resourcefulness.

His companion was swart and bandy-legged, with rat-eyes and a much-broken hooked nose. His defiant air was obviously a pretence, a weapon of protection borrowed from that world of snarl and snap, of physical bluff and physical menace, in which he had always lived. His name was Gus Rose.

Leaving the café they sauntered down Sixth Avenue, wielding toothpicks with great gusto and complete detachment.

'Where to?' asked Rose, in a tone which implied that he would not be surprised if Key suggested the South Sea Islands.

'What you say we see if we can getta holda some liquor?' Pro-hibition[9] was not yet. The ginger in the suggestion was caused by the law forbidding the selling of liquor to soldiers.

Rose agreed enthusiastically.

'I got an idea,' continued Key, after a moment's thought, 'I got a brother somewhere.'

'In New York?'

'Yeah. He's an old fella.' He meant that he was an elder brother. 'He's a waiter in a hash joint.'

'Maybe he can get us some.'

'I'll say he can!'

'B'lieve me, I'm goin' to get this darn uniform off me tomorra. Never get me in it again, neither. I'm goin' to get me some regular clothes.'

'Say, maybe I'm not.'

As their combined finances were something less than five dollars, this intention can be taken largely as a pleasant game of words, harmless and consoling. It seemed to please both of them, however, for they reinforced it with chuckling and mention of personages high in biblical circles, adding such further emphasis as 'Oh, boy!' 'You know!' and 'I'll say so!' repeated many times over.

The entire mental pabulum of these two men consisted of an offended nasal comment extended through the years upon the institution – army, business, or poorhouse – which kept them alive, and toward their immediate superior in that institution. Until that very morning the institution had been the 'government' and the immediate superior had been the 'cap'n' – from these two they had glided out and were now in the vaguely uncomfortable state before they should adopt their next bondage. They were uncertain, resentful, and somewhat ill at ease. This they hid by pretending an elaborate relief at being out of the army, and by assuring each other that military discipline should never again rule their stubborn, liberty-loving wills. Yet, as a matter of fact, they would have felt more at home in a prison than in this new-found and unquestionable freedom.

Suddenly Key increased his gait. Rose, looking up and following his glance, discovered a crowd that was collecting fifty yards down the street. Key chuckled and began to run in the direction of the crowd; Rose thereupon also chuckled and his short bandy legs twinkled beside the long, awkward strides of his companion.

Reaching the outskirts of the crowd they immediately became an indistinguishable part of it. It was composed of ragged civilians somewhat the worse for liquor, and of soldiers representing many divisions and many stages of sobriety, all clustered around a gesticulating little Jew with long black whiskers, who was waving his arms and delivering an excited but succinct harangue. Key and Rose, having wedged themselves into the approximate parquet, scrutinised him with acute suspicion, as his words penetrated their common consciousness.

' – What have you got outa the war?' he was crying fiercely. 'Look arounja, look arounja! Are you rich? Have you got a lot of money offered you? – no; you're lucky if you're alive and got both your legs; you're lucky if you came back an' find your wife ain't gone off with some other fella that had the money to buy himself out of the war! That's when you're lucky! Who got anything out of it except J. P. Morgan[10] an' John D. Rockerfeller[11]?'

At this point the little Jew's oration was interrupted by the hostile impact of a fist upon the point of his bearded chin and he toppled backward to a sprawl on the pavement.

'God-damn Bolsheviki!' cried the big soldier-blacksmith who had delivered the blow. There was a rumble of approval, the crowd closed in nearer.

The Jew staggered to his feet, and immediately went down again before a half-dozen reaching-in fists. This time he stayed down, breathing heavily, blood oozing from his lip where it was cut within and without.

There was a riot of voices, and in a minute Rose and Key found themselves flowing with the jumbled crowd down Sixth Avenue under the leadership of a thin civilian in a slouch hat and the brawny soldier who had summarily ended the oration. The crowd had marvellously swollen to formidable proportions and a stream of more non-committal citizens followed it along the sidewalks lending their moral support by intermittent huzzas.

'Where we goin'?' yelled Key to the man nearest him.

His neighbour pointed up to the leader in the slouch hat. 'That guy knows where there's a lot of 'em! We're goin' to show em!'

'We're goin' to show 'em!' whispered Key delightedly to Rose, who repeated the phrase rapturously to a man on the other side.

Down Sixth Avenue swept the procession, joined here and there by soldiers and marines, and now and then by civilians, who came up with the inevitable cry that they were just out of the army themselves, as if presenting it as a card of admission to a newly formed Sporting and Amusement Club.

Then the procession swerved down a cross street and headed for Fifth Avenue and the word filtered here and there that they were bound for a Red meeting at Tolliver Hall.

'Where is it?'

The question went up the line and a moment later the answer floated back. Tolliver Hall was down on 10th Street. There was a bunch of other sojers who was goin' to break it up and was down there now!

But 10th Street had a far-away sound and at the word a general groan went up and a score of the procession dropped out. Among these were Rose and Key, who slowed down to a saunter and let the more enthusiastic sweep on by.

'I'd rather get some liquor,' said Key, as they halted and made their way to the sidewalk amid cries of 'Shell hole!' and 'Quitters!'

'Does your brother work around here?' asked Rose, assuming the air of one passing from the superficial to the eternal.

'He oughta,' replied Key. 'I ain't seen him for a coupla years. I been out to Pennsylvania since. Maybe he don't work at night anyhow. It's right along here. He can get us some o'right if he ain't gone.'

They found the place after a few minutes' patrol of the street – a shoddy tablecloth restaurant between Fifth Avenue and Broadway. Here Key went inside to enquire for his brother, George, while Rose waited on the sidewalk.

'He ain't here no more,' said Key emerging. 'He's a waiter up to Delmonico's.'

Rose nodded wisely, as if he'd expected as much. One should not be surprised at a capable man changing jobs occasionally. He knew a waiter once – there ensued a long conversation as they walked as to whether waiters made more in actual wages than in tips – it was decided that it depended on the social tone of the joint wherein the waiter laboured. After having given each other vivid pictures of millionaires dining at Delmonico's and throwing away fifty-dollar bills after their first quart of champagne, both men thought privately of becoming waiters. In fact, Key's narrow brow was secreting a resolution to ask his brother to get him a job.

'A waiter can drink up all the champagne those fellas leave in bottles,' suggested Rose with some relish, and then added as an afterthought, 'Oh, boy!'

By the time they reached Delmonico's it was half-past ten, and they were surprised to see a stream of taxis driving up to the door one after the other and emitting marvellous, hatless young ladies, each one attended by a stiff young gentleman in evening clothes.

'It's a party,' said Rose with some awe. 'Maybe we better not go in. He'll be busy.'

'No, he won't. He'll be o'right.'

After some hesitation they entered what appeared to them to be the least elaborate door and, indecision falling upon them immediately, stationed themselves nervously in an inconspicuous corner of the small dining-room in which they found themselves. They took off their caps and held them in their hands. A cloud of gloom fell upon them and both started when a door at one end of the room crashed open, emitting a comet-like waiter who streaked across the floor and vanished through another door on the other side.

There had been three of these lightning passages before the seekers mustered the acumen to hail a waiter. He turned, looked at them suspiciously, and then approached with soft, catlike steps, as if prepared at any moment to turn and flee.

'Say,' began Key, 'say, do you know my brother? He's a waiter here.'

'His name is Key,' annotated Rose.

Yes, the waiter knew Key. He was upstairs, he thought. There was a big dance going on in the main ballroom. He'd tell him.

Ten minutes later George Key appeared and greeted his brother with the utmost suspicion; his first and most natural thought being that he was going to be asked for money.

George was tall and weak chinned, but there his resemblance to his brother ceased. The waiter's eyes were not dull, they were alert and twinkling, and his manner was suave, indoor, and faintly superior. They exchanged formalities. George was married and had three children. He seemed fairly interested, but not impressed, by the news that Carrol had been abroad in the army. This disappointed Carrol.

'George,' said the younger brother, these amenities having been disposed of, 'we want to get some booze, and they won't sell us none. Can you get us some?'

George considered.

'Sure. Maybe I can. It may be half an hour, though.'

'All right,' agreed Carrol, 'we'll wait.'

At this Rose started to sit down in a convenient chair, but was hailed to his feet by the indignant George.

'Hey! Watch out, you! Can't sit down here! This room's all set for a twelve o'clock banquet.'

'I ain't going to hurt it,' said Rose resentfully. 'I been through the delouser.'

'Never mind,' said George sternly, 'if the head waiter seen me here talkin' he'd romp all over me.'

'Oh.'

The mention of the head waiter was full explanation to the other two; they fingered their overseas caps nervously and waited for a suggestion.

'I tell you,' said George, after a pause, 'I got a place you can wait; you just come here with me.'

They followed him out the far door, through a deserted pantry and up a pair of dark winding stairs, emerging finally into a small room chiefly furnished by piles of pails and stacks of scrubbing brushes, and illuminated by a single dim electric light. There he left them, after soliciting two dollars and agreeing to return in half an hour with a quart of whiskey.

'George is makin' money, I bet,' said Key gloomily as he seated himself on an inverted pail. 'I bet he's making fifty dollars a week.'

Rose nodded his head and spat.

'I bet he is, too.'

'What'd he say the dance was of?'

'A lot of college fellas. Yale College.'

They both nodded solemnly at each other.

'Wonder where that crowda sojers is now?'

'I don't know. I know that's too damn long to walk for me.'

'Me too. You don't catch me walkin' that far.'

Ten minutes later restlessness seized them.

'I'm goin' to see what's out here,' said Rose, stepping cautiously towards the other door.

It was a swinging door of green baize and he pushed it open a cautious inch.

'See anything?'

For answer Rose drew in his breath sharply.

'Doggone! Here's some liquor, I'll say!'

'Liquor?'

Key joined Rose at the door, and looked eagerly.

'I'll tell the world that's liquor,' he said, after a moment of concentrated gazing.

It was a room about twice as large as the one they were in – and in it was prepared a radiant feast of spirits. There were long walls of alternating bottles set along two white covered tables: whiskey, gin, brandy, French and Italian vermouths, and orange juice, not to mention an array of syphons and two great empty punch-bowls. The room was as yet uninhabited.

'It's for this dance they're just starting,' whispered Key; 'hear the violins playin'? Say, boy, I wouldn't mind havin' a dance.'

They closed the door softly and exchanged a glance of mutual comprehension. There was no need of feeling each other out.

'I'd like to get my hands on a coupla those bottles,' said Rose emphatically.

'Me too.'

'Do you suppose we'd get seen?'

Key considered.

'Maybe we better wait till they start drinkin' 'em. They got 'em all laid out now, and they know how many of them there are.'

They debated this point for several minutes. Rose was all for getting his hands on a bottle now and tucking it under his coat before anyone came into the room. Key, however, advocated caution. He was afraid he might get his brother in trouble. If they waited till some of the bottles were opened it'd be all right to take one, and everybody'd think it was one of the college fellas.

While they were still engaged in argument George Key hurried through the room and, barely grunting at them, disappeared by way of the green-baize door. A minute later they heard several corks pop, and then the sound of crackling ice and splashing liquid. George was mixing the punch.

The soldiers exchanged delighted grins.

'Oh, boy!' whispered Rose.

George reappeared.

'Just keep low, boys,' he said quickly. 'I'll have your stuff for you in five minutes.'

He disappeared through the door by which he had come.

As soon as his footsteps receded down the stairs, Rose, after a cautious look, darted into the room of delights and reappeared with a bottle in his hand.

'Here's what I say,' he said, as they sat radiantly digesting their first drink. 'We'll wait till he comes up, and we'll ask him if we can't just stay here and drink what he brings us – see. We'll tell him we haven't got any place to drink it – see. Then we can sneak in there whenever there ain't nobody in that there room and tuck a bottle under our coats. We'll have enough to last us a coupla days – see?'

'Sure,' agreed Rose enthusiastically. 'Oh, boy! And if we want to we can sell it to sojers any time we want to.'

They were silent for a moment thinking rosily of this idea. Then Key reached up and unhooked the collar of his O. D.[12] coat.

'It's hot in here, ain't it?'

Rose agreed earnestly.

'Hot as hell.'

CHAPTER 4

SHE WAS STILL quite angry when she came out of the dressing-room and crossed the intervening parlour of politeness that opened on to the hall – angry not so much at the actual happening which was, after all, the merest commonplace of her social existence, but because it had occurred on this particular night. She had no quarrel with herself. She had acted with that correct mixture of dignity and reticent pity which she always employed. She had succinctly and deftly snubbed him.

It had happened when their taxi was leaving the Biltmore – hadn't gone half a block. He had lifted his right arm awkwardly – she was on his right side – and attempted to settle it snugly around the crimson fur-trimmed opera cloak she wore. This in itself had been a mistake. It was inevitably more graceful for a young man attempting to embrace a young lady of whose acquiescence he was not certain, to first put his far arm around her. It avoided that awkward movement of raising the near arm.

His second *faux pas*[13] was unconscious. She had spent the afternoon at the hairdresser's; the idea of any calamity overtaking her hair was extremely repugnant yet as Peter made his unfortunate attempt the point of his elbow had just faintly brushed it. That was his second *faux pas*. Two were quite enough.

He had begun to murmur. At the first murmur she had decided that he was nothing but a college boy – Edith was twenty-two, and anyhow, this dance, first of its kind since the war, was reminding her, with the accelerating rhythm of its associations, of something else – of another dance and another man, a man for whom her feelings had been little more than a sad-eyed, adolescent mooniness. Edith Bradin was falling in love with her recollection of Gordon Sterrett.

So she came out of the dressing-room at Delmonico's and stood for a second in the doorway looking over the shoulders of a black dress in front of her at the groups of Yale men who flitted like dignified black moths around the head of the stairs. From the room she had left drifted out the heavy fragrance left by the passage to and fro of many scented young beauties – rich perfumes and the fragile memory-laden dust of fragrant powders. This odour drifting out acquired the tang of cigarette smoke in the hall, and then settled sensuously down the stairs and permeated the ballroom where the Gamma Psi dance was to be held. It was an odour she knew well, exciting, stimulating, restlessly sweet – the odour of a fashionable dance.

She thought of her own appearance. Her bare arms and shoulders were powdered to a creamy white. She knew they looked very soft and would gleam like milk against the black backs that were to silhouette them tonight. The hairdressing had been a success; her reddish mass of hair was piled and crushed and creased to an arrogant marvel of mobile curves. Her lips were finely made of deep carmine; the irises of her eyes were delicate, breakable blue, like china eyes. She was a complete, infinitely delicate, quite perfect thing of beauty, flowing in an even line from a complex coiffure to two small slim feet.

She thought of what she would say tonight at this revel, faintly presaged already by the sounds of high and low laughter and slippered footsteps, and movements of couples up and down the stairs. She would talk the language she had talked for many years – her line – made up of the current expressions, bits of journalese and college slang strung together into an intrinsic whole, careless, faintly provocative, delicately sentimental. She smiled faintly as she heard a girl sitting on the stairs near her say: 'You don't know the half of it, dearie!'

And as she smiled her anger melted for a moment, and closing her eyes she drew in a deep breath of pleasure. She dropped her arms to her sides until they were faintly touching the sleek sheath that covered and suggested her figure. She had never felt her own softness so much nor so enjoyed the whiteness of her own arms.

'I smell sweet,' she said to herself simply, and then came another thought – 'I'm made for love.'

She liked the sound of this and thought it again; then in inevitable succession came her new-born riot of dreams about Gordon. The twist of her imagination which, two months before, had disclosed to her her unguessed desire to see him again, seemed now to have been leading up to this dance, this hour.

For all her sleek beauty, Edith was a grave, slow-thinking girl. There was a streak in her of that same desire to ponder, of that adolescent idealism that had turned her brother socialist and pacifist. Henry Bradin had left Cornell, where he had been an instructor in economics, and had come to New York to pour the latest cures for incurable evils into the columns of a radical weekly newspaper.

Edith, less fatuously, would have been content to cure Gordon Sterrett. There was a quality of weakness in Gordon that she wanted to take care of; there was a helplessness in him that she wanted to protect. And she wanted someone she had known a long while, someone who had loved her a long while. She was a little tired; she wanted to get married. Out of a pile of letters, half a dozen pictures and as many memories, and this weariness, she had decided that next time she saw Gordon their relations were going to be changed. She would say something that would change them. There was this evening. This was her evening. All evenings were her evenings.

Then her thoughts were interrupted by a solemn undergraduate with a hurt look and an air of strained formality who presented himself before her and bowed unusually low. It was the man she had come with, Peter Himmel. He was tall and humorous, with horn-rimmed glasses and an air of attractive whimsicality. She suddenly rather disliked him – probably because he had not succeeded in kissing her.

'Well,' she began, 'are you still furious at me?'

'Not at all.'

She stepped forward and took his arm.

'I'm sorry,' she said softly. 'I don't know why I snapped out that way. I'm in a bum humour tonight for some strange reason. I'm sorry.'

'S'all right,' he mumbled, 'don't mention it.'

He felt disagreeably embarrassed. Was she rubbing in the fact of his late failure?

'It was a mistake,' she continued, on the same consciously gentle key. 'We'll both forget it.' For this he hated her.

A few minutes later they drifted out on the floor while the dozen swaying, sighing members of the specially hired jazz orchestra informed the crowded ballroom that 'if a saxophone and me are left alone why then two is compan–ee!'

A man with a moustache cut in.

'Hello,' he began reprovingly. 'You don't remember me.'

'I can't just think of your name,' she said lightly – 'and I know you so well.'

'I met you up at – ' His voice trailed disconsolately off as a man with very fair hair cut in. Edith murmured a conventional, 'Thanks, loads – cut in later,' to the *inconnu*.[14]

The very fair man insisted on shaking hands enthusiastically. She placed him as one of the numerous Jims of her acquaintance – last name a mystery. She remembered even that he had a peculiar rhythm in dancing and found as they started that she was right.

'Going to be here long?' he breathed confidentially.

She leaned back and looked up at him.

'Couple of weeks.'

'Where are you?'

'Biltmore. Call me up some day.'

'I mean it,' he assured her. 'I will. We'll go to tea.'

'So do I – Do.'

A dark man cut in with intense formality.

'You don't remember me, do you?' he said gravely.

'I should say I do. Your name's Harlan.'

'No–ope. Barlow.'

'Well, I knew there were two syllables anyway. You're the boy that played the ukulele so well up at Howard Marshall's house party.'

'I played – but not – '

A man with prominent teeth cut in. Edith inhaled a slight cloud of whiskey. She liked men to have had something to drink; they were so much more cheerful, and appreciative, and complimentary – much easier to talk to.

'My name's Dean, Philip Dean,' he said cheerfully. 'You don't remember me, I know, but you used to come up to New Haven with a fellow I roomed with senior year, Gordon Sterrett.'

Edith looked up quickly.

'Yes, I went up with him twice – to the Pump and Slipper and the Junior prom.'

'You've seen him, of course,' said Dean carelessly. 'He's here tonight. I saw him just a minute ago.'

Edith started. Yet she had felt quite sure he would be here.

'Why no, I haven't – '

A fat man with red hair cut in.

'Hello, Edith,' he began.

'Why – hello there – '

She slipped, stumbled lightly.

'I'm sorry, dear,' she murmured mechanically.

She had seen Gordon – Gordon very white and listless, leaning against the side of a doorway, smoking and looking into the ballroom. Edith could see that his face was thin and wan – that the hand he raised to his lips with a cigarette was trembling. They were dancing quite close to him now.

' – They invite so darn many extra fellas that you –' the short man was saying.

'Hello, Gordon,' called Edith over her partner's shoulder. Her heart was pounding wildly.

His large dark eyes were fixed on her. He took a step in her direction. Her partner turned her away – she heard his voice bleating –

' – but half the stags[15] get lit and leave before long, so – '

Then a low tone at her side.

'May I, please?'

She was dancing suddenly with Gordon; one of his arms was around her; she felt it tighten spasmodically; felt his hand on her back with the fingers spread. Her hand holding the little lace handkerchief was crushed in his.

'Why, Gordon,' she began breathlessly.

'Hello, Edith.'

She slipped again – was tossed forward by her recovery until her face touched the black cloth of his dinner coat. She loved him – she knew she loved him – then for a minute there was silence while a strange feeling of uneasiness crept over her. Something was wrong.

Of a sudden her heart wrenched and turned over as she realised what it was. He was pitiful and wretched, a little drunk, and miserably tired.

'Oh – ' she cried involuntarily.

His eyes looked down at her. She saw suddenly that they were blood-streaked and rolling uncontrollably.

'Gordon,' she murmured, 'we'll sit down, I want to sit down.'

They were nearly in mid-floor, but she had seen two men start toward her from opposite sides of the room, so she halted, seized Gordon's limp hand and led him bumping through the crowd, her mouth tight shut, her face a little pale under her rouge, her eyes trembling with tears.

She found a place high up on the soft-carpeted stairs, and he sat down heavily beside her.

'Well,' he began, staring at her unsteadily, 'I certainly am glad to see you, Edith.'

She looked at him without answering. The effect of this on her was immeasurable. For years she had seen men in various stages of intoxication, from uncles all the way down to chauffeurs, and her feelings had varied from amusement to disgust, but here for the first time she was seized with a new feeling – an unutterable horror.

'Gordon,' she said accusingly and almost crying, 'you look like the devil.'

He nodded. 'I've had trouble, Edith.'

'Trouble?'

'All sorts of trouble. Don't you say anything to the family, but I'm all gone to pieces. I'm a mess, Edith.'

His lower lip was sagging. He seemed scarcely to see her.

'Can't you – can't you,' she hesitated, 'can't you tell me about it, Gordon? You know I'm always interested in you.'

She bit her lip – she had intended to say something stronger, but found at the end that she couldn't bring it out.

Gordon shook his head dully. 'I can't tell you. You're a good woman. I can't tell a good woman the story.'

'Rot,' she said, defiantly. 'I think it's a perfect insult to call anyone a good woman in that way. It's a slam. You've been drinking, Gordon.'

'Thanks.' He inclined his head gravely. 'Thanks for the information.'

'Why do you drink?'

'Because I'm so damn miserable.'

'Do you think drinking's going to make it any better?'

'What you doing – trying to reform me?'

'No; I'm trying to help you, Gordon. Can't you tell me about it?'

'I'm in an awful mess. Best thing you can do is to pretend not to know me.'

'Why, Gordon?'

'I'm sorry I cut in on you – it's unfair to you. You're a pure woman – and all that sort of thing. Here, I'll get someone else to dance with you.'

He rose clumsily to his feet, but she reached up and pulled him down beside her on the stairs.

'Here, Gordon. You're ridiculous. You're hurting me. You're acting like a – like a crazy man – '

'I admit it. I'm a little crazy. Something's wrong with me, Edith. There's something left me. It doesn't matter.'

'It does, tell me.'

'Just that. I was always queer – little bit different from other boys. All right in college, but now it's all wrong. Things have been snapping inside me for four months like little hooks on a dress, and it's about to come off when a few more hooks go. I'm very gradually going loony.'

He turned his eyes full on her and began to laugh, and she shrank away from him.

'What *is* the matter?'

'Just me,' he repeated. 'I'm going loony. This whole place is like a dream to me – this Delmonico's – '

As he talked she saw he had changed utterly. He wasn't at all light and gay and careless – a great lethargy and discouragement had come over him. Revulsion seized her, followed by a faint, surprising boredom. His voice seemed to come out of a great void.

'Edith,' he said, 'I used to think I was clever, talented, an artist. Now I know I'm nothing. Can't draw, Edith. Don't know why I'm telling you this.'

She nodded absently.

'I can't draw, I can't do anything. I'm poor as a church mouse.' He laughed, bitterly and rather too loud. 'I've become a damn beggar, a leech on my friends. I'm a failure. I'm poor as hell.'

Her distaste was growing. She barely nodded this time, waiting for her first possible cue to rise.

Suddenly Gordon's eyes filled with tears.

'Edith,' he said, turning to her with what was evidently a strong effort at self-control, 'I can't tell you what it means to me to know there's one person left who's interested in me.'

He reached out and patted her hand, and involuntarily she drew it away.

'It's mighty fine of you,' he repeated.

'Well,' she said slowly, looking him in the eye, 'anyone's always glad to see an old friend – but I'm sorry to see you like this, Gordon.'

There was a pause while they looked at each other, and the momentary eagerness in his eyes wavered. She rose and stood looking at him, her face quite expressionless.

'Shall we dance?' she suggested, coolly.

– Love is fragile – she was thinking – but perhaps the pieces are saved, the things that hovered on lips, that might have been said. The new love-words, the tenderness learned, and treasured up for the next lover.

CHAPTER 5

PETER HIMMEL, escort to the lovely Edith, was unaccustomed to being snubbed; having been snubbed, he was hurt and embarrassed, and ashamed of himself. For a matter of two months he had been on special delivery terms with Edith Bradin and knowing that the one excuse and explanation of the special delivery letter is its value in sentimental correspondence, he had believed himself quite sure of his ground. He searched in vain for any reason why she should have taken this attitude in the matter of a simple kiss.

Therefore when he was cut in on by the man with the moustache he went out into the hall and, making up a sentence, said it over to himself several times. Considerably deleted, this was it: 'Well, if any girl ever led a man on and then jilted him, she did – and she has no kick coming if I go out and get beautifully boiled.'

So he walked through the supper room into a small room adjoining it, which he had located earlier in the evening. It was a room in which there were several large bowls of punch flanked by many bottles. He took a seat beside the table which held the bottles.

At the second highball, boredom, disgust, the monotony of time, the turbidity of events, sank into a vague background before which glittering cobwebs formed. Things became reconciled to themselves, things lay quietly on their shelves; the troubles of the day arranged themselves in trim formation and at his curt wish of dismissal, marched off and disappeared. And with the departure of worry came brilliant, permeating symbolism. Edith became a flighty, negligible girl, not to be worried over; rather to be laughed at. She fitted like a figure of his own dream into the surface world forming about him. He himself became in a measure symbolic, a type of the continent bacchanal, the brilliant dreamer at play.

Then the symbolic mood faded and as he sipped his third highball his imagination yielded to the warm glow and he lapsed into a state similar to floating on his back in pleasant water. It was at this point that he noticed that a green baize door near him was open about two inches, and that through the aperture a pair of eyes were watching him intently.

'Hm,' murmured Peter calmly.

The green door closed – and then opened again – a bare half-inch this time.

'Peek-a-boo,' murmured Peter.

The door remained stationary and then he became aware of a series of tense intermittent whispers.

'One guy.'

'What's he doin'?'

'He's sittin' lookin'.'

'He better beat it off. We gotta get another li'l' bottle.'

Peter listened while the words filtered into his consciousness.

'Now this,' he thought, 'is most remarkable.'

He was excited. He was jubilant. He felt that he had stumbled upon a mystery. Affecting an elaborate carelessness he arose and walked around the table – then, turning quickly, pulled open the green door, precipitating Private Rose into the room.

Peter bowed.

'How do you do?' he said.

Private Rose set one foot slightly in front of the other, poised for fight, flight, or compromise.

'How do you do?' repeated Peter politely.

'I'm o'right.'

'Can I offer you a drink?'

Private Rose looked at him searchingly, suspecting possible sarcasm.

'O'right,' he said finally.

Peter indicated a chair.

'Sit down.'

'I got a friend,' said Rose, 'I got a friend in there.' He pointed to the green door.

'By all means let's have him in.'

Peter crossed over, opened the door and welcomed in Private Key, very suspicious and uncertain and guilty. Chairs were found and the three took their seats around the punch-bowl. Peter gave them each a highball and offered them a cigarette from his case. They accepted both with some diffidence.

'Now,' continued Peter easily, 'may I ask why you gentlemen prefer to lounge away your leisure hours in a room which is chiefly furnished, as far as I can see, with scrubbing brushes. And when the human race has progressed to the stage where seventeen thousand chairs are manufactured on every day except Sunday – ' he paused. Rose and Key regarded him vacantly. 'Will you tell me,' went on Peter, 'why you choose to rest yourselves on articles intended for the transportation of water from one place to another?'

At this point Rose contributed a grunt to the conversation.

'And lastly,' finished Peter, 'will you tell me why, when you are in a building beautifully hung with enormous candelabra, you prefer to spend these evening hours under one anaemic electric light?'

Rose looked at Key; Key looked at Rose. They laughed; they laughed uproariously; they found it was impossible to look at each other without laughing. But they were not laughing with this man – they were laughing at him. To them a man who talked after this fashion was either raving drunk or raving crazy.

'You are Yale men, I presume,' said Peter, finishing his highball and preparing another.

They laughed again.

'Na–ah.'

'So? I thought perhaps you might be members of that lowly section of the university known as the Sheffield Scientific School.'

'Na–ah.'

'Hm. Well, that's too bad. No doubt you are Harvard men, anxious to preserve your incognito in this – this paradise of violet blue, as the newspapers say.'

'Na-ah,' said Key scornfully, 'we was just waitin' for somebody.'

'Ah,' exclaimed Peter, rising and filling their glasses, 'very interestin'. Had a date with a scrublady, eh?'

They both denied this indignantly.

'It's all right,' Peter reassured them, 'don't apologise. A scrub-lady's as good as any lady in the world. Kipling says,[16] "Any lady and Judy o'Grady under the skin." '

'Sure,' said Key, winking broadly at Rose.

'My case, for instance,' continued Peter, finishing his glass. 'I got a girl up there that's spoiled. Spoildest darn girl I ever saw. Refused to kiss me; no reason whatsoever. Led me on deliberately to think sure I want to kiss you and then plunk! Threw me over! What's the younger generation comin' to?'

'Say tha's hard luck,' said Key – 'that's awful hard luck.'

'Oh boy!' said Rose.

'Have another?' said Peter.

'We got in a sort of fight for a while,' said Key after a pause, 'but it was too far away.'

'A fight? – tha's stuff!' said Peter, seating himself unsteadily. 'Fight 'em all! I was in the army.'

'This was a Bolshevik fella.'

'Tha's stuff!' exclaimed Peter, enthusiastic. 'That's what I say! Kill the Bolsheviki.[17] Exterminate 'em!'

'We're Americuns,' said Rose, implying a sturdy, defiant patriotism.

'Sure,' said Peter. 'Greatest race in the world! We're all Americuns! Have another.'

They had another.

CHAPTER 6

AT ONE O'CLOCK a special orchestra, special even in a day of special orchestras, arrived at Delmonico's, and its members, seating themselves arrogantly around the piano, took up the burden of providing music for the Gamma Psi Fraternity. They were headed by a famous flute-player, distinguished throughout New York for his feat of standing on his head and shimmying with his shoulders while he played the latest jazz on his flute. During his performance the lights were extinguished except for the spotlight on the flute-player and another roving beam that threw flickering shadows and changing kaleidoscopic colours over the massed dancers.

Edith had danced herself into that tired, dreamy state habitual only with débutantes, a state equivalent to the glow of a noble soul after several long highballs. Her mind floated vaguely on the bosom of her music; her partners changed with the unreality of phantoms under the colourful shifting dusk, and to her present coma it seemed as if days had passed since the dance began. She had talked on many fragmentary subjects with many men. She had been kissed once and made love[18] to six times. Earlier in the evening different undergraduates had danced with her, but now, like all the more popular girls there, she had her own entourage – that is, half a dozen gallants had singled her out or were alternating her charms with those of some other chosen beauty; they cut in on her in regular, inevitable succession.

Several times she had seen Gordon – he had been sitting a long time on the stairway with his palm to his head, his dull eyes fixed at an infinite speck on the floor before him, very depressed, he looked, and quite drunk – but Edith each time had averted her glance, hurriedly. All that seemed long ago; her mind was passive now, her senses were lulled to trancelike sleep; only her feet danced and her voice talked on in hazy sentimental banter.

But Edith was not nearly so tired as to be incapable of moral indignation when Peter Himmel cut in on her, sublimely and happily drunk. She gasped and looked up at him.

'Why, *Peter*!'

'I'm a li'l stewed, Edith.'

'Why, Peter, you're a *peach*, you are! Don't you think it's a bum way of doing – when you're with me?'

Then she smiled unwillingly, for he was looking at her with owlish sentimentality varied with a silly spasmodic smile.

'Darlin' Edith,' he began earnestly, 'you know I love you, don't you?'

'You tell it well.'

'I love you – and I merely wanted you to kiss me,' he added sadly.

His embarrassment, his shame, were both gone. She was a mos' beautiful girl in whole worl'. Mos' beautiful eyes, like stars above. He wanted to 'pologise – firs', for presuming to try to kiss her; second, for drinking – but he'd been so discouraged 'cause he had thought she was mad at him –

The red-fat man cut in, and looking up at Edith smiled radiantly.

'Did you bring anyone?' she asked.

No. The red-fat man was a stag.

'Well, would you mind – would it be an awful bother for you to – to take me home tonight?' (this extreme diffidence was a charming affectation on Edith's part – she knew that the red-fat man would immediately dissolve into a paroxysm of delight).

'Bother? Why, good Lord, I'd be darn glad to! You know I'd be darn glad to.'

'Thanks *loads!* You're awfully sweet.'

She glanced at her wrist-watch. It was half-past one. And, as she said 'half-past one' to herself, it floated vaguely into her mind that her brother had told her at luncheon that he worked in the office of his newspaper until after one-thirty every evening.

Edith turned suddenly to her current partner.

'What street is Delmonico's on, anyway?'

'Street? Oh, why Fifth Avenue, of course.'

'I mean, what cross street?'

'Why – let's see – it's on 44th Street.'

This verified what she had thought. Henry's office must be across the street and just around the corner, and it occurred to her immediately that she might slip over for a moment and surprise him, float in on him, a shimmering marvel in her new crimson opera cloak and 'cheer him up'. It was exactly the sort of thing Edith revelled in doing – an unconventional, jaunty thing. The idea reached out and gripped at her imagination – after an instant's hesitation she had decided.

'My hair is just about to tumble entirely down,' she said pleasantly to her partner; 'would you mind if I go and fix it?'

'Not at all.'

'You're a peach.'

A few minutes later, wrapped in her crimson opera cloak, she flitted down a side-stairs, her cheeks glowing with excitement at her little adventure. She ran by a couple who stood at the door – a weak-chinned waiter and an over-rouged young lady, in hot dispute – and opening the outer door stepped into the warm May night.

CHAPTER 7

THE OVER-ROUGED young lady followed her with a brief, bitter glance – then turned again to the weak-chinned waiter and took up her argument.

'You better go up and tell him I'm here,' she said defiantly, 'or I'll go up myself.'

'No, you don't!' said George sternly.

The girl smiled sardonically.

'Oh, I don't, don't I? Well, let me tell you I know more college fellas and more of 'em know me, and are glad to take me out on a party, than you ever saw in your whole life.'

'Maybe so – '

'Maybe so,' she interrupted. 'Oh, it's all right for any of 'em like

that one that just ran out – God knows where *she* went – it's all right
for them that are asked here to come or go as they like – but when I
want to see a friend they have some cheap, ham-slinging, bring-me-
a-doughnut waiter to stand here and keep me out.'

'See here,' said the elder Key indignantly, 'I can't lose my job.
Maybe this fella you're talking about doesn't want to see you.'

'Oh, he wants to see me all right.'

'Anyway, how could I find him in all that crowd?'

'Oh, he'll be there,' she asserted confidently. 'You just ask anybody for Gordon Sterrett and they'll point him out to you. They all
know each other, those fellas.'

She produced a mesh bag, and taking out a dollar bill handed it to
George.

'Here,' she said, 'here's a bribe. You find him and give him
my message. You tell him if he isn't here in five minutes I'm
coming up.'

George shook his head pessimistically, considered the question
for a moment, wavered violently, and then withdrew.

In less than the allotted time Gordon came downstairs. He was
drunker than he had been earlier in the evening and in a different
way. The liquor seemed to have hardened on him like a crust. He
was heavy and lurching – almost incoherent when he talked.

' 'Lo, Jewel,' he said thickly. 'Came right away. Jewel, I couldn't
get that money. Tried my best.'

'Money nothing!' she snapped. 'You haven't been near me for ten
days. What's the matter?'

He shook his head slowly.

'Been very low, Jewel. Been sick.'

'Why didn't you tell me if you were sick. I don't care about the
money that bad. I didn't start bothering you about it at all until you
began neglecting me.'

Again he shook his head.

'Haven't been neglecting you. Not at all.'

'Haven't! You haven't been near me for three weeks, unless you
been so drunk you didn't know what you were doing.'

'Been sick, Jewel,' he repeated, turning his eyes upon her wearily.

'You're well enough to come and play with your society friends here
all right. You told me you'd meet me for dinner, and you said you'd
have some money for me. You didn't even bother to ring me up.'

'I couldn't get any money.'

'Haven't I just been saying that doesn't matter? I wanted to see you, Gordon, but you seem to prefer your somebody else.'

He denied this bitterly.

'Then get your hat and come along,' she suggested.

Gordon hesitated – and she came suddenly close to him and slipped her arms around his neck.

'Come on with me, Gordon,' she said in a half whisper. 'We'll go over to Devineries' and have a drink, and then we can go up to my apartment.'

'I can't, Jewel – '

'You can,' she said intensely.

'I'm sick as a dog!'

'Well, then, you oughtn't to stay here and dance.'

With a glance around him in which relief and despair were mingled, Gordon hesitated; then she suddenly pulled him to her and kissed him with soft, pulpy lips.

'All right,' he said heavily. 'I'll get my hat.'

CHAPTER 8

WHEN EDITH came out into the clear blue of the May night she found the Avenue deserted. The windows of the big shops were dark; over their doors were drawn great iron masks until they were only shadowy tombs of the late day's splendour. Glancing down towards 42nd Street she saw a commingled blur of lights from the all-night restaurants. Over on Sixth Avenue the elevated,[19] a flare of fire, roared across the street between the glimmering parallels of light at the station and streaked along into the crisp dark. But at 44th Street it was very quiet.

Pulling her cloak close about her Edith darted across the Avenue. She started nervously as a solitary man passed her and said in a hoarse whisper – 'Where bound, kiddo?' She was reminded of a night in her childhood when she had walked around the block in her pyjamas and a dog had howled at her from a mystery-big back yard.

In a minute she had reached her destination, a two-storey, comparatively old building on 44th, in the upper windows of which she thankfully detected a wisp of light. It was bright enough outside for her to make out the sign beside the window – the *New York Trumpet*.

She stepped inside a dark hall and after a second saw the stairs in the corner.

Then she was in a long, low room furnished with many desks and hung on all sides with file copies of newspapers. There were only two occupants. They were sitting at different ends of the room, each wearing a green eye-shade and writing by a solitary desk light.

For a moment she stood uncertainly in the doorway, and then both men turned around simultaneously and she recognised her brother.

'Why, Edith!' He rose quickly and approached her in surprise, removing his eye-shade. He was tall, lean, and dark, with black, piercing eyes under very thick glasses. They were far-away eyes that seemed always fixed just over the head of the person to whom he was talking.

He put his hands on her arms and kissed her cheek.

'What is it?' he repeated in some alarm.

'I was at a dance across at Delmonico's, Henry,' she said excitedly, 'and I couldn't resist tearing over to see you.'

'I'm glad you did.' His alertness gave way quickly to a habitual vagueness. 'You oughtn't to be out alone at night though, ought you?'

The man at the other end of the room had been looking at them curiously, but at Henry's beckoning gesture he approached. He was loosely fat with little twinkling eyes, and, having removed his collar and tie, he gave the impression of a Middle-Western farmer on a Sunday afternoon.

'This is my sister,' said Henry. 'She dropped in to see me.'

'How do you do?' said the fat man, smiling. 'My name's Bartholomew, Miss Bradin. I know your brother has forgotten it long ago.'

Edith laughed politely.

'Well,' he continued, 'not exactly gorgeous quarters we have here, are they?'

Edith looked around the room.

'They seem very nice,' she replied. 'Where do you keep the bombs?'

'The bombs?' repeated Bartholomew, laughing. 'That's pretty good – the bombs. Did you hear her, Henry? She wants to know where we keep the bombs. Say, that's pretty good.'

Edith swung herself around on to a vacant desk and sat dangling her feet over the edge. Her brother took a seat beside her.

'Well,' he asked, absent mindedly, 'how do you like New York this trip?'

'Not bad. I'll be over at the Biltmore with the Hoyts until Sunday. Can't you come to luncheon tomorrow?'

He thought a moment.

'I'm especially busy,' he objected, 'and I hate women in groups.'

'All right,' she agreed, unruffled. 'Let's you and me have luncheon together.'

'Very well.'

'I'll call for you at twelve.'

Bartholomew was obviously anxious to return to his desk, but apparently considered that it would be rude to leave without some parting pleasantry.

'Well' – he began awkwardly.

They both turned to him.

'Well, we – we had an exciting time earlier in the evening.'

The two men exchanged glances.

'You should have come earlier,' continued Bartholomew, somewhat encouraged. 'We had a regular vaudeville.'

'Did you really?'

'A serenade,' said Henry. 'A lot of soldiers gathered down there in the street and began to yell at the sign.'

'Why?' she demanded.

'Just a crowd,' said Henry, abstractedly. 'All crowds have to howl. They didn't have anybody with much initiative in the lead, or they'd probably have forced their way in here and smashed things up.'

'Yes,' said Bartholomew, turning again to Edith, 'you should have been here.'

He seemed to consider this a sufficient cue for withdrawal, for he turned abruptly and went back to his desk.

'Are the soldiers all set against the Socialists?' demanded Edith of her brother. 'I mean do they attack you violently and all that?'

Henry replaced his eye-shade and yawned.

'The human race has come a long way,' he said casually, 'but most of us are throwbacks; the soldiers don't know what they want, or what they hate, or what they like. They're used to acting in large bodies, and they seem to have to make demonstrations. So it happens to be against us. There've been riots all over the city tonight. It's May Day, you see.'

'Was the disturbance here pretty serious?'

'Not a bit,' he said scornfully. 'About twenty-five of them stopped in the street about nine o'clock, and began to bellow at the moon.'

'Oh – ' She changed the subject. 'You're glad to see me, Henry?'

'Why, sure.'

'You don't seem to be.'

'I am.'

'I suppose you think I'm a – a waster. Sort of the World's Worst Butterfly.'

Henry laughed.

'Not at all. Have a good time while you're young. Why? Do I seem like the priggish and earnest youth?'

'No – ' she paused ' – but somehow I began thinking how absolutely different the party I'm on is from – from all your purposes. It seems sort of – of incongruous, doesn't it? – me being at a party like that, and you over here working for a thing that'll make that sort of party impossible ever any more, if your ideas work.'

'I don't think of it that way. You're young, and you're acting just as you were brought up to act. Go ahead have a good time.'

Her feet, which had been idly swinging, stopped and her voice dropped a note.

'I wish you'd – you'd come back to Harrisburg and have a good time. Do you feel sure that you're on the right track – '

'You're wearing beautiful stockings,' he interrupted. 'What on earth are they?'

'They're embroidered,' she replied, glancing down. 'Aren't they cunning?' She raised her skirts and uncovered slim, silk-sheathed calves. 'Or do you disapprove of silk stockings?'

He seemed slightly exasperated, bent his dark eyes on her piercingly.

'Are you trying to make me out as criticising you in any way, Edith?'

'Not at all – '

She paused. Bartholomew had uttered a grunt. She turned and saw that he had left his desk and was standing at the window.

'What is it?' demanded Henry.

'People,' said Bartholomew, and then after an instant: 'Whole jam of them. They're coming from Sixth Avenue.'

'People.'

The fat man pressed his nose to the pane.

'Soldiers, by God!' he said emphatically. 'I had an idea they'd come back.'

Edith jumped to her feet, and running over joined Bartholomew at the window.

'There's a lot of them!' she cried excitedly. 'Come here, Henry!'

Henry readjusted his shade, but kept his seat.

'Hadn't we better turn out the lights?' suggested Bartholomew.

'No. They'll go away in a minute.'

'They're not,' said Edith, peering from the window. 'They're not even thinking of going away. There's more of them coming. Look – there's a whole crowd turning the corner of Sixth Avenue.'

By the yellow glow and blue shadows of the street lamp she could see that the sidewalk was crowded with men. They were mostly in uniform, some sober, some enthusiastically drunk, and over the whole swept an incoherent clamour and shouting.

Henry rose, and going to the window exposed himself as a long silhouette against the office lights. Immediately the shouting became a steady yell, and a rattling fusillade of small missiles, corners of tobacco plugs, cigarette-boxes, and even pennies beat against the window. The sounds of the racket now began floating up the stairs as the folding doors revolved.

'They're coming up!' cried Bartholomew.

Edith turned anxiously to Henry.

'They're coming up, Henry.'

From downstairs in the lower hall their cries were now quite audible.

' – God-damn Socialists!'

'Pro-Germans! Boche-lovers!'[20]

'Second floor, front! Come on.'

'We'll get the sons – '

The next five minutes passed in a dream. Edith was conscious that the clamour burst suddenly upon the three of them like a cloud of rain, that there was a thunder of many feet on the stairs, that Henry had seized her arm and drawn her back towards the rear of the office. Then the door opened and an overflow of men were forced into the room – not the leaders, but simply those who happened to be in front.

'Hello, Bo!'

'Up late, ain't you?'

'You an' your girl. Damn you!'

She noticed that two very drunken soldiers had been forced to the front, where they wobbled fatuously – one of them was short and dark, the other was tall and weak of chin.

Henry stepped forward and raised his hand.

'Friends!' he said.

The clamour faded into a momentary stillness, punctuated with mutterings.

'Friends!' he repeated, his far away eyes fixed over the heads of the crowd, 'you're injuring no one but yourselves by breaking in here tonight. Do we look like rich men? Do we look like Germans? I ask you in all fairness – '

'Pipe down!'

'I'll say you do!'

'Say, who's your lady friend, buddy?'

A man in civilian clothes, who had been pawing over a table, suddenly held up a newspaper.

'Here it is!' he shouted. 'They wanted the Germans to win the war!'

A new overflow from the stairs was shouldered in and of a sudden the room was full of men all closing around the pale little group at the back. Edith saw that the tall soldier with the weak chin was still in front. The short dark one had disappeared.

She edged slightly backward, stood close to the open window, through which came a clear breath of cool night air.

Then the room was a riot. She realised that the soldiers were surging forward, glimpsed the fat man swinging a chair over his head – instantly the lights went out, and she felt the push of warm bodies under rough cloth, and her ears were full of shouting and trampling and hard breathing.

A figure flashed by her out of nowhere, tottered, was edged sideways, and of a sudden disappeared helplessly out through the open window with a frightened, fragmentary cry that died staccato on the bosom of the clamour. By the faint light streaming from the building backing on the area Edith had a quick impression that it had been the tall soldier with the weak chin.

Anger rose astonishingly in her. She swung her arms wildly, edged blindly towards the thickest of the scuffling. She heard grunts, curses, the muffled impacts of fists.

'Henry!' she called frantically, 'Henry!'

Then, it was minutes later, she felt suddenly that there were other figures in the room. She heard a voice, deep, bullying, authoritative; she saw yellow rays of light sweeping here and there in the fracas. The cries became more scattered. The scuffling increased and then stopped.

Suddenly the lights were on and the room was full of policemen, clubbing left and right. The deep voice boomed out: 'Here now! Here now! Here now!'

And then: 'Quiet down and get out! Here now!'

The room seemed to empty like a washbowl. A policeman fast-grappled in the corner released his hold on his soldier antagonist and started him with a shove towards the door. The deep voice continued. Edith perceived now that it came from a bull-necked police captain standing near the door.

'Here now! This is no way! One of your own sojers got shoved out of the back window an' killed hisself!'

'Henry!' called Edith, 'Henry!'

She beat wildly with her fists on the back of the man in front of her; she brushed between two others; fought, shrieked, and beat her way to a very pale figure sitting on the floor close to a desk.

'Henry,' she cried passionately, 'what's the matter? What's the matter? Did they hurt you?'

His eyes were shut. He groaned and then looking up said disgustedly –

'They broke my leg. My God, the fools!'

'Here now!' called the police captain. 'Here now! Here now!'

CHAPTER 9

CHILDS', 59TH STREET, at eight o'clock of any morning differs from its sisters by less than the width of their marble tables or the degree of polish on the frying-pans. You will see there a crowd of poor people with sleep in the corners of their eyes, trying to look straight before them at their food so as not to see the other poor people. But Childs', 59th, four hours earlier is quite unlike any Childs' restaurant from Portland, Oregon, to Portland, Maine. Within its pale but sanitary walls one finds a noisy medley of chorus girls, college boys, débutantes, rakes, *filles de joie*[21] – a not unrepresentative mixture of the gayest of Broadway, and even of Fifth Avenue.

In the early morning of May the second it was unusually full. Over the marble-topped tables were bent the excited faces of flappers[22] whose fathers owned individual villages. They were eating buckwheat cakes and scrambled eggs with relish and gusto, an accomplishment that it would have been utterly impossible for them to repeat in the same place four hours later.

Almost the entire crowd were from the Gamma Psi dance at Delmonico's except for several chorus girls from a midnight revue who sat at a side table and wished they'd taken off a little more make-up after the show. Here and there a drab, mouse-like figure, desperately out of place, watched the butterflies with a weary, puzzled curiosity. But the drab figure was the exception. This was the morning after May Day, and celebration was still in the air.

Gus Rose, sober but a little dazed, must be classed as one of the drab figures. How he had got himself from 44th Street to 59th Street after the riot was only a hazy half-memory. He had seen the body of Carrol Key put in an ambulance and driven off, and then he had started uptown with two or three soldiers. Somewhere between 44th Street and 59th Street the other soldiers had met some women and disappeared. Rose had wandered to Columbus Circle and chosen the gleaming lights of Childs' to minister to his craving for coffee and doughnuts. He walked in and sat down.

All around him floated airy, inconsequential chatter and high-pitched laughter. At first he failed to understand, but after a puzzled five minutes he realised that this was the aftermath of some gay party. Here and there a restless, hilarious young man wandered fraternally and familiarly between the tables, shaking hands indiscriminately and pausing occasionally for a facetious chat, while excited waiters, bearing cakes and eggs aloft, swore at him silently, and bumped him out of the way. To Rose, seated at the most inconspicuous and least crowded table, the whole scene was a colourful circus of beauty and riotous pleasure.

He became gradually aware, after a few moments, that the couple seated diagonally across from him, with their backs to the crowd, where not the least interesting pair in the room. The man was drunk. He wore a dinner coat with a dishevelled tie and shirt swollen by spillings of water and wine. His eyes, dim and bloodshot, roved unnaturally from side to side. His breath came short between his lips.

'He's been on a spree!' thought Rose.

The woman was almost if not quite sober. She was pretty, with dark eyes and feverish high colour, and she kept her active eyes fixed on her companion with the alertness of a hawk. From time to time she would lean and whisper intently to him, and he would answer by inclining his head heavily or by a particularly ghoulish and repellent wink.

Rose scrutinised them dumbly for some minutes, until the woman gave him a quick, resentful look; then he shifted his gaze to two of the most conspicuously hilarious of the promenaders who were on a protracted circuit of the tables. To his surprise he recognised in one of them the young man by whom he had been so ludicrously entertained at Delmonico's. This started him thinking of Key with a vague sentimentality, not unmixed with awe. Key was dead. He had fallen thirty-five feet and split his skull like a cracked coconut.

'He was a darn good guy,' thought Rose mournfully. 'He was a darn good guy, o'right. That was awful hard luck about him.'

The two promenaders approached and started down between Rose's table and the next, addressing friends and strangers alike with jovial familiarity. Suddenly Rose saw the fair-haired one with the prominent teeth stop, look unsteadily at the man and girl opposite, and then begin to move his head disapprovingly from side to side.

The man with the bloodshot eyes looked up.

'Gordy,' said the promenader with the prominent teeth, 'Gordy.'

Prominent Teeth shook his finger pessimistically at the pair, giving the woman a glance of aloof condemnation.

'What'd I tell you, Gordy?'

Gordon stirred in his seat.

'Go to hell!' he said.

Dean continued to stand there shaking his finger. The woman began to get angry.

'You go away!' she cried fiercely. 'You're drunk, that's what you are!'

'So's he,' suggested Dean, staying the motion of his finger and pointing it at Gordon.

Peter Himmel ambled up, owlish now and oratorically inclined.

'Here now,' he began, as if called upon to deal with some petty dispute between children. 'Wha's all trouble?'

'You take your friend away,' said Jewel tartly. 'He's bothering us.'

'What's 'at?'

'You heard me!' she said shrilly. 'I said to take your drunken friend away.'

Her rising voice rang out above the clatter of the restaurant and a waiter came hurrying up.

'You gotta be more quiet!'

'That fella's drunk,' she cried. 'He's insulting us.'

'Ah–ha, Gordy,' persisted the accused. 'What'd I tell you.' He turned to the waiter. 'Gordy an' I friends. Been tryin' help him, haven't I, Gordy?'

Gordy looked up.

'Help me? Hell, no!'

Jewel rose suddenly, and seizing Gordon's arm assisted him to his feet.

'Come on, Gordy!' she said, leaning towards him and speaking in a half whisper. 'Let's get out of here. This fella's got a mean drunk on.'

Gordon allowed himself to be urged to his feet and started towards the door. Jewel turned for a second and addressed the provoker of their flight.

'I know all about you!' she said fiercely. 'Nice friend, you are, I'll say. He told me about you.'

Then she seized Gordon's arm, and together they made their way through the curious crowd, paid their check, and went out.

'You'll have to sit down,' said the waiter to Peter after they had gone.

'What's 'at? Sit down?'

'Yes – or get out.'

Peter turned to Dean.

'Come on,' he suggested. 'Let's beat up this waiter.'

'All right.'

They advanced towards him, their faces grown stern. The waiter retreated.

Peter suddenly reached over to a plate on the table beside him and picking up a handful of hash tossed it into the air. It descended as a languid parabola in snowflake effect on the heads of those near by.

'Hey! Ease up!'

'Put him out!'

'Sit down, Peter!'

'Cut out that stuff!'

Peter laughed and bowed.

'Thank you for your kind applause, ladies and gents. If someone will lend me some more hash and a tall hat we will go on with the act.'

The bouncer hustled up.

'You've gotta get out!' he said to Peter.

'Hell, no!'

'He's my friend!' put in Dean indignantly.

A crowd of waiters were gathering. 'Put him out!'

'Better go, Peter.'

There was a short struggle and the two were edged and pushed towards the door.

'I got a hat and coat here!' cried Peter.

'Well, go get 'em and be spry about it!'

The bouncer released his hold on Peter, who, adopting a ludicrous air of extreme cunning, rushed immediately around to the other table, where he burst into derisive laughter and thumbed his nose at the exasperated waiters.

'Think I just better wait a l'il' longer,' he announced.

The chase began. Four waiters were sent around one way and four another. Dean caught hold of two of them by the coat, and another struggle took place before the pursuit of Peter could be resumed; he was finally pinioned after overturning a sugar-bowl and several cups of coffee. A fresh argument ensued at the cashier's desk, where Peter attempted to buy another dish of hash to take with him and throw at policemen.

But the commotion upon his exit proper was dwarfed by another phenomenon which drew admiring glances and a prolonged involuntary 'Oh–h–h!' from every person in the restaurant.

The great plate-glass front had turned to a deep creamy blue, the colour of a Maxfield Parrish[23] moonlight – a blue that seemed to press close upon the pane as if to crowd its way into the restaurant. Dawn had come up in Columbus Circle, magical, breathless dawn, silhouetting the great statue of the immortal Christopher, and mingling in a curious and uncanny manner with the fading yellow electric light inside.

CHAPTER 10

MR IN AND MR OUT are not listed by the census-taker. You will search for them in vain through the social register or the births, marriages and deaths, or the grocer's credit list. Oblivion has swallowed them and the testimony that they ever existed at all is vague and shadowy, and inadmissible in a court of law. Yet I have it upon the best authority that for a brief space Mr In and Mr Out lived, breathed, answered to their names, and radiated vivid personalities of their own.

During the brief span of their lives they walked in their native garments down the great highway of a great nation; were laughed at, sworn at, chased, and fled from. Then they passed and were heard of no more.

They were already taking form dimly, when a taxicab with the top open breezed down Broadway in the faintest glimmer of May dawn. In this car sat the souls of Mr In and Mr Out discussing with amazement the blue light that had so precipitately coloured the sky behind the statue of Christopher Columbus, discussing with bewilderment the old, grey faces of the early risers which skimmed palely along the street like blown bits of paper on a grey lake. They were agreed on all things, from the absurdity of the bouncer in Childs' to the absurdity of the business of life. They were dizzy with the extreme maudlin happiness that the morning had awakened in their glowing souls. Indeed, so fresh and vigorous was their pleasure in living that they felt it should be expressed by loud cries.

'Ye–ow–ow!' hooted Peter, making a megaphone with his hands – and Dean joined in with a call that, though equally significant and symbolic, derived its resonance from its very inarticulateness.

'Yo–ho! Yea! Yoho! Yo–buba!'

Fifty-third Street was a bus with a dark, bobbed-hair beauty atop; 52nd was a street cleaner who dodged, escaped, and sent up a yell of, 'Look where you're aimin'!' in a pained and grieved voice. At 50th Street a group of men on a very white sidewalk in front of a very white building turned to stare after them, and shouted: 'Some party, boys!'

At 49th Street Peter turned to Dean. 'Beautiful morning,' he said gravely, squinting up his owlish eyes.

'Probably is.'

'Go get some breakfast, hey?'

Dean agreed – with additions.

'Breakfast and liquor.'

'Breakfast and liquor,' repeated Peter, and they looked at each other, nodding. 'That's logical.'

Then they both burst into loud laughter.

'Breakfast and liquor! Oh, gosh!'

'No such thing,' announced Peter.

'Don't serve it? Ne'mind. We force 'em serve it. Bring pressure bear.'

'Bring logic bear.'

The taxi cut suddenly off Broadway, sailed along a cross street, and stopped in front of a heavy tomblike building in Fifth Avenue.

'What's idea?'

The taxi-driver informed them that this was Delmonico's.

This was somewhat puzzling. They were forced to devote several minutes to intense concentration, for if such an order had been given there must have been a reason for it.

'Somep'm 'bouta coat,' suggested the taxi-man.

That was it. Peter's overcoat and hat. He had left them at Delmonico's. Having decided this, they disembarked from the taxi and strolled towards the entrance arm in arm.

'Hey!' said the taxi-driver.

'Huh?'

'You better pay me.'

They shook their heads in shocked negation.

'Later, not now – we give orders, you wait.'

The taxi-driver objected; he wanted his money now. With a scornful condescension of men exercising tremendous self-control they paid him.

Inside Peter groped in vain through a dim, deserted check-room in search of his coat and derby.

'Gone, I guess. Somebody stole 'em.'

'Some Sheff student.'

'All probability.'

'Never mind,' said Dean, nobly. 'I'll leave mine here too – then we'll both be dressed the same.'

He removed his overcoat and hat and was hanging them up when his roving glance was caught and held magnetically by two large squares of cardboard tacked to the two coat-room doors. The one on the left-hand bore the word 'In' in big black letters, and the one on the right-hand door flaunted the equally emphatic word 'Out'.

'Look!' he exclaimed happily –

Peter's eyes followed his pointing finger.

'What?'

'Look at the signs. Let's take 'em.'

'Good idea.'

'Probably pair very rare an' valuable signs. Probably come in handy.'

Peter removed the left-hand sign from the door and endeavoured to conceal it about his person. The sign being of considerable proportions, this was a matter of some difficulty. An idea flung itself at him, and with an air of dignified mystery he turned his back. After an instant he wheeled dramatically around, and stretching out his arms displayed himself to the admiring Dean. He had inserted the sign in his vest, completely covering his shirt front. In effect, the word 'In' had been painted upon his shirt in large black letters.

'Yoho!' cheered Dean. 'Mister In.'

He inserted his own sign in like manner.

'Mister Out!' he announced triumphantly. 'Mr In meet Mr Out.'

They advanced and shook hands. Again laughter overcame them and they rocked in a shaken spasm of mirth.

'Yoho!'

'We probably get a flock of breakfast.'

'We'll go – go to the Commodore.'

Arm in arm they sallied out the door, and turning east on 44th Street set out for the Commodore.

As they came out a short dark soldier, very pale and tired, who had been wandering listlessly along the sidewalk, turned to look at them.

He started over as though to address them, but as they immediately bent on him glances of withering unrecognition, he waited until they had started unsteadily down the street, and then followed at about forty paces, chuckling to himself and saying, 'Oh, boy!' over and over under his breath, in delighted, anticipatory tones.

Mr In and Mr Out were meanwhile exchanging pleasantries concerning their future plans.

'We want liquor; we want breakfast. Neither without the other. One and indivisible.'

'We want both 'em!'

'Both 'em!'

It was quite light now, and passers-by began to bend curious eyes on the pair. Obviously they were engaged in a discussion which afforded each of them intense amusement, for occasionally a fit of laughter would seize upon them so violently that, still with their arms interlocked, they would bend nearly double.

Reaching the Commodore, they exchanged a few spicy epigrams with the sleepy-eyed doorman, navigated the revolving door with some difficulty, and then made their way through a thinly populated but startled lobby to the dining-room, where a puzzled waiter showed them to an obscure table in a corner. They studied the bill of fare helplessly, telling over the items to each other in puzzled mumbles.

'Don't see any liquor here,' said Peter reproachfully.

The waiter became audible but unintelligible.

'Repeat,' continued Peter, with patient tolerance, 'that there seems to be unexplained and quite distasteful lack of liquor upon bill of fare.'

'Here!' said Dean confidently, 'let me handle him.' He turned to the waiter – 'Bring us – bring us – ' he scanned the bill of fare anxiously. 'Bring us a quart of champagne and a – a – probably ham sandwich.'

The waiter looked doubtful.

'Bring it!' roared Mr In and Mr Out in chorus.

The waiter coughed and disappeared. There was a short wait during which they were subjected without their knowledge to a careful scrutiny by the head waiter. Then the champagne arrived, and at the sight of it Mr In and Mr Out became jubilant.

'Imagine their objecting to us having champagne for breakfast – jus' imagine.'

They both concentrated upon the vision of such an awesome possibility, but the feat was too much for them. It was impossible for their joint imaginations to conjure up a world where anyone might object to anyone else having champagne for breakfast. The waiter drew the cork with an enormous *pop* – and their glasses immediately foamed with pale yellow froth.

'Here's health, Mr In.'

'Here's the same to you, Mr Out.'

The waiter withdrew; the minutes passed; the champagne became low in the bottle.

'It's – it's mortifying,' said Dean suddenly.

'Wha's mortifying?'

'The idea their objecting us having champagne breakfast.'

'Mortifying?' Peter considered. 'Yes, tha's word – mortifying.'

Again they collapsed into laughter, howled, swayed, rocked back and forth in their chairs, repeating the word 'mortifying' over and over to each other – each repetition seeming to make it only more brilliantly absurd.

After a few more gorgeous minutes they decided on another quart. Their anxious waiter consulted his immediate superior, and this discreet person gave implicit instructions that no more champagne should be served. Their check was brought.

Five minutes later, arm in arm, they left the Commodore and made their way through a curious, staring crowd along 42nd Street, and up Vanderbilt Avenue to the Biltmore. There, with sudden cunning, they rose to the occasion and traversed the lobby, walking fast and standing unnaturally erect.

Once in the dining-room they repeated their performance. They were torn between intermittent convulsive laughter and sudden spasmodic discussions of politics, college, and the sunny state of their dispositions. Their watches told them it was now nine o'clock, and a dim idea was born in them that they were on a memorable party, something that they would remember always. They lingered over the second bottle. Either of them had only to mention the word 'mortifying' to send them both into riotous gasps. The dining-room was whirring and shifting now; a curious lightness permeated and rarefied the heavy air.

They paid their check and walked out into the lobby.

It was at this moment that the exterior doors revolved for the thousandth time that morning, and admitted into the lobby a very pale young beauty with dark circles under her eyes, attired in a much-rumpled evening dress. She was accompanied by a plain stout man, obviously not an appropriate escort.

At the top of the stairs this couple encountered Mr In and Mr Out.

'Edith,' began Mr In, stepping towards her hilariously and making a sweeping bow, 'darling, good morning.'

The stout man glanced questioningly at Edith, as if merely asking her permission to throw this man summarily out of the way.

' 'Scuse familiarity,' added Peter, as an afterthought. 'Edith, good morning.'

He seized Dean's elbow and impelled him into the foreground.

'Meet Mr Out, Edith, my bes' frien'. Inseparable. Mr In and Mr Out.'

Mr Out advanced and bowed; in fact, he advanced so far and bowed so low that he tipped slightly forward and only kept his balance by placing a hand lightly on Edith's shoulder.

'I'm Mr Out, Edith,' he mumbled pleasantly. ' 'S Misterin 'n' Misterout.'

' 'Smisterinanout,' said Peter proudly.

But Edith stared straight by them, her eyes fixed on some infinite speck in the gallery above her. She nodded slightly to the stout man, who advanced bull-like and with a sturdy brisk gesture pushed Mr In and Mr Out to either side. Through this alley he and Edith walked.

But ten paces farther on Edith stopped again – stopped and pointed to a short, dark soldier who was eyeing the crowd in general, and the tableau of Mr In and Mr Out in particular, with a sort of puzzled, spellbound awe.

'There,' cried Edith. 'See there!'

Her voice rose, became somewhat shrill. Her pointing finger shook slightly.

'There's the soldier who broke my brother's leg.'

There were a dozen exclamations; a man in a cutaway coat left his place near the desk and advanced alertly; the stout person made a sort of lightning-like spring towards the short, dark soldier, and then the lobby closed around the little group and blotted them from the sight of Mr In and Mr Out.

But to Mr In and Mr Out this event was merely a parti-coloured iridescent segment of a whirring, spinning world.

They heard loud voices; they saw the stout man spring; the picture suddenly blurred.

Then they were in an elevator bound skyward.

'What floor, please?' said the elevator man.

'Any floor,' said Mr In.

'Top floor,' said Mr Out.

'This is the top floor,' said the elevator man.

'Have another floor put on,' said Mr Out.

'Higher,' said Mr In.

'Heaven,' said Mr Out.

IN A BEDROOM of a small hotel just off Sixth Avenue Gordon Sterrett awoke with a pain in the back of his head and a sick throbbing in all his veins. He looked at the dusky grey shadows in the corners of the room and at a raw place on a large leather chair in the corner where it had long been in use. He saw clothes, dishevelled, rumpled clothes on the floor and he smelt stale cigarette smoke and stale liquor. The windows were tight shut. Outside the bright sunlight had thrown a dust-filled beam across the sill – a beam broken by the head of the wide wooden bed in which he had slept. He lay very quiet – comatose, drugged, his eyes wide, his mind clicking wildly like an unoiled machine.

It must have been thirty seconds after he perceived the sunbeam with the dust in it and the rip on the large leather chair that he had the sense of life close beside him, and it was another thirty seconds after that before he realised he was irrevocably married to Jewel Hudson.

He went out half an hour later and bought a revolver at a sporting-goods store. Then he took a taxi to the room where he had been living on East 27th Street, and, leaning across the table that held his drawing materials, fired a cartridge into his head just behind the temple.

The Diamond as Big as the Ritz

CHAPTER I

JOHN T. UNGER came from a family that had been well known in Hades[24] – a small town on the Mississippi River – for several generations. John's father had held the amateur golf championship through many a heated contest; Mrs Unger was known 'from hot-box to hotbed', as the local phrase went, for her political addresses; and young John T. Unger, who had just turned sixteen, had danced all the latest dances from New York before he put on long trousers. And now, for a certain time, he was to be away from home. That respect for a New England education which is the bane of all provincial places, which drains them yearly of their most promising young men, had seized upon his parents. Nothing would suit them but that he should go to St Midas's[25] School near Boston – Hades was too small to hold their darling and gifted son.

Now in Hades – as you know if you ever have been there – the names of the more fashionable preparatory schools and colleges mean very little. The inhabitants have been so long out of the world that, though they make a show of keeping up to date in dress and manners and literature, they depend to a great extent on hearsay, and a function that in Hades would be considered elaborate would doubtless be hailed by a Chicago beef-princess as 'perhaps a little tacky'.

John T. Unger was on the eve of departure. Mrs Unger, with maternal fatuity, packed his trunks full of linen suits and electric fans, and Mr Unger presented his son with an asbestos pocketbook stuffed with money.

'Remember, you are always welcome here,' he said. 'You can be sure, boy, that we'll keep the home fires burning.'[26]

'I know,' answered John huskily.

'Don't forget who you are and where you come from,' continued his father proudly, 'and you can do nothing to harm you. You are an Unger – from Hades.'

So the old man and the young shook hands and John walked away
with tears streaming from his eyes. Ten minutes later he had passed
outside the city limits, and he stopped to glance back for the last
time. Over the gates the old-fashioned Victorian motto seemed
strangely attractive to him. His father had tried time and time
again to have it changed to something with a little more push and
verve about it, such as 'Hades – Your opportunity', or else a plain
'Welcome' sign set over a hearty handshake pricked out in electric
lights. The old motto was a little depressing, Mr Unger had
thought – but now . . .

So John took his look and then set his face resolutely towards his
destination. And, as he turned away, the lights of Hades against the
sky seemed full of a warm and passionate beauty.

St Midas's School is half an hour from Boston in a Rolls-Pierce
motor car. The actual distance will never be known, for no one,
except John T. Unger, had ever arrived there save in a Rolls-Pierce
and probably no one ever will again. St Midas's is the most expensive
and the most exclusive boys' preparatory school in the world.

John's first two years there passed pleasantly. The fathers of all
the boys were money-kings and John spent his summers visiting at
fashionable resorts. While he was very fond of all the boys he
visited, their fathers struck him as being much of a piece, and in his
boyish way he often wondered at their exceeding sameness. When
he told them where his home was they would ask jovially, 'Pretty hot
down there?' and John would muster a faint smile and answer, 'It
certainly is.' His response would have been heartier had they not all
made this joke – at best varying it with, 'Is it hot enough for you
down there?' which he hated just as much.

In the middle of his second year at school, a quiet, handsome boy
named Percy Washington had been put in John's form. The new-
comer was pleasant in his manner and exceedingly well dressed even
for St Midas's, but for some reason he kept aloof from the other
boys. The only person with whom he was intimate was John T.
Unger, but even to John he was entirely uncommunicative concerning his home or his family. That he was wealthy went without
saying, but beyond a few such deductions John knew little of his
friend, so it promised rich confectionery for his curiosity when
Percy invited him to spend the summer at his home 'in the West'.
He accepted, without hesitation.

It was only when they were in the train that Percy became, for the first time, rather communicative. One day while they were eating lunch in the dining-car and discussing the imperfect characters of several of the boys at school, Percy suddenly changed his tone and made an abrupt remark.

'My father,' he said, 'is by far the richest man in the world.'

'Oh,' said John, politely. He could think of no answer to make to this confidence. He considered 'That's very nice', but it sounded hollow, and he was on the point of saying 'Really?' but refrained since it would seem to question Percy's statement. And such an astounding statement could scarcely be questioned.

'By far the richest,' repeated Percy.

'I was reading in the *World Almanack*,' began John, 'that there was one man in America with an income of over five million a year and four men with incomes of over three million a year, and – '

'Oh, they're nothing,' Percy's mouth was a half-moon of scorn. 'Catch-penny capitalists, financial small-fry, petty merchants, and money-lenders. My father could buy them out and not know he'd done it.'

'But how does he – '

'Why haven't they put down *his* income tax? Because he doesn't pay any. At least he pays a little one – but he doesn't pay any on his *real* income.'

'He must be very rich,' said John simply. 'I'm glad. I like very rich people. The richer a fella is, the better I like him.' There was a look of passionate frankness upon his dark face. 'I visited the Schnlitzer-Murphys last Easter. Vivian Schnlitzer-Murphy had rubies as big as hen's eggs, and sapphires that were like globes with lights inside them – '

'I love jewels,' agreed Percy enthusiastically. 'Of course I wouldn't want anyone at school to know about it, but I've got quite a collection myself. I used to collect them instead of stamps.'

'And diamonds,' continued John eagerly. 'The Schnlitzer-Murphys had diamonds as big as walnuts – '

'That's nothing.' Percy had leaned forward and dropped his voice to a low whisper. 'That's nothing at all. My father has a diamond bigger than the Ritz-Carlton Hotel.'

THE MONTANA SUNSET lay between two mountains like a gigantic bruise from which dark arteries spread themselves over a poisoned sky. An immense distance under the sky crouched the village of Fish, minute, dismal, and forgotten. There were twelve men, so it was said, in the village of Fish, twelve sombre and inexplicable souls who sucked a lean milk from the almost literally bare rock upon which a mysterious populatory force had begotten them. They had become a race apart, these twelve men of Fish, like some species developed by an early whim of nature, which on second thought had abandoned them to struggle and extermination.

Out of the blue-black bruise in the distance crept a long line of moving lights upon the desolation of the land, and the twelve men of Fish gathered like ghosts at the shanty depot to watch the passing of the seven o'clock train, the Transcontinental Express from Chicago. Six times or so a year the Transcontinental Express, through some inconceivable jurisdiction, stopped at the village of Fish, and when this occurred a figure or so would disembark, mount into a buggy that always appeared from out of the dusk, and drive off towards the bruised sunset. The observation of this pointless and preposterous phenomenon had become a sort of cult among the men of Fish. To observe, that was all; there remained in them none of the vital quality of illusion which would make them wonder or speculate, else a religion might have grown up around these mysterious visitations. But the men of Fish were beyond all religion – the barest and most savage tenets of even Christianity could gain no foothold on that barren rock – so there was no altar, no priest, no sacrifice; only each night at seven the silent concourse by the shanty depot, a congregation who lifted up a prayer of dim, anaemic wonder.

On this June night, the Great Brakeman, whom, had they deified anyone, they might well have chosen as their celestial protagonist, had ordained that the seven o'clock train should leave its human (or inhuman) deposit at Fish. At two minutes after seven Percy Washington and John T. Unger disembarked, hurried past the spellbound, the agape, the fearsome eyes of the twelve men of Fish, mounted into a buggy which had obviously appeared from nowhere, and drove away.

After half an hour, when the twilight had coagulated into dark, the silent Negro who was driving the buggy hailed an opaque body somewhere ahead of them in the gloom. In response to his cry, it turned upon them a luminous disk which regarded them like a malignant eye out of the unfathomable night. As they came closer, John saw that it was the tail-light of an immense automobile, larger and more magnificent than any he had ever seen. Its body was of gleaming metal richer than nickel and lighter than silver, and the hubs of the wheels were studded with iridescent geometric figures of green and yellow – John did not dare to guess whether they were glass or jewel.

Two Negroes, dressed in glittering livery such as one sees in pictures of royal processions in London, were standing at attention beside the car and as the two young men dismounted from the buggy they were greeted in some language which the guest could not understand, but which seemed to be an extreme form of the Southern Negro's dialect.

'Get in,' said Percy to his friend, as their trunks were tossed to the ebony roof of the limousine. 'Sorry we had to bring you this far in that buggy, but of course it wouldn't do for the people on the train or those Godforsaken fellas in Fish to see this automobile.'

'Gosh! What a car!' This ejaculation was provoked by its interior. John saw that the upholstery consisted of a thousand minute and exquisite tapestries of silk, woven with jewels and embroideries, and set upon a background of cloth of gold. The two armchair seats in which the boys luxuriated were covered with stuff that resembled duvetyn,[27] but seemed woven in numberless colours of the ends of ostrich feathers.

'What a car!' cried John again, in amazement.

'This thing?' Percy laughed. 'Why, it's just an old junk we use for a station wagon.'

By this time they were gliding along through the darkness towards the break between the two mountains.

'We'll be there in an hour and a half,' said Percy, looking at the clock. 'I may as well tell you it's not going to be like anything you ever saw before.'

If the car was any indication of what John would see, he was prepared to be astonished indeed. The simple piety prevalent in

Hades has the earnest worship of and respect for riches as the first article of its creed – had John felt otherwise than radiantly humble before them, his parents would have turned away in horror at the blasphemy.

They had now reached and were entering the break between the two mountains and almost immediately the way became much rougher.

'If the moon shone down here, you'd see that we're in a big gulch,' said Percy, trying to peer out of the window. He spoke a few words into the mouthpiece and immediately the footman turned on a searchlight and swept the hillsides with an immense beam.

'Rocky, you see. An ordinary car would be knocked to pieces in half an hour. In fact it'd take a tank to navigate it unless you knew the way. You notice we're going uphill now.'

They were obviously ascending, and within a few minutes the car was crossing a high rise, where they caught a glimpse of a pale moon newly risen in the distance. The car stopped suddenly and several figures took shape out of the dark beside it – these were Negroes also. Again the two young men were saluted in the same dimly recognisable dialect; then the Negroes set to work and four immense cables dangling from overhead were attached with hooks to the hubs of the great jewelled wheels. At a resounding 'Hey–yah!' John felt the car being lifted slowly from the ground – up and up – clear of the tallest rocks on both sides – then higher, until he could see a wavy, moonlit valley stretched out before him in sharp contrast to the quagmire of rocks that they had just left. Only on one side was there still rock – and then suddenly there was no rock beside them or anywhere around.

It was apparent that they had surmounted some immense knife-blade of stone, projecting perpendicularly into the air. In a moment they were going down again, and finally with a soft bump they were landed upon the smooth earth.

'The worst is over,' said Percy, squinting out the window. 'It's only five miles from here, and our own road – tapestry brick – all the way. This belongs to us. This is where the United States ends, father says.'

'Are we in Canada?'

'We are not. We're in the middle of the Montana Rockies. But you are now on the only five square miles of land in the country that's never been surveyed.'

'Why hasn't it? Did they forget it?'

'No,' said Percy, grinning, 'they tried to do it three times. The first time my grandfather corrupted a whole department of the State survey; the second time he had the official maps of the United States tinkered with – that held them for fifteen years. The last time was harder. My father fixed it so that their compasses were in the strongest magnetic field ever artificially set up. He had a whole set of surveying instruments made with a slight defection that would allow for this territory not to appear, and he substituted them for the ones that were to be used. Then he had a river deflected and he had what looked like a village built up on its banks – so that they'd see it, and think it was a town ten miles farther up the valley. There's only one thing my father's afraid of,' he concluded, 'only one thing in the world that could be used to find us out.'

'What's that?'

Percy sank his voice to a whisper.

'Aeroplanes,' he breathed. 'We've got half a dozen anti-aircraft guns and we've arranged it so far – but there've been a few deaths and a great many prisoners. Not that we mind that, you know, father and I, but it upsets mother and the girls, and there's always the chance that some time we won't be able to arrange it.'

Shreds and tatters of chinchilla, courtesy clouds in the green moon's heaven, were passing the green moon like precious Eastern stuffs paraded for the inspection of some Tartar Khan. It seemed to John that it was day, and that he was looking at some lads sailing above him in the air, showering down tracts and patent-medicine circulars, with their messages of hope for despairing, rockbound hamlets. It seemed to him that he could see them look down out of the clouds and stare – and stare at whatever there was to stare at in this place whither he was bound. What then? Were they induced to land by some insidious device, there to be immured far from patent medicines and from tracts until the judgement day – or, should they fail to fall into the trap, did a quick puff of smoke and the sharp round of a splitting shell bring them drooping to earth – and 'upset' Percy's mother and sisters. John shook his head and the wraith of a hollow laugh issued silently from his parted lips. What desperate transaction lay hidden here? What amoral expedient of a bizarre Croesus?[28] What terrible and golden mystery? . . .

The chinchilla clouds had drifted past now and outside the Montana night was bright as day. The tapestry brick of the road was smooth to the tread of the great tyres as they rounded a still, moonlit lake; they passed into darkness for a moment, a pine grove, pungent and cool, then they came out into a broad avenue of lawn and John's exclamation of pleasure was simultaneous with Percy's taciturn, 'We're home.'

Full in the light of the stars, an exquisite château rose from the borders of the lake, climbed in marble radiance half the height of an adjoining mountain, then melted in grace, in perfect symmetry, in translucent feminine languor, into the massed darkness of a forest of pine. The many towers, the slender tracery of the sloping parapets, the chiselled wonder of a thousand yellow windows with their oblongs and hectagons and triangles of golden light, the shattered softness of the intersecting planes of starshine and blue shade, all trembled on John's spirit like a chord of music. On one of the towers, the tallest, the blackest at its base, an arrangement of exterior lights at the top made a sort of floating fairyland – and as John gazed up in warm enchantment the faint *acciaccare*[29] sound of violins drifted down in a rococo harmony that was like nothing he had ever heard before. Then in a moment the car stopped before wide, high marble steps around which the night air was fragrant with a host of flowers. At the top of the steps two great doors swung silently open and amber light flooded out upon the darkness, silhouetting the figure of an exquisite lady with black, high-piled hair, who held out her arms towards them.

'Mother,' Percy was saying, 'this is my friend, John Unger, from Hades.'

Afterwards John remembered that first night as a daze of many colours, of quick sensory impressions, of music soft as a voice in love, and of the beauty of things, lights and shadows, and motions and faces. There was a white-haired man who stood drinking a many-hued cordial from a crystal thimble set on a golden stem. There was a girl with a flowery face, dressed like Titania[30] with braided sapphires in her hair. There was a room where the solid, soft gold of the walls yielded to the pressure of his hand, and a room that was like a platonic conception[31] of the ultimate prison – ceiling, floor, and all, it was lined with an unbroken mass of diamonds, diamonds of every size and shape, until, lit with tall violet lamps in the corners, it dazzled the eyes with a whiteness that could be compared only with itself, beyond human wish or dream.

Through a maze of these rooms the two boys wandered. Sometimes the floor under their feet would flame in brilliant patterns from lighting below, patterns of barbaric clashing colours, of pastel delicacy, of sheer whiteness, or of subtle and intricate mosaic, surely from some mosque on the Adriatic Sea. Sometimes beneath layers of thick crystal he would see blue or green water swirling, inhabited by vivid fish and growths of rainbow foliage. Then they would be treading on furs of every texture and colour or along corridors of palest ivory, unbroken as though carved complete from the gigantic tusks of dinosaurs extinct before the age of man . . .

Then a hazily remembered transition, and they were at dinner – where each plate was of two almost imperceptible layers of solid diamond between which was curiously worked a filigree of emerald design, a shaving sliced from green air. Music, plangent and unobtrusive, drifted down through far corridors – his chair, feathered and curved insidiously to his back, seemed to engulf and overpower him as he drank his first glass of port. He tried drowsily to answer a question that had been asked him, but the honeyed luxury that clasped his body added to the illusion of sleep – jewels, fabrics, wines and metals blurred before his eyes into a sweet mist . . .

'Yes,' he replied with a polite effort, 'it certainly is hot enough for me down there.'

He managed to add a ghostly laugh; then, without movement, without resistance, he seemed to float off and away, leaving an iced dessert that was pink as a dream . . . He fell asleep.

When he awoke he knew that several hours had passed. He was in a great quiet room with ebony walls and a dull illumination that was too faint, too subtle, to be called a light. His young host was standing over him.

'You fell asleep at dinner,' Percy was saying. 'I nearly did, too – it was such a treat to be comfortable again after this year of school. Servants undressed and bathed you while you were sleeping.'

'Is this a bed or a cloud?' sighed John. 'Percy, Percy before you go, I want to apologise.'

'For what?'

'For doubting you when you said you had a diamond as big as the Ritz-Carlton Hotel.'

Percy smiled.

'I thought you didn't believe me. It's that mountain, you know.'

'What mountain?'

'The mountain the château rests on. It's not very big for a

mountain. But except about fifty feet of sod and gravel on top it's solid diamond. One diamond, one cubic mile without a flaw. Aren't you listening? Say – '

But John T. Unger had again fallen asleep.

CHAPTER 3

MORNING. As he awoke he perceived drowsily that the room had at the same moment become dense with sunlight. The ebony panels of one wall had slid aside on a sort of track, leaving his chamber half open to the day. A large Negro in a white uniform stood beside his bed.

'Good-evening,' muttered John, summoning his brains from the wild places.

'Good-morning, sir. Are you ready for your bath, sir? Oh, don't get up – I'll put you in, if you'll just unbutton your pyjamas – there. Thank you, sir.'

John lay quietly as his pyjamas were removed – he was amused and delighted; he expected to be lifted like a child by this black Gargantua[32] who was tending him, but nothing of the sort happened; instead he felt the bed tilt up slowly on its side – he began to roll, startled at first, in the direction of the wall, but when he reached the wall its drapery gave way, and sliding two yards farther down a fleecy incline he plumped gently into water the same temperature as his body.

He looked about him. The runway or rollway on which he had arrived had folded gently back into place. He had been projected into another chamber and was sitting in a sunken bath with his head just above the level of the floor. All about him, lining the walls of the room and the sides and bottom of the bath itself, was a blue aquarium, and gazing through the crystal surface on which he sat, he could see fish swimming among amber lights and even gliding without curiosity past his outstretched toes, which were separated from them only by the thickness of the crystal. From overhead, sunlight came down through sea-green glass.

'I suppose, sir, that you'd like hot rose-water and soapsuds this morning, sir – and perhaps cold salt water to finish?'

The Negro was standing beside him.

'Yes,' agreed John, smiling inanely, 'as you please.' Any idea of ordering this bath according to his own meagre standards of living would have been priggish and not a little wicked.

The Negro pressed a button and a warm rain began to fall, apparently from overhead, but really, so John discovered after a moment, from a fountain arrangement near by. The water turned to a pale rose colour and jets of liquid soap spurted into it from four miniature walrus heads at the corners of the bath. In a moment a dozen little paddle-wheels, fixed to the sides, had churned the mixture into a radiant rainbow of pink foam which enveloped him softly with its delicious lightness, and burst in shining, rosy bubbles here and there about him.

'Shall I turn on the moving-picture machine, sir?' suggested the Negro deferentially. 'There's a good one-reel comedy in this machine today, or I can put in a serious piece in a moment, if you prefer it.'

'No, thanks,' answered John, politely but firmly. He was enjoying his bath too much to desire any distraction. But distraction came. In a moment he was listening intently to the sound of flutes from just outside, flutes dripping a melody that was like a waterfall, cool and green as the room itself, accompanying a frothy piccolo, in play more fragile than the lace of suds that covered and charmed him.

After a cold salt-water bracer and a cold fresh finish, he stepped out and into a fleecy robe, and upon a couch covered with the same material he was rubbed with oil, alcohol, and spice. Later he sat in a voluptuous chair while he was shaved and his hair was trimmed.

'Mr Percy is waiting in your sitting-room,' said the Negro, when these operations were finished. 'My name is Gygsum, Mr Unger, sir. I am to see Mr Unger every morning.'

John walked out into the brisk sunshine of his living-room, where he found breakfast waiting for him and Percy, gorgeous in white-kid knickerbockers, smoking in an easy-chair.

CHAPTER 4

THIS IS A STORY of the Washington family as Percy sketched it for John during breakfast.

The father of the present Mr Washington had been a Virginian, a direct descendant of George Washington and Lord Baltimore. At the close of the Civil War he was a twenty-five-year-old Colonel with a played-out plantation and about a thousand dollars in gold.

Fitz-Norman Culpepper Washington, for that was the young colonel's name, decided to present the Virginia estate to his younger brother and go West. He selected two dozen of the most faithful blacks, who, of course, worshipped him, and bought twenty-five tickets to the West, where he intended to take out land in their names and start a sheep and cattle ranch.

When he had been in Montana for less than a month and things were going very poorly indeed, he stumbled on his great discovery. He had lost his way when riding in the hills, and after a day without food he began to grow hungry. As he was without his rifle, he was forced to pursue a squirrel, and in the course of the pursuit he noticed that it was carrying something shiny in its mouth. Just before it vanished into its hole – for Providence did not intend that this squirrel should alleviate his hunger – it dropped its burden. Sitting down to consider the situation Fitz-Norman's eye was caught by a gleam in the grass beside him. In ten seconds he had completely lost his appetite and gained one hundred thousand dollars. The squirrel which had refused with annoying persistence to become food, had made him a present of a large and perfect diamond.

Late that night he found his way to camp and twelve hours later all the males among his darkies were back by the squirrel hole digging furiously at the side of the mountain. He told them he had discovered a rhinestone mine, and, as only one or two of them had ever seen even a small diamond before, they believed him, without question. When the magnitude of his discovery became apparent to him, he found himself in a quandary. The mountain was a diamond – it was literally nothing else but solid diamond. He filled four saddle bags full of glittering samples and started on horseback for St Paul. There he managed to dispose of half a dozen small stones – when he tried a larger one a storekeeper fainted and Fitz-Norman was arrested as a public disturber. He escaped from jail and caught the train for New York, where he sold a few medium-sized diamonds and received in exchange about two hundred thousand dollars in gold. But he did not dare to produce any exceptional gems – in fact, he left New York just in time. Tremendous excitement had been created in jewellery circles, not so much by the size of his diamonds as by their appearance in the city from mysterious sources. Wild rumours became current that a diamond mine had been discovered in the Catskills, on the Jersey coast, on Long Island, beneath Washington Square. Excursion trains, packed with men carrying picks and shovels began to leave New York hourly, bound for various neighbouring El Dorados.[33] But by that time young Fitz-Norman was on his way back to Montana.

By the end of a fortnight he had estimated that the diamond in the mountain was approximately equal in quantity to all the rest of the diamonds known to exist in the world. There was no valuing it by any regular computation, however, for it was *one solid diamond* – and if it were offered for sale not only would the bottom fall out of the market, but also, if the value should vary with its size in the usual arithmetical progression, there would not be enough gold in the world to buy a tenth part of it. And what could anyone do with a diamond that size?

It was an amazing predicament. He was, in one sense, the richest man that ever lived – and yet was he worth anything at all? If his secret should transpire there was no telling to what measures the Government might resort in order to prevent a panic, in gold as well as in jewels. They might take over the claim immediately and institute a monopoly.

There was no alternative – he must market his mountain in secret. He sent South for his younger brother and put him in charge of his coloured following – darkies who had never realised that slavery was abolished. To make sure of this, he read them a proclamation that he had composed, which announced that General Forrest[34] had reorganised the shattered Southern armies and defeated the North in one pitched battle. The Negroes believed him implicitly. They passed a vote declaring it a good thing and held revival services immediately.

Fitz-Norman himself set out for foreign parts with one hundred thousand dollars and two trunks filled with rough diamonds of all sizes. He sailed for Russia in a Chinese junk and six months after his departure from Montana he was in St Petersburg. He took obscure lodgings and called immediately upon the court jeweller, announcing that he had a diamond for the Czar. He remained in St Petersburg for two weeks, in constant danger of being murdered, living from lodging to lodging, and afraid to visit his trunks more than three or four times during the whole fortnight.

On his promise to return in a year with larger and finer stones, he was allowed to leave for India. Before he left, however, the Court Treasurers had deposited to his credit, in American banks, the sum of fifteen million dollars under four different aliases.

He returned to America in 1868, having been gone a little over two years. He had visited the capitals of twenty-two countries and talked with five emperors, eleven kings, three princes, a shah, a khan, and a sultan. At that time, Fitz-Norman estimated his own wealth at one billion dollars. One fact worked consistently against the disclosure of his secret. No one of his larger diamonds remained in the public eye for a week before being invested with a history of enough fatalities, amours, revolutions, and wars to have occupied it from the days of the first Babylonian Empire.[35]

From 1870 until his death in 1900, the history of Fitz-Norman Washington was a long epic in gold. There were side issues, of course – he evaded the surveys, he married a Virginia lady, by whom he had a single son, and he was compelled, due to a series of unfortunate complications, to murder his brother, whose unfortunate habit of drinking himself into an indiscreet stupor had several times endangered their safety. But very few other murders stained these happy years of progress and expansion.

Just before he died he changed his policy, and with all but a few million dollars of his outside wealth bought up rare minerals in bulk, which he deposited in the safety vaults of banks all over the world, marked as bric-à-brac. His son, Braddock Tarleton Washington, followed this policy on an even more intensive scale. The minerals were converted into the rarest of all elements – radium – so that the equivalent of a billion dollars in gold could be placed in a receptacle no bigger than a cigar box.

When Fitz-Norman had been dead three years his son, Braddock, decided that the business had gone far enough. The amount of wealth that he and his father had taken out of the mountain was beyond all exact computation. He kept a notebook in cipher in which he set down the approximate quantity of radium in each of the thousand banks he patronised, and recorded the alias under which it was held. Then he did a very simple thing – he sealed up the mine.

He sealed up the mine. What had been taken out of it would support all the Washingtons yet to be born in unparalleled luxury for generations. His one care must be the protection of his secret, lest in the possible panic attendant on its discovery he should be reduced with all the property-holders in the world to utter poverty.

This was the family among whom John T. Unger was staying. This was the story he heard in his silver-walled living-room the morning after his arrival.

CHAPTER 5

AFTER BREAKFAST, John found his way out of the great marble entrance, and looked curiously at the scene before him. The whole valley, from the diamond mountain to the steep granite cliff five miles away, still gave off a breath of golden haze which hovered idly above the fine sweep of lawns and lakes and gardens. Here and there clusters of elms made delicate groves of shade, contrasting strangely with the tough masses of pine forest that held the hills in a grip of dark-blue green. Even as John looked he saw three fawns in single file patter out from one clump about a half-mile away and disappear with awkward gaiety into the black-ribbed half-light of another. John would not have been surprised to see a goat foot-piping his way among the trees or to catch a glimpse of pink nymph-skin and flying yellow hair between the greenest of the green leaves.

In some such cool hope he descended the marble steps, disturbing the sleep of two silky Russian wolfhounds at the bottom, and set off along a walk of white and blue brick that seemed to lead in no particular direction.

He was enjoying himself as much as he was able. It is youth's felicity as well as its insufficiency that it can never live in the present, but must always be measuring up the day against its own radiantly imagined future – flowers and gold, girls and stars, they are only pre-figurations and prophecies of that incomparable, unattainable young dream.

John rounded a soft corner where the massed rose bushes filled the air with heavy scent, and struck off across a park towards a patch of moss under some trees. He had never lain upon moss, and he wanted to see whether it was really soft enough to justify the use of its name as an adjective. Then he saw a girl coming towards him over the grass. She was the most beautiful person he had ever seen.

She was dressed in a white little gown that came just below her knees, and a wreath of mignonettes clasped with blue slices of sapphire bound up her hair. Her pink bare feet scattered the dew before them as she came. She was younger than John – not more than sixteen.

'Hello,' she cried softly, 'I'm Kismine.'

She was much more than that to John already. He advanced towards her, scarcely moving as he drew near lest he should tread on her bare toes.

'You haven't met me,' said her soft voice. Her blue eyes added, 'Oh, but you've missed a great deal!' . . . 'You met my sister, Jasmine, last night. I was sick with lettuce poisoning,' went on her soft voice, and her eyes continued, 'and when I'm sick I'm sweet – and when I'm well.'

'You have made an enormous impression on me,' said John's eyes, 'and I'm not so slow myself' – 'How do you do?' said his voice. 'I hope you're better this morning.' 'You darling,' added his eyes tremulously.

John observed that they had been walking along the path. On her suggestion they sat down together upon the moss, the softness of which he failed to determine.

He was critical about women. A single defect – a thick ankle, a hoarse voice, a glass eye – was enough to make him utterly indifferent. And here for the first time in his life he was beside a girl who seemed to him the incarnation of physical perfection.

'Are you from the East?' asked Kismine with charming interest.

'No,' answered John simply. 'I'm from Hades.'

Either she had never heard of Hades, or she could think of no pleasant comment to make upon it, for she did not discuss it further.

'I'm going East to school this fall,' she said. 'D'you think I'll like it? I'm going to New York to Miss Bulge's. It's very strict, but you see over the weekends I'm going to live at home with the family in our New York house, because father heard that the girls had to go walking two by two.'

'Your father wants you to be proud,' observed John.

'We are,' she answered, her eyes shining with dignity. 'None of us has ever been punished. Father said we never should be. Once when my sister Jasmine was a little girl she pushed him downstairs and he just got up and limped away.

'Mother was – well, a little startled,' continued Kismine, 'when she heard that you were from – from where you *are* from, you know. She said that when she was a young girl – but then, you see, she's a Spaniard and old-fashioned.'

'Do you spend much time out here?' asked John, to conceal the fact that he was somewhat hurt by this remark. It seemed an unkind allusion to his provincialism.

'Percy and Jasmine and I are here every summer, but next summer Jasmine is going to Newport. She's coming out in London a year from this fall. She'll be presented at Court.'

'Do you know,' began John hesitantly, 'you're much more sophisticated than I thought you were when I first saw you?'

'Oh, no, I'm not,' she exclaimed hurriedly. 'Oh, I wouldn't think of being. I think that sophisticated young people are *terribly* common, don't you? I'm not at all, really. If you say I am, I'm going to cry.'

She was so distressed that her lip was trembling. John was impelled to protest: 'I didn't mean that; I only said it to tease you.'

'Because I wouldn't mind if I *were*,' she persisted, 'but I'm *not*. I'm very innocent and girlish. I never smoke, or drink, or read anything except poetry. I know scarcely any mathematics or chemistry. I dress *very* simply – in fact, I scarcely dress at all. I think sophisticated is the last thing you can say about me. I believe that girls ought to enjoy their youths in a wholesome way.'

'I do too,' said John heartily.

Kismine was cheerful again. She smiled at him, and a stillborn tear dripped from the corner of one blue eye.

'I like you,' she whispered, intimately. 'Are you going to spend all your time with Percy while you're here, or will you be nice to me? Just think – I'm absolutely fresh ground. I've never had a boy in love with me in all my life. I've never been allowed even to *see* boys alone – except Percy. I came all the way out here into this grove hoping to run into you, where the family wouldn't be around.'

Deeply flattered, John bowed from the hips as he had been taught at dancing school in Hades.

'We'd better go now,' said Kismine sweetly. 'I have to be with mother at eleven. You haven't asked me to kiss you once. I thought boys always did that nowadays.'

John drew himself up proudly.

'Some of them do,' he answered, 'but not me. Girls don't do that sort of thing – in Hades.'

Side by side they walked back towards the house.

CHAPTER 4

JOHN STOOD FACING Mr Braddock Washington in the full sunlight. The elder man was about forty with a proud, vacuous face, intelligent eyes, and a robust figure. In the mornings he smelt of horses – the best horses. He carried a plain walking-stick of grey birch with a single large opal for a grip. He and Percy were showing John around.

'The slaves' quarters are there.' His walking-stick indicated a cloister of marble on their left that ran in graceful Gothic along the side of the mountain. 'In my youth I was distracted for a while from the business of life by a period of absurd idealism. During that time they lived in luxury. For instance, I equipped every one of their rooms with a tile bath.'

'I suppose,' ventured John, with an ingratiating laugh, 'that they used the bathtubs to keep coal in. Mr Schnlitzer-Murphy told me that once he – '

'The opinions of Mr Schnlitzer-Murphy are of little importance, I should imagine,' interrupted Braddock Washington, coldly. 'My slaves did not keep coal in their bathtubs. They had orders to bathe every day, and they did. If they hadn't I might have ordered a sulphuric acid shampoo. I discontinued the baths for quite another reason. Several of them caught cold and died. Water is not good for certain races – except as a beverage.'

John laughed, and then decided to nod his head in sober agreement. Braddock Washington made him uncomfortable.

'All these Negroes are descendants of the ones my father brought North with him. There are about two hundred and fifty now. You notice that they've lived so long apart from the world that their original dialect has become an almost indistinguishable patois. We bring a few of them up to speak English – my secretary and two or three of the house servants.

'This is the golf-course,' he continued, as they strolled along the velvet winter grass. 'It's all a green, you see – no fairway, no rough, no hazards.'

He smiled pleasantly at John.

'Many men in the cage, father?' asked Percy suddenly.

Braddock Washington stumbled, and let forth an involuntary curse.

'One less than there should be,' he ejaculated darkly – and then added after a moment, 'We've had difficulties.'

'Mother was telling me,' exclaimed Percy, 'that Italian teacher – '

'A ghastly error,' said Braddock Washington angrily. 'But of course there's a good chance that we may have got him. Perhaps he fell somewhere in the woods or stumbled over a cliff. And then there's always the probability that if he did get away his story wouldn't be believed. Nevertheless, I've had two dozen men looking for him in different towns around here.'

'And no luck?'

'Some. Fourteen of them reported to my agent that they'd each killed a man answering to that description, but of course it was probably only the reward they were after – '

He broke off. They had come to a large cavity in the earth about the circumference of a merry-go-round and covered by a strong iron grating. Braddock Washington beckoned to John, and pointed his cane down through the grating. John stepped to the edge and gazed. Immediately his ears were assailed by a wild clamour from below.

'Come on down to Hell!'

'Hello, kiddo, how's the air up there?'

'Hey! Throw us a rope!'

'Got an old doughnut, Buddy, or a couple of second-hand sandwiches?'

'Say, fella, if you'll push down that guy you're with, we'll show you a quick disappearance scene.'

'Paste him one for me, will you?'

It was too dark to see clearly into the pit below, but John could tell from the coarse optimism and rugged vitality of the remarks and voices that they proceeded from middle-class Americans of the more spirited type. Then Mr Washington put out his cane and touched a button in the grass, and the scene below sprang into light.

'These are some adventurous mariners who had the misfortune to discover El Dorado,' he remarked.

Below them there had appeared a large hollow in the earth shaped like the interior of a bowl. The sides were steep and apparently of polished glass, and on its slightly concave surface stood about two dozen men clad in the half-costume, half-uniform, of aviators. Their upturned faces, lit with wrath, with malice, with despair, with cynical humour, were covered by long growths of beard, but with the exception of a few who had pined perceptibly away, they seemed to be a well-fed, healthy lot.

Braddock Washington drew a garden chair to the edge of the pit and sat down.

'Well, how are you, boys?' he enquired genially.

A chorus of execration, in which all joined except a few too dispirited to cry out, rose up into the sunny air, but Braddock Washington heard it with unruffled composure. When its last echo had died away he spoke again.

'Have you thought up a way out of your difficulty?'

From here and there among them a remark floated up.

'We decided to stay here for love!'

'Bring us up there and we'll find us a way!'

Braddock Washington waited until they were again quiet. Then he said: 'I've told you the situation. I don't want you here. I wish to heaven I'd never seen you. Your own curiosity got you here, and any time that you can think of a way out which protects me and my interests I'll be glad to consider it. But so long as you confine your efforts to digging tunnels – yes, I know about the new one you've started – you won't get very far. This isn't as hard on you as you make it out, with all your howling for the loved ones at home. If you were the type who worried much about the loved ones at home, you'd never have taken up aviation.'

A tall man moved apart from the others, and held up his hand to call his captor's attention to what he was about to say.

'Let me ask you a few questions!' he cried. 'You pretend to be a fair-minded man.'

'How absurd. How could a man of my position be fair-minded towards you? You might as well speak of a Spaniard being fair-minded towards a piece of steak.'

At this harsh observation the faces of the two dozen steaks fell, but the tall man continued: 'All right!' he cried. 'We've argued this out before. You're not a humanitarian and you're not fair-minded, but you're human – at least you say you are – and you ought to be able to put yourself in our place for long enough to think how – how – how – '

'How what?' demanded Washington, coldly.

' – how unnecessary – '

'Not to me.'

'Well – how cruel – '

'We've covered that. Cruelty doesn't exist where self-preservation is involved. You've been soldiers: you know that. Try another.'

'Well, then, how stupid.'

'There,' admitted Washington, 'I grant you that. But try to think of an alternative. I've offered to have all or any of you painlessly executed if you wish. I've offered to have your wives, sweethearts, children, and mothers kidnapped and brought out here. I'll enlarge your place down there and feed and clothe you the rest of your lives. If there was some method of producing permanent amnesia I'd have all of you operated on and released immediately, somewhere outside of my preserves. But that's as far as my ideas go.'

'How about trusting us not to peach on you?' cried someone.

'You don't proffer that suggestion seriously,' said Washington, with an expression of scorn. 'I did take out one man to teach my daughter Italian. Last week he got away.'

A wild yell of jubilation went up suddenly from two dozen throats and a pandemonium of joy ensued. The prisoners clog-danced and cheered and yodelled and wrestled with one another in a sudden uprush of animal spirits. They even ran up the glass sides of the bowl as far as they could, and slid back to the bottom upon the natural cushions of their bodies. The tall man started a song in which they all joined –

> 'Oh, we'll hang the Kaiser
> On a sour apple tree – '

Braddock Washington sat in inscrutable silence until the song was over.

'You see,' he remarked, when he could gain a modicum of attention. 'I bear you no ill-will. I like to see you enjoying yourselves. That's why I didn't tell you the whole story at once. The man – what was his name? Critchtichiello? – was shot by some of my agents in fourteen different places.'

Not guessing that the places referred to were cities, the tumult of rejoicing subsided immediately.

'Nevertheless,' cried Washington with a touch of anger, 'he tried to run away. Do you expect me to take chances with any of you after an experience like that?'

Again a series of ejaculations went up.

'Sure!'

'Would your daughter like to learn Chinese?'

'Hey, I can speak Italian! My mother was a wop.'

'Maybe she'd like t'learna speak N'Yawk!'

'If she's the little one with the big blue eyes I can teach her a lot of things better than Italian.'

'I know some Irish songs – and I could hammer brass once't.'

Mr Washington reached forward suddenly with his cane and pushed the button in the grass so that the picture below went out instantly, and there remained only that great dark mouth covered dismally with the black teeth of the grating.

'Hey!' called a single voice from below, 'you ain't goin' away without givin' us your blessing?'

But Mr Washington, followed by the two boys, was already strolling on towards the ninth hole of the golf-course, as though the pit and its contents were no more than a hazard over which his facile iron had triumphed with ease.

CHAPTER 7

JULY UNDER THE LEE of the diamond mountain was a month of blanket nights and of warm, glowing days. John and Kismine were in love. He did not know that the little gold football (inscribed with the legend Pro deo et patria et St Mida[36]) which he had given her rested on a platinum chain next to her bosom. But it did. And she for her part was not aware that a large sapphire which had dropped one day from her simple coiffure was stowed away tenderly in John's jewel-box.

Late one afternoon when the ruby and ermine music-room was quiet, they spent an hour there together. He held her hand and she gave him such a look that he whispered her name aloud. She bent towards him – then hesitated.

'Did you say "Kismine"?' she asked softly, 'or – '

She had wanted to be sure. She thought she might have mis-understood.

Neither of them had ever kissed before, but in the course of an hour it seemed to make little difference.

The afternoon drifted away. That night when a last breath of music drifted down from the highest tower, they each lay awake, happily dreaming over the separate minutes of the day. They had decided to be married as soon as possible.

CHAPTER 8

EVERY DAY Mr Washington and the two young men went hunting or fishing in the deep forests or played golf around the somnolent course – games which John diplomatically allowed his host to win – or swam in the mountain coolness of the lake. John found Mr Washington a somewhat exacting personality – utterly uninterested in any ideas or opinions except his own. Mrs Washington was aloof and reserved at all times. She was apparently indifferent to her two daughters, and entirely absorbed in her son Percy, with whom she held interminable conversations in rapid Spanish at dinner.

Jasmine, the elder daughter, resembled Kismine in appearance – except that she was somewhat bow-legged, and terminated in large hands and feet – but was utterly unlike her in temperament. Her favourite books had to do with poor girls who kept house for widowed fathers. John learned from Kismine that Jasmine had never recovered from the shock and disappointment caused her by the termination of the World War, just as she was about to start for Europe as a canteen expert. She had even pined away for a time, and Braddock Washington had taken steps to promote a new war in the Balkans – but she had seen a photograph of some wounded Serbian soldiers and lost interest in the whole proceedings. But Percy and Kismine seemed to have inherited the arrogant attitude in all its harsh magnificence from their father. A chaste and consistent selfishness ran like a pattern through their every idea.

John was enchanted by the wonders of the château and the valley. Braddock Washington, so Percy told him, had caused to be kidnapped a landscape gardener, an architect, a designer of stage settings, and a French decadent poet left over from the last century. He had put his entire force of Negroes at their disposal, guaranteed to supply them with any materials that the world could offer, and left them to work out some ideas of their own. But one by one they had shown their uselessness. The decadent poet had at once begun bewailing his separation from the boulevards in spring – he made some vague remarks about spices, apes and ivories, but said nothing that was of any practical value. The stage designer on his part wanted to make the whole valley a series of tricks and sensational effects – a state of things that the Washingtons would soon have grown tired of. And as for the architect and the landscape gardener, they thought only in terms of convention. They must make this like this and that like that.

But they had, at least, solved the problem of what was to be done with them – they all went mad early one morning after spending the night in a single room trying to agree upon the location of a fountain, and were now confined comfortably in an insane asylum at Westport, Connecticut.

'But,' enquired John curiously, 'who did plan all your wonderful reception rooms and halls, and approaches and bathrooms – ?'

'Well,' answered Percy, 'I blush to tell you, but it was a moving-picture fella. He was the only man we found who was used to playing with an unlimited amount of money, though he did tuck his napkin in his collar and couldn't read or write.'

As August drew to a close John began to regret that he must soon go back to school. He and Kismine had decided to elope the following June.

'It would be nicer to be married here,' Kismine confessed, 'but of course I could never get father's permission to marry you at all. Next to that I'd rather elope. It's terrible for wealthy people to be married in America at present – they always have to send out bulletins to the Press saying that they're going to be married in remnants, when what they mean is just a peck of old second-hand pearls and some used lace worn once by the Empress Eugènie.'[37]

'I know,' agreed John fervently. 'When I was visiting the Schnlitzer-Murphys, the eldest daughter, Gwendolyn, married a man whose father owns half of West Virginia. She wrote home saying what a tough struggle it was carrying on on his salary as a bank clerk – and then she ended up by saying that "Thank God, I have four good maids anyhow, and that helps a little." '

'It's absurd,' commented Kismine. 'Think of the millions and millions of people in the world, labourers and all, who get along with only two maids.'

One afternoon late in August a chance remark of Kismine's changed the face of the entire situation, and threw John into a state of terror.

They were in their favourite grove, and between kisses John was indulging in some romantic forebodings which he fancied added poignancy to their relations.

'Sometimes I think we'll never marry,' he said sadly. 'You're too wealthy, too magnificent. No one as rich as you are can be like other girls. I should marry the daughter of some well-to-do wholesale hardware man from Omaha or Sioux City, and be content with her half-million.'

'I knew the daughter of a wholesale hardware man once,' remarked Kismine. 'I don't think you'd have been contented with her. She was a friend of my sister's. She visited here.'

'Oh, then you've had other guests?' exclaimed John in surprise.

Kismine seemed to regret her words.

'Oh, yes,' she said hurriedly, 'we've had a few.'

'But aren't you – wasn't your father afraid they'd talk outside?'

'Oh, to some extent, to some extent,' she answered. 'Let's talk about something pleasanter.'

But John's curiosity was aroused.

'Something pleasanter!' he demanded. 'What's unpleasant about that? Weren't they nice girls?'

To his great surprise Kismine began to weep.

'Yes – th–that's the – the whole t–trouble. I grew qu–quite attached to some of them. So did Jasmine, but she kept inv–viting them anyway. I couldn't understand it.

A dark suspicion was born in John's heart.

'Do you mean that they *told*, and your father had them – removed?'

'Worse than that,' she muttered brokenly. 'Father took no chances – and Jasmine kept writing them to come, and they had *such* a good time!'

She was overcome by a paroxysm of grief.

Stunned with the horror of this revelation, John sat there open-mouthed, feeling the nerves of his body twitter like so many sparrows perched upon his spinal column.

'Now, I've told you, and I shouldn't have,' she said, calming suddenly and drying her dark blue eyes.

'Do you mean to say that your father had them *murdered* before they left?'

She nodded.

'In August usually – or early in September. It's only natural for us to get all the pleasure out of them that we can first.'

'How abominable! How – why, I must be going crazy! Did you really admit that – '

'I did,' interrupted Kismine, shrugging her shoulders. 'We can't very well imprison them like those aviators, where they'd be a continual reproach to us every day. And it's always been made easier for Jasmine and me, because father had it done sooner than we expected. In that way we avoided any farewell scene – '

'So you murdered them! Uh!' cried John.

'It was done very nicely. They were drugged while they were asleep – and their families were always told that they died of scarlet fever in Butte.'

'But – I fail to understand why you kept on inviting them!'

'I didn't,' burst out Kismine. 'I never invited one. Jasmine did. And they always had a very good time. She'd give them the nicest presents towards the last. I shall probably have visitors too – I'll harden up to it. We can't let such an inevitable thing as death stand in the way of enjoying life while we have it. Think how lonesome it'd be out here if we never had *any*one. Why, father and mother have sacrificed some of their best friends just as we have.'

'And so,' cried John accusingly, 'and so you were letting me make love to you and pretending to return it, and talking about marriage, all the time knowing perfectly well that I'd never get out of here alive – '

'No,' she protested passionately. 'Not any more. I did at first. You were here. I couldn't help that, and I thought your last days might as well be pleasant for both of us. But then I fell in love with you, and – and I'm honestly sorry you're going to – going to be put away – though I'd rather you'd be put away than ever kiss another girl.'

'Oh, you would, would you?' cried John ferociously.

'Much rather. Besides, I've always heard that a girl can have more fun with a man whom she knows she can never marry. Oh, why did I tell you? I've probably spoiled your whole good time now, and we were really enjoying things when you didn't know it. I knew it would make things sort of depressing for you.'

'Oh, you did, did you?' John's voice trembled with anger. 'I've heard about enough of this. If you haven't any more pride and decency than to have an affair with a fellow that you know isn't much better than a corpse, I don't want to have any more to do with you!'

'You're not a corpse!' she protested in horror. 'You're not a corpse! I won't have you saying that I kissed a corpse!'

'I said nothing of the sort!'

'You did! You said I kissed a corpse!'

'I didn't!'

Their voices had risen, but upon a sudden interruption they both subsided into immediate silence. Footsteps were coming along the path in their direction, and a moment later the rose bushes were parted displaying Braddock Washington, whose intelligent eyes set in his good-looking vacuous face were peering in at them.

'Who kissed a corpse?' he demanded in obvious disapproval.

'Nobody,' answered Kismine quickly. 'We were just joking.'

'What are you two doing here, anyhow?' he demanded gruffly. 'Kismine, you ought to be – to be reading or playing golf with your sister. Go read! Go play golf! Don't let me find you here when I come back!'

Then he bowed at John and went up the path.

'See?' said Kismine crossly, when he was out of hearing. 'You've spoiled it all. We can never meet any more. He won't let me meet you. He'd have you poisoned if he thought we were in love.'

'We're not, any more!' cried John fiercely, 'so he can set his mind at rest upon that. Moreover, don't fool yourself that I'm going to stay around here. Inside of six hours I'll be over those mountains, if I have to gnaw a passage through them, and on my way East.'

They had both got to their feet, and at this remark Kismine came close and put her arm through his.

'I'm going, too.'

'You must be crazy – '

'Of course I'm going,' she interrupted patiently.

'You most certainly are not. You – '

'Very well,' she said quietly, 'we'll catch up with father now and talk it over with him.'

Defeated, John mustered a sickly smile.

'Very well, dearest,' he agreed, with pale and unconvincing affection, 'we'll go together.'

His love for her returned and settled placidly on his heart. She was his – she would go with him to share his dangers. He put his arms about her and kissed her fervently. After all she loved him; she had saved him, in fact.

Discussing the matter, they walked slowly back towards the château. They decided that since Braddock Washington had seen them together they had best depart the next night. Nevertheless, John's lips were unusually dry at dinner, and he nervously emptied a great spoonful of peacock soup into his left lung. He had to be carried into the turquoise and sable card-room and pounded on the back by one of the under-butlers, which Percy considered a great joke.

CHAPTER 9

LONG AFTER MIDNIGHT John's body gave a nervous jerk, and he sat suddenly upright, staring into the veils of somnolence that draped the room. Through the squares of blue darkness that were his open windows, he had heard a faint far-away sound that died upon a bed of wind before identifying itself on his memory, clouded with uneasy dreams. But the sharp noise that had succeeded it was nearer, was just outside the room – the click of a turned knob, a footstep, a whisper, he could not tell; a hard lump gathered in the pit of his stomach, and his whole body ached in the moment that he strained agonisingly to hear. Then one of the veils seemed to dissolve, and he saw a vague figure standing by the door, a figure only faintly limned and blocked in upon the darkness, mingled so with the folds of the drapery as to seem distorted, like a reflection seen in a dirty pane of glass.

With a sudden movement of fright or resolution John pressed the button by his bedside, and the next moment he was sitting in the green sunken bath of the adjoining room, waked into alertness by the shock of the cold water which half filled it.

He sprang out and, his wet pyjamas scattering a heavy trickle of water behind him, ran for the aquamarine door which he knew led out on to the ivory landing of the second floor. The door opened noiselessly. A single crimson lamp burning in a great dome above lit the magnificent sweep of the carved stairways with a poignant beauty. For a moment John hesitated, appalled by the silent splendour massed about him, seeming to envelop in its gigantic folds and contours the solitary drenched little figure shivering upon the ivory landing. Then simultaneously two things happened. The door of his own sitting-room swung open, precipitating three naked Negroes into the hall – and, as John swayed in wild terror towards the stairway, another door slid back in the wall on the other side of the corridor, and John saw Braddock Washington standing in the lighted lift, wearing a fur coat and a pair of riding boots which reached to his knees and displayed, above, the glow of his rose-coloured pyjamas.

On the instant the three Negroes – John had never seen any of them before, and it flashed through his mind that they must be the professional executioners – paused in their movement towards John, and turned expectantly to the man in the lift, who burst out with an imperious command: 'Get in here! All three of you! Quick as hell!'

Then, within the instant, the three Negroes darted into the cage, the oblong of light was blotted out as the lift door slid shut, and John was again alone in the hall. He slumped weakly down against an ivory stair.

It was apparent that something portentous had occurred, something which, for the moment at least, had postponed his own petty disaster. What was it? Had the Negroes risen in revolt? Had the aviators forced aside the iron bars of the grating? Or had the men of Fish stumbled blindly through the hills and gazed with bleak, joyless eyes upon the gaudy valley? John did not know. He heard a faint whir of air as the lift whizzed up again, and then, a moment later, as it descended. It was probable that Percy was hurrying to his father's assistance, and it occurred to John that this was his opportunity to join Kismine and plan an immediate escape. He waited until the lift had been silent for several minutes; shivering a little with the night cool that whipped in through his wet pyjamas, he returned to his room and dressed himself quickly. Then he mounted a long flight of stairs and turned down the corridor carpeted with Russian sable[38] which led to Kismine's suite.

The door of her sitting-room was open and the lamps were lighted. Kismine, in an angora[39] kimono, stood near the window of the room in a listening attitude, and as John entered noiselessly, she turned towards him.

'Oh, it's you!' she whispered, crossing the room to him. 'Did you hear them?'

'I heard your father's slaves in my – '

'No,' she interrupted excitedly. 'Aeroplanes!'

'Aeroplanes? Perhaps that was the sound that woke me.'

'There're at least a dozen. I saw one a few moments ago dead against the moon. The guard back by the cliff fired his rifle and that's what roused father. We're going to open on them right away.'

'Are they here on purpose?'

'Yes – it's that Italian who got away – '

Simultaneously with her last word, a succession of sharp cracks tumbled in through the open window. Kismine uttered a little cry, took a penny with fumbling fingers from a box on her dresser, and ran to one of the electric lights. In an instant the entire château was in darkness – she had blown out the fuse.

'Come on!' she cried to him. 'We'll go up to the roof garden, and watch it from there!'

Drawing a cape about her, she took his hand, and they found their way out the door. It was only a step to the tower lift, and as she pressed the button that shot them upward, he put his arms around her in the darkness and kissed her mouth. Romance had come to John Unger at last. A minute later they had stepped out upon the star-white platform. Above, under the misty moon, sliding in and out of the patches of cloud that eddied below it, floated a dozen dark-winged bodies in a constant circling course. From here and there in the valley flashes of fire leaped towards them, followed by sharp detonations. Kismine clapped her hands with pleasure which, a moment later, turned to dismay as the aeroplanes at some pre-arranged signal began to release their bombs and the whole of the valley became a panorama of deep reverberant sound and lurid light.

Before long the aim of the attackers became concentrated upon the points where the anti-aircraft guns were situated, and one of them was almost immediately reduced to a giant cinder to lie smouldering in a park of rose bushes.

'Kismine,' begged John, 'you'll be glad when I tell you that this attack came on the eve of my murder. If I hadn't heard that guard shoot off his gun back by the pass I should now be stone dead – '

'I can't hear you!' cried Kismine, intent on the scene before her. 'You'll have to talk louder!'

'I simply said,' shouted John, 'that we'd better get out before they begin to shell the château!'

Suddenly the whole portico of the Negro quarters cracked asunder, a geyser of flame shot up from under the colonnades, and great fragments of jagged marble were hurled as far as the borders of the lake.

'There go fifty thousand dollars' worth of slaves,' cried Kismine, 'at pre-war prices. So few Americans have any respect for property.'

John renewed his efforts to compel her to leave. The aim of the aeroplanes was becoming more precise minute by minute, and only two of the anti-aircraft guns were still retaliating. It was obvious that the garrison, encircled with fire, could not hold out much longer.

'Come on!' cried John, pulling Kismine's arm, 'we've got to go. Do you realise that those aviators will kill you without question if they find you?'

She consented reluctantly.

'We'll have to wake Jasmine!' she said, as they hurried towards the lift. Then she added in a sort of childish delight: 'We'll be poor, won't we? Like people in books. And I'll be an orphan and utterly free. Free and poor! What fun!' She stopped and raised her lips to him in a delighted kiss.

'It's impossible to be both together,' said John grimly. 'People have found that out. And I should choose to be free as preferable of the two. As an extra caution you'd better lump the contents of your jewel-box into your pockets.'

Ten minutes later the two girls met John in the dark corridor and they descended to the main floor of the château. Passing for the last time through the magnificence of the splendid halls, they stood for a moment out on the terrace, watching the burning Negro quarters and the flaming embers of two planes which had fallen on the other side of the lake. A solitary gun was still keeping up a sturdy popping, and the attackers seemed timorous about descending lower, but sent their thunderous fireworks in a circle around it, until any chance shot might annihilate its Ethiopian crew.

John and the two sisters, passed down the marble steps, turned sharply to the left, and began to ascend a narrow path that wound like a garter about the diamond mountain. Kismine knew a heavily wooded spot halfway up where they could lie concealed and yet be able to observe the wild night in the valley – finally to make an escape, when it should be necessary, along a secret path laid in a rocky gully.

IT WAS THREE O'CLOCK when they attained their destination. The obliging and phlegmatic Jasmine fell off to sleep immediately, leaning against the trunk of a large tree, while John and Kismine sat, his arm around her, and watched the desperate ebb and flow of the dying battle among the ruins of a vista that had been a garden spot that morning. Shortly after four o'clock the last remaining gun gave out a clanging sound and went out of action in a swift tongue of red smoke. Though the moon was down, they saw that the flying bodies were circling closer to the earth. When the planes had made certain that the beleaguered possessed no further resources, they would land and the dark and glittering reign of the Washingtons would be over.

With the cessation of the firing the valley grew quiet. The embers of the two aeroplanes glowed like the eyes of some monster crouching in the glass. The château stood dark and silent, beautiful without light as it had been beautiful in the sun, while the woody rattles of Nemesis[40] filled the air above with a growing and receding complaint. Then John perceived that Kismine, like her sister, had fallen sound asleep.

It was long after four when he became aware of footsteps along the path they had lately followed, and he waited in breathless silence until the persons to whom they belonged had passed the vantage-point he occupied. There was a faint stir in the air now that was not of human origin, and the dew was cold; he knew that the dawn would break soon. John waited until the steps had gone a safe distance up the mountain and were inaudible. Then he followed. About halfway to the steep summit the trees fell away and a hard saddle of rock spread itself over the diamond beneath. Just before he reached this point he slowed down his pace, warned by an animal sense that there was life just ahead of him. Coming to a high boulder, he lifted his head gradually above its edge. His curiosity was rewarded; this is what he saw: Braddock Washington was standing there motionless, silhouetted against the grey sky without sound or sign of life. As the dawn came up out of the east, lending a cold green colour to the earth, it brought the solitary figure into insignificant contrast with the new day.

While John watched, his host remained for a few moments absorbed in some inscrutable contemplation; then he signalled to the two Negroes who crouched at his feet to lift the burden which lay between them. As they struggled upright, the first yellow beam of the sun struck through the innumerable prisms of an immense and exquisitely chiselled diamond – and a white radiance was kindled that glowed upon the air like a fragment of the morning star. The bearers staggered beneath its weight for a moment – then their rippling muscles caught and hardened under the wet shine of the skins and the three figures were again motionless in their defiant impotency before the heavens.

After a while the white man lifted his head and slowly raised his arms in a gesture of attention, as one who would call a great crowd to hear – but there was no crowd, only the vast silence of the mountain and the sky, broken by faint bird voices down among the trees. The figure on the saddle of rock began to speak ponderously and with an inextinguishable pride.

'You out there – ' he cried in a trembling voice. 'You there – !' He paused, his arms still uplifted, his head held attentively as though he were expecting an answer. John strained his eyes to see whether there might be men coming down the mountain, but the mountain was bare of human life. There was only sky and a mocking flute of wind along the tree-tops. Could Washington be praying? For a moment John wondered. Then the illusion passed – there was something in the man's whole attitude antithetical to prayer.

'Oh, you above there!'

The voice was become strong and confident. This was no forlorn supplication. If anything, there was in it a quality of monstrous condescension.

'You there – '

Words, too quickly uttered to be understood, flowing one into the other . . . John listened breathlessly, catching a phrase here and there, while the voice broke off, resumed, broke off again – now strong and argumentative, now coloured with a slow, puzzled impatience. Then a conviction commenced to dawn on the single listener, and as realisation crept over him a spray of quick blood rushed through his arteries. Braddock Washington was offering a bribe to God!

That was it – there was no doubt. The diamond in the arms of his slaves was some advance sample, a promise of more to follow.

That, John perceived after a time, was the thread running through his sentences. Prometheus Enriched[41] was calling to witness forgotten sacrifices, forgotten rituals, prayers obsolete before the birth of Christ. For a while his discourse took the form of reminding God of this gift or that which Divinity had deigned to accept from men – great churches if he would rescue cities from the plague, gifts of myrrh and gold, of human lives and beautiful women and captive armies, of children and queens, of beasts of the forest and field, sheep and goats, harvests and cities, whole conquered lands that had been offered up in lust or blood for His appeasal, buying a meed's worth of alleviation from the Divine wrath – and now he, Braddock Washington, Emperor of Diamonds, king and priest of the age of gold, arbiter of splendour and luxury, would offer up a treasure such as princes before him had never dreamed of, offer it up not in suppliance, but in pride.

He would give to God, he continued, getting down to specifications, the greatest diamond in the world. This diamond would be cut with many more thousand facets than there were leaves on a tree, and yet the whole diamond would be shaped with the perfection of a stone no bigger than a fly. Many men would work upon it for many years. It would be set in a great dome of beaten gold, wonderfully carved and equipped with gates of opal and crusted sapphire. In the middle would be hollowed out a chapel presided over by an altar of iridescent, decomposing, ever-changing radium which would burn out the eyes of any worshipper who lifted up his head from prayer – and on this altar there would be slain for the amusement of the Divine Benefactor any victim He should choose, even though it should be the greatest and most powerful man alive.

In return he asked only a simple thing, a thing that for God would be absurdly easy – only that matters should be as they were yesterday at this hour and that they should so remain. So very simple! Let but the heavens open, swallowing these men and their aeroplanes – and then close again. Let him have his slaves once more, restored to life and well.

There was no one else with whom he had ever needed to treat or bargain.

He doubted only whether he had made his bribe big enough. God had His price, of course. God was made in man's image, so it had been said: He must have His price. And the price would be rare –

no cathedral whose building consumed many years, no pyramid constructed by ten thousand workmen, would be like this cathedral, this pyramid.

He paused here. That was his proposition. Everything would be up to specifications and there was nothing vulgar in his assertion that it would be cheap at the price. He implied that Providence could take it or leave it.

As he approached the end his sentences became broken, became short and uncertain, and his body seemed tense, seemed strained to catch the slightest pressure or whisper of life in the spaces around him. His hair had turned gradually white as he talked, and now he lifted his head high to the heavens like a prophet of old – magnificently mad.

Then, as John stared in giddy fascination, it seemed to him that a curious phenomenon took place somewhere around him. It was as though the sky had darkened for an instant, as though there had been a sudden murmur in a gust of wind, a sound of far-away trumpets, a sighing like the rustle of a great silken robe – for a time the whole of nature round about partook of this darkness: the birds' song ceased, the trees were still, and far over the mountain there was a mutter of dull, menacing thunder.

That was all. The wind died along the tall grasses of the valley. The dawn and the day resumed their place in time, and the risen sun sent hot waves of yellow mist that made its path bright before it. The leaves laughed in the sun, and their laughter shook the trees until each bough was like a girls' school in fairyland. God had refused to accept the bribe.

For another moment John watched the triumph of the day. Then, turning, he saw a flutter of brown down by the lake, then another flutter, then another, like the dance of golden angels alighting from the clouds. The aeroplanes had come to earth.

John slid off the boulder and ran down the side of the mountain to the clump of trees, where the two girls were awake and waiting for him. Kismine sprang to her feet, the jewels in her pockets jingling, a question on her parted lips, but instinct told John that there was no time for words. They must get off the mountain without losing a moment. He seized a hand of each, and in silence they threaded the tree-trunks, washed with light now and with the rising mist. Behind them from the valley came no sound at all, except the complaint of the peacocks far away and the pleasant undertone of morning.

When they had gone about a half a mile, they avoided the park land and entered a narrow path that led over the next rise of ground. At the highest point of this they paused and turned around. Their eyes rested upon the mountainside they had just left – oppressed by some dark sense of tragic impendency.

Clear against the sky a broken, white-haired man was slowly descending the steep slope, followed by two gigantic and emotionless Negroes, who carried a burden between them which still flashed and glittered in the sun. Halfway down two other figures joined them – John could see that they were Mrs Washington and her son, upon whose arm she leaned. The aviators had clambered from their machines to the sweeping lawn in front of the château, and with rifles in hand were starting up the diamond mountain in skirmishing formation.

But the little group of five which had formed farther up and was engrossing all the watchers' attention had stopped upon a ledge of rock. The Negroes stooped and pulled up what appeared to be a trap-door in the side of the mountain. Into this they all disappeared, the white-haired man first, then his wife and son, finally the two Negroes, the glittering tips of whose jewelled head-dresses caught the sun for a moment before the trap-door descended and engulfed them all.

Kismine clutched John's arm.

'Oh,' she cried wildly, 'where are they going? What are they going to do?'

'It must be some underground way of escape – '

A little scream from the two girls interrupted his sentence.

'Don't you see?' sobbed Kismine hysterically. 'The mountain is wired!'

Even as she spoke John put up his hands to shield his sight. Before their eyes the whole surface of the mountain had changed suddenly to a dazzling burning yellow, which showed up through the jacket of turf as light shows through a human hand. For a moment the intolerable glow continued, and then like an extinguished filament it disappeared, revealing a black waste from which blue smoke arose slowly, carrying off with it what remained of vegetation and of human flesh. Of the aviators there was left neither blood nor bone – they were consumed as completely as the five souls who had gone inside.

Simultaneously, and with an immense concussion, the château literally threw itself into the air, bursting into flaming fragments as it rose, and then tumbling back upon itself in a smoking pile that lay projecting half into the water of the lake. There was no fire – what smoke there was drifted off mingling with the sunshine, and for a few minutes longer a powdery dust of marble drifted from the great featureless pile that had once been the house of jewels. There was no more sound and the three people were alone in the valley.

CHAPTER 9

AT SUNSET John and his two companions reached the high cliff which had marked the boundaries of the Washingtons' dominion, and looking back found the valley tranquil and lovely in the dusk. They sat down to finish the food which Jasmine had brought with her in a basket.

'There!' she said, as she spread the tablecloth and put the sandwiches in a neat pile upon it. 'Don't they look tempting? I always think that food tastes better outdoors.'

'With that remark,' remarked Kismine, 'Jasmine enters the middle class.'

'Now,' said John eagerly, 'turn out your pockets and let's see what jewels you brought along. If you made a good selection we three ought to live comfortably all the rest of our lives.'

Obediently Kismine put her hand in her pocket and tossed two handfuls of glittering stones before him.

'Not so bad,' cried John, enthusiastically. 'They aren't very big, but – Hello!' His expression changed as he held one of them up to the declining sun. 'Why, these aren't diamonds! There's something the matter!'

'By golly!' exclaimed Kismine, with a startled look. 'What an idiot I am!'

'Why, these are rhinestones!' cried John.

'I know.' She broke into a laugh. 'I opened the wrong drawer. They belonged on the dress of a girl who visited Jasmine. I got her to give them to me in exchange for diamonds. I'd never seen anything but precious stones before.'

'And this is what you brought?'

'I'm afraid so. She fingered the brilliants wistfully. 'I think I like these better. I'm a little tired of diamonds.'

'Very well,' said John gloomily. 'We'll have to live in Hades. And you will grow old telling incredulous women that you got the wrong drawer. Unfortunately your father's bank-books were consumed with him.'

'Well, what's the matter with Hades?'

'If I come home with a wife at my age my father is just as liable as not to cut me off with a hot coal, as they say down there.'

Jasmine spoke up.

'I love washing,' she said quietly. 'I have always washed my own handkerchiefs. I'll take in laundry and support you both.'

'Do they have washwomen in Hades?' asked Kismine innocently.

'Of course,' answered John. 'It's just like anywhere else.'

'I thought – perhaps it was too hot to wear any clothes.'

John laughed.

'Just try it!' he suggested. 'They'll run you out before you're half started.'

'Will father be there?' she asked.

John turned to her in astonishment.

'Your father is dead,' he replied sombrely. 'Why should he go to Hades? You have it confused with another place that was abolished long ago.'

After supper they folded up the tablecloth and spread their blankets for the night.

'What a dream it was,' Kismine sighed, gazing up at the stars. 'How strange it seems to be here with one dress and a penniless fiancé!

'Under the stars,' she repeated. 'I never noticed the stars before. I always thought of them as great big diamonds that belonged to someone. Now they frighten me. They make me feel that it was all a dream, all my youth.'

'It *was* a dream,' said John quietly. 'Everybody's youth is a dream, a form of chemical madness.'

'How pleasant then to be insane!'

'So I'm told,' said John gloomily. 'I don't know any longer. At any rate, let us love for a while, for a year or so, you and me. That's a form of divine drunkenness that we can all try. There are only diamonds in the whole world, diamonds and perhaps the shabby gift of disillusion. Well, I have that last and I will make the usual nothing of it.' He shivered. 'Turn up your coat collar, little girl, the night's full of chill and you'll get pneumonia. His was a great sin who first invented consciousness. Let us lose it for a few hours.'

So wrapping himself in his blanket he fell off to sleep.

The Rich Boy

CHAPTER I

BEGIN WITH AN INDIVIDUAL, and before you know it you find that you have created a type; begin with a type, and you find that you have created – nothing. That is because we are all queer fish, queerer behind our faces and voices than we want anyone to know or than we know ourselves. When I hear a man proclaiming himself an 'average, honest, open fellow', I feel pretty sure that he has some definite and perhaps terrible abnormality which he has agreed to conceal – and his protestation of being average and honest and open is his way of reminding himself of his misprision.

There are no types, no plurals. There is a rich boy, and this is his and not his brothers' story. All my life I have lived among his brothers but this one has been my friend. Besides, if I wrote about his brothers I should have to begin by attacking all the lies that the poor have told about the rich and the rich have told about themselves – such a wild structure they have erected that when we pick up a book about the rich, some instinct prepares us for unreality. Even the intelligent and impassioned reporters of life have made the country of the rich as unreal as fairyland.

Let me tell you about the very rich. They are different from you and me. They possess and enjoy early, and it does something to them, makes them soft where we are hard, and cynical where we are trustful, in a way that, unless you were born rich, it is very difficult to understand. They think, deep in their hearts, that they are better than we are because we had to discover the compensations and refuges of life for ourselves. Even when they enter deep into our world or sink below us, they still think that they are better than we are. They are different. The only way I can describe young Anson Hunter is to approach him as if he were a foreigner and cling stubbornly to my point of view. If I accept his for a moment I am lost – I have nothing to show but a preposterous movie.

CHAPTER 2

ANSON WAS THE ELDEST of six children who would some day divide a fortune of fifteen million dollars, and he reached the age of reason – is it seven? – at the beginning of the century when daring young women were already gliding along Fifth Avenue in electric 'mobiles'. In those days he and his brother had an English governess who spoke the language very clearly and crisply and well, so that the two boys grew to speak as she did – their words and sentences were all crisp and clear and not run together as ours are. They didn't talk exactly like English children but acquired an accent that is peculiar to fashionable people in the city of New York.

In the summer the six children were moved from the house on 71st Street to a big estate in northern Connecticut. It was not a fashionable locality – Anson's father wanted to delay as long as possible his children's knowledge of that side of life. He was a man somewhat superior to his class, which composed New York society, and to his period, which was the snobbish and formalised vulgarity of the Gilded Age,[42] and he wanted his sons to learn habits of concentration and have sound constitutions and grow up into right-living and successful men. He and his wife kept an eye on them as well as they were able until the two older boys went away to school, but in huge establishments this is difficult – it was much simpler in the series of small and medium-sized houses in which my own youth was spent – I was never far out of the reach of my mother's voice, of the sense of her presence, her approval or disapproval.

Anson's first sense of his superiority came to him when he realised the half-grudging American deference that was paid to him in the Connecticut village. The parents of the boys he played with always enquired after his father and mother, and were vaguely excited when their own children were asked to the Hunters' house. He accepted this as the natural state of things, and a sort of impatience with all groups of which he was not the centre – in money, in position, in authority – remained with him for the rest of his life. He disdained to struggle with other boys for precedence – he expected it to be given him freely, and when it wasn't he withdrew into his family. His family was sufficient, for in the East money is still a somewhat feudal thing, a clan-forming thing. In the snobbish West, money separates families to form 'sets'.

At eighteen, when he went to New Haven, Anson was tall and thickset, with a clear complexion and a healthy colour from the ordered life he had led in school. His hair was yellow and grew in a funny way on his head, his nose was beaked – these two things kept him from being handsome – but he had a confident charm and a certain brusque style, and the upper-class men who passed him on the street knew without being told that he was a rich boy and had gone to one of the best schools. Nevertheless, his very superiority kept him from being a success in college – the independence was mistaken for egotism, and the refusal to accept Yale standards with the proper awe seemed to belittle all those who had. So, long before he graduated, he began to shift the centre of his life to New York.

He was at home in New York – there was his own house with 'the kind of servants you can't get any more' – and his own family, of which, because of his good humour and a certain ability to make things go, he was rapidly becoming the centre, and the débutante parties, and the correct manly world of the men's clubs, and the occasional wild spree with the gallant girls whom New Haven only knew from the fifth row. His aspirations were conventional enough – they included even the irreproachable shadow he would someday marry – but they differed from the aspirations of the majority of young men in that there was no mist over them, none of that quality which is variously known as 'idealism' or 'illusion'. Anson accepted without reservation the world of high finance and high extravagance, of divorce and dissipation, of snobbery and of privilege. Most of our lives end as a compromise – it was as a compromise that his life began.

He and I first met in the late summer of 1917 when he was just out of Yale, and, like the rest of us, was swept up into the systematised hysteria of the war. In the blue-green uniform of the naval aviation he came down to Pensacola, where the hotel orchestras played *I'm Sorry, Dear*, and we young officers danced with the girls. Everyone liked him, and though he ran with the drinkers and wasn't an especially good pilot, even the instructors treated him with a certain respect. He was always having long talks with them in his confident, logical voice – talks which ended by his getting himself, or, more frequently, another officer, out of some impending trouble. He was convivial, bawdy, robustly avid for pleasure, and we were all surprised when he fell in love with a conservative and rather proper girl.

Her name was Paula Legendre, a dark, serious beauty from somewhere in California. Her family kept a winter residence just outside of town, and in spite of her primness she was enormously popular; there is a large class of men whose egotism can't endure humour in a woman. But Anson wasn't that sort, and I couldn't understand the attraction of her 'sincerity' – that was the thing to say about her – for his keen and somewhat sardonic mind.

Nevertheless, they fell in love – and on her terms. He no longer joined the twilight gathering at the De Soto Bar,[43] and whenever they were seen together they were engaged in a long, serious dialogue, which must have gone on several weeks. Long afterward he told me that it was not about anything in particular but was composed on both sides of immature and even meaningless statements – the emotional content that gradually came to fill it grew up not out of the words but out of its enormous seriousness. It was a sort of hypnosis. Often it was interrupted, giving way to that emasculated humour we call fun; when they were alone it was resumed again, solemn, low-keyed, and pitched so as to give each other a sense of unity in feeling and thought. They came to resent any interruptions of it, to be unresponsive to facetiousness about life, even to the mild cynicism of their contemporaries. They were only happy when the dialogue was going on, and its seriousness bathed them like the amber glow of an open fire. Toward the end there came an interruption they did not resent – it began to be interrupted by passion.

Oddly enough, Anson was as engrossed in the dialogue as she and as profoundly affected by it, yet at the same time aware that on his side much was insincere, and on hers much was merely simple. At first, too, he despised her emotional simplicity as well, but with his love her nature deepened and blossomed, and he could despise it no longer. He felt that if he could enter into Paula's warm safe life he would be happy. The long preparation of the dialogue removed any constraint – he taught her some of what he had learned from more adventurous women, and she responded with a rapt holy intensity. One evening after a dance they agreed to marry, and he wrote a long letter about her to his mother. The next day Paula told him that she was rich, that she had a personal fortune of nearly a million dollars.

It was exactly as if they could say, 'Neither of us has anything: we shall be poor together' – just as delightful that they should be rich instead. It gave them the same communion of adventure. Yet when Anson got leave in April, and Paula and her mother accompanied him North, she was impressed with the standing of his family in New York and with the scale on which they lived. Alone with Anson for the first time in the rooms where he had played as a boy, she was filled with a comfortable emotion, as though she were pre-eminently safe and taken care of. The pictures of Anson in a skullcap at his first school, of Anson on horseback with the sweetheart of a mysterious forgotten summer, of Anson in a gay group of ushers and bridesmaids at a wedding, made her jealous of his life apart from her in the past, and so completely did his authoritative person seem to sum up and typify these possessions of his that she was inspired with the idea of being married immediately and returning to Pensacola as his wife.

But an immediate marriage wasn't discussed – even the engagement was to be secret until after the war. When she realised that only two days of his leave remained, her dissatisfaction crystallised in the intention of making him as unwilling to wait as she was. They were driving to the country for dinner and she determined to force the issue that night.

Now a cousin of Paula's was staying with them at the Ritz, a severe, bitter girl who loved Paula but was somewhat jealous of her impressive engagement, and as Paula was late in dressing, the cousin, who wasn't going to the party, received Anson in the parlour of the suite.

Anson had met friends at five o'clock and drunk freely and indiscreetly with them for an hour. He left the Yale Club at a proper time, and his mother's chauffeur drove him to the Ritz, but his usual capacity was not in evidence, and the impact of the steam-heated sitting-room made him suddenly dizzy. He knew it, and he was both amused and sorry.

Paula's cousin was twenty-five, but she was exceptionally naïve, and at first failed to realise what was up. She had never met Anson before, and she was surprised when he mumbled strange information and nearly fell off his chair, but until Paula appeared it didn't occur to her that what she had taken for the odour of a dry-cleaned uniform was really whiskey. But Paula understood as soon as she appeared; her only thought was to get Anson away before her mother saw him, and at the look in her eyes the cousin understood too.

When Paula and Anson descended to the limousine they found two men inside, both asleep; they were the men with whom he had been drinking at the Yale Club, and they were also going to the party. He had entirely forgotten their presence in the car. On the way to Hempstead they awoke and sang. Some of the songs were rough, and though Paula tried to reconcile herself to the fact that Anson had few verbal inhibitions, her lips tightened with shame and distaste.

Back at the hotel the cousin, confused and agitated, considered the incident, and then walked into Mrs Legendre's bedroom, saying: 'Isn't he funny?'

'Who is funny?'

'Why – Mr Hunter. He seemed so funny.'

Mrs Legendre looked at her sharply.

'How is he funny?'

'Why, he said he was French. I didn't know he was French.'

'That's absurd. You must have misunderstood.' She smiled: 'It was a joke.'

The cousin shook her head stubbornly.

'No. He said he was brought up in France. He said he couldn't speak any English, and that's why he couldn't talk to me. And he couldn't!'

Mrs Legendre looked away with impatience just as the cousin added thoughtfully, 'Perhaps it was because he was so drunk', and walked out of the room.

This curious report was true. Anson, finding his voice thick and uncontrollable, had taken the unusual refuge of announcing that he spoke no English. Years afterwards he used to tell that part of the story, and he invariably communicated the uproarious laughter which the memory aroused in him.

Five times in the next hour Mrs Legendre tried to get Hempstead on the phone. When she succeeded, there was a ten-minute delay before she heard Paula's voice on the wire.

'Cousin Jo told me Anson was intoxicated.'

'Oh, no . . . '

'Oh, yes. Cousin Jo says he was intoxicated. He told her he was French, and fell off his chair and behaved as if he was very intoxicated. I don't want you to come home with him.'

'Mother, he's all right! Please don't worry about – '

'But I do worry. I think it's dreadful. I want you to promise me not to come home with him.'

'I'll take care of it, mother . . . '

'I don't want you to come home with him.'

'All right, mother. Goodbye.'

'Be sure now, Paula. Ask someone to bring you.'

Deliberately Paula took the receiver from her ear and hung it up. Her face was flushed with helpless annoyance. Anson was stretched out asleep in a bedroom upstairs, while the dinner-party below was proceeding lamely toward conclusion.

The hour's drive had sobered him somewhat – his arrival was merely hilarious – and Paula hoped that the evening was not spoiled, after all, but two imprudent cocktails before dinner completed the disaster. He talked boisterously and somewhat offensively to the party at large for fifteen minutes, and then slid silently under the table; like a man in an old print – but, unlike an old print, it was rather horrible without being at all quaint. None of the young girls present remarked upon the incident – it seemed to merit only silence. His uncle and two other men carried him upstairs, and it was just after this that Paula was called to the phone.

An hour later Anson awoke in a fog of nervous agony, through which he perceived after a moment the figure of his Uncle Robert standing by the door.

' . . . I said are you better?'

'What?'

'Do you feel better, old man?'

'Terrible,' said Anson.

'I'm going to try you on another bromo-seltzer.[44] If you can hold it down, it'll do you good to sleep.'

With an effort Anson slid his legs from the bed and stood up.

'I'm all right,' he said dully.

'Take it easy.'

'I thin' if you gave me a glass brandy I could go downstairs.'

'Oh, no – '

'Yes, that's the only thin'. I'm all right now . . . I suppose I'm in Dutch[45] dow' there.'

'They know you're a little under the weather,' said his uncle deprecatingly. 'But don't worry about it. Schuyler didn't even get here. He passed away in the locker-room over at the Links.'

Indifferent to any opinion, except Paula's, Anson was nevertheless determined to save the debris of the evening, but when after a cold bath he made his appearance most of the party had already left. Paula got up immediately to go home.

In the limousine the old serious dialogue began. She had known that he drank, she admitted, but she had never expected anything like this – it seemed to her that perhaps they were not suited to each other, after all. Their ideas about life were too different, and so forth. When she finished speaking, Anson spoke in turn, very soberly. Then Paula said she'd have to think it over; she wouldn't decide tonight; she was not angry but she was terribly sorry. Nor would she let him come into the hotel with her, but just before she got out of the car she leaned and kissed him unhappily on the cheek.

The next afternoon Anson had a long talk with Mrs Legendre while Paula sat listening in silence. It was agreed that Paula was to brood over the incident for a proper period and then, if mother and daughter thought it best, they would follow Anson to Pensacola. On his part he apologised with sincerity and dignity – that was all; with every card in her hand Mrs Legendre was unable to establish any advantage over him. He made no promises, showed no humility, only delivered a few serious comments on life which brought him off with rather a moral superiority at the end. When they came South three weeks later, neither Anson in his satisfaction nor Paula in her relief at the reunion realised that the psychological moment had passed for ever.

CHAPTER 4

HE DOMINATED and attracted her, and at the same time filled her with anxiety. Confused by his mixture of solidity and self-indulgence, of sentiment and cynicism – incongruities which her gentle mind was unable to resolve – Paula grew to think of him as two alternating personalities. When she saw him alone, or at a formal party, or with his casual inferiors, she felt a tremendous pride in his strong, attractive presence, the paternal, understanding stature of his mind.

In other company she became uneasy when what had been a fine imperviousness to mere gentility showed its other face. The other face was gross, humorous, reckless of everything but pleasure. It startled her mind temporarily away from him, even led her into a short, covert experiment with an old beau, but it was no use – after four months of Anson's enveloping vitality there was an anaemic pallor in all other men.

In July he was ordered abroad, and their tenderness and desire reached a crescendo. Paula considered a last-minute marriage – decided against it only because there were always cocktails on his breath now, but the parting itself made her physically ill with grief. After his departure she wrote him long letters of regret for the days of love they had missed by waiting. In August Anson's plane slipped down into the North Sea. He was pulled on to a destroyer after a night in the water and sent to hospital with pneumonia; the armistice was signed before he was finally sent home.

Then, with every opportunity given back to them, with no material obstacle to overcome, the secret weavings of their temperaments came between them, drying up their kisses and their tears, making their voices less loud to one another, muffling the intimate chatter of their hearts until the old communication was only possible by letters, from far away. One afternoon a society reporter waited for two hours in the Hunters' house for a confirmation of their engagement. Anson denied it; nevertheless an early issue carried the report as a leading paragraph – they were 'constantly seen together at Southampton, Hot Springs, and Tuxedo Park'. But the serious dialogue had turned a corner into a long-sustained quarrel, and the affair was almost played out. Anson got drunk flagrantly and missed an engagement with her, whereupon Paula made certain behaviouristic demands. His despair was helpless before his pride and his knowledge of himself: the engagement was definitely broken.

'Dearest,' said their letters now, 'Dearest, Dearest, when I wake up in the middle of the night and realise that after all it was not to be, I feel that I want to die. I can't go on living any more. Perhaps when we meet this summer we may talk things over and decide differently – we were so excited and sad that day, and I don't feel that I can live all my life without you. You speak of other people. Don't you know there are no other people for me, but only you . . . '

But as Paula drifted here and there around the East she would sometimes mention her gaieties to make him wonder. Anson was too acute to wonder. When he saw a man's name in her letters he felt more sure of her and a little disdainful – he was always superior to such things. But he still hoped that they would someday marry.

Meanwhile he plunged vigorously into all the movement and glitter of post-bellum New York, entering a brokerage house, joining half a dozen clubs, dancing late, and moving in three worlds – his own world, the world of young Yale graduates, and that section of the half-world which rests one end on Broadway. But there was always a thorough and infractible eight hours devoted to his work in Wall Street, where the combination of his influential family connection, his sharp intelligence, and his abundance of sheer physical energy brought him almost immediately forward. He had one of those invaluable minds with partitions in it; sometimes he appeared at his office refreshed by less than an hour's sleep, but such occurrences were rare. So early as 1920 his income in salary and commissions exceeded twelve thousand dollars.

As the Yale tradition slipped into the past he became more and more of a popular figure among his classmates in New York, more popular than he had ever been in college. He lived in a great house, and had the means of introducing young men into other great houses. Moreover, his life already seemed secure, while theirs, for the most part, had arrived again at precarious beginnings. They commenced to turn to him for amusement and escape, and Anson responded readily, taking pleasure in helping people and arranging their affairs.

There were no men in Paula's letters now, but a note of tenderness ran through them that had not been there before. From several sources he heard that she had 'a heavy beau', Lowell Thayer, a Bostonian of wealth and position, and though he was sure she still loved him, it made him uneasy to think that he might lose her, after all. Save for one unsatisfactory day, she had not been in New York for almost five months, and as the rumours multiplied he became increasingly anxious to see her. In February he took his vacation and went down to Florida.

Palm Beach sprawled plump and opulent between the sparkling sapphire of Lake Worth, flawed here and there by houseboats at anchor, and the great turquoise bar of the Atlantic Ocean. The huge bulks of the Breakers and the Royal Poinciana rose as twin paunches from the bright level of the sand, and around them clustered the Dancing Glade, Bradley's House of Chance, and a dozen modistes and milliners with goods at triple prices from New York. Upon the trellised veranda of the Breakers two hundred women stepped right, stepped left, wheeled, and slid in that then celebrated calisthenic known as the double-shuffle, while in half-time to the music two thousand bracelets clicked up and down on two hundred arms.

At the Everglades Club after dark Paula and Lowell Thayer and Anson and a casual fourth played bridge with hot cards. It seemed to Anson that her kind, serious face was wan and tired – she had been around now for four, five, years. He had known her for three.

'Two spades.'

'Cigarette? . . . Oh, I beg your pardon. By me.'

'By.'

'I'll double three spades.'

There were a dozen tables of bridge in the room, which was filling up with smoke. Anson's eyes met Paula's, held them persistently even when Thayer's glance fell between them . . .

'What was bid?' he asked abstractedly.

'Rose of Washington Square'

sang the young people in the corners:

'I'm withering there
In basement air – '

The smoke banked like fog, and the opening of a door filled the room with blown swirls of ectoplasm. Little Bright Eyes streaked past the tables seeking Mr Conan Doyle[46] among the Englishmen who were posing as Englishmen about the lobby.

'You could cut it with a knife.'

' . . . cut it with a knife.'

' . . . a knife.'

At the end of the rubber Paula suddenly got up and spoke to Anson in a tense, low voice. With scarcely a glance at Lowell Thayer, they walked out the door and descended a long flight of stone steps – in a moment they were walking hand in hand along the moonlit beach.

'Darling, darling . . . ' They embraced recklessly, passionately, in a shadow . . . Then Paula drew back her face to let his lips say what she wanted to hear – she could feel the words forming as they kissed again . . . Again she broke away, listening, but as he pulled her close once more she realised that he had said nothing – only 'Darling! Darling!' in that deep, sad whisper that always made her cry. Humbly, obediently, her emotions yielded to him and the tears streamed down her face, but her heart kept on crying: 'Ask me – oh, Anson, ask me!'

'Paula . . . *Paula!*'

The words wrung her heart like hands, and Anson, feeling her tremble, knew that emotion was enough. He need say no more, commit their destinies to no practical enigma. Why should he, when he might hold her so, biding his own time, for another year – for ever? He was considering them both, her more than himself. For a moment, when she said suddenly that she must go back to her hotel, he hesitated, thinking first, 'This is the moment, after all,' and then: 'No, let it wait – she is mine . . . '

He had forgotten that Paula too was worn away inside with the strain of three years. Her mood passed for ever in the night.

He went back to New York next morning filled with a certain restless dissatisfaction. Late in April, without warning, he received a telegram from Bar Harbour in which Paula told him that she was engaged to Lowell Thayer, and that they would be married immediately in Boston. What he never really believed could happen had happened at last.

Anson filled himself with whiskey that morning, and going to the office, carried on his work without a break rather with a fear of what would happen if he stopped. In the evening he went out as usual, saying nothing of what had occurred; he was cordial, humorous, unabstracted. But one thing he could not help – for three days, in any place, in any company, he would suddenly bend his head into his hands and cry like a child.

CHAPTER 5

IN 1922 when Anson went abroad with the junior partner to investigate some London loans, the journey intimated that he was to be taken into the firm. He was twenty-seven now, a little heavy without being definitely stout, and with a manner older than his years. Old people and young people liked him and trusted him, and mothers felt safe when their daughters were in his charge, for he had a way, when he came into a room, of putting himself on a footing with the oldest and most conservative people there. 'You and I,' he seemed to say, 'we're solid. We understand.'

He had an instinctive and rather charitable knowledge of the weaknesses of men and women, and, like a priest, it made him the more concerned for the maintenance of outward forms. It was typical of him that every Sunday morning he taught in a fashionable Episcopal Sunday-school – even though a cold shower and a quick change into a cutaway coat were all that separated him from the wild night before.

After his father's death he was the practical head of his family, and, in effect, guided the destinies of the younger children. Through a complication his authority did not extend to his father's estate, which was administered by his Uncle Robert, who was the horsey member of the family, a good-natured, hard-drinking member of that set which centres about Wheatley Hills.

Uncle Robert and his wife, Edna, had been great friends of Anson's youth, and the former was disappointed when his nephew's superiority failed to take a horsey form. He backed him for a city club which was the most difficult in America to enter – one could only join if one's family had 'helped to build up New York' (or, in other words, were rich before 1880) – and when Anson, after his election, neglected it for the Yale Club, Uncle Robert gave him a little talk on the subject. But when on top of that Anson declined to enter Robert Hunter's own conservative and somewhat neglected brokerage house, his manner grew cooler. Like a primary teacher who has taught all he knew, he slipped out of Anson's life.

There were so many friends in Anson's life – scarcely one for whom he had not done some unusual kindness and scarcely one whom he did not occasionally embarrass by his bursts of rough conversation or his habit of getting drunk whenever and however he liked. It annoyed him when anyone else blundered in that regard – about his own lapses he was always humorous. Odd things happened to him and he told them with infectious laughter.

I was working in New York that spring, and I used to lunch with him at the Yale Club, which my university was sharing until the completion of our own. I had read of Paula's marriage, and one afternoon, when I asked him about her, something moved him to tell me the story. After that he frequently invited me to family dinners at his house and behaved as though there was a special relation between us, as though with his confidence a little of that consuming memory had passed into me.

I found that despite the trusting mothers, his attitude toward girls was not indiscriminately protective. It was up to the girl – if she showed an inclination toward looseness, she must take care of herself, even with him.

'Life,' he would explain sometimes, 'has made a cynic of me.'

By life he meant Paula. Sometimes, especially when he was drinking, it became a little twisted in his mind, and he thought that she had callously thrown him over.

This 'cynicism', or rather his realisation that naturally fast girls were not worth sparing, led to his affair with Dolly Karger. It wasn't his only affair in those years, but it came nearest to touching him deeply, and it had a profound effect upon his attitude toward life.

Dolly was the daughter of a notorious 'publicist' who had married into society. She herself grew up into the Junior League, came out at the Plaza, and went to the Assembly; and only a few old families like the Hunters could question whether or not she 'belonged', for her picture was often in the papers, and she had more enviable attention than many girls who undoubtedly did. She was dark-haired, with carmine lips and a high, lovely colour, which she concealed under pinkish-grey powder all through the first year out, because high colour was unfashionable – Victorian-pale was the thing to be. She wore black, severe suits and stood with her hands in her pockets leaning a little forward, with a humorous restraint on her face. She danced exquisitely – better than anything she liked to dance – better than anything except making love. Since she was ten she had always been in love, and, usually, with some boy who didn't respond to her. Those who did – and there were many – bored her after a brief encounter, but for her failures she reserved the warmest spot in her heart. When she met them she would always try once more – sometimes she succeeded, more often she failed.

It never occurred to this gypsy of the unattainable that there was a certain resemblance in those who refused to love her – they shared a hard intuition that saw through to her weakness, not a weakness of emotion but a weakness of rudder. Anson perceived this when he first met her, less than a month after Paula's marriage. He was drinking rather heavily, and he pretended for a week that he was falling in love with her. Then he dropped her abruptly and forgot – immediately he took up the commanding position in her heart.

Like so many girls of that day Dolly was slackly and indiscreetly wild. The unconventionality of a slightly older generation had been simply one facet of a post-war movement to discredit obsolete manners – Dolly's was both older and shabbier, and she saw in Anson the two extremes which the emotionally shiftless woman seeks, an abandon to indulgence alternating with a protective strength. In his character she felt both the sybarite and the solid rock, and these two satisfied every need of her nature.

She felt that it was going to be difficult, but she mistook the reason – she thought that Anson and his family expected a more spectacular marriage, but she guessed immediately that her advantage lay in his tendency to drink.

They met at the large débutante dances, but as her infatuation increased they managed to be more and more together. Like most mothers, Mrs Karger believed that Anson was exceptionally reliable, so she allowed Dolly to go with him to distant country clubs and suburban houses without enquiring closely into their activities or questioning her explanations when they came in late. At first these explanations might have been accurate, but Dolly's worldly ideas of capturing Anson were soon engulfed in the rising sweep of her emotion. Kisses in the back of taxis and motor cars were no longer enough; they did a curious thing:

They dropped out of their world for a while and made another world just beneath it where Anson's tippling and Dolly's irregular hours would be less noticed and commented on. It was composed, this world, of varying elements – several of Anson's Yale friends and their wives, two or three young brokers and bond salesmen, and a handful of unattached men, fresh from college, with money and a propensity to dissipation. What this world lacked in spaciousness and scale it made up for by allowing them a liberty that it scarcely permitted itself. Moreover, it centred around them and permitted Dolly the pleasure of a faint condescension – a pleasure which Anson, whose whole life was a condescension from the certitudes of his childhood, was unable to share.

He was not in love with her, and in the long feverish winter of their affair he frequently told her so. In the spring he was weary – he wanted to renew his life at some other source – moreover, he saw that either he must break with her now or accept the responsibility of a definite seduction. Her family's encouraging attitude precipitated his decision – one evening when Mr Karger knocked discreetly at the library door to announce that he had left a bottle of old brandy in the dining-room, Anson felt that life was hemming him in. That night he wrote her a short letter in which he told her that he was going on his vacation, and that in view of all the circumstances they had better meet no more.

It was June. His family had closed up the house and gone to the country, so he was living temporarily at the Yale Club. I had heard about his affair with Dolly as it developed – accounts salted with humour, for he despised unstable women, and granted them no place in the social edifice in which he believed – and when he told me that night that he was definitely breaking with her I was glad. I had seen Dolly here and there, and each time with a feeling of pity at the hopelessness of her struggle, and of shame at knowing so much about her that I had no right to know. She was what is known as 'a pretty little thing', but there was a certain recklessness which rather fascinated me. Her dedication to the goddess of waste would have been less obvious had she been less spirited – she would most certainly throw herself away, but I was glad when I heard that the sacrifice would not be consummated in my sight.

Anson was going to leave the letter of farewell at her house next morning. It was one of the few houses left open in the Fifth Avenue district, and he knew that the Kargers, acting upon erroneous information from Dolly, had forgone a trip abroad to give their daughter her chance. As he stepped out the door of the Yale Club into Madison Avenue the postman passed him, and he followed him back inside. The first letter that caught his eye was in Dolly's hand.

He knew what it would be – a lonely and tragic monologue, full of the reproaches he knew, the invoked memories, and 'I wonder if's – all the immemorial intimacies that he had communicated to Paula Legendre in what seemed another age. Thumbing over some bills, he brought it on top again and opened it. To his surprise it was a short, somewhat formal note, which said that Dolly would be unable to go to the country with him for the weekend, because Perry Hull from Chicago had unexpectedly come to town. It added that Anson had brought this on himself: ' – if I felt that you loved me as I love you I would go with you at any time, any place, but Perry is *so* nice, and he so much wants me to marry him – '

Anson smiled contemptuously – he had had experience with such decoy epistles. Moreover, he knew how Dolly had laboured over this plan, probably sent for the faithful Perry and calculated the time of his arrival – even laboured over the note so that it would make him jealous without driving him away. Like most compromises, it had neither force nor vitality but only a timorous despair.

Suddenly he was angry. He sat down in the lobby and read it again. Then he went to the phone, called Dolly and told her in his clear, compelling voice that he had received her note and would call for her at five o'clock as they had previously planned. Scarcely waiting for the pretended uncertainty of her 'Perhaps I can see you for an hour', he hung up the receiver and went down to his office. On the way he tore his own letter into bits and dropped it in the street.

He was not jealous – she meant nothing to him – but at her pathetic ruse everything stubborn and self-indulgent in him came to the surface. It was a presumption from a mental inferior and it could not be overlooked. If she wanted to know to whom she belonged she would see.

He was on the doorstep at quarter-past five. Dolly was dressed for the street, and he listened in silence to the paragraph of 'I can only see you for an hour', which she had begun on the phone.

'Put on your hat, Dolly,' he said, 'we'll take a walk.'

They strolled up Madison Avenue and over to Fifth while Anson's shirt dampened upon his portly body in the deep heat. He talked little, scolding her, making no love to her, but before they had walked six blocks she was his again, apologising for the note, offering not to see Perry at all as an atonement, offering anything. She thought that he had come because he was beginning to love her.

'I'm hot,' he said when they reached 71st Street. 'This is a winter suit. If I stop by the house and change, would you mind waiting for me downstairs? I'll only be a minute.'

She was happy; the intimacy of his being hot, of any physical fact about him, thrilled her. When they came to the iron-grated door and Anson took out his key she experienced a sort of delight.

Downstairs it was dark, and after he ascended in the lift Dolly raised a curtain and looked out through opaque lace at the houses over the way. She heard the lift machinery stop, and with the notion of teasing him pressed the button that brought it down. Then on what was more than an impulse she got into it and sent it up to what she guessed was his floor.

'Anson,' she called, laughing a little.

'Just a minute,' he answered from his bedroom . . . then after a brief delay: 'Now you can come in.'

He had changed and was buttoning his vest.

'This is my room,' he said lightly. 'How do you like it?'

She caught sight of Paula's picture on the wall and stared at it in fascination, just as Paula had stared at the pictures of Anson's childish sweethearts five years before. She knew something about Paula – sometimes she tortured herself with fragments of the story.

Suddenly she came close to Anson, raising her arms. They embraced. Outside the area window a soft artificial twilight already hovered, though the sun was still bright on a back roof across the way. In half an hour the room would be quite dark. The uncalculated opportunity overwhelmed them, made them both breathless, and they clung more closely. It was imminent, inevitable. Still holding one another, they raised their heads – their eyes fell together upon Paula's picture, staring down at them from the wall.

Suddenly Anson dropped his arms, and sitting down at his desk tried the drawer with a bunch of keys.

'Like a drink?' he asked in a gruff voice.

'No, Anson.'

He poured himself half a tumbler of whiskey, swallowed it, and then opened the door into the hall.

'Come on,' he said.

Dolly hesitated.

'Anson – I'm going to the country with you tonight, after all. You understand that, don't you?'

'Of course,' he answered brusquely.

In Dolly's car they rode on to Long Island, closer in their emotions than they had ever been before. They knew what would happen – not with Paula's face to remind them that something was lacking, but when they were alone in the still, hot, Long Island night they did not care.

The estate in Port Washington where they were to spend the weekend belonged to a cousin of Anson's who had married a Montana copper operator. An interminable drive began at the lodge and twisted under imported poplar saplings toward a huge, pink Spanish house. Anson had often visited there before.

After dinner they danced at the Linx Club. About midnight Anson assured himself that his cousins would not leave before two – then he explained that Dolly was tired; he would take her home and return to the dance later. Trembling a little with excitement, they got into a borrowed car together and drove to Port Washington. As they reached the lodge he stopped and spoke to the nightwatchman.

'When are you making a round, Carl?'

'Right away.'

'Then you'll be here till everybody's in?'

'Yes, sir.'

'All right. Listen: if any automobile, no matter whose it is, turns in at this gate, I want you to phone the house immediately.' He put a five dollar bill into Carl's hand. 'Is that clear?'

'Yes, Mr Anson.' Being of the Old World, he neither winked nor smiled. Yet Dolly sat with her face turned slightly away.

Anson had a key. Once inside he poured a drink for both of them – Dolly left hers untouched – then he ascertained definitely the location of the phone, and found that it was within easy hearing distance of their rooms, both of which were on the first floor.

Five minutes later he knocked at the door of Dolly's room.

'Anson?' He went in, closing the door behind him. She was in bed, leaning up anxiously with elbows on the pillow; sitting beside her he took her in his arms.

'Anson, darling.'

He didn't answer.

'Anson . . . Anson! I love you . . . Say you love me. Say it now – can't you say it now? Even if you don't mean it?'

He did not listen. Over her head he perceived that the picture of Paula was hanging here upon this wall.

He got up and went close to it. The frame gleamed faintly with thrice-reflected moonlight – within was a blurred shadow of a face that he saw he did not know. Almost sobbing, he turned around and stared with abomination at the little figure on the bed.

'This is all foolishness,' he said thickly. 'I don't know what I was thinking about. I don't love you and you'd better wait for somebody that loves you. I don't love you a bit, can't you understand?'

His voice broke, and he went hurriedly out. Back in the saloon he was pouring himself a drink with uneasy fingers, when the front door opened suddenly, and his cousin came in.

'Why, Anson, I hear Dolly's sick,' she began solicitously. 'I hear she's sick . . . '

'It was nothing,' he interrupted, raising his voice so that it would carry into Dolly's room. 'She was a little tired. She went to bed.'

For a long time afterward Anson believed that a protective God sometimes interfered in human affairs. But Dolly Karger, lying awake and staring at the ceiling, never again believed in anything at all.

WHEN DOLLY married during the following autumn, Anson was in London on business. Like Paula's marriage, it was sudden, but it affected him in a different way. At first he felt that it was funny, and had an inclination to laugh when he thought of it. Later it depressed him – it made him feel old.

There was something repetitive about it – why, Paula and Dolly had belonged to different generations. He had a foretaste of the sensation of a man of forty who hears that the daughter of an old flame has married. He wired congratulations and, as was not the case with Paula, they were sincere – he had never really hoped that Paula would be happy.

When he returned to New York, he was made a partner in the firm, and, as his responsibilities increased, he had less time on his hands. The refusal of a life-insurance company to issue him a policy made such an impression on him that he stopped drinking for a year, and claimed that he felt better physically, though I think he missed the convivial recounting of those Celliniesque[47] adventures which, in his early twenties, had played such a part in his life. But he never abandoned the Yale Club. He was a figure there, a personality, and the tendency of his class, who were now seven years out of college, to drift away to more sober haunts was checked by his presence.

His day was never too full nor his mind too weary to give any sort of aid to anyone who asked it. What had been done at first through pride and superiority had become a habit and passion. And there was always something – a younger brother in trouble at New Haven, a quarrel to be patched up between a friend and his wife, a position to be found for this man, an investment for that. But his speciality was the solving of problems for young married people. Young married people fascinated him and their apartments were almost sacred to him – he knew the story of their love-affair, advised them where to live and how, and remembered their babies' names. Toward young wives his attitude was circumspect: he never abused the trust which their husbands – strangely enough in view of his unconcealed irregularities – invariably reposed in him.

He came to take a vicarious pleasure in happy marriages, and to be inspired to an almost equally pleasant melancholy by those that went astray. Not a season passed that he did not witness the collapse of an affair that perhaps he himself had fathered. When Paula was divorced and almost immediately remarried to another Bostonian, he talked about her to me all one afternoon. He would never love anyone as he had loved Paula, but he insisted that he no longer cared.

'I'll never marry,' he came to say; 'I've seen too much of it, and I know a happy marriage is a very rare thing. Besides, I'm too old.'

But he did believe in marriage. Like all men who spring from a happy and successful marriage, he believed in it passionately – nothing he had seen would change his belief, his cynicism dissolved upon it like air. But he did really believe he was too old. At twenty-eight he began to accept with equanimity the prospect of marrying without romantic love; he resolutely chose a New York girl of his own class, pretty, intelligent, congenial, above reproach and set about falling in love with her. The things he had said to Paula with sincerity, to other girls with grace, he could no longer say at all without smiling, or with the force necessary to convince.

'When I'm forty,' he told his friends, 'I'll be ripe. I'll fall for some chorus girl like the rest.'

Nevertheless, he persisted in his attempt. His mother wanted to see him married, and he could now well afford it – he had a seat on the Stock Exchange, and his earned income came to twenty-five thousand a year. The idea was agreeable: when his friends – he spent most of his time with the set he and Dolly had evolved – closed themselves in behind domestic doors at night, he no longer rejoiced in his freedom. He even wondered if he should have married Dolly. Not even Paula had loved him more, and he was learning the rarity, in a single life, of encountering true emotion.

Just as this mood began to creep over him a disquieting story reached his ear. His Aunt Edna, a woman just this side of forty, was carrying on an open intrigue with a dissolute, hard-drinking young man named Cary Sloane. Everyone knew of it except Anson's Uncle Robert, who for fifteen years had talked long in clubs and taken his wife for granted.

Anson heard the story again and again with increasing annoyance. Something of his old feeling for his uncle came back to him, a feeling that was more than personal, a reversion towards that family solidarity on which he had based his pride. His intuition singled out the essential point of the affair, which was that his uncle shouldn't be hurt. It was his first experiment in unsolicited meddling, but with his knowledge of Edna's character he felt that he could handle the matter better than a district judge or his uncle.

His uncle was in Hot Springs. Anson traced down the sources of the scandal so that there should be no possibility of mistake and then he called Edna and asked her to lunch with him at the Plaza next day. Something in his tone must have frightened her, for she was reluctant, but he insisted, putting off the date until she had no excuse for refusing.

She met him at the appointed time in the Plaza lobby, a lovely, faded, grey-eyed blonde in a coat of Russian sable. Five great rings, cold with diamonds and emeralds, sparkled on her slender hands. It occurred to Anson that it was his father's intelligence and not his uncle's that had earned the fur and the stones, the rich brilliance that buoyed up her passing beauty.

Though Edna scented his hostility, she was unprepared for the directness of his approach.

'Edna, I'm astonished at the way you've been acting,' he said in a strong, frank voice. 'At first I couldn't believe it.'

'Believe what?' she demanded sharply.

'You needn't pretend with me, Edna, I'm talking about Cary Sloane. Aside from any other consideration, I didn't think you could treat Uncle Robert – '

'Now look here, Anson – ' she began angrily, but his peremptory voice broke through hers: ' – and your children in such a way. You've been married eighteen years, and you're old enough to know better.'

'You can't talk to me like that! You – '

'Yes, I can. Uncle Robert has always been my best friend.' He was tremendously moved. He felt a real distress about his uncle, about his three young cousins.

Edna stood up, leaving her crab-flake cocktail untasted.

'This is the silliest thing – '

'Very well, if you won't listen to me I'll go to Uncle Robert and tell him the whole story – he's bound to hear it sooner or later. And afterward I'll go to old Moses Sloane.'

Edna faltered back into her chair.

'Don't talk so loud,' she begged him. Her eyes blurred with tears. 'You have no idea how your voice carries. You might have chosen a less public place to make all these crazy accusations.'

He didn't answer.

'Oh, you never liked me, I know,' she went on. 'You're just taking advantage of some silly gossip to try and break up the only interesting friendship I've ever had. What did I ever do to make you hate me so?'

Still Anson waited. There would be the appeal to his chivalry, then to his pity, finally to his superior sophistication – when he had shouldered his way through all these there would be admissions, and he could come to grips with her. By being silent, by being impervious, by returning constantly to his main weapon, which was his own true emotion, he bullied her into frantic despair as the luncheon hour slipped away. At two o'clock she took out a mirror and a handkerchief, shined away the marks of her tears and powdered the slight hollows where they had lain. She had agreed to meet him at her own house at five.

When he arrived she was stretched on a chaise-longue which was covered with cretonne for the summer, and the tears he had called up at luncheon seemed still to be standing in her eyes. Then he was aware of Cary Sloane's dark, anxious presence upon the cold hearth.

'What's this idea of yours?' broke out Sloane immediately. 'I understand you invited Edna to lunch and then threatened her on the basis of some cheap scandal.'

Anson sat down.

'I have no reason to think it's only scandal.'

'I hear you're going to take it to Robert Hunter, and to my father.'

Anson nodded.

'Either you break it off – or I will,' he said.

'What God-damned business is it of yours, Hunter?'

'Don't lose your temper, Cary,' said Edna nervously. 'It's only a question of showing him how absurd – '

'For one thing, it's my name that's being handed around,' interrupted Anson. 'That's all that concerns you, Cary.'

'Edna isn't a member of your family.'

'She most certainly is!' His anger mounted. 'Why – she owes this house and the rings on her fingers to my father's brains. When Uncle Robert married her she didn't have a penny.'

They all looked at the rings as if they had a significant bearing on the situation. Edna made a gesture to take them from her hand.

'I guess they're not the only rings in the world,' said Sloane.

'Oh, this is absurd,' cried Edna. 'Anson, will you listen to me? I've found out how the silly story started. It was a maid I discharged who went right to the Chilicheffs – all these Russians pump things out of their servants and then put a false meaning on them.' She brought down her fist angrily on the table: 'And after Robert lent them the limousine for a whole month when we were South last winter – '

'Do you see?' demanded Sloane eagerly. 'This maid got hold of the wrong end of the thing. She knew that Edna and I were friends, and she carried it to the Chilicheffs. In Russia they assume that if a man and a woman – '

He enlarged the theme to a disquisition upon social relations in the Caucasus.

'If that's the case it better be explained to Uncle Robert,' said Anson dryly, 'so that when the rumours do reach him he'll know they're not true.'

Adopting the method he had followed with Edna at luncheon he let them explain it all away. He knew that they were guilty and that presently they would cross the line from explanation into justification and convict themselves more definitely than he could ever do. By seven they had taken the desperate step of telling him the truth – Robert Hunter's neglect, Edna's empty life, the casual dalliance that had flamed up into passion – but like so many true stories it had the misfortune of being old, and its enfeebled body beat helplessly against the armour of Anson's will. The threat to go to Sloane's father sealed their helplessness, for the latter, a retired cotton broker out of Alabama, was a notorious fundamentalist who controlled his son by a rigid allowance and the promise that at his next vagary the allowance would stop for ever.

They dined at a small French restaurant, and the discussion continued – at one time Sloane resorted to physical threats, a little later they were both imploring him to give them time. But Anson was obdurate. He saw that Edna was breaking up, and that her spirit must not be refreshed by any renewal of their passion.

At two o'clock in a small nightclub on 53rd Street, Edna's nerves suddenly collapsed, and she cried to go home. Sloane had been drinking heavily all evening, and he was faintly maudlin, leaning on the table and weeping a little with his face in his hands. Quickly Anson gave them his terms. Sloane was to leave town for six months, and he must be gone within forty-eight hours. When he returned there was to be no resumption of the affair, but at the end of a year Edna might, if she wished, tell Robert Hunter that she wanted a divorce and go about it in the usual way.

He paused, gaining confidence from their faces for his final word.

'Or there's another thing you can do,' he said slowly. 'If Edna wants to leave her children, there's nothing I can do to prevent your running off together.'

'I want to go home!' cried Edna again. 'Oh, haven't you done enough to us for one day?'

Outside it was dark, save for a blurred glow from Sixth Avenue down the street. In that light those two who had been lovers looked for the last time into each other's tragic faces, realising that between them there was not enough youth and strength to avert their eternal parting. Sloane walked suddenly off down the street and Anson tapped a dozing taxi-driver on the arm.

It was almost four; there was a patient flow of cleaning water along the ghostly pavement of Fifth Avenue, and the shadows of two night women flitted over the dark façade of St Thomas's church. Then the desolate shrubbery of Central Park, where Anson had often played as a child, and the mounting numbers, significant as names, of the marching streets. This was his city, he thought, where his name had flourished through five generations. No change could alter the permanence of its place here, for change itself was the essential substratum by which he and those of his name identified themselves with the spirit of New York. Resourcefulness and a powerful will – for his threats in weaker hands would have been less than nothing – had beaten the gathering dust from his uncle's name, from the name of his family, from even this shivering figure that sat beside him in the car.

Cary Sloane's body was found next morning on the lower shelf of a pillar of Queensboro Bridge. In the darkness and in his excitement he had thought that it was the water flowing black beneath him, but in less than a second it made no possible difference – unless he had planned to think one last thought of Edna, and call out her name as he struggled feebly in the water.

ANSON NEVER BLAMED himself for his part in this affair – the situation which brought it about had not been of his making. But the just suffer with the unjust, and he found that his oldest and somehow his most precious friendship was over. He never knew what distorted story Edna told, but he was welcome in his uncle's house no longer.

Just before Christmas Mrs Hunter retired to a select Episcopal heaven, and Anson became the responsible head of his family. An unmarried aunt who had lived with them for years ran the house, and attempted with helpless inefficiency to chaperone the younger girls. All the children were less self-reliant than Anson, more conventional both in their virtues and in their shortcomings. Mrs Hunter's death had postponed the début of one daughter and the wedding of another. Also it had taken something deeply material from all of them, for with her passing the quiet, expensive superiority of the Hunters came to an end.

For one thing, the estate, considerably diminished by two inheritance taxes and soon to be divided among six children, was not a notable fortune any more. Anson saw a tendency in his youngest sisters to speak rather respectfully of families that hadn't 'existed' twenty years ago. His own feeling of precedence was not echoed in them – sometimes they were conventionally snobbish, that was all. For another thing, this was the last summer they would spend on the Connecticut estate; the clamour against it was too loud: 'Who wants to waste the best months of the year shut up in that dead old town?' Reluctantly he yielded – the house would go into the market in the fall, and next summer they would rent a smaller place in Westchester County. It was a step down from the expensive simplicity of his father's idea, and, while he sympathised with the revolt, it also annoyed him; during his mother's lifetime he had gone up there at least every other weekend – even in the gayest summers.

Yet he himself was part of this change, and his strong instinct for life had turned him in his twenties from the hollow obsequies of that abortive leisure class. He did not see this clearly – he still felt that there was a norm, a standard of society. But there was no norm, it was doubtful if there ever had been a true norm in New York. The few who still paid and fought to enter a particular set succeeded only to find that as a society it scarcely functioned – or, what was more alarming, that the Bohemia from which they fled sat above them at table.

At twenty-nine Anson's chief concern was his own growing loneliness. He was sure now that he would never marry. The number of weddings at which he had officiated as best man or usher was past all counting – there was a drawer at home that bulged with the official neckties of this or that wedding-party, neckties standing for romances that had not endured a year, for couples who had passed completely from his life. Scarf-pins, gold pencils, cuff-buttons, presents from a generation of grooms had passed through his jewel-box and been lost – and with every ceremony he was less and less able to imagine himself in the groom's place. Under his hearty goodwill toward all those marriages there was despair about his own.

And as he neared thirty he became not a little depressed at the inroads that marriage, especially lately, had made upon his friendships. Groups of people had a disconcerting tendency to dissolve and disappear. The men from his own college – and it was upon them he had expended the most time and affection – were the most elusive of all. Most of them were drawn deep into domesticity, two were dead, one lived abroad, one was in Hollywood writing continuities for pictures that Anson went faithfully to see.

Most of them, however, were permanent commuters with an intricate family life centring around some suburban country club, and it was from these that he felt his estrangement most keenly.

In the early days of their married life they had all needed him; he gave them advice about their slim finances, he exorcised their doubts about the advisability of bringing a baby into two rooms and a bath, especially he stood for the great world outside. But now their financial troubles were in the past and the fearfully expected child had evolved into an absorbing family. They were always glad to see old Anson, but they dressed up for him and tried to impress him with their present importance, and kept their troubles to themselves. They needed him no longer.

A few weeks before his thirtieth birthday the last of his early and intimate friends was married. Anson acted in his usual role of best man, gave his usual silver tea-service, and went down to the usual Homeric[48] to say goodbye. It was a hot Friday afternoon in May, and as he walked from the pier he realised that Saturday closing had begun and he was free until Monday morning.

'Go where?' he asked himself.

The Yale Club, of course; bridge until dinner, then four or five raw cocktails in somebody's room and a pleasant confused evening. He regretted that this afternoon's groom wouldn't be along – they had always been able to cram so much into such nights: they knew how to attach women and how to get rid of them, how much consideration any girl deserved from their intelligent hedonism. A party was an adjusted thing – you took certain girls to certain places and spent just so much on their amusement; you drank a little, not much, more than you ought to drink, and at a certain time in the morning you stood up and said you were going home. You avoided college boys, sponges, future engagements, fights, sentiment, and indiscretions. That was the way it was done. All the rest was dissipation.

In the morning you were never violently sorry – you made no resolutions, but if you had overdone it and your heart was slightly out of order, you went on the wagon for a few days without saying anything about it, and waited until an accumulation of nervous boredom projected you into another party.

The lobby of the Yale Club was unpopulated. In the bar three very young alumni looked up at him, momentarily and without curiosity.

'Hello, there, Oscar,' he said to the bartender. 'Mr Cahill been around this afternoon?'

'Mr Cahill's gone to New Haven.'

'Oh . . . that so?'

'Gone to the ball game. Lot of men gone up.'

Anson looked once again into the lobby, considered for a moment, and then walked out and over to Fifth Avenue. From the broad window of one of his clubs – one that he had scarcely visited in five years – a grey man with watery eyes stared down at him. Anson looked quickly away – that figure sitting in vacant resignation, in supercilious solitude, depressed him. He stopped and, retracing his steps, started over 47th Street toward Teak Warden's apartment. Teak and his wife had once been his most familiar friends – it was a household where he and Dolly Karger had been used to go in the days of their affair. But Teak had taken to drink, and his wife had remarked publicly that Anson was a bad influence on him. The remark reached Anson in an exaggerated form – when it was finally cleared up, the delicate spell of intimacy was broken, never to be renewed.

'Is Mr Warden at home?' he enquired.

'They've gone to the country.'

The fact unexpectedly cut at him. They were gone to the country and he hadn't known. Two years before he would have known the date, the hour, come up at the last moment for a final drink, and planned his first visit to them. Now they had gone without a word.

Anson looked at his watch and considered a weekend with his family, but the only train was a local that would jolt through the aggressive heat for three hours. And tomorrow in the country, and Sunday – he was in no mood for porch-bridge with polite undergraduates, and dancing after dinner at a rural roadhouse, a diminutive of gaiety which his father had estimated too well.

'Oh, no,' he said to himself . . . 'No.'

He was a dignified, impressive young man, rather stout now, but otherwise unmarked by dissipation. He could have been cast for a pillar of something – at times you were sure it was not society, at others nothing else – for the law, for the church. He stood for a few minutes motionless on the sidewalk in front of a 47th Street apartment-house; for almost the first time in his life he had nothing whatever to do.

Then he began to walk briskly up Fifth Avenue, as if he had just been reminded of an important engagement there. The necessity of dissimulation is one of the few characteristics that we share with dogs, and I think of Anson on that day as some well-bred specimen who had been disappointed at a familiar back door. He was going to see Nick, once a fashionable bartender in demand at all private dances, and now employed in cooling non-alcoholic champagne among the labyrinthine cellars of the Plaza Hotel.

'Nick,' he said, 'what's happened to everything?'

'Dead,' Nick said.

'Make me a whiskey sour.' Anson handed a pint bottle over the counter. 'Nick, the girls are different; I had a little girl in Brooklyn and she got married last week without letting me know.'

'That a fact? Ha-ha-ha,' responded Nick diplomatically. 'Slipped it over on you.'

'Absolutely,' said Anson. 'And I was out with her the night before.'

'Ha–ha–ha,' said Nick, 'ha–ha–ha!'

'Do you remember the wedding, Nick, in Hot Springs where I had the waiters and the musicians singing "God save the King"?'

'Now where was that, Mr Hunter?' Nick concentrated doubtfully. 'Seems to me that was – '

'Next time they were back for more, and I began to wonder how much I'd paid them,' continued Anson.

' – seems to me that was at Mr Trenholm's wedding.'

'Don't know him,' said Anson decisively. He was offended that a strange name should intrude upon his reminiscences; Nick perceived this.

'Na – aw – ' he admitted, 'I ought to know that. It was one of *your* crowd – Brakins . . . Baker – '

'Bicker Baker,' said Anson responsively. 'They put me in a hearse after it was over and covered me up with flowers and drove me away.'

'Ha–ha–ha,' said Nick. 'Ha–ha–ha.'

Nick's simulation of the old family servant paled presently and Anson went upstairs to the lobby. He looked around – his eyes met the glance of an unfamiliar clerk at the desk, then fell upon a flower from the morning's marriage hesitating in the mouth of a brass cuspidor. He went out and walked slowly toward the blood-red sun over Columbus Circle. Suddenly he turned around and, retracing his steps to the Plaza, immured himself in a telephone-booth.

Later he said that he tried to get me three times that afternoon, that he tried everyone who might be in New York – men and girls he had not seen for years, an artist's model of his college days whose faded number was still in his address book – Central told him that even the exchange existed no longer. At length his quest roved into the country, and he held brief disappointing conversations with emphatic butlers and maids. So-and-so was out, riding, swimming, playing golf, sailed to Europe last week. Who shall I say phoned?

It was intolerable that he should pass the evening alone – the private reckonings which one plans for a moment of leisure lose every charm when the solitude is enforced. There were always women of a sort, but the ones he knew had temporarily vanished, and to pass a New York evening in the hired company of a stranger never occurred to him – he would have considered that that was something shameful and secret, the diversion of a travelling salesman in a strange town.

Anson paid the telephone bill – the girl tried unsuccessfully to joke with him about its size – and for the second time that afternoon started to leave the Plaza and go he knew not where. Near the revolving door the figure of a woman, obviously with child, stood sideways to the light – a sheer beige cape fluttered at her shoulders when the door turned and, each time, she looked impatiently toward it as if she were weary of waiting. At the first sight of her a strong nervous thrill of familiarity went over him, but not until he was within five feet of her did he realise that it was Paula.

'Why, Anson Hunter!'

His heart turned over.

'Why, Paula – '

'Why, this is wonderful. I can't believe it, *Anson*!'

She took both his hands, and he saw in the freedom of the gesture that the memory of him had lost poignancy to her. But not to him – he felt that old mood that she evoked in him stealing over his brain, that gentleness with which he had always met her optimism as if afraid to mar its surface.

'We're at Rye for the summer. Pete had to come East on business – you know of course I'm Mrs Peter Hagerty now – so we brought the children and took a house. You've got to come out and see us.'

'Can I?' he asked directly. 'When?'

'When you like. Here's Pete.' The revolving door functioned, giving up a fine tall man of thirty with a tanned face and a trim moustache. His immaculate fitness made a sharp contrast with Anson's increasing bulk, which was obvious under the faintly tight cutaway coat.

'You oughtn't to be standing,' said Hagerty to his wife. 'Let's sit down here.' He indicated lobby chairs, but Paula hesitated.

'I've got to go right home,' she said. 'Anson, why don't you – why don't you come out and have dinner with us tonight! We're just getting settled, but if you can stand that – '

Hagerty confirmed the invitation cordially.

'Come out for the night.'

Their car waited in front of the hotel, and Paula with a tired gesture sank back against silk cushions in the corner. 'There's so much I want to talk to you about,' she said, 'it seems hopeless.'

'I want to hear about you.'

'Well' – she smiled at Hagerty – 'that would take a long time too. I have three children – by my first marriage. The oldest is five, then four, then three.' She smiled again. 'I didn't waste much time having them, did I?'

'Boys?'

'A boy and two girls. Then – oh, a lot of things happened, and I got a divorce in Paris a year ago and married Pete. That's all – except that I'm awfully happy.'

In Rye they drove up to a large house near the Beach Club, from which there issued presently three dark, slim children who broke from an English governess and approached them with an esoteric cry. Abstractedly and with difficulty, Paula took each one into her arms, a caress which they accepted stiffly, as they had evidently been told not to bump into Mummy. Even against their fresh faces Paula's skin showed scarcely any weariness – for all her physical languor she seemed younger than when he had last seen her at Palm Beach seven years ago.

At dinner she was preoccupied, and afterward, during the homage to the radio, she lay with closed eyes on the sofa, until Anson wondered if his presence at this time were not an intrusion. But at nine o'clock, when Hagerty rose and said pleasantly that he was going to leave them by themselves for a while, she began to talk slowly about herself and the past.

'My first baby,' she said – 'the one we call Darling, the biggest little girl – I wanted to die when I knew I was going to have her, because Lowell was like a stranger to me. It didn't seem as though she could be my own. I wrote you a letter and tore it up. Oh, you were *so* bad to me, Anson.'

It was the dialogue again, rising and falling. Anson felt a suddenly quickening of memory.

'Weren't you engaged once?' she asked – 'a girl named Dolly something?'

'I wasn't ever engaged. I tried to be engaged, but I never loved anybody but you, Paula.'

'Oh,' she said. Then after a moment: 'This baby is the first one I ever really wanted. You see, I'm in love now – at last.'

He didn't answer, shocked at the treachery of her remembrance. She must have seen that the 'at last' bruised him, for she continued: 'I was infatuated with you, Anson – you could make me do anything you liked. But we wouldn't have been happy. I'm not smart enough for you. I don't like things to be complicated like you do.' She paused. 'You'll never settle down,' she said.

The phrase struck at him from behind – it was an accusation that of all accusations he had never merited.

'I could settle down if women were different,' he said. 'If I didn't understand so much about them, if women didn't spoil you for other women, if they had only a little pride. If I could go to sleep for a while and wake up into a home that was really mine – why, that's what I'm made for, Paula, that's what women have seen in me and liked in me. It's only that I can't get through the preliminaries any more.'

Hagerty came in a little before eleven; after a whiskey Paula stood up and announced that she was going to bed. She went over and stood by her husband.

'Where did you go, dearest?' she demanded.

'I had a drink with Ed Saunders.'

'I was worried. I thought maybe you'd run away.' She rested her head against his coat. 'He's sweet, isn't he, Anson?' she demanded.

'Absolutely,' said Anson, laughing.

She raised her face to her husband. 'Well, I'm ready,' she said.

She turned to Anson: 'Do you want to see our family gymnastic stunt?'

'Yes,' he said in an interested voice.

'All right. Here we go!'

Hagerty picked her up easily in his arms.

'This is called the family acrobatic stunt,' said Paula. 'He carries me upstairs. Isn't it sweet of him?'

'Yes,' said Anson.

Hagerty bent his head slightly until his face touched Paula's.

'And I love him,' she said. 'I've just been telling you, haven't I, Anson?'

'Yes,' he said.

'He's the dearest thing that ever lived in this world; aren't you, darling? . . . Well, good-night. Here we go. Isn't he strong?'

'Yes,' Anson said.

'You'll find a pair of Pete's pyjamas laid out for you. Sweet dreams – see you at breakfast.'

'Yes,' Anson said.

CHAPTER 8

THE OLDER MEMBERS of the firm insisted that Anson should go abroad for the summer. He had scarcely had a vacation in seven years, they said. He was stale and needed a change. Anson resisted.

'If I go,' he declared, 'I won't come back any more.'

'That's absurd, old man. You'll be back in three months with all this depression gone. Fit as ever.'

'No.' He shook his head stubbornly. 'If I stop, I won't go back to work. If I stop, that means I've given up – I'm through.'

'We'll take a chance on that. Stay six months if you like – we're not afraid you'll leave us. Why, you'd be miserable if you didn't work.'

They arranged his passage for him. They liked Anson – everyone liked Anson – and the change that had been coming over him cast a sort of pall over the office. The enthusiasm that had invariably signalled up business, the consideration toward his equals and his inferiors, the lift of his vital presence – within the past four months his intense nervousness had melted down these qualities into the fussy pessimism of a man of forty. On every transaction in which he was involved he acted as a drag and a strain.

'If I go I'll never come back,' he said.

Three days before he sailed Paula Legendre Hagerty died in childbirth. I was with him a great deal then, for we were crossing together, but for the first time in our friendship he told me not a word of how he felt, nor did I see the slightest sign of emotion. His chief preoccupation was with the fact that he was thirty years old – he would turn the conversation to the point where he could remind you of it and then fall silent, as if he assumed that the statement would start a chain of thought sufficient to itself. Like his partners, I was amazed at the change in him, and I was glad when the *Paris* moved off into the wet space between the worlds, leaving his principality behind.

'How about a drink?' he suggested.

We walked into the bar with that defiant feeling that characterises the day of departure and ordered four Martinis. After one cocktail a change came over him – he suddenly reached across and slapped my knee with the first joviality I had seen him exhibit for months.

'Did you see the girl in the red tam?' he demanded, 'the one with the high colour who had the two police dogs down to bid her goodbye.'

'She's pretty,' I agreed.

'I looked her up in the purser's office and found out that she's alone. I'm going down to see the steward in a few minutes. We'll have dinner with her tonight.'

After a while he left me, and within an hour he was walking up and down the deck with her, talking to her in his strong, clear voice. Her red tam was a bright spot of colour against the steel-grey sea, and from time to time she looked up with a flashing bob of her head, and smiled with amusement and interest, and anticipation. At dinner we had champagne, and were very joyous – afterward Anson ran the pool with infectious gusto, and several people who had seen me with him asked me his name. He and the girl were talking and laughing together on a lounge in the bar when I went to bed.

I saw less of him on the trip than I had hoped. He wanted to arrange a foursome, but there was no one available, so I saw him only at meals. Sometimes, though, he would have a cocktail in the bar, and he told me about the girl in the red tam, and his adventures with her, making them all bizarre and amusing, as he had a way of doing, and I was glad that he was himself again, or at least the self that I knew, and with which I felt at home. I don't think he was ever happy unless someone was in love with him, responding to him like filings to a magnet, helping him to explain himself, promising him something. What it was I do not know. Perhaps they promised that there would always be women in the world who would spend their brightest, freshest, rarest hours to nurse and protect that superiority he cherished in his heart.

Crazy Sunday

CHAPTER I

IT WAS SUNDAY – not a day, but rather a gap between two other days. Behind, for all of them, lay sets and sequences, the long waits under the crane that swung the microphone, the hundred miles a day by automobiles to and fro across a county, the struggles of rival ingenuities in the conference rooms, the ceaseless compromise, the clash and strain of many personalities fighting for their lives. And now Sunday, with individual life starting up again, with a glow kindling in eyes that had been glazed with monotony the afternoon before. Slowly as the hours waned they came awake like *Puppenfeen*[49] in a toy shop: an intense colloquy in a corner, lovers disappearing to neck in a hall. And the feeling of, 'Hurry, it's not too late, but for God's sake hurry before the blessed forty hours of leisure are over.'

Joel Coles was writing continuity. He was twenty-eight and not yet broken by Hollywood. He had had what were considered nice assignments since his arrival six months before and he submitted his scenes and sequences with enthusiasm. He referred to himself modestly as a hack but really did not think of it that way. His mother had been a successful actress; Joel had spent his childhood between London and New York trying to separate the real from the unreal, or at least to keep one guess ahead. He was a handsome man with the pleasant cow-brown eyes that in 1913 had gazed out at Broadway audiences from his mother's face.

When the invitation came it made him sure that he was getting somewhere. Ordinarily he did not go out on Sundays but stayed sober and took work home with him. Recently they had given him a Eugene O'Neill play destined for a very important lady indeed. Everything he had done so far had pleased Miles Calman, and Miles Calman was the only director on the lot who did not work under a supervisor and was responsible to the money men alone. Everything was clicking into place in Joel's career. ('This is Mr Calman's secretary. Will you come to tea from four to six Sunday – he lives in Beverly Hills, number —.')

Joel was flattered. It would be a party out of the top-drawer. It was a tribute to himself as a young man of promise. The Marion Davies[50] crowd, the high-hats, the big currency numbers, perhaps even Dietrich[51] and Garbo[52] and the Marquis, people who were not seen everywhere, would probably be at Calman's.

'I won't take anything to drink,' he assured himself. Calman was audibly tired of rummies, and thought it was a pity the industry could not get along without them.

Joel agreed that writers drank too much – he did himself, but he wouldn't this afternoon. He wished Miles would be within hearing when the cocktails were passed to hear his succinct, unobtrusive, 'No, thank you.'

Miles Calman's house was built for great emotional moments – there was an air of listening, as if the far silences of its vistas hid an audience, but this afternoon it was thronged, as though people had been bidden rather than asked. Joel noted with pride that only two other writers from the studio were in the crowd, an ennobled limey and, somewhat to his surprise, Nat Keogh, who had evoked Calman's impatient comment on drunks.

Stella Calman (Stella Walker, of course) did not move on to her other guests after she spoke to Joel. She lingered – she looked at him with the sort of beautiful look that demands some sort of acknowledgement and Joel drew quickly on the dramatic adequacy inherited from his mother: 'Well, you look about sixteen! Where's your kiddy car?' She was visibly pleased; she lingered. He felt that he should say something more, something confident and easy – he had first met her when she was struggling for bits in New York. At that moment a tray slid up and Stella put a cocktail glass into his hand.

'Everybody's afraid, aren't they?' he said, looking at it absently. 'Everybody watches for everybody else's blunders, or tries to make sure they're with people that'll do them credit. Of course that's not true in your house,' he covered himself hastily. 'I just meant generally in Hollywood.'

Stella agreed. She presented several people to Joel as if he were very important. Reassuring himself that Miles was at the other side of the room, Joel drank the cocktail.

'So you have a baby?' he said. 'That's the time to look out. After a pretty woman has had her first child, she's very vulnerable, because she wants to be reassured about her own charm. She's got to have some new man's unqualified devotion to prove to herself she hasn't lost anything.'

'I never get anybody's unqualified devotion,' Stella said rather resentfully.

'They're afraid of your husband.'

'You think that's it?' She wrinkled her brow over the idea; then the conversation was interrupted at the exact moment Joel would have chosen.

Her attentions had given him confidence. Not for him to join safe groups, to slink to refuge under the wings of such acquaintances as he saw about the room. He walked to the window and looked out towards the Pacific, colourless under its sluggish sunset. It was good here – the American Riviera and all that, if there were ever time to enjoy it. The handsome, well-dressed people in the room, the lovely girls, and the – well, the lovely girls. You couldn't have everything.

He saw Stella's fresh boyish face, with the tired eyelid that always drooped a little over one eye, moving about among her guests and he wanted to sit with her and talk a long time as if she were a girl instead of a name; he followed her to see if she paid anyone as much attention as she had paid him. He took another cocktail – not because he needed confidence but because she had given him so much of it. Then he sat down beside the director's mother.

'Your son's gotten to be a legend, Mrs Calman – Oracle and a Man of Destiny and all that. Personally, I'm against him but I'm in a minority. What do you think of him? Are you impressed? Are you surprised how far he's gone?'

'No, I'm not surprised,' she said calmly. 'We always expected a lot from Miles.'

'Well now, that's unusual,' remarked Joel. 'I always think all mothers are like Napoleon's mother. My mother didn't want me to have anything to do with the entertainment business. She wanted me to go to West Point and be safe.'

'We always had every confidence in Miles.'

He stood by the built-in bar of the dining-room with the good-humoured, heavy-drinking, highly paid Nat Keogh.

' – I made a hundred grand during the year and lost forty grand gambling, so now I've hired a manager.'

'You mean an agent,' suggested Joel.

'No, I've got that too. I mean a manager. I make over everything to my wife and then he and my wife get together and hand me out the money. I pay him five thousand a year to hand me out my money.'

'You mean your agent.'

'No, I mean my manager, and I'm not the only one – a lot of other irresponsible people have him'

'Well, if you're irresponsible why are you responsible enough to hire a manager?'

'I'm just irresponsible about gambling. Look here – '

A singer performed; Joel and Nat went forward with the others to listen.

CHAPTER 2

THE SINGING REACHED Joel vaguely; he felt happy and friendly towards all the people gathered there, people of bravery and industry, superior to bourgeoisie that outdid them in ignorance and loose living, risen to a position of the highest prominence in a nation that for a decade had wanted only to be entertained. He liked them – he loved them. Great waves of good feeling flowed through him.

As the singer finished his number and there was a drift towards the hostess to say goodbye, Joel had an idea. He would give them *Building It Up*, his own composition. It was his only parlour trick, it had amused several parties and it might please Stella Walker. Possessed by the hunch, his blood throbbing with the scarlet corpuscles of exhibitionism, he sought her.

'Of course,' she cried. 'Please! Do you need anything?'

'Someone has to be the secretary that I'm supposed to be dictating to.'

'I'll be her.'

As the word spread, the guests in the hall, already putting on their coats to leave, drifted back and Joel faced the eyes of many strangers. He had a dim foreboding, realising that the man who had just performed was a famous radio entertainer. Then someone said, 'Sh!' and he was alone with Stella, the centre of a sinister Indian-like half-circle. Stella smiled up at him expectantly – he began.

His burlesque was based upon the cultural limitations of Mr Dave

Silverstein, an independent producer; Silverstein was presumed to be dictating a letter outlining a treatment of a story he had bought.

' – a story of divorce, the younger generation, and the Foreign Legion,' he heard his voice saying, with the intonations of Mr Silverstein. 'But we got to build it up, see?'

A sharp pang of doubt struck through him. The faces surrounding him in the gently moulded light were intent and curious, but there was no ghost of a smile anywhere; directly in front, the Great Lover of the screen glared at him with an eye as keen as the eye of a potato. Only Stella Walker looked up at him with a radiant, never faltering smile.

'If we make him a Menjou type,[53] then we get a sort of Michael Arlen[54] only with a Honolulu atmosphere.'

Still not a ripple in front, but in the rear a rustling, a perceptible shift towards the left, towards the front door.

' – then she says she feels this sex appil for him and he burns out and says, "Oh, go on destroy yourself – " '

At some point he heard Nat Keogh snicker and here and there were a few encouraging faces, but as he finished he had the sickening realisation that he had made a fool of himself in view of an important section of the picture world, upon whose favour depended his career.

For a moment he existed in the midst of a confused silence, broken by a general trek for the door. He felt the undercurrent of derision that rolled through the gossip; then – all this was in the space of ten seconds – the Great Lover, his eye hard and empty as the eye of a needle, shouted, 'Boo! Boo!' voicing in an overtone what he felt was the mood of the crowd. It was the resentment of the professional towards the amateur, of the community towards the stranger, the thumbs-down of the clan.

Only Stella Walker was still standing near and thanking him as if he had been an unparalleled success, as if it hadn't occurred to her that anyone hadn't liked it. As Nat Keogh helped him into his overcoat, a great wave of self-disgust swept over him and he clung desperately to his rule of never betraying an inferior emotion until he no longer felt it.

'I was a flop,' he said lightly, to Stella. 'Never mind, it's a good number when appreciated. Thanks for your co-operation.'

The smile did not leave her face – he bowed rather drunkenly and Nat drew him towards the door . . .

The arrival of his breakfast awakened him into a broken and ruined world. Yesterday he was himself, a point of fire against an industry, today he felt that he was pitted under an enormous disadvantage against those faces, against individual contempt and collective sneer. Worse than that, to Miles Calman he was become one of those rummies, stripped of dignity, whom Calman regretted he was compelled to use. To Stella Walker on whom he had forced a martyrdom to preserve the courtesy of her house – her opinion he did not dare to guess. His gastric juices ceased to flow and he set his poached eggs back on the telephone table. He wrote:

> DEAR MILES – You can imagine my profound self-disgust. I confess to a taint of exhibitionism, but at six o'clock in the afternoon, in broad daylight! Good God! My apologies to your wife.
>
> Yours ever,   JOEL COLES

Joel emerged from his office on the lot only to slink like a malefactor to the tobacco store. So suspicious was his manner that one of the studio police asked to see his admission card. He had decided to eat lunch outside when Nat Keogh, confident and cheerful, overtook him.

'What do you mean you're in permanent retirement? What if that Three-Piece Suit did boo you?

'Why, listen,' he continued, drawing Joel into the studio restaurant. 'The night of one of his premières at Grauman's, Joe Squires kicked his tail while he was bowing to the crowd. The ham said Joe'd hear from him later but when Joe called him up at eight o'clock next day and said, "I thought I was going to hear from you," he hung up the phone.'

The preposterous story cheered Joel, and he found a gloomy consolation in staring at the group at the next table, the sad, lovely Siamese twins, the mean dwarfs, the proud giant from the circus picture. But looking beyond at the yellow-stained faces of pretty women, their eyes all melancholy and startling with mascara, their ball gowns garish in full day, he saw a group who had been at Calman's and winced.

'Never again,' he exclaimed aloud, 'absolutely my last social appearance in Hollywood!'

The following morning a telegram was waiting for him at his office:

You were one of the most agreeable people at our party. Expect you at my sister June's buffet supper next Sunday.

STELLA WALKER CALMAN

The blood rushed fast through his veins for a feverish minute. Incredulously he read the telegram over.

'Well, that's the sweetest thing I ever heard of in my life!'

CHAPTER 3

CRAZY SUNDAY again. Joel slept until eleven, then he read a newspaper to catch up with the past week. He lunched in his room on trout, avocado salad, and a pint of California wine. Dressing for the tea, he selected a pin-check suit, a blue shirt, a burnt orange tie. There were dark circles of fatigue under his eyes. In his second-hand car he drove to the Riviera apartments. As he was introducing himself to Stella's sister, Miles and Stella arrived in riding clothes – they had been quarrelling fiercely most of the afternoon on all the dirt roads back of Beverly Hills.

Miles Calman, tall, nervous, with a desperate humour and the unhappiest eyes Joel ever saw, was an artist from the top of his curiously shaped head to his niggerish feet. Upon these last he stood firmly – he had never made a cheap picture though he had sometimes paid heavily for the luxury of making experimental flops. In spite of his excellent company, one could not be with him long without realising that he was not a well man.

From the moment of their entrance Joel's day bound itself up inextricably with theirs. As he joined the group around them Stella turned away from it with an impatient little tongue click – and Miles Calman said to the man who happened to be next to him: 'Go easy on Eva Goebel. There's hell to pay about her at home.' Miles turned to Joel, 'I'm sorry I missed you at the office yesterday. I spent the afternoon at the analyst's.'

'You being psychoanalysed?'

'I have been for months. First I went for claustrophobia, now I'm trying to get my whole life cleared up. They say it'll take over a year.'

'There's nothing the matter with your life,' Joel assured him.

'Oh, no? Well, Stella seems to think so. Ask anybody – they can all tell you about it,' he said bitterly.

A girl perched herself on the arm of Miles's chair; Joel crossed to Stella, who stood disconsolately by the fire.

'Thank you for your telegram,' he said. 'It was darn sweet. I can't imagine anybody as good-looking as you are being so good-humoured.'

She was a little lovelier than he had ever seen her and perhaps the unstinted admiration in his eyes prompted her to unload on him – it did not take long, for she was obviously at the emotional bursting point.

' – and Miles has been carrying on this thing for two years, and I never knew. Why, she was one of my best friends, always in the house. Finally when people began to come to me, Miles had to admit it.'

She sat down vehemently on the arm of Joel's chair. Her riding breeches were the colour of the chair and Joel saw that the mass of her hair was made up of some strands of red gold and some of pale gold, so that it could not be dyed, and that she had on no make-up. She was that good-looking –

Still quivering with the shock of her discovery, Stella found unbearable the spectacle of a new girl hovering over Miles; she led Joel into a bedroom, and seated at either end of a big bed they went on talking. People on their way to the washroom glanced in and made wisecracks, but Stella, emptying out her story, paid no attention. After a while Miles stuck his head in the door and said, 'There's no use trying to explain something to Joel in half an hour that I don't understand myself and the psychoanalyst says will take a whole year to understand.'

She talked on as if Miles were not there. She loved Miles, she said – under considerable difficulties she had always been faithful to him.

'The psychoanalyst told Miles that he had a mother complex. In his first marriage he transferred his mother complex to his wife, you see – and then his sex turned to me. But when we married the thing repeated itself – he transferred his mother complex to me and all his libido turned towards this other woman.'

Joel knew that this probably wasn't gibberish – yet it sounded like gibberish. He knew Eva Goebel; she was a motherly person, older and probably wiser than Stella, who was a golden child.

Miles now suggested impatiently that Joel come back with them since Stella had so much to say, so they drove out to the mansion in Beverly Hills. Under the high ceilings the situation seemed more dignified and tragic. It was an eerie bright night with the dark very clear outside of all the windows and Stella all rose-gold raging and crying around the room. Joel did not quite believe in picture actresses' grief. They have other preoccupations – they are beautiful rose-gold figures blown full of life by writers and directors, and after hours they sit around and talk in whispers and giggle innuendoes, and the ends of many adventures flow through them.

Sometimes he pretended to listen and instead thought how well she was got up – sleek breeches with a matched set of legs in them, an Italian-coloured sweater with a little high neck, and a short brown chamois coat. He couldn't decide whether she was an imitation of an English lady or an English lady was an imitation of her. She hovered somewhere between the realest of realities and the most blatant of impersonations.

'Miles is so jealous of me that he questions everything I do,' she cried scornfully. 'When I was in New York I wrote him that I'd been to the theatre with Eddie Baker. Miles was so jealous he phoned me ten times in one day.'

'I was wild,' Miles snuffled sharply, a habit he had in times of stress. 'The analyst couldn't get any results for a week.'

Stella shook her head despairingly. 'Did you expect me just to sit in the hotel for three weeks?'

'I don't expect anything. I admit that I'm jealous. I try not to be. I worked on that with Dr Bridgebane, but it didn't do any good. I was jealous of Joel this afternoon when you sat on the arm of his chair.'

'You were?' She started up. 'You were! Wasn't there somebody on the arm of your chair? And did you speak to me for two hours?'

'You were telling your troubles to Joel in the bedroom.'

'When I think that that woman' – she seemed to believe that to omit Eva Goebel's name would be to lessen her reality – 'used to come here – '

'All right – all right,' said Miles wearily. 'I've admitted everything and I feel as bad about it as you do.' Turning to Joel he began talking about pictures, while Stella moved restlessly along the far walls, her hands in her breeches pockets.

'They've treated Miles terribly,' she said, coming suddenly back into the conversation as if they'd never discussed her personal affairs. 'Dear, tell him about old Beltzer trying to change your picture.'

As she stood hovering protectively over Miles, her eyes flashing with indignation in his behalf, Joel realised that he was in love with her. Stifled with excitement he got up to say good-night.

With Monday the week resumed its workaday rhythm, in sharp contrast to the theoretical discussions, the gossip and scandal of Sunday; there was the endless detail of script revision – 'Instead of a lousy dissolve, we can leave her voice on the soundtrack and cut to a medium shot of the taxi from Bell's angle or we can simply pull the camera back to include the station, hold it a minute, and then pan to the row of taxis' – by Monday afternoon Joel had again forgotten that people whose business was to provide entertainment were ever privileged to be entertained. In the evening he phoned Miles's house. He asked for Miles but Stella came to the phone.

'Do things seem better?'

'Not particularly. What are you doing next Saturday evening?'

'Nothing.'

'The Perrys are giving a dinner and theatre party and Miles won't be here – he's flying to South Bend to see the Notre Dame–California game. I thought you might go with me in his place.'

After a long moment Joel said, 'Why – surely. If there's a conference I can't make dinner but I can get to the theatre.'

'Then I'll say we can come.'

Joel walked to his office. In view of the strained relations of the Calmans, would Miles be pleased, or did she intend that Miles shouldn't know of it? That would be out of the question – if Miles didn't mention it Joel would. But it was an hour or more before he could get down to work again.

Wednesday there was a four-hour wrangle in a conference room crowded with planets and nebulae of cigarette smoke. Three men and a woman paced the carpet in turn, suggesting or condemning, speaking sharply or persuasively, confidently or despairingly. At the end Joel lingered to talk to Miles.

The man was tired – not with the exaltation of fatigue but life-tired, with his lids sagging and his beard prominent over the blue shadows near his mouth.

'I hear you're flying to the Notre Dame game.'

Miles looked beyond him and shook his head.

'I've given up the idea.'

'Why?'

'On account of you.' Still he did not look at Joel.

'What the hell, Miles?'

'That's why I've given it up.' He broke into a perfunctory laugh at himself. 'I can't tell what Stella might do just out of spite – she's invited you to take her to the Perrys, hasn't she? I wouldn't enjoy the game.'

The fine instinct that moved swiftly and confidently on the set, muddled so weakly and helplessly through his personal life.

'Look, Miles,' Joel said frowning. 'I've never made any passes whatsoever at Stella. If you're really seriously cancelling your trip on account of me, I won't go to the Perrys with her. I won't see her. You can trust me absolutely.'

Miles looked at him, carefully now.

'Maybe.' He shrugged his shoulders. 'Anyhow there'd just be somebody else. I wouldn't have any fun.'

'You don't seem to have much confidence in Stella. She told me she'd always been true to you.'

'Maybe she has.' In the last few minutes several more muscles had sagged around Miles's mouth. 'But how can I ask anything of her after what's happened? How can I expect her – ' He broke off and his face grew harder as he said, 'I'll tell you one thing, right or wrong and no matter what I've done, if I ever had anything on her I'd divorce her. I can't have my pride hurt – that would be the last straw.'

His tone annoyed Joel, but he said: 'Hasn't she calmed down about the Eva Goebel thing?'

'No.' Miles snuffled pessimistically. 'I can't get over it either.'

'I thought it was finished.'

'I'm trying not to see Eva again, but you know it isn't easy just to drop something like that – it isn't some girl I kissed last night in a taxi. The psychoanalyst says – '

'I know,' Joel interrupted. 'Stella told me.' This was depressing. 'Well, as far as I'm concerned if you go to the game I won't see Stella. And I'm sure Stella has nothing on her conscience about anybody.'

'Maybe not,' Miles repeated listlessly. 'Anyhow I'll stay and take her to the party. Say,' he said suddenly, 'I wish you'd come too. I've got to have somebody sympathetic to talk to. That's the trouble – I've influenced Stella in everything. Especially I've influenced her so that she likes all the men I like – it's very difficult.'

'It must be,' Joel agreed.

JOEL COULD NOT GET to the dinner. Self-conscious in his silk hat against the unemployment, he waited for the others in front of the Hollywood Theatre and watched the evening parade: obscure replicas of bright, particular picture stars, spavined men in polo coats, a stomping dervish with the beard and staff of an apostle, a pair of chic Filipinos in collegiate clothes, reminder that this corner of the Republic opened to the seven seas, a long fantastic carnival of young shouts which proved to be a fraternity initiation The line split to pass two smart limousines that stopped at the kerb.

There she was, in a dress like ice-water, made in a thousand pale-blue pieces, with icicles trickling at the throat. He started forward.

'So you like my dress?'

'Where's Miles?'

'He flew to the game after all. He left yesterday morning – at least I think – ' She broke off. 'I just got a telegram from South Bend saying that he's starting back. I forgot – you know all these people?'

The party of eight moved into the theatre.

Miles had gone after all and Joel wondered if he should have come. But during the performance, with Stella a profile under the pure grain of light hair, he thought no more about Miles. Once he turned and looked at her and she looked back at him, smiling and meeting his eyes for as long as he wanted. Between the acts they smoked in the lobby and she whispered: 'They're all going to the opening of Jack Johnson's⁵⁵ night club – I don't want to go, do you?'

'Do we have to?'

'I suppose not.' She hesitated. 'I'd like to talk to you. I suppose we could go to our house – if I were only sure – '

Again she hesitated and Joel asked: 'Sure of what?'

'Sure that – oh, I'm haywire, I know, but how can I be sure Miles went to the game?'

'You mean you think he's with Eva Goebel?'

'No, not so much that – but supposing he was here watching everything I do. You know Miles does odd things sometimes. Once he wanted a man with a long beard to drink tea with him and he sent down to the casting agency for one, and drank tea with him all afternoon.'

'That's different. He sent you a wire from South Bend – that proves he's at the game.'

After the play they said good-night to the others at the kerb and were answered by looks of amusement. They slid off along the golden garish thoroughfare through the crowd that had gathered around Stella.

'You see he could arrange the telegrams,' Stella said, 'very easily.'

That was true. And with the idea that perhaps her uneasiness was justified, Joel grew angry: if Miles had trained a camera on them he felt no obligations towards Miles. Aloud he said: 'That's nonsense.'

There were Christmas trees already in the shop windows and the full moon over the boulevard was only a prop, as scenic as the giant boudoir lamps of the corners. On into the dark foliage of Beverly Hills that flamed as eucalyptus by day, Joel saw only the flash of a white face under his own, the arc of her shoulder. She pulled away suddenly and looked up at him.

'Your eyes are like your mother's,' she said. 'I used to have a scrapbook full of pictures of her.'

'Your eyes are like your own and not a bit like any other eyes,' he answered.

Something made Joel look out into the grounds as they went into the house, as if Miles were lurking in the shrubbery. A telegram waited on the hall table. She read aloud:

'Chicago. Home tomorrow night. Thinking of you. Love – MILES.'

'You see,' she said, throwing the slip back on the table, 'he could easily have faked that.' She asked the butler for drinks and sandwiches and ran upstairs, while Joel walked into the empty reception rooms. Strolling about he wandered to the piano where he had stood in disgrace two Sundays before.

'Then we could put over,' he said aloud, 'a story of divorce, the younger generation, and the Foreign Legion.'

His thoughts jumped to another telegram.

'You were one of the most agreeable people at our party – '

An idea occurred to him. If Stella's telegram had been purely a gesture of courtesy then it was likely that Miles had inspired it, for it was Miles who had invited him. Probably Miles had said: 'Send him a wire – he's miserable – he thinks he's queered himself.'

It fitted in with, 'I've influenced Stella in everything. Especially I've influenced her so that she likes all the men I like.' A woman would do a thing like that because she felt sympathetic – only a man would do it because he felt responsible.

When Stella came back into the room he took both her hands.

'I have a strange feeling that I'm a sort of pawn in a spite game you're playing against Miles,' he said.

'Help yourself to a drink.'

'And the odd thing is that I'm in love with you anyhow.'

The telephone rang and she freed herself to answer it.

'Another wire from Miles,' she announced. 'He dropped it, or it says he dropped it, from the aeroplane at Kansas City.'

'I suppose he asked to be remembered to me.'

'No, he just said he loved me. I believe he does. He's so very weak.'

'Come sit beside me,' Joel urged her.

It was early. And it was still a few minutes short of midnight a half-hour later, when Joel walked to the cold hearth, and said tersely: 'Meaning that you haven't any curiosity about me?'

'Not at all. You attract me a lot and you know it. The point is that I suppose I really do love Miles.'

'Obviously.'

'And tonight I feel uneasy about everything.'

He wasn't angry – he was even faintly relieved that a possible entanglement was avoided. Still, as he looked at her, the warmth and softness of her body thawing her cold blue costume, he knew she was one of the things he would always regret.

'I've got to go,' he said. 'I'll phone a taxi.'

'Nonsense – there's a chauffeur on duty.'

He winced at her readiness to have him go, and seeing this she kissed him lightly and said, 'You're sweet, Joel.' Then suddenly three things happened: he took down his drink at a gulp, the phone rang loud through the house, and a clock in the hall struck in trumpet notes.

Nine – ten – eleven – twelve –

CHAPTER 5

IT WAS SUNDAY AGAIN. Joel realised that he had come to the theatre this evening with the work of the week still hanging about him like cerements. He had made love to Stella as he might attack some matter to be cleaned up hurriedly before the day's end. But this was Sunday – the lovely, lazy perspective of the next twenty-four hours unrolled before him – every minute was something to be approached with lulling indirection, every moment held the germ of innumerable possibilities. Nothing was impossible – everything was just beginning. He poured himself another drink.

With a sharp moan, Stella slipped forward inertly by the telephone. Joel picked her up and laid her on the sofa. He squirted soda-water on a handkerchief and slapped it over her face. The telephone mouthpiece was still grinding and he put it to his ear.

' – the plane fell just this side of Kansas City. The body of Miles Calman has been identified and – '

He hung up the receiver.

'Lie still,' he said, stalling, as Stella opened her eyes.

'Oh, what's happened?' she whispered. 'Call them back. Oh, what's happened?'

'I'll call them right away. What's your doctor's name?'

'Did they say Miles was dead?'

'Lie quiet – is there a servant still up?'

'Hold me – I'm frightened.'

He put his arm around her.

'I want the name of your doctor,' he said sternly. 'It may be a mistake but I want someone here.'

'It's Dr – oh, God, is Miles dead?'

Joel ran upstairs and searched through strange medicine cabinets for spirits of ammonia. When he came down Stella cried: 'He isn't dead – I know he isn't. This is part of his scheme. He's torturing me. I know he's alive. I can feel he's alive.'

'I want to get hold of some close friend of yours, Stella. You can't stay here alone tonight.'

'Oh, no,' she cried. 'I can't see anybody. You stay, I haven't got any friend.' She got up, tears streaming down her face. 'Oh, Miles is my only friend. He's not dead – he can't be dead. I'm going there right away and see. Get a train. You'll have to come with me.'

'You can't. There's nothing to do tonight. I want you to tell me the name of some woman I can call: Lois? Joan? Carmel? Isn't there somebody?'

Stella stared at him blindly.

'Eva Goebel was my best friend,' she said.

Joel thought of Miles, his sad and desperate face in the office two days before. In the awful silence of his death all was clear about him. He was the only American-born director with both an interesting temperament and an artistic conscience. Meshed in an industry, he had paid with his ruined nerves for having no resilience, no healthy cynicism, no refuge – only a pitiful and precarious escape.

There was a sound at the outer door – it opened suddenly, and there were footsteps in the hall.

'Miles!' Stella screamed. 'Is it you, Miles? Oh, it's Miles.'

A telegraph boy appeared in the doorway.

'I couldn't find the bell. I heard you talking inside.'

The telegram was a duplicate of the one that had been phoned. While Stella read it over and over, as though it were a black lie, Joel telephoned. It was still early and he had difficulty getting anyone; when finally he succeeded in finding some friends he made Stella take a stiff drink.

'You'll stay here, Joel,' she whispered, as though she were half-asleep. 'You won't go away. Miles liked you – he said you – ' She shivered violently, 'Oh, my God, you don't know how alone I feel.' Her eyes closed, 'Put your arms around me. Miles had a suit like that.' She started bolt upright. 'Think of what he must have felt. He was afraid of almost everything, anyhow.'

She shook her head dazedly. Suddenly she seized Joel's face and held it close to hers.

'You won't go. You like me – you love me, don't you? Don't call up anybody. Tomorrow's time enough. You stay here with me tonight.'

He stared at her, at first incredulously, and then with shocked understanding. In her dark groping Stella was trying to keep Miles alive by sustaining a situation in which he had figured – as if Miles's mind could not die so long as the possibilities that had worried him still existed. It was a distraught and tortured effort to stave off the realisation that he was dead.

Resolutely Joel went to the phone and called a doctor.

'Don't, oh, don't call anybody!' Stella cried. 'Come back here and put your arms around me.'

'Is Dr Bales in?'

'Joel,' Stella cried. 'I thought I could count on you. Miles liked you. He was jealous of you – Joel, come here.'

Ah then – if he betrayed Miles she would be keeping him alive – for if he were really dead how could he be betrayed?

' – has just had a very severe shock. Can you come at once, and get hold of a nurse?'

'Joel!'

Now the doorbell and the telephone began to ring intermittently, and automobiles were stopping in front of the door.

'But you're not going,' Stella begged him. 'You're going to stay, aren't you?'

'No,' he answered. 'But I'll be back, if you need me.'

Standing on the steps of the house which now hummed and palpitated with the life that flutters around death like protective leaves, he began to sob a little in his throat.

'Everything he touched he did something magical to,' he thought. 'He even brought that little gamin alive and made her a sort of masterpiece.'

And then: 'What a hell of a hole he leaves in this damn wilderness – already!'

And then with a certain bitterness, 'Oh, yes, I'll be back – I'll be back!'

An Alcoholic Case

CHAPTER I

'LET – GO – THAT – oh–h–h! Please, now, will you? *Don't* start drinking again! Come on – give me the bottle. I told you I'd stay awake givin' it to you. Come on. If you're like that away – then what are you going to be like when you go home. Come on – leave it with me – I'll leave half in the bottle. Pul–lease. You know what Dr Carter says – I'll stay awake and give it to you, or else fix some of it in the bottle – come on – like I told you, I'm too tired to be fightin' you all night . . . All right, drink your fool self to death.'

'Would you like some beer?' he asked.

'No, I don't want any beer. Oh, to think that I have to look at you drunk again. My God!'

'Then I'll drink the Coca-Cola.'

The girl sat down panting on the bed.

'Don't you believe in anything?' she demanded.

'Nothing you believe in – please – it'll spill.'

She had no business there, she thought, no business trying to help him. Again they struggled, but after this time he sat with his head in his hands awhile, before he turned around once more.

'Once more you try to get it I'll throw it down,' she said quickly. 'I will – on the tiles in the bathroom.'

'Then I'll step on the broken glass – or you'll step on it.'

'Then let go – oh, you promised – '

Suddenly she dropped it like a torpedo, sliding underneath her hand and slithering with a flash of red and black and the words SIR GALAHAD, DISTILLED LOUISVILLE GIN. He took it by the neck and tossed it through the open door to the bathroom.

It was on the floor in pieces and everything was silent for a while and she read *Gone with the Wind*[56] about things so lovely that had happened long ago. She began to worry that he would have to go into the bathroom and might cut his feet, and looked up from time to time to see if he would go in. She was very sleepy – the last time she looked up he was crying and he looked like an old Jewish man she had nursed once in California; he had had to go to the bathroom many times. On this case she was unhappy all the time but she thought: 'I guess if I hadn't liked him I wouldn't have stayed on the case.'

With a sudden resurgence of conscience she got up and put a chair in front of the bathroom door. She had wanted to sleep because he had got her up early that morning to get a paper with the story of the Yale–Dartmouth game in it and she hadn't been home all day. That afternoon a relative of his had come to see him and she had waited outside in the hall where there was a draught with no sweater to put over her uniform.

As well as she could she arranged him for sleeping, put a robe over his shoulders as he sat slumped over his writing table, and one on his knees. She sat down in the rocker but she was no longer sleepy; there was plenty to enter on the chart and treading lightly about she found a pencil and put it down: *Pulse 120; Respiration 25; Temp. 98 – 98.4 – 98.2; Remarks –*

She could make so many: *Tried to get bottle of gin. Threw it away and broke it.*

She corrected it to read: *In the struggle it dropped and was broken. Patient was generally difficult.*

She started to add as part of her report: *I never want to go on an alcoholic case again*, but that wasn't in the picture. She knew she could wake herself at seven and clean up everything before his niece awakened. It was all part of the game. But when she sat down in the chair she looked at his face, white and exhausted, and counted his breathing again, wondering why it had all happened. He had been so nice today, drawn her a whole strip of his cartoon just for fun and given it to her. She was going to have it framed and hang it in her room. She felt again his thin wrists wrestling against her wrist and remembered the awful things he had said, and she thought too of what the doctor had said to him yesterday: 'You're too good a man to do this to yourself.'

She was tired and didn't want to clean up the glass on the bath-room floor, because as soon as he breathed evenly she wanted to get him over to the bed. But she decided finally to clean up the glass first; on her knees, searching for a last piece of it, she thought: This isn't what I ought to be doing. And this isn't what *he* ought to be doing.

Resentfully she stood up and regarded him. Through the thin delicate profile of his nose came a light snore, sighing, remote, inconsolable. The doctor had shaken his head in a certain way, and she knew that really it was a case that was beyond her. Besides, on her card at the agency was written, on the advice of her elders, 'No Alcoholics'.

She had done her whole duty, but all she could think of was that when she was struggling about the room with him with that gin bottle there had been a pause when he asked her if she had hurt her elbow against a door and that she had answered: 'You don't know how people talk about you, no matter how you think of yourself –' when she knew he had a long time ceased to care about such things.

The glass was all collected – as she got out a broom to make sure, she realised that the glass, in its fragments, was less than a window through which they had seen each other for a moment. He did not know about her sister, and Bill Markoe whom she had almost married, and she did not know what had brought him to this pitch, when there was a picture on his bureau of his young wife and his two sons and him, all trim and handsome as he must have been five years ago. It was so utterly senseless – as she put a bandage on her finger where she had cut it while picking up the glass she made up her mind she would never take an alcoholic case again.

CHAPTER 2

IT WAS EARLY the next evening. Some Halloween jokester had split the side windows of the bus and she shifted back to the Negro section in the rear for fear the glass might fall out. She had her patient's cheque but no way to cash it at this hour; there was a quarter and a penny in her purse.

Two nurses she knew were waiting in the hall of Mrs Hixson's Agency.

'What kind of case have you been on?'

'Alcoholic,' she said.

'Oh, yes – Gretta Hawks told me about it – you were on with that cartoonist who lives at the Forest Park Inn.'

'Yes, I was.'

'I hear he's pretty fresh.'

'He's never done anything to bother me,' she lied. 'You can't treat them as if they were committed – '

'Oh, don't get bothered – I just heard that around town – oh, you know – they want you to play around with them – '

'Oh, be quiet,' she said, surprised at her own rising resentment.

In a moment Mrs Hixson came out and, asking the other two to wait, signalled her into the office.

'I don't like to put young girls on such cases,' she began. 'I got your call from the hotel.'

'Oh, it wasn't bad, Mrs Hixson. He didn't know what he was doing and he didn't hurt me in any way. I was thinking much more of my reputation with you. He was really nice all day yesterday. He drew me – '

'I didn't want to send you on that case.' Mrs Hixson thumbed through the registration cards. 'You take TB cases, don't you? Yes, I see you do. Now here's one – '

The phone rang in a continuous chime. The nurse listened as Mrs Hixson's voice said precisely: 'I will do what I can – that is simply up to the doctor . . . That is beyond my jurisdiction . . . Oh, hello, Hattie, no, I can't now. Look, have you got any nurse that's good with alcoholics? There's somebody up at the Forest Park Inn who needs somebody. Call back will you?'

She put down the receiver. 'Suppose you wait outside. What sort of man is this, anyhow? Did he act indecently?'

'He held my hand away,' she said, 'so I couldn't give him an injection.'

'Oh, an invalid he-man,' Mrs Hixson grumbled. 'They belong in sanatoria. I've got a case coming along in two minutes that you can get a little rest on. It's an old woman – '

The phone rang again. 'Oh, hello, Hattie . . . Well, how about that big Svensen girl? She ought to be able to take care of any alcoholic . . . How about Josephine Markham? Doesn't she live in your apartment house? . . . Get her to the phone.' Then after a moment, 'Jo, would you care to take the case of a well-known cartoonist, or artist, whatever they call themselves, at Forest Park Inn? . . . No, I don't know, but Dr Carter is in charge and will be around about ten o'clock.'

There was a long pause; from time to time Mrs Hixson spoke: 'I see . . . Of course, I understand your point of view. Yes, but this isn't supposed to be dangerous – just a little difficult. I never like to send

girls to a hotel because I know what riff-raff you're liable to run
into . . . No, I'll find somebody. Even at this hour. Never mind and
thanks. Tell Hattie I hope that the hat matches the négligé . . .'

Mrs Hixson hung up the receiver and made notations on the pad
before her. She was a very efficient woman. She had been a nurse and
had gone through the worst of it, had been a proud, idealistic,
overworked probationer, suffered the abuse of smart internees and
the insolence of her first patients, who thought that she was something to be taken into camp immediately for premature commitment
to the service of old age. She swung around suddenly from the desk.

'What kind of cases do you want? I told you I have a nice old
woman –'

The nurse's brown eyes were alight with a mixture of thoughts –
the movie she had just seen about Pasteur[57] and the book they had all
read about Florence Nightingale[58] when they were student nurses.
And their pride, swinging across the streets in the cold weather at
Philadelphia General, as proud of their new capes as débutantes in
their furs going into balls at the hotels.

'I – I think I would like to try the case again,' she said amid a
cacophony of telephone bells. 'I'd just as soon go back if you can't
find anybody else.'

'But one minute you say you'll never go on an alcoholic case again
and the next minute you say you want to go back to one.'

'I think I overestimated how difficult it was. Really, I think I could
help him.'

'That's up to you. But if he tried to grab your wrists.'

'But he couldn't,' the nurse said. 'Look at my wrists: I played
basketball at Waynesboro High for two years. I'm quite able to take
care of him.'

Mrs Hixson looked at her for a long minute. 'Well, all right,' she
said. 'But just remember that nothing they say when they're drunk is
what they mean when they're sober – I've been all through that;
arrange with one of the servants that you can call on him, because
you never can tell – some alcoholics are pleasant and some of them
are not, but all of them can be rotten.'

'I'll remember,' the nurse said.

It was an oddly clear night when she went out, with slanting
particles of thin sleet making white of a blue-black sky. The bus was
the same that had taken her into town, but there seemed to be more
windows broken now and the bus driver was irritated and talked

about what terrible things he would do if he caught any kids. She knew he was just talking about the annoyance in general, just as she had been thinking about the annoyance of an alcoholic. When she came up to the suite and found him all helpless and distraught she would despise him and be sorry for him.

Getting off the bus, she went down the long steps to the hotel, feeling a little exalted by the chill in the air. She was going to take care of him because nobody else would, and because the best people of her profession had been interested in taking care of the cases that nobody else wanted.

She knocked at his study door, knowing just what she was going to say.

He answered it himself. He was in dinner clothes even to a derby hat – but minus his studs and tie.

'Oh, hello,' he said casually. 'Glad you're back. I woke up a while ago and decided I'd go out. Did you get a night nurse?'

'I'm the night nurse too,' she said. 'I decided to stay on twenty-four-hour duty.'

He broke into a genial, indifferent smile.

'I saw you were gone, but something told me you'd come back. Please find my studs. They ought to be either in a little tortoiseshell box or – '

He shook himself a little more into his clothes, and hoisted the cuffs up inside his coat sleeves.

'I thought you had quit me,' he said casually.

'I thought I had, too.'

'If you look on that table,' he said, 'you'll find a whole strip of cartoons that I drew you.'

'Who are you going to see?' she asked.

'It's the President's secretary,' he said. 'I had an awful time trying to get ready. I was about to give up when you came in. Will you order me some sherry?'

'One glass,' she agreed wearily.

From the bathroom he called presently: 'Oh, nurse, nurse, light of my life, where is another stud?'

'I'll put it in.'

In the bathroom she saw the pallor and the fever on his face and smelled the mixed peppermint and gin on his breath.

'You'll come up soon?' she asked. 'Dr Carter's coming at ten.'

'What nonsense! You're coming down with me.'

'Me?' she exclaimed. 'In a sweater and skirt? Imagine!'

'Then I won't go.'

'All right then, go to bed. That's where you belong anyhow. Can't you see these people tomorrow?'

'No, of course not!'

She went behind him and reaching over his shoulder tied his tie – his shirt was already thumbed out of press where he had put in the studs, and she suggested: 'Won't you put on another one, if you've got to meet some people you like?'

'All right, but I want to do it myself.'

'Why can't you let me help you?' she demanded in exasperation. 'Why can't you let me help you with your clothes? What's a nurse for – what good am I doing?'

He sat down suddenly on the toilet seat.

'All right – go on.'

'Now don't grab my wrist,' she said, and then, 'Excuse me.'

'Don't worry. It didn't hurt. You'll see in a minute.'

She had the coat, vest, and stiff shirt off him but before she could pull his undershirt over his head he dragged at his cigarette, delaying her.

'Now watch this,' he said. 'One – two – three.'

She pulled up the undershirt; simultaneously he thrust the crimson-grey point of the cigarette like a dagger against his heart. It crushed out against a copper plate on his left rib about the size of a silver dollar, and he said 'Ouch!' as a stray spark fluttered down against his stomach.

Now was the time to be hard-boiled, she thought. She knew there were three medals from the war in his jewel box, but she had risked many things herself: tuberculosis among them and one time something worse, though she had not known it and had never quite forgiven the doctor for not telling her.

'You've had a hard time with that, I guess,' she said lightly as she sponged him. 'Won't it ever heal?'

'Never. That's a copper plate.'

'Well, it's no excuse for what you're doing to yourself.'

He bent his great brown eyes on her, shrewd – aloof, confused. He signalled to her, in one second, his Will to Die, and for all her training and experience she knew she could never do anything constructive with him. He stood up, steadying himself on the wash-basin and fixing his eyes on some place just ahead.

'Now, if I'm going to stay here you're not going to get at that liquor,' she said.

Suddenly she knew he wasn't looking for that. He was looking at the corner where he had thrown the bottle the night before. She stared at his handsome face, weak and defiant – afraid to turn even halfway because she knew that death was in that corner where he was looking. She knew death – she had heard it, smelt its unmistakable odour, but she had never seen it before it entered into anyone, and she knew this man saw it in the corner of his bathroom; that it was standing there looking at him while he spat from a feeble cough and rubbed the result into the braid of his trousers. It shone there crackling for a moment as evidence of the last gesture he ever made.

She tried to express it next day to Mrs Hixson: 'It's not like anything you can beat – no matter how hard you try. This one could have twisted my wrists until he strained them and that wouldn't matter so much to me. It's just that you can't really help them and it's so discouraging – it's all for nothing.'

The Lees of Happiness

CHAPTER I

IF YOU SHOULD LOOK through the files of old magazines for the first years of the present century you would find, sandwiched in between the stories of Richard Harding Davis[59] and Frank Norris[60] and others long since dead, the work of one Jeffrey Curtain: a novel or two, and perhaps three or four dozen short stories. You could, if you were interested, follow them along until say, 1908, when they suddenly disappeared.

When you had read them all you would have been quite sure that here were no masterpieces – here were passably amusing stories, a bit out of date now, but doubtless the sort that would then have whiled away a dreary half-hour in a dental office. The man who did them was of good intelligence, talented, glib, probably young. In the samples of his work you found there would have been nothing to stir you to more than a faint interest in the whims of life – no deep interior laughs, no sense of futility, or hint of tragedy.

After reading them you would yawn and put the number back in the files, and perhaps, if you were in some library reading-room, you would decide that by way of variety you would look at a newspaper of the period and see whether the Japs had taken Port Arthur.[61] But if by any chance the newspaper you had chosen was the right one and had crackled open at the theatrical page, your eyes would have been arrested and held, and for at least a minute you would have forgotten Port Arthur as quickly as you forgot Château Thierry.[62] For you would, by this fortunate chance, be looking at the portrait of an exquisite woman.

Those were the days of *Floradora* and of sextets, of pinched-in waists and blown-out sleeves, of almost bustles and absolute ballet skirts, but here, without doubt, disguised as she might be by the unaccustomed stiffness and old fashion of her costume, was a butter-fly of butterflies. Here was the gaiety of the period – the soft wine of eyes, the songs that flurried hearts, the toasts and the bouquets, the dances and the dinners. Here was a Venus of the hansom cab, the Gibson girl[63] in her glorious prime. Here was . . .

. . . here was, you find by looking at the name beneath, one Roxanne Milbank, who had been chorus girl and understudy in *The Daisy Chain*, but who, by reason of an excellent performance when the star was indisposed, had gained a leading part.

You would look again – and wonder why you had never heard of her. Why did her name not linger in popular songs and vaudeville jokes and cigar bands, and the memory of that gay old uncle of yours along with Lillian Runssell and Stella Mayhew and Anna Held?[64] Roxanne Milbank – whither had she gone? What dark trap-door had opened suddenly and swallowed her up? Her name was certainly not in last Sunday's supplement on that list of actresses married to English noblemen. No doubt she was dead – poor beautiful young lady – and quite forgotten.

I am hoping too much. I am having you stumble on Jeffrey Curtain's stories and Roxanne Milbank's picture. It would be incredible that you should find a newspaper item six months later, a single item two inches by four, which informed the public of the marriage, very quietly, of Miss Roxanne Milbank, who had been on tour with *The Daisy Chain*, to Mr Jeffrey Curtain, the popular author. 'Mrs Curtain,' it added dispassionately, 'will retire from the stage.'

It was a marriage of love. He was sufficiently spoiled to be charming; she was ingenuous enough to be irresistible. Like two floating logs they met in a head-on rush, caught, and sped along together. Yet had Jeffrey Curtain kept at scrivening for two-score years he could not have put a quirk into one of his stories weirder than the quirk that came into his own life. Had Roxanne Milbank played three dozen parts and filled five thousand houses she could never have had a role with more happiness and more despair than were in the fate prepared for Roxanne Curtain.

For a year they lived in hotels, travelled to California, to Alaska, to Florida, to Mexico, loved and quarrelled gently, and gloried in the golden triflings of his wit with her beauty – they were young and gravely passionate; they demanded everything and then yielded everything again in ecstasies of unselfishness and pride. She loved the swift tones of his voice and his frantic, unfounded jealousy. He loved her dark radiance, the white irises of her eyes, the warm, lustrous enthusiasm of her smile.

'Don't you like her?' he would demand rather excitedly and shyly; 'Isn't she wonderful? Did you ever see – '

'Yes,' they would answer, grinning. 'She's a wonder. You're lucky.'

The year passed. They tired of hotels. They bought an old house and twenty acres near the town of Marlowe, half an hour from Chicago; bought a little car, and moved out riotously with a pioneering hallucination that would have confounded Balboa.[65]

'Your room will be here!' they cried in turn.

– And then:

'And my room here!'

'And the nursery here when we have children.'

'And we'll build a sleeping porch – oh, next year.'

They moved out in April. In July Jeffrey's closest friend, Harry Cromwell, came to spend a week – they met him at the end of the long lawn and hurried him proudly to the house.

Harry was married also. His wife had had a baby some six months before and was still recuperating at her mother's in New York. Roxanne had gathered from Jeffrey that Harry's wife was not as attractive as Harry – Jeffrey had met her once and considered her – 'shallow'. But Harry had been married nearly two years and was apparently happy, so Jeffrey guessed that she was probably all right . . .

'I'm making biscuits,' chattered Roxanne gravely. 'Can your wife make biscuits? The cook is showing me how. I think every woman should know how to make biscuits. It sounds so utterly disarming. A woman who can make biscuits can surely do no – '

'You'll have to come out here and live,' said Jeffrey. 'Get a place out in the country like us, for you and Kitty.'

'You don't know Kitty. She hates the country. She's got to have her theatres and vaudevilles.'

'Bring her out,' repeated Jeffrey. 'We'll have a colony. There's an awfully nice crowd here already. Bring her out!'

They were at the porch steps now and Roxanne made a brisk gesture toward a dilapidated structure on the right.

'The garage,' she announced. 'It will also be Jeffrey's writing-room within the month. Meanwhile dinner is at seven. Meanwhile to that I will mix a cocktail.'

The two men ascended to the second floor – that is, they ascended halfway, for at the first landing Jeffrey dropped his guest's suitcase and in a cross between a query and a cry exclaimed: 'For God's sake, Harry, how do you like her?'

'We will go upstairs,' answered his guest, 'and we will shut the door.'

Half an hour later as they were sitting together in the library Roxanne reissued from the kitchen, bearing before her a pan of biscuits. Jeffrey and Harry rose.

'They're beautiful, dear,' said the husband, intensely.

'Exquisite,' murmured Harry.

Roxanne beamed.

'Taste one. I couldn't bear to touch them before you'd seen them all and I can't bear to take them back until I find what they taste like.'

'Like manna, darling.'

Simultaneously the two men raised the biscuits to their lips, nibbled tentatively. Simultaneously they tried to change the subject. But Roxanne, undeceived, set down the pan and seized a biscuit. After a second her comment rang out with lugubrious finality: 'Absolutely bum!'

'Really – ?'

'Why, I didn't notice – '

Roxanne roared.

'Oh, I'm useless,' she cried laughing. 'Turn me out, Jeffrey – I'm a parasite; I'm no good – '

Jeffrey put his arm around her.

'Darling, I'll eat your biscuits.'

'They're beautiful, anyway,' insisted Roxanne.

'They're – they're decorative,' suggested Harry.

Jeffrey took him up wildly.

'That's the word. They're decorative; they're masterpieces. We'll use them.'

He rushed to the kitchen and returned with a hammer and a handful of nails.

'We'll use them, by golly, Roxanne! We'll make a frieze out of them.'

'Don't!' wailed Roxanne. 'Our beautiful house.'

'Never mind. We're going to have the library repapered in October. Don't you remember?'

'Well – '

Bang! The first biscuit was impaled to the wall, where it quivered for a moment like a live thing.

Bang! . . .

When Roxanne returned with a second round of cocktails the biscuits were in a perpendicular row, twelve of them, like a collection of primitive spearheads.

'Roxanne,' exclaimed Jeffrey, 'you're an artist! Cook? – nonsense! You shall illustrate my books!'

During dinner the twilight faltered into dusk, and later it was a starry dark outside, filled and permeated with the frail gorgeousness of Roxanne's white dress and her tremulous, low laugh.

– Such a little girl she is, thought Harry. Not as old as Kitty.

He compared the two. Kitty – nervous without being sensitive, temperamental without temperament, a woman who seemed to flit and never light – and Roxanne, who was as young as a spring night, and summed up in her own adolescent laughter.

– A good match for Jeffrey, he thought again. Two very young people, the sort who'll stay very young until they suddenly find themselves old.

Harry thought these things between his constant thoughts about Kitty. He was depressed about Kitty. It seemed to him that she was well enough to come back to Chicago and bring his little son. He was thinking vaguely of Kitty when he said good-night to his friend's wife and his friend at the foot of the stairs.

'You're our first real house guest,' called Roxanne after him. 'Aren't you thrilled and proud?'

When he was out of sight around the stair corner she turned to Jeffrey, who was standing beside her resting his hand on the end of the banister.

'Are you tired, my dearest?'

Jeffrey rubbed the centre of his forehead with his fingers.

'A little. How did you know?'

'Oh, how could I help knowing about you?'

'It's a headache,' he said moodily. 'Splitting. I'll take some aspirin.'

She reached over and snapped out the light, and with his arm tight about her waist they walked up the stairs together.

HARRY'S WEEK PASSED. They drove about the dreaming lanes or idled in cheerful inanity upon lake or lawn. In the evening Roxanne, sitting inside, played to them while the ashes whitened on the glowing ends of their cigars. Then came a telegram from Kitty saying that she wanted Harry to come East and get her, so Roxanne and Jeffrey were left alone in that privacy of which they never seemed to tire.

'Alone' thrilled them again. They wandered about the house, each feeling intimately the presence of the other; they sat on the same side of the table like honeymooners; they were intensely absorbed, intensely happy.

The town of Marlowe, though a comparatively old settlement, had only recently acquired a 'society'. Five or six years before, alarmed at the smoky swelling of Chicago, two or three young married couples, 'bungalow people', had moved out; their friends had followed. The Jeffrey Curtains found an already formed 'set' prepared to welcome them; a country club, ballroom, and golf-links yawned for them, and there were bridge parties, and poker parties, and parties where they drank beer, and parties where they drank nothing at all.

It was at a poker party that they found themselves a week after Harry's departure. There were two tables, and a good proportion of the young wives were smoking and shouting their bets, and being very daringly mannish for those days.

Roxanne had left the game early and taken to perambulation; she wandered into the pantry and found herself some grape juice – beer gave her a headache – and then passed from table to table, looking over shoulders at the hands, keeping an eye on Jeffrey and being pleasantly unexcited and content. Jeffrey, with intense concentration, was raising a pile of chips of all colours, and Roxanne knew by the deepened wrinkle between his eyes that he was interested. She liked to see him interested in small things.

She crossed over quietly and sat down on the arm of his chair.

She sat there five minutes, listening to the sharp intermittent comments of the men and the chatter of the women, which rose from the table like soft smoke – and yet scarcely hearing either. Then quite innocently she reached out her hand, intending to place it on Jeffrey's shoulder – as it touched him he started of a sudden, gave a short grunt, and, sweeping back his arm furiously, caught her a glancing blow on her elbow.

There was a general gasp. Roxanne regained her balance, gave a little cry, and rose quickly to her feet. It had been the greatest shock of her life. This, from Jeffrey, the heart of kindness, of consideration – this instinctively brutal gesture.

The gasp became a silence. A dozen eyes were turned on Jeffrey, who looked up as though seeing Roxanne for the first time. An expression of bewilderment settled on his face.

'Why – Roxanne – ' he said haltingly.

Into a dozen minds entered a quick suspicion, a rumour of scandal. Could it be that behind the scenes with this couple, apparently so in love, lurked some curious antipathy? Why else this streak of fire across such a cloudless heaven?

'Jeffrey!' – Roxanne's voice was pleading – startled and horrified, yet she knew that it was a mistake. Not once did it occur to her to blame him or to resent it. Her word was a trembling supplication – 'Tell me, Jeffrey,' it said, 'tell Roxanne, your own Roxanne.'

'Why, Roxanne – ' began Jeffrey again. The bewildered look changed to pain. He was clearly as startled as she. 'I didn't intend that,' he went on; 'you startled me. You – I felt as if someone were attacking me. I – how – why, how idiotic!'

'Jeffrey!' Again the word was a prayer, incense offered up to a high God through this new and unfathomable darkness.

They were both on their feet, they were saying goodbye, faltering, apologising, explaining. There was no attempt to pass it off easily. That way lay sacrilege. Jeffrey had not been feeling well, they said. He had become nervous. Back of both their minds was the unexplained horror of that blow – the marvel that there had been for an instant something between them – his anger and her fear – and now to both a sorrow, momentary, no doubt, but to be bridged at once, at once, while there was yet time. Was that swift water lashing under their feet, the fierce glint of some unchartered chasm?

Out in their car under the harvest moon he talked brokenly. It was just incomprehensible to him, he said. He had been thinking of the poker game – absorbed – and the touch on his shoulder had seemed like an attack. An attack! He clung to that word, flung it up as a shield. He had hated what touched him. With the impact of his hand it had gone, that – nervousness. That was all he knew.

Both their eyes filled with tears and they whispered love there under the broad night as the serene streets of Marlowe sped by. Later, when they went to bed, they were quite calm. Jeffrey was to take a week off all work – was simply to loll, and sleep, and go on long walks until this nervousness left him. When they had decided this safety settled down upon Roxanne. The pillows underhead became soft and friendly; the bed on which they lay seemed wide, and white, and sturdy beneath the radiance that streamed in at the window.

Five days later, in the first cool of late afternoon, Jeffrey picked up an oak chair and sent it crashing through his own front window. Then he lay down on the couch like a child, weeping piteously and begging to die. A blood clot the size of a marble had broken in his brain.

CHAPTER 3

THERE IS A SORT OF waking nightmare that sets in sometimes when one has missed a sleep or two, a feeling that comes with extreme fatigue and a new sun, that the quality of the life around has changed. It is a fully articulate conviction that somehow the existence one is then leading is a branch shoot of life and is related to life only as a moving picture or a mirror – that the people, and streets, and houses are only projections from a very dim and chaotic past. It was in such a state that Roxanne found herself during the first months of Jeffrey's illness. She slept only when she was utterly exhausted; she awoke under a cloud. The long, sober-voiced consultations, the faint aura of medicine in the halls, the sudden tiptoeing in a house that had echoed to many cheerful footsteps, and, most of all, Jeffrey's white face amid the pillows of the bed they had shared – these things subdued her and made her indelibly older. The doctors held out hope, but that was all. A long rest, they said, and quiet. So responsibility came to Roxanne. It was she who paid the bills, pored over his bank-book, corresponded with his publishers. She was in the kitchen constantly. She learned from the nurse how to prepare his meals and after the first month took complete charge of the sickroom. She had had to let the nurse go for reasons of economy. One of the two coloured girls left at the same time. Roxanne was realising that they had been living from short story to short story.

The most frequent visitor was Harry Cromwell. He had been shocked and depressed by the news, and though his wife was now living with him in Chicago he found time to come out several times a month. Roxanne found his sympathy welcome – there was some quality of suffering in the man, some inherent pitifulness that made her comfortable when he was near. Roxanne's nature had suddenly deepened. She felt sometimes that with Jeffrey she was losing her children also, those children that now most of all she needed and should have had.

It was six months after Jeffrey's collapse and when the nightmare had faded, leaving not the old world but a new one, greyer and colder, that she went to see Harry's wife. Finding herself in Chicago with an extra hour before train time, she decided out of courtesy to call.

As she stepped inside the door she had an immediate impression that the apartment was very like some place she had seen before – and almost instantly she remembered a round-the-corner bakery of her childhood, a bakery full of rows and rows of pink frosted cakes – a stuffy pink, pink as a food, pink triumphant, vulgar, and odious.

And this apartment was like that. It was pink. It smelled pink!

Mrs Cromwell, attired in a wrapper of pink and black, opened the door. Her hair was yellow, heightened, Roxanne imagined, by a dash of peroxide in the rinsing water every week. Her eyes were a thin waxen blue – she was pretty and too consciously graceful. Her cordiality was strident and intimate, hostility melted so quickly to hospitality that it seemed they were both merely in the face and voice – never touching nor touched by the deep core of egotism beneath.

But to Roxanne these things were secondary; her eyes were caught and held in uncanny fascination by the wrapper. It was vilely unclean. From its lowest hem up four inches it was sheerly dirty with the blue dust of the floor; for the next three inches it was grey – then it shaded off into its natural colour, which was – pink. It was dirty at the sleeves, too, and at the collar – and when the woman turned to lead the way into the parlour, Roxanne was sure that her neck was dirty.

A one-sided rattle of conversation began. Mrs Cromwell became explicit about her likes and dislikes, her head, her stomach, her teeth, her apartment – avoiding with a sort of insolent meticulousness any inclusion of Roxanne with life, as if presuming that Roxanne, having been dealt a blow, wished life to be carefully skirted.

Roxanne smiled. That kimono! That neck!

After five minutes a little boy toddled into the parlour – a dirty little boy clad in dirty pink rompers. His face was smudgy – Roxanne wanted to take him into her lap and wipe his nose; other parts in the vicinity of his head needed attention, his tiny shoes were kicked out at the toes. Unspeakable!

'What a darling little boy!' exclaimed Roxanne, smiling radiantly. 'Come here to me.'

Mrs Cromwell looked coldly at her son.

'He *will* get dirty. Look at that face!' She held her head on one side and regarded it critically.

'Isn't he a *darling*?' repeated Roxanne.

'Look at his rompers,' frowned Mrs Cromwell.

'He needs a change, don't you, George?'

George stared at her curiously. To his mind the word rompers connotated a garment extraneously smeared, as this one.

'I tried to make him look respectable this morning,' complained Mrs Cromwell as one whose patience had been sorely tried, 'and I found he didn't have any more rompers – so rather than have him go around without any I put him back in those – and his face – '

'How many pairs has he?' Roxanne's voice was pleasantly curious. 'How many feather fans have you?' she might have asked.

'Oh – ' Mrs Cromwell considered, wrinkling her pretty brow. 'Five, I think. Plenty, I know.'

'You can get them for fifty cents a pair.'

Mrs Cromwell's eyes showed surprise – and the faintest superiority. The price of rompers!

'Can you really? I had no idea. He ought to have plenty, but I haven't had a minute all week to send the laundry out.' Then, dismissing the subject as irrelevant, 'I must show you some things – '

They rose and Roxanne followed her past an open bathroom door whose garment-littered floor showed indeed that the laundry hadn't been sent out for some time, into another room that was, so to speak, the quintessence of pinkness. This was Mrs Cromwell's room.

Here the hostess opened a closet door and displayed before Roxanne's eyes an amazing collection of lingerie. There were dozens of filmy marvels of lace and silk, all clean, unruffled, seemingly not yet touched. On hangers beside them were three new evening dresses.

'I have some beautiful things,' said Mrs Cromwell, 'but not much of a chance to wear them. Harry doesn't care about going out.' Spite crept into her voice. 'He's perfectly content to let me play nursemaid and housekeeper all day and loving wife in the evening.'

Roxanne smiled again.

'You've got some beautiful clothes here.'

'Yes, I have. Let me show you – '

'Beautiful,' repeated Roxanne, interrupting, 'but I'll have to run if I'm going to catch my train.'

She felt that her hands were trembling. She wanted to put them on this woman and shake her – shake her. She wanted her locked up somewhere and set to scrubbing floors.

'Beautiful,' she repeated, 'and I just came in for a moment.'

'Well, I'm sorry Harry isn't here.'

They moved toward the door.

' – and, oh,' said Roxanne with an effort – yet her voice was still gentle and her lips were smiling – 'I think it's Argile's where you can get those rompers. Goodbye.'

It was not until she had reached the station and bought her ticket to Marlowe that Roxanne realised it was the first five minutes in six months that her mind had been off Jeffrey.

CHAPTER 4

A WEEK LATER Harry appeared at Marlowe, arrived unexpectedly at five o'clock, and coming up the walk sank into a porch chair in a state of exhaustion. Roxanne herself had had a busy day and was worn out. The doctors were coming at five-thirty, bringing a celebrated nerve specialist from New York. She was excited and thoroughly depressed, but Harry's eyes made her sit down beside him.

'What's the matter?'

'Nothing, Roxanne,' he denied. 'I came to see how Jeff was doing. Don't you bother about me.'

'Harry,' insisted Roxanne, 'there's something the matter.'

'Nothing,' he repeated. 'How's Jeff?'

Anxiety darkened her face.

'He's a little worse, Harry. Dr Jewett has come on from New York. They thought he could tell me something definite. He's going to try and find whether this paralysis has anything to do with the original blood clot.'

Harry rose.

'Oh, I'm sorry,' he said jerkily. 'I didn't know you expected a consultation. I wouldn't have come. I thought I'd just rock on your porch for an hour – '

'Sit down,' she commanded.

Harry hesitated.

'Sit down, Harry, dear boy.' Her kindness flooded out now – enveloped him. 'I know there's something the matter. You're white as a sheet. I'm going to get you a cool bottle of beer.'

All at once he collapsed into his chair and covered his face with his hands.

'I can't make her happy,' he said slowly. 'I've tried and I've tried. This morning we had some words about breakfast – I'd been getting my breakfast downtown – and well, just after I went to the office she left the house, went East to her mother's with George and a suitcase full of lace underwear.'

'Harry!'

'And I don't know – '

There was a crunch on the gravel, a car turning into the drive. Roxanne uttered a little cry.

'It's Dr Jewett.'

'Oh, I'll – '

'You'll wait, won't you?' she interrupted abstractedly. He saw that his problem had already died on the troubled surface of her mind.

There was an embarrassing minute of vague, elided introductions, and then Harry followed the party inside and watched them disappear up the stairs. He went into the library and sat down on the big sofa.

For an hour he watched the sun creep up the patterned folds of the chintz curtains. In the deep quiet a trapped wasp buzzing on the inside of the window-pane assumed the proportions of a clamour. From time to time another buzzing drifted down from upstairs, resembling several more larger wasps caught on larger window-panes. He heard low footfalls, the clink of bottles, the clamour of pouring water.

What had he and Roxanne done that life should deal these crashing blows to them? Upstairs there was taking place a living inquest on the soul of his friend; he was sitting here in a quiet room listening to the plaint of a wasp, just as when he was a boy he had been compelled by a strict aunt to sit hour-long on a chair and atone for some misbehaviour. But who had put him here? What ferocious aunt had leaned out of the sky to make him atone for – what?

About Kitty he felt a great hopelessness. She was too expensive – that was the irremediable difficulty. Suddenly he hated her. He wanted to throw her down and kick at her – to tell her she was a cheat and a leech – that she was dirty. Moreover, she must give him his boy.

He rose and began pacing up and down the room. Simultaneously he heard someone begin walking along the hallway upstairs in exact tune with him. He found himself wondering if they would walk in time until the person reached the end of the hall.

Kitty had gone to her mother. God help her, what a mother to go to! He tried to imagine the meeting: the abused wife collapsing upon the mother's breast. He could not. That Kitty was capable of any deep grief was unbelievable. He had gradually grown to think of her as something unapproachable and callous. She would get a divorce, of course, and eventually she would marry again. He began to consider this. Whom would she marry? He laughed bitterly, stopped; a picture flashed before him of Kitty's arms around some man whose face he could not see, of Kitty's lips pressed close to other lips in what was surely passion.

'God!' he cried aloud. 'God! God! God!'

Then the pictures came thick and fast. The Kitty of this morning faded; the soiled kimono rolled up and disappeared; the pouts, and rages, and tears all were washed away. Again she was Kitty Carr – Kitty Carr with yellow hair and great baby eyes. Ah, she had loved him, she had loved him.

After a while he perceived that something was amiss with him, something that had nothing to do with Kitty or Jeff, something of a different genre. Amazingly it burst on him at last; he was hungry. Simple enough! He would go into the kitchen in a moment and ask the coloured cook for a sandwich. After that he must go back to the city.

He paused at the wall, jerked at something round, and, fingering it absently, put it to his mouth and tasted it as a baby tastes a bright toy. His teeth closed on it – Ah!

She'd left that damn kimono, that dirty pink kimono. She might have had the decency to take it with her, he thought. It would hang in the house like a corpse of their sick alliance. He would try to throw it away, but he would never be able to bring himself to move it. It would be like Kitty, soft and pliable, withal impervious. You couldn't move Kitty; you couldn't reach Kitty. There was nothing there to reach. He understood that perfectly – he had understood it all along.

He reached to the wall for another biscuit and with an effort pulled it out, nail and all. He carefully removed the nail from the centre, wondering idly if he had eaten the nail with the first biscuit. Preposterous! He would have remembered – it was a huge nail. He felt his stomach. He must be very hungry. He considered – remembered – yesterday he had had no dinner. It was the girl's day out and Kitty had lain in her room eating chocolate drops. She had said she felt 'smothery' and couldn't bear having him near her. He had given George a bath and put him to bed, and then laid down on the couch intending to rest a minute before getting his own dinner. There he had fallen asleep and awakened about eleven, to find that there was nothing in the ice-box except a spoonful of potato salad. This he had eaten, together with some chocolate drops that he found on Kitty's bureau. This morning he had breakfast hurriedly downtown before going to the office. But at noon, beginning to worry about Kitty, he had decided to go home and take her out to lunch. After that there had been the note on his pillow. The pile of lingerie in the closet was gone – and she had left instructions for sending her trunk.

He had never been so hungry, he thought.

At five o'clock, when the visiting nurse tiptoed downstairs, he was sitting on the sofa staring at the carpet.

'Mr Cromwell?'

'Yes?'

'Oh, Mrs Curtain won't be able to see you at dinner. She's not well. She told me to tell you that the cook will fix you something and that there's a spare bedroom.'

'She's sick, you say?'

'She's lying down in her room. The consultation is just over.'

'Did they – did they decide anything?'

'Yes,' said the nurse softly. 'Dr Jewett says there's no hope. Mr Curtain may live indefinitely, but he'll never see again or move again or think. He'll just breathe.'

'Just breathe?'

'Yes.'

For the first time the nurse noted that beside the writing-desk where she remembered that she had seen a line of a dozen curious round objects she had vaguely imagined to be some exotic form of decoration, there was now only one. Where the others had been, there was now a series of little nail-holes.

Harry followed her glance dazedly and then rose to his feet.

'I don't believe I'll stay. I believe there's a train.'

She nodded. Harry picked up his hat.

'Goodbye,' she said pleasantly.

'Goodbye,' he answered, as though talking to himself and, evidently moved by some involuntary necessity, he paused on his way to the door and she saw him pluck the last object from the wall and drop it into his pocket.

Then he opened the screen door and, descending the porch steps, passed out of her sight.

CHAPTER 5

AFTER A WHILE the coat of clean white paint on the Jeffrey Curtain house made a definite compromise with the suns of many Julys and showed its good faith by turning grey. It scaled – huge peelings of very brittle old paint leaned over backward like aged men practising grotesque gymnastics and finally dropped to a mouldy death in the overgrown grass beneath. The paint on the front pillars became streaky; the white ball was knocked off the left-hand doorpost; the green blinds darkened, then lost all pretence of colour.

It began to be a house that was avoided by the tender minded – some church bought a lot diagonally opposite for a graveyard, and this, combined with 'the place where Mrs Curtain stays with that living corpse', was enough to throw a ghostly aura over that quarter of the road. Not that she was left alone. Men and women came to see her, met her downtown, where she went to do her marketing, brought her home in their cars – and came in for a moment to talk and to rest, in the glamour that still played in her smile. But men who did not know her no longer followed her with admiring glances in the street; a diaphanous veil had come down over her beauty, destroying its vividness, yet bringing neither wrinkles nor fat.

She acquired a character in the village – a group of little stories were told of her: how when the country was frozen over one winter so that no wagons nor automobiles could travel, she taught herself to skate so that she could make quick time to the grocer and druggist, and not leave Jeffrey alone for long. It was said that every night since his paralysis she slept in a small bed beside his bed, holding his hand.

Jeffrey Curtain was spoken of as though he were already dead. As the years dropped by those who had known him died or moved away – there were but half a dozen of the old crowd who had drunk cocktails together, called each other's wives by their first names, and thought that Jeff was about the wittiest and most talented fellow that Marlowe had ever known. Now, to the casual visitor, he was merely the reason that Mrs Curtain excused herself sometimes and hurried upstairs; he was a groan or a sharp cry borne to the silent parlour on the heavy air of a Sunday afternoon.

He could not move; he was stone blind, dumb, and totally unconscious. All day he lay in his bed, except for a shift to his wheelchair every morning while she straightened the room. His paralysis was creeping slowly toward his heart. At first – for the first year – Roxanne had received the faintest answering pressure sometimes when she held his hand – then it had gone, ceased one evening, and never come back, and through two nights Roxanne lay wide-eyed, staring into the dark and wondering what had gone, what fraction of his soul had taken flight, what last grain of comprehension those shattered broken nerves still carried to the brain.

After that hope died. Had it not been for her unceasing care the last spark would have gone long before. Every morning she shaved and bathed him, shifted him with her own hands from bed to chair and back to bed. She was in his room constantly, bearing medicine, straightening a pillow, talking to him almost as one talks to a nearly human dog, without hope of response or appreciation, but with the dim persuasion of habit, a prayer when faith has gone.

Not a few people, one celebrated nerve specialist among them, gave her a plain impression that it was futile to exercise so much care, that if Jeffrey had been conscious he would have wished to die, that if his spirit were hovering in some wider air it would agree to no such sacrifice from her, it would fret only for the prison of its body to give it full release.

'But you see,' she replied, shaking her head gently, 'when I married Jeffrey it was – until I ceased to love him.'

'But,' was protested, in effect, 'you can't love that.'

'I can love what it once was. What else is there for me to do?'

The specialist shrugged his shoulders and went away to say that Mrs Curtain was a remarkable woman and just about as sweet as an angel – but, he added, it was a terrible pity.

'There must be some man, or a dozen, just crazy to take care of her . . .'

Casually – there were. Here and there someone began in hope – and ended in reverence. There was no love in the woman except, strangely enough, for life, for the people in the world, from the tramp to whom she gave food she could ill afford, to the butcher who sold her a cheap cut of steak across the meaty board. The other phase was sealed up somewhere in that expressionless mummy who lay with his face turned ever toward the light as mechanically as a compass needle and waited dumbly for the last wave to wash over his heart.

After eleven years he died in the middle of a May night, when the scent of the syringa hung upon the window-sill and a breeze wafted in the shrillings of the frogs and cicadas outside. Roxanne awoke at two, and realised with a start she was alone in the house at last.

CHAPTER 4

AFTER THAT she sat on her weather-beaten porch through many afternoons, gazing down across the fields that undulated in a slow descent to the white and green town. She was wondering what she would do with her life. She was thirty-six – handsome, strong, and free. The years had eaten up Jeffrey's insurance; she had reluctantly parted with the acres to right and left of her, and had even placed a small mortgage on the house.

With her husband's death had come a great physical restlessness. She missed having to care for him in the morning, she missed her rush to town, and the brief and therefore accentuated neighbourly meetings in the butcher's and grocer's; she missed the cooking for two, the preparation of delicate liquid food for him. One day, consumed with energy, she went out and spaded up the whole garden, a thing that had not been done for years.

And she was alone at night in the room that had seen the glory of her marriage and then the pain. To meet Jeff again she went back in spirit to that wonderful year, that intense, passionate absorption and companionship, rather than looked forward to a problematical meeting hereafter; she awoke often to lie and wish for that presence beside her – inanimate yet breathing – still Jeff.

One afternoon six months after his death she was sitting on the porch, in a black dress which took away the faintest suggestion of plumpness from her figure. It was Indian summer – golden brown all about her; a hush broken by the sighing of leaves; westward a four o'clock sun dripping streaks of red and yellow over a flaming sky. Most of the birds had gone – only a sparrow that had built itself a nest on the cornice of a pillar kept up an intermittent cheeping varied by occasional fluttering sallies overhead. Roxanne moved her chair to where she could watch him and her mind idled drowsily on the bosom of the afternoon.

Harry Cromwell was coming out from Chicago to dinner. Since his divorce over eight years before he had been a frequent visitor. They had kept up what amounted to a tradition between them: when he arrived they would go to look at Jeff; Harry would sit down on the edge of the bed and in a hearty voice ask: 'Well, Jeff, old man, how do you feel today?'

Roxanne, standing beside, would look intently at Jeff, dreaming that some shadowy recognition of this former friend had passed across that broken mind – but the head, pale, carven, would only move slowly in its sole gesture toward the light as if something behind the blind eyes were groping for another light long since gone out.

These visits stretched over eight years – at Easter, Christmas, Thanksgiving, and on many a Sunday Harry had arrived, paid his call on Jeff, and then talked for a long while with Roxanne on the porch. He was devoted to her. He made no pretence of hiding, no attempt to deepen, this relation. She was his best friend as the mass of flesh on the bed there had been his best friend. She was peace, she was rest; she was the past. Of his own tragedy she alone knew.

He had been at the funeral, but since then the company for which he worked had shifted him to the East and only a business trip had brought him to the vicinity of Chicago. Roxanne had written him to come when he could – after a night in the city he had caught a train out.

They shook hands and he helped her move two rockers together.
'How's George?'
'He's fine, Roxanne. Seems to like school.'
'Of course, it was the only thing to do, to send him.'
'Of course – '

'You miss him horribly, Harry?'

'Yes – I do miss him. He's a funny boy – '

He talked a lot about George. Roxanne was interested. Harry must bring him out on his next vacation. She had only seen him once in her life – a child in dirty rompers.

She left him with the newspaper while she prepared dinner – she had four chops tonight and some late vegetables from her own garden. She put it all on and then called him, and sitting down together they continued their talk about George.

'If I had a child – ' she would say.

Afterward, Harry having given her what slender advice he could about investments, they walked through the garden, pausing here and there to recognise what had once been a cement bench or where the tennis-court had lain . . .

'Do you remember – '

Then they were off on a flood of reminiscences: the day they had taken all the snapshots and Jeff had been photographed astride the calf; and the sketch Harry had made of Jeff and Roxanne, lying sprawled in the grass, their heads almost touching. There was to have been a covered lattice connecting the barn-studio with the house, so that Jeff could get there on wet days – the lattice had been started, but nothing remained except a broken triangular piece that still adhered to the house and resembled a battered chicken coop.

'And those mint juleps!'[66]

'And Jeff's notebook! Do you remember how we'd laugh, Harry, when we'd get it out of his pocket and read aloud a page of material. And how frantic he used to get?'

'Wild! He was such a kid about his writing.'

They were both silent a moment, and then Harry said: 'We were to have a place out here, too. Do you remember? We were to buy the adjoining twenty acres. And the parties we were going to have!'

Again there was a pause, broken this time by a low question from Roxanne.

'Do you ever hear of her, Harry?'

'Why – yes,' he admitted placidly. 'She's in Seattle. She's married again to a man named Horton, a sort of lumber king. He's a great deal older than she is, I believe.'

'And she's behaving?'

'Yes – that is, I've heard so. She has everything, you see. Nothing much to do except dress up for this fellow at dinner-time.'

'I see.'

Without effort he changed the subject.

'Are you going to keep the house?'

'I think so,' she said, nodding. 'I've lived here so long, Harry, it'd seem terrible to move. I thought of trained nursing, but of course that'd mean leaving. I've about decided to be a boarding-house lady.'

'Live in one?'

'No. Keep one. Is there such an anomaly as a boarding-house lady? Anyway I'd have a Negress and keep about eight people in the summer and two or three, if I can get them, in the winter. Of course I'll have to have the house repainted and gone over inside.'

Harry considered.

'Roxanne, why – naturally, you know best what you can do, but it does seem a shock, Roxanne. You came here as a bride.'

'Perhaps,' she said, 'that's why I don't mind remaining here as a boarding-house lady.'

'I remember a certain batch of biscuits.'

'Oh, those biscuits,' she cried. 'Still, from all I heard about the way you devoured them, they couldn't have been so bad. I was *so* low that day, yet somehow I laughed when the nurse told me about those biscuits.'

'I noticed that the twelve nail-holes are still in the library wall where Jeff drove them.'

'Yes.'

It was getting very dark now, a crispness settled in the air; a little gust of wind sent down a last spray of leaves. Roxanne shivered slightly.

'We'd better go in.'

He looked at his watch.

'It's late. I've got to be leaving. I go East tomorrow.'

'Must you?'

They lingered for a moment just below the stoop, watching a moon that seemed full of snow float out of the distance where the lake lay. Summer was gone and now Indian summer. The grass was cold and there was no mist and no dew. After he left she would go in and light the gas and close the shutters, and he would go down the path and on to the village. To these two life had come quickly and gone, leaving not bitterness, but pity; not disillusion, but only pain. There was already enough moonlight when they shook hands for each to see the gathered kindness in the other's eyes.

The Lost Decade

ALL SORTS OF PEOPLE came into the offices of the newsweekly and Orrison Brown had all sorts of relations with them. Outside of office hours he was 'one of the editors' – during work time he was simply a curly-haired man who a year before had edited the Dartmouth *Jack-o-Lantern* and was now only too glad to take the undesirable assignments around the office, from straightening out illegible copy to playing call boy without the title.

He had seen this visitor go into the editor's office – a pale tall man of forty with blond statuesque hair and a manner that was neither shy nor timid, nor other-worldly like a monk, but something of all three. The name on his card, Louis Trimble, evoked some vague memory, but having nothing to start on, Orrison did not puzzle over it – until a buzzer sounded on his desk, and previous experience warned him that Mr Trimble was to be his first course at lunch.

'Mr Trimble – Mr Brown,' said the source of all luncheon money. 'Orrison – Mr Trimble's been away a long time. Or he *feels* it's a long time – almost twelve years. Some people would consider themselves lucky to've missed the last decade.'

'That's so,' said Orrison.

'I can't lunch today,' continued his chief. 'Take him to Voisin or 21 or anywhere he'd like. Mr Trimble feels there're lots of things he hasn't seen.'

Trimble demurred politely.

'Oh, I can get around.'

'I know it, old boy. Nobody knew this place like you did once – and if Brown tries to explain the horseless carriage just send him back here to me. And you'll be back yourself by four, won't you?'

Orrison got his hat.

'You've been away ten years?' he asked while they went down in the elevator.

'They'd begun the Empire State Building,' said Trimble. 'What does that add up to?'

'About 1928. But as the chief said, you've been lucky to miss a lot.' As a feeler he added, 'Probably had more interesting things to look at.'

'Can't say I have.'

They reached the street and the way Trimble's face tightened at the roar of traffic made Orrison take one more guess.

'You've been out of civilisation?'

'In a sense.' The words were spoken in such a measured way that Orrison concluded this man wouldn't talk unless he wanted to – and simultaneously wondered if he could have possibly spent the thirties in a prison or an insane asylum.

'This is the famous 21,' he said. 'Do you think you'd rather eat somewhere else?'

Trimble paused, looking carefully at the brownstone house.

'I can remember when the name 21 got to be famous,' he said, 'about the same year as Moriarty's.' Then he continued almost apologetically, 'I thought we might walk up Fifth Avenue about five minutes and eat wherever we happened to be. Some place with young people to look at.'

Orrison gave him a quick glance and once again thought of bars and grey walls and bars; he wondered if his duties included introducing Mr Trimble to complaisant girls. But Mr Trimble didn't look as if that was in his mind – the dominant expression was of absolute and deep-seated curiosity and Orrison attempted to connect the name with Admiral Byrd's[67] hideout at the South Pole or flyers lost in Brazilian jungles. He was, or he had been, quite a fellow – that was obvious. But the only definite clue to his environment – and to Orrison the clue that led nowhere – was his countryman's obedience to the traffic lights and his predilection for walking on the side next to the shops and not the street. Once he stopped and gazed into a haberdasher's window.

'Crêpe ties,' he said. 'I haven't seen one since I left college.'

'Where'd you go?'

'Massachusetts Tech.'

'Great place.'

'I'm going to take a look at it next week. Let's eat somewhere along here – ' they were in the upper Fifties ' – you choose.'

There was a good restaurant with a little awning just around the corner.

'What do you want to see most?' Orrison asked, as they sat down.

Trimble considered.

'Well – the back of people's heads,' he suggested. 'Their necks – how their heads are joined to their bodies. I'd like to hear what those two little girls are saying to their father. Not exactly what they're saying but whether the words float or submerge, how their mouths shut when they've finished speaking. Just a matter of rhythm – Cole Porter[68] came back to the States in 1928 because he felt that there were new rhythms around.'

Orrison was sure he had his clue now, and with nice delicacy did not pursue it by a millimetre – even suppressing a sudden desire to say there was a fine concert in Carnegie Hall tonight.

'The weight of spoons,' said Trimble, 'so light. A little bowl with a stick attached. The cast in that waiter's eye. I knew him once but he wouldn't remember me.'

But as they left the restaurant the same waiter looked at Trimble rather puzzled as if he almost knew him. When they were outside Orrison laughed: 'After ten years people will forget.'

'Oh, I had dinner there last May – ' He broke off in an abrupt manner.

It was all kind of nutsy, Orrison decided – and changed himself suddenly into a guide.

'From here you get a good candid focus on Rockefeller Centre,' he pointed out with spirit ' – and the Chrysler Building and the Armistead Building, the daddy of all the new ones.'

'The Armistead Building,' Trimble rubber-necked obediently. 'Yes – I designed it.'

Orrison shook his head cheerfully – he was used to going out with all kinds of people. But that stuff about having been in the restaurant last May . . .

He paused by the brass entablature in the cornerstone of the building. 'Erected 1928,' it said.

Trimble nodded.

'But I was taken drunk that year – every-which-way drunk. So I never saw it before now.'

'Oh.' Orrison hesitated. 'Like to go in now?'

'I've been in it – lots of times. But I've never seen it. And now it isn't what I want to see. I wouldn't ever be able to see it now. I simply want to see how people walk and what their clothes and shoes and hats are made of. And their eyes and hands. Would you mind shaking hands with me?'

'Not at all, sir.'

'Thanks. Thanks. That's very kind. I suppose it looks strange – but people will think we're saying goodbye. I'm going to walk up the avenue for a while, so we *will* say goodbye. Tell your office I'll be in at four.'

Orrison looked after him when he started out, half expecting him to turn into a bar. But there was nothing about him that suggested or ever had suggested drink.

'Jesus!' he said to himself. 'Drunk for ten years.'

He felt suddenly of the texture of his own coat and then he reached out and pressed his thumb against the granite of the building by his side.

Babylon[69] Revisited

I

'AND WHERE'S Mr Campbell?' Charlie asked.

'Gone to Switzerland. Mr Campbell's a pretty sick man, Mr Wales.'

'I'm sorry to hear that. And George Hardt?' Charlie enquired.

'Back in America, gone to work.'

'And where is the Snow Bird?'

'He was in here last week. Anyway, his friend, Mr Schaeffer, is in Paris.'

Two familiar names from the long list of a year and a half ago. Charlie scribbled an address in his notebook and tore out the page.

'If you see Mr Schaeffer, give him this,' he said. 'It's my brother-in-law's address. I haven't settled on a hotel yet.'

He was not really disappointed to find Paris was so empty. But the stillness in the Ritz bar was strange and portentous. It was not an American bar any more – he felt polite in it, and not as if he owned it. It had gone back into France. He felt the stillness from the moment he got out of the taxi and saw the doorman, usually in a frenzy of activity at this hour, gossiping with a *chasseur*[70] by the servants' entrance.

Passing through the corridor, he heard only a single, bored voice in the once-clamorous women's room. When he turned into the bar he travelled the twenty feet of green carpet with his eyes fixed straight ahead by old habit; and then, with his foot firmly on the rail, he turned and surveyed the room, encountering only a single pair of eyes that fluttered up from a newspaper in the corner. Charlie asked for the head barman, Paul, who in the latter days of the bull market had come to work in his own custom-built car – disembarking, however, with due nicety at the nearest corner. But Paul was at his country house today and Alix giving him information.

'No, no more,' Charlie said, 'I'm going slow these days.'

Alix congratulated him: 'You were going pretty strong a couple of years ago.'

'I'll stick to it all right,' Charlie assured him. 'I've stuck to it for over a year and a half now.'

'How do you find conditions in America?'

'I haven't been to America for months. I'm in business in Prague, representing a couple of concerns there. They don't know about me down there.'

Alix smiled.

'Remember the night of George Hardt's bachelor dinner here?' said Charlie. 'By the way, what's become of Claude Fessenden?'

Alix lowered his voice confidentially: 'He's in Paris, but he doesn't come here any more. Paul doesn't allow it. He ran up a bill of thirty thousand francs, charging all his drinks and his lunches, and usually his dinner, for more than a year. And when Paul finally told him he had to pay, he gave him a bad cheque.' Alix shook his head sadly. 'I don't understand it, such a dandy fellow. Now he's all bloated up – ' He made a plump apple of his hands.

Charlie watched a group of strident queens installing themselves in a corner.

'Nothing affects them,' he thought. 'Stocks rise and fall, people loaf or work, but they go on for ever.' The place oppressed him. He called for the dice and shook with Alix for the drink.

'Here for long, Mr Wales?'

'I'm here for four or five days to see my little girl.'

'Oh-h! You have a little girl?'

Outside, the fire-red, gas-blue, ghost-green signs shone smokily through the tranquil rain. It was late afternoon and the streets were in movement; the bistros gleamed. At the corner of the Boulevard des Capucines he took a taxi. The Place de la Concorde moved by in pink majesty; they crossed the logical Seine, and Charlie felt the sudden provincial quality of the Left Bank.

Charlie directed his taxi to the Avenue de l'Opéra, which was out of his way. But he wanted to see the blue hour spread over the magnificent façade, and imagine that the cab horns, playing end-lessly the first few bars of Le Plus que Lent,[71] were the trumpets of the Second Empire.[72] They were closing the iron grill in front of Brentano's Bookstore, and people were already at dinner behind the trim little bourgeois hedge of Duval's. He had never eaten at a really cheap restaurant in Paris. Five-course dinner, four francs fifty, eighteen cents, wine included. For some odd reason he wished that he had.

As they rolled on to the Left Bank and he felt its sudden provincialism, he thought, 'I spoiled this city for myself. I didn't realise
it, but the days came along one after another, and then two years
were gone, and everything was gone, and I was gone.'

He was thirty-five, and good to look at. The Irish mobility of his
face was sobered by a deep wrinkle between his eyes. As he rang his
brother-in-law's bell in the Rue Palatine, the wrinkle deepened till it
pulled down his brow; he felt a cramping sensation in his belly.
From behind the maid who opened the door darted a lovely little
girl of nine who shrieked, 'Daddy!' and flew up, struggling like a fish
into his arms. She pulled his head around by one ear and set her
cheek against his.

'My old pie,' he said.

'Oh, daddy, daddy, daddy, daddy, dads, dads, dads!'

She drew him into the salon, where the family waited, a boy and
a girl his daughter's age, his sister-in-law and her husband. He
greeted Marion with his voice pitched carefully to avoid either
feigned enthusiasm or dislike, but her response was more frankly
tepid, though she minimised her expression of unalterable distrust
by directing her regard toward his child. The two men clasped
hands in a friendly way and Lincoln Peters rested his for a moment
on Charlie's shoulder.

The room was warm and comfortably American. The three children
moved intimately about, playing through the yellow oblongs that led
to other rooms; the cheer of six o'clock spoke in the eager smacks of
the fire and the sounds of French activity in the kitchen. But Charlie
did not relax; his heart sat up rigidly in his body and he drew
confidence from his daughter, who from time to time came close to
him, holding in her arms the doll he had brought.

'Really extremely well,' he declared in answer to Lincoln's question.
'There's a lot of business there that isn't moving at all, but we're
doing even better than ever. In fact, damn well. I'm bringing my
sister over from America next month to keep house for me. My
income last year was bigger than it was when I had money. You see,
the Czechs – '

His boasting was for a specific purpose; but after a moment,
seeing a faint restiveness in Lincoln's eye, he changed the subject:
'Those are fine children of yours, well brought up, good manners.'

'We think Honoria's a great little girl too.'

Marion Peters came back from the kitchen. She was a tall woman

with worried eyes, who had once possessed a fresh American loveliness. Charlie had never been sensitive to it and was always surprised
when people spoke of how pretty she had been. From the first there
had been an instinctive antipathy between them.

'Well, how do you find Honoria?' she asked.

'Wonderful. I was astonished how much she's grown in ten
months. All the children are looking well.'

'We haven't had a doctor for a year. How do you like being back
in Paris?'

'It seems very funny to see so few Americans around.'

'I'm delighted,' Marion said vehemently. 'Now at least you can go
into a store without their assuming you're a millionaire. We've
suffered like everybody, but on the whole it's a good deal pleasanter.'

'But it was nice while it lasted,' Charlie said. 'We were a sort of
royalty, almost infallible, with a sort of magic around us. In the bar
this afternoon' – he stumbled, seeing his mistake – 'there wasn't a
man I knew.'

She looked at him keenly. 'I should think you'd have had enough
of bars.'

'I only stayed a minute. I take one drink every afternoon, and no
more.'

'Don't you want a cocktail before dinner?' Lincoln asked.

'I take only one drink every afternoon, and I've had that.'

'I hope you keep to it,' said Marion.

Her dislike was evident in the coldness with which she spoke, but
Charlie only smiled, he had larger plans. Her very aggressiveness
gave him an advantage, and he knew enough to wait. He wanted
them to initiate the discussion of what they knew had brought him
to Paris.

At dinner he couldn't decide whether Honoria was most like him
or her mother. Fortunate if she didn't combine the traits of both
that had brought them to disaster. A great wave of protectiveness
went over him. He thought he knew what to do for her. He believed
in character; he wanted to jump back a whole generation and trust in
character again as the eternally valuable element. Everything else
wore out.

He left soon after dinner, but not to go home. He was curious to
see Paris by night with clearer and more judicious eyes than those of
other days. He bought a *strapontin*[73] for the Casino and watched
Josephine Baker[74] go through her chocolate arabesques.

After an hour he left and strolled toward Montmartre, up the Rue Pigalle into the Place Blanche. The rain had stopped and there were a few people in evening clothes disembarking from taxis in front of cabarets, and *cocottes*[75] prowling singly or in pairs, and many Negroes. He passed a lighted door from which issued music, and stopped with the sense of familiarity; it was Bricktop's, where he had parted with so many hours and so much money. A few doors farther on he found another ancient rendezvous and incautiously put his head inside. Immediately an eager orchestra burst into sound, a pair of professional dancers leaped to their feet and a maître d'hôtel swooped toward him, crying, 'Crowd just arriving, sir!' But he withdrew quickly.

'You have to be damn drunk,' he thought.

Zelli's was closed, the bleak and sinister cheap hotels surrounding it were dark; up in the Rue Blanche there was more light and a local, colloquial French crowd. The Poet's Cave had disappeared, but the two great mouths of the Café of Heaven and the Café of Hell still yawned – even devoured, as he watched, the meagre contents of a tourist bus – a German, a Japanese, and an American couple who glanced at him with frightened eyes.

So much for the effort and ingenuity of Montmartre. All the catering to vice and waste was on an utterly childish scale, and he suddenly realised the meaning of the word 'dissipate' – to dissipate into thin air; to make nothing out of something. In the little hours of the night every move from place to place was an enormous human jump, an increase of paying for the privilege of slower and slower motion.

He remembered thousand-franc notes given to an orchestra for playing a single number, hundred-franc notes tossed to a doorman for calling a cab.

But it hadn't been given for nothing.

It had been given, even the most wildly squandered sum, as an offering to destiny that he might not remember the things most worth remembering, the things that now he would always remember – his child taken from his control, his wife escaped to a grave in Vermont.

In the glare of a *brasserie* a woman spoke to him. He bought her some eggs and coffee, and then, eluding her encouraging stare, gave her a twenty-franc note and took a taxi to his hotel.

He woke upon a fine fall day—football weather. The depression of yesterday was gone and he liked the people on the streets. At noon he sat opposite Honoria at Le Grand Vatel, the only restaurant he could think of not reminiscent of champagne dinners and long luncheons that began at two and ended in a blurred and vague twilight.

'Now, how about vegetables? Oughtn't you to have some vegetables?'

'Well, yes.'

'Here's *épinards* and *chou-fleur* and carrots and *haricots*.'[76]

'I'd like *chou-fleur*.'

'Wouldn't you like to have two vegetables?'

'I usually only have one at lunch.'

The waiter was pretending to be inordinately fond of children.

'*Qu'elle est mignonne la petite! Elle parle exactement comme une Française*.'[77]

'How about dessert? Shall we wait and see?'

The waiter disappeared. Honoria looked at her father expectantly.

'What are you going to do?'

'First, we're going to that toy store in the Rue Saint-Honoré and buy you anything you like. And then we're going to the vaudeville at the Empire.'

She hesitated. 'I like it about the vaudeville, but not the toy store.'

'Why not?'

'Well, you brought me this doll.' She had it with her. 'And I've got lots of things. And we're not rich any more, are we?'

'We never were. But today you are to have anything you want.'

'All right,' she agreed resignedly.

When there had been her mother and a French nurse he had been inclined to be strict; now he extended himself, reached out for a new tolerance; he must be both parents to her and not shut any of her out of communication.

'I want to get to know you,' he said gravely. 'First let me introduce myself. My name is Charles J. Wales, of Prague.'

'Oh, daddy!' her voice cracked with laughter.

'And who are you, please?' he persisted, and she accepted a role immediately: 'Honoria Wales, Rue Palatine, Paris.'

'Married or single?'

'No, not married. Single.'

He indicated the doll. 'But I see you have a child, madame.'

Unwilling to disinherit it, she took it to her heart and thought quickly: 'Yes, I've been married, but I'm not married now. My husband is dead.'

He went on quickly, 'And the child's name?'

'Simone. That's after my best friend at school.'

'I'm very pleased that you're doing so well at school.'

'I'm third this month,' she boasted. 'Elsie' – that was her cousin – 'is only about eighteenth, and Richard is about at the bottom.'

'You like Richard and Elsie, don't you?'

'Oh, yes. I like Richard quite well and I like her all right.'

Cautiously and casually he asked: 'And Aunt Marion and Uncle Lincoln – which do you like best?'

'Oh, Uncle Lincoln, I guess.'

He was increasingly aware of her presence. As they came in, a murmur of ' . . . adorable' followed them, and now the people at the next table bent all their silences upon her, staring as if she were something no more conscious than a flower.

'Why don't I live with you?' she asked suddenly. 'Because mamma's dead?'

'You must stay here and learn more French. It would have been hard for daddy to take care of you so well.'

'I don't really need much taking care of any more. I do everything for myself.'

Going out of the restaurant, a man and a woman unexpectedly hailed him.

'Well, the old Wales!'

'Hello there, Lorraine . . . Dunc.'

Sudden ghosts out of the past: Duncan Schaeffer, a friend from college. Lorraine Quarries, a lovely, pale blonde of thirty; one of a crowd who had helped them make months into days in the lavish times of three years ago.

'My husband couldn't come this year,' she said, in answer to his question. 'We're poor as hell. So he gave me two hundred a month and told me I could do my worst on that . . . This your little girl?'

'What about coming back and sitting down?' Duncan asked.

'Can't do it.' He was glad for an excuse. As always, he felt Lorraine's passionate, provocative attraction, but his own rhythm was different now.

'Well, how about dinner?' she asked.

'I'm not free. Give me your address and let me call you.'

'Charlie, I believe you're sober,' she said judicially. 'I honestly believe he's sober, Dunc. Pinch him and see if he's sober.'

Charlie indicated Honoria with his head. They both laughed.

'What's your address?' said Duncan sceptically.

He hesitated, unwilling to give the name of his hotel.

'I'm not settled yet. I'd better call you. We're going to see the vaudeville at the Empire.'

'There! That's what I want to do,' Lorraine said. 'I want to see some clowns and acrobats and jugglers. That's just what we'll do, Dunc.'

'We've got to do an errand first,' said Charlie. 'Perhaps we'll see you there.'

'All right, you snob . . . Goodbye, beautiful little girl.'

'Goodbye.'

Honoria bobbed politely.

Somehow, an unwelcome encounter. They liked him because he was functioning, because he was serious; they wanted to see him, because he was stronger than they were now, because they wanted to draw a certain sustenance from his strength.

At the Empire, Honoria proudly refused to sit upon her father's folded coat. She was already an individual with a code of her own, and Charlie was more and more absorbed by the desire of putting a little of himself into her before she crystallised utterly. It was hopeless to try to know her in so short a time.

Between the acts they came upon Duncan and Lorraine in the lobby where the band was playing.

'Have a drink?'

'All right, but not up at the bar. We'll take a table.'

'The perfect father.'

Listening abstractedly to Lorraine, Charlie watched Honoria's eyes leave their table, and he followed them wistfully about the room, wondering what they saw. He met her glance and she smiled. 'I liked that lemonade,' she said.

What had she said? What had he expected? Going home in a taxi afterward, he pulled her over until her head rested against his chest.

'Darling, do you ever think about your mother?'

'Yes, sometimes,' she answered vaguely.

'I don't want you to forget her. Have you got a picture of her?'

'Yes, I think so. Anyhow, Aunt Marion has. Why don't you want me to forget her?'

'She loved you very much.'

'I loved her too.'

They were silent for a moment.

'Daddy, I want to come and live with you,' she said suddenly.

His heart leaped; he had wanted it to come like this.

'Aren't you perfectly happy?'

'Yes, but I love you better than anybody. And you love me better than anybody, don't you, now that mummy's dead?'

'Of course I do. But you won't always like me best, honey. You'll grow up and meet somebody your own age and go marry him and forget you ever had a daddy.'

'Yes, that's true,' she agreed tranquilly.

He didn't go in. He was coming back at nine o'clock and he wanted to keep himself fresh and new for the thing he must say then.

'When you're safe inside, just show yourself in that window.'

'All right. Goodbye, dads, dads, dads, dads.'

He waited in the dark street until she appeared, all warm and glowing, in the window above and kissed her fingers out into the night.

3

They were waiting. Marion sat behind the coffee service in a dignified black dinner dress that just faintly suggested mourning. Lincoln was walking up and down with the animation of one who had already been talking. They were as anxious as he was to get into the question. He opened it almost immediately.

'I suppose you know what I want to see you about – why I really came to Paris.'

Marion played with the black stars on her necklace and frowned.

'I'm awfully anxious to have a home,' he continued. 'And I'm awfully anxious to have Honoria in it. I appreciate your taking in Honoria for her mother's sake, but things have changed now' – he hesitated and then continued more forcibly – 'changed radically with me, and I want to ask you to reconsider the matter. It would be silly for me to deny that about three years ago I was acting badly – '

Marion looked up at him with hard eyes.

' – but all that's over. As I told you, I haven't had more than a drink a day for over a year, and I take that drink deliberately, so that the idea of alcohol won't get too big in my imagination. You see the idea?'

'No,' said Marion succinctly.

'It's a sort of stunt I set myself. It keeps the matter in proportion.'

'I get you,' said Lincoln. 'You don't want to admit it's got any attraction for you.'

'Something like that. Sometimes I forget and don't take it. But I try to take it. Anyhow, I couldn't afford to drink in my position. The people I represent are more than satisfied with what I've done, and I'm bringing my sister over from Burlington to keep house for me, and I want awfully to have Honoria too. You know that even when her mother and I weren't getting along well we never let anything that happened touch Honoria. I know she's fond of me and I know I'm able to take care of her and – well, there you are. How do you feel about it?'

He knew that now he would have to take a beating. It would last an hour or two hours, and it would be difficult, but if he modulated his inevitable resentment to the chastened attitude of the reformed sinner, he might win his point in the end.

Keep your temper, he told himself. You don't want to be justified. You want Honoria.

Lincoln spoke first: 'We've been talking it over ever since we got your letter last month. We're happy to have Honoria here. She's a dear little thing, and we're glad to be able to help her, but of course that isn't the question – '

Marion interrupted suddenly. 'How long are you going to stay sober, Charlie?' she asked.

'Permanently, I hope.'

'How can anybody count on that?'

'You know I never did drink heavily until I gave up business and came over here with nothing to do. Then Helen and I began to run around with – '

'Please leave Helen out of it. I can't bear to HEAR you talk about her like that.'

He stared at her grimly; he had never been certain how fond of each other the sisters were in life.

'My drinking only lasted about a year and a half – from the time we came over until I – collapsed.'

'It was time enough.'

'It was time enough,' he agreed.

'My duty is entirely to Helen,' she said. 'I try to think what she would have wanted me to do. Frankly, from the night you did that terrible thing you haven't really existed for me. I can't help that. She was my sister.'

'Yes.'

'When she was dying she asked me to look out for Honoria. If you hadn't been in a sanatorium then, it might have helped matters.'

He had no answer.

'I'll never in my life be able to forget the morning when Helen knocked at my door, soaked to the skin and shivering, and said you'd locked her out.'

Charlie gripped the sides of the chair. This was more difficult than he expected; he wanted to launch out into a long expostulation and explanation, but he only said: 'The night I locked her out – ' and she interrupted, 'I don't feel up to going over that again.'

After a moment's silence Lincoln said: 'We're getting off the subject. You want Marion to set aside her legal guardianship and give you Honoria. I think the main point for her is whether she has confidence in you or not.'

'I don't blame Marion,' Charlie said slowly, 'but I think she can have entire confidence in me. I had a good record up to three years ago. Of course, it's within human possibilities I might go wrong any time. But if we wait much longer I'll lose Honoria's childhood and my chance for a home.' He shook his head, 'I'll simply lose her, don't you see?'

'Yes, I see,' said Lincoln.

'Why didn't you think of all this before?' Marion asked.

'I suppose I did, from time to time, but Helen and I were getting along badly. When I consented to the guardianship, I was flat on my back in a sanatorium and the market had cleaned me out. I knew I'd acted badly, and I thought if it would bring any peace to Helen, I'd agree to anything. But now it's different. I'm functioning, I'm behaving damn well, so far as – '

'Please don't swear at me,' Marion said.

He looked at her, startled. With each remark the force of her dislike became more and more apparent. She had built up all her fear of life into one wall and faced it toward him. This trivial reproof was possibly the result of some trouble with the cook several hours before. Charlie became increasingly alarmed at leaving Honoria in this atmosphere of hostility against himself; sooner or later it would come out in a word here, a shake of the head there, and some of that distrust would be irrevocably implanted in Honoria. But he pulled his temper down out of his face and shut it up inside him, he had won a point, for Lincoln realised the absurdity of Marion's remark and asked her lightly since when she had objected to the word 'damn'.

'Another thing,' Charlie said: 'I'm able to give her certain advantages now. I'm going to take a French governess to Prague with me. I've got a lease on a new apartment – '

He stopped, realising that he was blundering. They couldn't be expected to accept with equanimity the fact that his income was again twice as large as their own.

'I suppose you can give her more luxuries than we can,' said Marion. 'When you were throwing away money we were living along watching every ten francs . . . I suppose you'll start doing it again.'

'Oh, no,' he said. 'I've learned. I worked hard for ten years, you know – until I got lucky in the market, like so many people. Terribly lucky. It won't happen again.'

There was a long silence. All of them felt their nerves straining, and for the first time in a year Charlie wanted a drink. He was sure now that Lincoln Peters wanted him to have his child.

Marion shuddered suddenly; part of her saw that Charlie's feet were planted on the earth now, and her own maternal feeling recognised the naturalness of his desire; but she had lived for a long time with a prejudice – a prejudice which was founded on a curious disbelief in her sister's happiness, and which, in the shock of one terrible night, had turned to hatred for him. It had all happened at a point in her life where the discouragement of ill health and adverse circumstances made it necessary for her to believe in tangible villainy and a tangible villain.

'I can't help what I think!' she cried out suddenly. 'How much you were responsible for Helen's death, I don't know. It's something you'll have to square with your own conscience.'

An electric current of agony surged through him; for a moment he was almost on his feet, an unuttered sound echoing in his throat. He hung on to himself for a moment, another moment.

'Hold on there,' said Lincoln uncomfortably. 'I never thought you were responsible for that.'

'Helen died of heart trouble,' Charlie said dully.

'Yes, heart trouble.' Marion spoke as if the phrase had another meaning for her.

Then, in the flatness that followed her outburst, she saw him plainly and she knew he had somehow arrived at control over the situation. Glancing at her husband, she found no help from him, and as abruptly as if it were a matter of no importance, she threw up the sponge.

'Do what you like!' she cried, springing up from her chair. 'She's your child. I'm not the person to stand in your way. I think if it were my child I'd rather see her – ' She managed to check herself. 'You two decide it. I can't stand this, I'm sick. I'm going to bed.'

She hurried from the room; after a moment Lincoln said: 'This has been a hard day for her. You know how strongly she feels – ' His voice was almost apologetic: 'When a woman gets an idea in her head.'

'Of course.'

'It's going to be all right. I think she sees now that you – can provide for the child, and so we can't very well stand in your way or Honoria's way.'

'Thank you, Lincoln.'

'I'd better go along and see how she is.'

'I'm going.'

He was still trembling when he reached the street, but a walk down the Rue Bonaparte to the *quais* set him up, and as he crossed the Seine, fresh and new by the *quai* lamps, he felt exultant. But back in his room he couldn't sleep. The image of Helen haunted him. Helen whom he had loved so until they had senselessly begun to abuse each other's love, tear it into shreds. On that terrible February night that Marion remembered so vividly, a slow quarrel had gone on for hours. There was a scene at the Florida, and then he attempted to take her home, and then she kissed young Webb at a table; after that there was what she had hysterically said. When he arrived home alone he turned the key in the lock in wild anger. How could he know she would arrive an hour later alone, that there would be a snowstorm in which she wandered about in slippers, too confused to find a taxi? Then the aftermath, her escaping pneumonia by a miracle, and all the attendant horror. They were 'reconciled', but that was the beginning of the end, and Marion, who had seen with her own eyes and who imagined it to be one of many scenes from her sister's martyrdom, never forgot.

Going over it again brought Helen nearer, and in the white, soft light that steals upon half-sleep near morning he found himself talking to her again. She said that he was perfectly right about Honoria and that she wanted Honoria to be with him. She said she was glad he was being good and doing better. She said a lot of other things – very friendly things – but she was in a swing in a white dress, and swinging faster and faster all the time, so that at the end he could not hear clearly all that she said.

4

He woke up feeling happy. The door of the world was open again. He made plans, vistas, futures for Honoria and himself, but suddenly he grew sad, remembering all the plans he and Helen had made. She had not planned to die. The present was the thing – work to do and someone to love. But not to love too much, for he knew the injury that a father can do to a daughter or a mother to a son by attaching them too closely: afterward, out in the world, the child would seek in the marriage partner the same blind tenderness and, failing probably to find it, turn against love and life.

It was another bright, crisp day. He called Lincoln Peters at the bank where he worked and asked if he could count on taking Honoria when he left for Prague. Lincoln agreed that there was no reason for delay. One thing – the legal guardianship. Marion wanted to retain that a while longer. She was upset by the whole matter, and it would oil things it she felt that the situation was still in her control for another year. Charlie agreed, wanting only the tangible, visible child.

Then the question of a governess. Charles sat in a gloomy agency and talked to a cross Béarnaise and to a buxom Breton[78] peasant, neither of whom he could have endured. There were others whom he would see tomorrow.

He lunched with Lincoln Peters at Griffons, trying to keep down his exultation.

'There's nothing quite like your own child,' Lincoln said. 'But you understand how Marion feels too.'

'She's forgotten how hard I worked for seven years there,' Charlie said. 'She just remembers one night.'

'There's another thing,' Lincoln hesitated. 'While you and Helen were tearing around Europe throwing money away, we were just getting along. I didn't touch any of the prosperity because I never got ahead enough to carry anything but my insurance. I think Marion felt there was some kind of injustice in it – you not even working toward the end, and getting richer and richer.'

'It went just as quick as it came,' said Charlie.

'Yes, a lot of it stayed in the hands of *chasseurs* and saxophone players and maîtres d'hôtel – well, the big party's over now. I just said that to explain Marion's feeling about those crazy years. If you drop in about six o'clock tonight before Marion's too tired, we'll settle the details on the spot.'

Back at his hotel, Charlie found a *pneumatique*[79] that had been re-directed from the Ritz bar where Charlie had left his address for the purpose of finding a certain man.

DEAR CHARLIE – You were so strange when we saw you the other day that I wondered if I did something to offend you. If so, I'm not conscious of it. In fact, I have thought about you too much for the last year, and it's always been in the back of my mind that I might see you if I came over here. We *did* have such good times that crazy spring, like the night you and I stole the butcher's tricycle, and the time we tried to call on the president and you had the old derby rim and the wire cane. Everybody seems so old lately, but I don't feel old a bit. Couldn't we get together some time today for old time's sake? I've got a vile hangover for the moment, but will be feeling better this afternoon and will look for you about five in the sweatshop at the Ritz.

Always devotedly,   LORRAINE

His first feeling was one of awe that he had actually, in his mature years, stolen a tricycle and pedalled Lorraine all over the Étoile between the small hours and dawn. In retrospect it was a nightmare. Locking out Helen didn't fit in with any other act of his life, but the tricycle incident did – it was one of many. How many weeks or months of dissipation to arrive at that condition of utter irresponsibility?

He tried to picture how Lorraine had appeared to him then – very attractive; Helen was unhappy about it, though she said nothing. Yesterday, in the restaurant, Lorraine had seemed trite, blurred, worn away. He emphatically did not want to see her, and he was glad Alix had not given away his hotel address. It was a relief to think instead of Honoria, to think of Sundays spent with her and of saying good-morning to her and of knowing she was there in his house at night, drawing her breath in the darkness.

At five he took a taxi and bought presents for all the Peterses – a piquant cloth doll, a box of Roman soldiers, Hewers for Marion, big linen handkerchiefs for Lincoln.

He saw, when he arrived in the apartment, that Marion had accepted the inevitable. She greeted him now as though he were a recalcitrant member of the family, rather than a menacing outsider. Honoria had been told she was going; Charlie was glad to see that her tact made her conceal her excessive happiness. Only on his lap did she whisper her delight and the question, 'When?' before she slipped away with the other children.

He and Marion were alone for a minute in the room, and on an impulse he spoke out boldly: 'Family quarrels are bitter things. They don't go according to any rules. They're not like aches or wounds, they're more like splits in the skin that won't heal because there's not enough material. I wish you and I could be on better terms.'

'Some things are hard to forget,' she answered. 'It's a question of confidence.' There was no answer to this and presently she asked, 'When do you propose to take her?'

'As soon as I can get a governess. I hoped the day after tomorrow.'

'That's impossible. I've got to get her things in shape. Not before Saturday.'

He yielded. Coming back into the room, Lincoln offered him a drink.

'I'll take my daily whiskey,' he said.

It was warm here, it was a home, people together by a fire. The children felt very safe and important; the mother and father were serious, watchful. They had things to do for the children more important than his visit here. A spoonful of medicine was, after all, more important than the strained relations between Marion and himself. They were not dull people, but they were very much in the grip of life and circumstances. He wondered if he couldn't do something to get Lincoln out of his rut at the bank.

A long peal at the doorbell; the *bonne à tout faire*[80] passed through and went down the corridor. The door opened upon another long ring, and then voices, and the three in the salon looked up expectantly; Richard moved to bring the corridor within his range of vision, and Marion rose. Then the maid came back along the corridor, closely followed by the voices, which developed under the light into Duncan Schaeffer and Lorraine Quarries.

They were gay, they were hilarious, they were roaring with laughter. For a moment Charlie was astounded; unable to understand how they had ferreted out the Peterses' address.

'Ah–h–h!' Duncan wagged his finger roguishly at Charlie. 'Ah–h–h!'

They both slid down another cascade of laughter. Anxious and at a loss, Charlie shook hands with them quickly and presented them to Lincoln and Marion. Marion nodded, scarcely speaking. She had drawn back a step toward the fire; her little girl stood beside her, and Marion put an arm about her shoulder.

With growing annoyance at the intrusion, Charlie waited for them to explain themselves.

After some concentration Duncan said: 'We came to invite you out to dinner. Lorraine and I insist that all this shishi, cagey business 'bout your address got to stop.'

Charlie came closer to them, as if to force them backward down the corridor.

'Sorry, but I can't. Tell me where you'll be and I'll phone you in half an hour.'

This made no impression. Lorraine sat down suddenly on the side of a chair, and focusing her eyes on Richard, cried, 'Oh, what a nice little boy! Come here, little boy.' Richard glanced at his mother, but did not move. With a perceptible shrug of her shoulders, Lorraine turned back to Charlie: 'Come and dine. Sure your cousins won' mine. See you so sel'om. Or solemn.'

'I can't,' said Charlie sharply, 'you two have dinner and I'll phone you.'

Her voice became suddenly unpleasant. 'All right, we'll go. But I remember once when you hammered on my door at four a.m. I was enough of a good sport to give you a drink. Come on, Dunc.'

Still in slow motion, with blurred, angry faces, with uncertain feet, they retired along the corridor.

'Good-night,' Charlie said.

'Good-night!' responded Lorraine emphatically.

When he went back into the salon Marion had not moved, only now her son was standing in the circle of her other arm. Lincoln was still swinging Honoria back and forth like a pendulum from side to side.

'What an outrage!' Charlie broke out. 'What an absolute outrage!'

Neither of them answered.

Charlie dropped into an armchair, picked up his drink, set it down again and said: 'People I haven't seen for two years having the colossal nerve – '

He broke off. Marion had made the sound 'Oh!' in one swift, furious breath, turned her body from him with a jerk and left the room.

Lincoln set down Honoria carefully.

'You children go in and start your soup,' he said, and when they obeyed, he said to Charlie: 'Marion's not well and she can't stand shocks. That kind of people make her really physically sick.'

'I didn't tell them to come here. They wormed your name out of somebody. They deliberately – '

'Well, it's too bad. It doesn't help matters. Excuse me a minute.'

Left alone, Charlie sat tense in his chair. In the next room he could hear the children eating, talking in monosyllables, already oblivious to the scene between their elders. He heard a murmur of conversation from a farther room and then the tinkling bell of a telephone receiver picked up, and in a panic he moved to the other side of the room and out of earshot.

In a minute Lincoln came back. 'Look here, Charlie, I think we'd better call off dinner for tonight. Marion's in bad shape.'

'Is she angry with me?'

'Sort of,' he said, almost roughly. 'She's not strong and – '

'You mean she's changed her mind about Honoria?'

'She's pretty bitter right now. I don't know. You phone me at the bank tomorrow.'

'I wish you'd explain to her I never dreamed these people would come here. I'm just as sore as you are.'

'I couldn't explain anything to her now.'

Charlie got up. He took his coat and hat and started down the corridor. Then he opened the door of the dining-room and said in a strange voice, 'Good-night, children.'

Honoria rose and ran around the table to hug him.

'Good-night, sweetheart,' he said vaguely, and then trying to make his voice more tender, trying to conciliate something, 'Good-night, dear children.'

5

Charlie went directly to the Ritz bar with the furious idea of finding Lorraine and Duncan, but they were not there, and he realised that in any case there was nothing he could do. He had not touched his drink at the Peterses', and now he ordered a whiskey and soda. Paul came over to say hello.

'It's a great change,' he said sadly. 'We do about half the business we did. So many fellows I hear about back in the States lost everything, maybe not in the first crash, but then in the second. Your friend George Hardt lost every cent, I hear. Are you back in the States?'

'No, I'm in business in Prague.'

'I heard that you lost a lot in the crash.'

'I did,' and he added grimly, 'but I lost everything I wanted in the boom.'

'Selling short.'

'Something like that.'

Again the memory of those days swept over him like a nightmare – the people they had met travelling; then people who couldn't add a row of figures or speak a coherent sentence. The little man Helen had consented to dance with at the ship's party, who had insulted her ten feet from the table; the women and girls carried screaming with drink or drugs out of public places –

– The men who locked their wives out in the snow, because the snow of twenty-nine wasn't real snow. If you didn't want it to be snow, you just paid some money.

He went to the phone and called the Peterses' apartment; Lincoln answered.

'I called up because this thing is on my mind. Has Marion said anything definite?'

'Marion's sick,' Lincoln answered shortly. 'I know this thing isn't altogether your fault, but I can't have her go to pieces about it. I'm afraid we'll have to let it slide for six months; I can't take the chance of working her up to this state again.'

'I see.'

'I'm sorry, Charlie.'

He went back to his table. His whiskey glass was empty, but he shook his head when Alix looked at it questioningly. There wasn't much he could do now except send Honoria some things; he would send her a lot of things tomorrow. He thought rather angrily that this was just money – he had given so many people money . . .

'No, no more,' he said to another waiter. 'What do I owe you?'

He would come back some day; they couldn't make him pay for ever. But he wanted his child and nothing was much good now, beside that fact. He wasn't young any more, with a lot of nice thoughts and dreams to have by himself. He was absolutely sure Helen wouldn't have wanted him to be so alone.

NOTES

THE CUT-GLASS BOWL (p. 23)

1 (p. 23) *Back Bay*   prestigious area of Boston

2 (p. 23) *ten little niggers*   reference to the rhyme, 'Ten little Indians [niggers] standing in a line; / One went home and then there were nine.'

3 (p. 26) *Morris chair*   named after William Morris (1834–96), English designer, craftsman, writer, and early Socialist

4 (p. 32) *Empire gown*   very formal gown deriving from Empress Josephine, wife of Napoleon I

5 (p. 36) *noveau rish*   nouveau-riche people who have new money as opposed to old-established money

MAY DAY (p. 43)

6 (p. 45) *Delmonico's*   one of New York City's most luxurious restaurants, with many rooms

7 (p. 50) *Gamma Psi dance*   fraternity dance

8 (p. 51) *gay*   disposed to have a good time

9 (p. 53) *Prohibition*   period 1919–33 when the sale of alcohol in the United States was banned by the Eighteenth Amendment to the Constitution

10 (p. 55) *J. P. Morgan*   American banker (1837–1913), one of the world's foremost financial figures during the first two decades of the twentieth century

11 (p. 55) *John D. Rockefeller*   American billionaire industrialist (1839–1937), founder of Standard Oil, the company which dominated the oil industry

12 (p. 59) *O.D.*   olive-drab, the colour of the enlisted man's uniform

13 (p. 60) *faux pas*   mistake, especially in terms of decorum

14 (p. 63) *inconnu*   unknown man

15 (p. 64) *the stags*   men hunting women

16 (p. 69) *Kipling says*   Rudyard Kipling (1865–1936) was an English writer; the quotation is from his poem 'The Ladies'.

17 (p. 70) *Bolsheviki*   plural of Bolshevik, name of a party led by Lenin which seized control of Russia in 1917 and eventually became the Communist Party

18 (p. 70) *made love to*   sweet-talked, chatted up

19 (p. 74) *the elevated*   elevated railroad line

20 (p. 78) *Boche-lovers*   Boche was hostile slang for Germans in World War I.

21 (p. 80) *filles de joie*   prostitutes

22 (p. 80) *flappers*   liberated young women looking for a good time

23 (p. 84) *Maxfield Parrish*   painter (1870–1966) and America's highest paid commercial artist in the 1920s. Some paintings gave the effect of stained glass.

THE DIAMOND AS BIG AS THE RITZ (p. 93)

24 (p. 93) *Hades*   abode of the dead; jokingly seen as hell, and therefore hot, in this story

25 (p. 93) *St Midas's*   Midas was the name of the fabled king of Phyrgia whose touch turned everything to gold.

26 (p. 93) *keep the home fires burning*   first line of a popular 1914 song, ending 'till the boys come home'; words by Lena Guilbert Ford, music by Ivor Novello

27 (p. 97) *duvetyn*   a smooth velvety fabric in various colours

28 (p. 99) *Croesus*   King of Lydia (500 BC) noted for his great wealth

29 (p. 100) *acciaccare*   Fitzgerald presumably means *acciaccatura*, a short grace-note.

30 (p. 100) *Titania*   Queen of the Fairies in Shakespeare's *A Midsummer Night's Dream*

31 (p. 100) *platonic conception*   ideal conception. The phrase is also used in the account of Gatsby (*The Great Gatsby*, Chapter 6).

32 (p. 102) *black Gargantua*   Gargantua is the name of the giant created by François Rabelais (1483–1553) in his comic satirical novel *Gargantua* (1534).

33 (p. 105) *El Dorados*   El Dorado is a mythical country containing great sources of wealth.

34 (p. 105) *General Forrest*   Confederate general in the American Civil War

35 (p. 106) *first Babylonian Empire*   around 500 BC

36 (p. 114) *Pro deo et patria et St Mida*   for god, nation and St Mida

37 (p. 116) *Empress Eugénie*   Eugénie (1826–1920), Empress of France and consort of Napoleon III

38 (p. 121) *Russian sable*   Sable is the fur of a small flesh-eating mammal.

39 (p. 121) *angora*   Angora is a silk-like goat's wool.

40 (p. 124) *Nemesis*   retributive justice

41 (p. 126) *Prometheus Enriched*   In Greek mythology Prometheus

was a great benefactor of mankind whom Zeus in punishment bound to a rock. Fitzgerald is evoking Aeschylus's *Prometheus Bound* and Shelley's *Prometheus Unbound*.

THE RICH BOY (p. 131)

42 (p. 132) *the Gilded Age* title of a novel (published in 1873) by Mark Twain and Charles Dudley Warner. It gave its name to the post-Civil War period in America when vast fortunes were made amid considerable corruption

43 (p. 134) *the De Soto Bar* Hernando De Soto (1500–42), Spanish explorer to what are now the Southern United States

44 (p. 137) *bromo-seltzer* cure for a hangover

45 (p. 137) *in Dutch* in trouble

46 (p. 141) *Mr Conan Doyle* Sir Arthur Conan Doyle (1859–1930), author of the Sherlock Holmes stories

47 (p. 150) *Celliniesque* like the wild escapades recounted in the *Autobiography* of Benvenuto Cellini (1500–71), Italian sculptor and metalsmith

48 (p. 157) *Homeric* big formal send-off

CRAZY SUNDAY (p. 167)

49 (p. 167) *Puppenfeen* fairy-dolls

50 (p. 168) *Marion Davies* actress (1897–1961) who became lover of William Randolph Hearst

51 (p. 168) *Dietrich* Marlene Dietrich (1901–92), German-born film star

52 (p. 168) *Garbo* Greta Garbo (1905–90), film star

53 (p. 171) *Menjou type* Adolphe Menjou (1890–1963), film actor who played dapper debonair men of the world

54 (p. 171) *Michael Arlen* English novelist (1895–1956)

55 (p. 178) *Jack Johnson's* Jack Johnson (1878–1946), African-American who became world heavyweight boxing champion

AN ALCOHOLIC CASE (p. 185)

56 (p. 185) *Gone with the Wind* written in 1936 by Margaret Mitchell (1900–49) and one of the most popular romantic novels ever published

57 (p. 189) *Pasteur* Louis Pasteur (1822–95), French chemist and originator of pasteurisation

58 (p. 189) *Florence Nightingale* English hospital reformer (1820–1910), founder of nursing as a profession

THE LEES OF HAPPINESS (p. 193)

59 (p. 193) *Richard Harding Davis*   famous foreign correspondent (1864–1916), who also wrote short stories and novels

60 (p. 193) *Frank Norris*   American novelist (1870–1902)

61 (p. 193) *the Japs had taken Port Arthur*   Chinese name Lushun, an important naval base contested in the Russo-Japanese War, 1904–5

62 (p. 193) *Château Thierry*   site of major World War 1 battle, July 1918

63 (p. 194) *the Gibson girl*   creation of illustrator Charles Dana Gibson (1867–1944), she was a thoroughly modern American athletic type

64 (p. 194) *Lillian Runssell and Stella Mayhew and Anna Held* actresses

65 (p. 195) *Balboa*   Vasco Núñez de Balboa (1475–1519), Spanish discoverer and soldier

66 (p. 211) *mint juleps*   sweet drink made with finely chopped mint

THE LOST DECADE (p. 213)

67 (p. 214) *Admiral Byrd*   Richard Evelyn Byrd (1888–1957), American naval explorer

68 (p. 215) *Cole Porter*   American composer and lyricist (1891–1964)

BABYLON REVISITED (p. 217)

69 (p. 217) *Babylon*   reference to Paris as a Babylon, a city associated by ancient Hebrews and Greeks with hedonism and materialism

70 (p. 217) *chasseur*   errand boy

71 (p. 218) *Le Plus que Lent*   well-known waltz by Debussy

72 (p. 218) *Second Empire*   the reign of Napoleon III (1851–70)

73 (p. 220) *strapontin*   folding chair

74 (p. 220) *Josephine Baker*   African-American jazz singer and dancer (1907–75), who was a star at the *Folies Bergère* in Paris

75 (p. 221) *cocottes*   prostitutes

76 (p. 222) *épinards, chou-fleur, haricots*   spinach, cauliflower, green beans

77 (p. 222) *'Qu'elle est . . . une Française'*   'How delightful the little girl is. She speaks exactly like a French girl.'

78 (p. 230) *Béarnaise, Breton*   Béarn and Breton are two regions of France.

79 (p. 231) *pneumatique*   a written note transmitted via pneumatic tube

80 (p. 233) *bonne à tout faire*   maid-of-all-work